Mary Victoria was born in 1973 in Turner's Falls, Massachusetts, in the United States. Despite this she managed to live most of her life in other places, including Cyprus, Canada, Sierra Leone, France and the UK. She studied animation and worked for ten years in the film industry before turning to full-time writing. She now lives in Wellington, New Zealand, with her husband and daughter.

BOOKS BY MARY VICTORIA

CHRONICLES OF THE TREE

Tymon's Flight (1)

Samiha's Song (2)

Oracle's Fire (3)

ORACLE'S FIRE

CHRONICLES *of the* TREE — BOOK THREE

MARY VICTORIA

HARPER
Voyager

Harper*Voyager*
An imprint of HarperCollins*Publishers*

First published in Australia in 2011
by HarperCollins*Publishers* Australia Pty Limited
ABN 36 009 913 517
harpercollins.com.au

HarperCollins*Publishers*
Level 13, 201 Elizabeth Street, Sydney NSW 2000, Australia
31 View Road, Glenfield, Auckland 0627, New Zealand
A 53, Sector 57, Noida, UP, India
77–85 Fulham Palace Road, London W6 8JB, United Kingdom
2 Bloor Street East, 20th floor, Toronto, Ontario M4W 1A8, Canada
10 East 53rd Street, New York NY 10022, USA

National Library of Australia Cataloguing-in-Publication data:

Victoria, Mary.
    Oracle's fire / Mary Victoria.
    ISBN: 978 0 7322 9100 6 (pbk.)
    Victoria, Mary. Chronicles of the tree ; bk. 3.
    Fantasy fiction.
NZ823.3

Cover design by Astred Hicks, Design Cherry
Cover illustration by Frank Victoria
Map by Frank Victoria
Typeset in Goudy 10/12pt by Letter Spaced
Printed and bound in Australia by Griffin Press
50gsm Bulky News used by HarperCollins*Publishers* is a natural,
recyclable product made from wood grown in sustainable plantation
forests. The manufacturing processes conform to the environmental
regulations in the country of origin, New Zealand.

5 4 3 2 1   11 12 13 14

For Frank

ORACLE'S FIRE

PROLOGUE

In the old country, thought Jedda, a man of principle was always considered a rebel. His integrity threatened those in power, who lived by corruption. As his existence was a constant reminder of what they were not, they were unable to rest until they had taken him apart, piece by piece.

First he would have his teaching post at the local school abolished. The dirty lice did not need to learn their letters, after all. If he then attempted to take up another trade — peddling recycled clothing, or selling bundles of loose bark for firewood, perhaps — his market stall would be routinely smashed and the goods destroyed. When poverty and ruin inevitably followed and he could not pay for his business licence, the authorities would confiscate his house as collateral on the debt. He would be forced into the streets with his young family to live as best he could, while his former neighbours and compatriots whispered to each other about the laziness of these filthy mystics who depended on handouts. Over the winter months his wife and infant daughter would die from exposure. He would become a husk of his former self, wandering with his surviving child from village to village and begging for alms, once a respected professor of the *gemhat* and *abjat* traditions, now a homeless drunk.

Let no one say Nurians knew about justice.

In the old country, if you were that other daughter, and unlucky enough to have inherited your father's stubborn character as well as his sharp mind, you would be unable to bear such insults. You would remember him as he had been, before the dust and the *kush* and the cold, hungry nights. In your innocence you might feel the first stirrings of power within you, and imagine you could one day rout the enemy, bringing your beloved parent dignity again. You would be full of dreams of righteousness and pride; you would be caught looking the wrong way at a foreign soldier and find yourself, a girl of ten summers, locked in a storeroom behind the army canteen and forced to endure whatever abuse the Argosians heaped upon you. The people in the garrison town where you were imprisoned would do nothing to help you, though some must have heard your cries. No one would tell your father where you were, and he would wander away, abandoning you at last. How he could justify such an action, what story of death or disloyalty he might have believed in order to accept your absence, would always remain a mystery. You would even begin to suspect he had sold you. Your fellow Nurians would let you rot in that storeroom for days until you found a way out on your own, clawing loose the grating on the window with your fingernails. The Sap helps those who help themselves.

Let no one wait for mercy in Nur.

Was it any surprise, then, that someone who had suffered what passed for a childhood in the old country might invent some story, some yarn about her parents dying in a pirate raid, in order to leave that pathetic history behind? Might such a person not jump at the promise of happiness, though it were given by the very invaders who had made her life a misery? She would only be betraying those who had so often betrayed her. And yet she would come to regret the choice. So it is when we deny a part of ourselves, even the worst part. Hail to Nur, thought Jedda bleakly, standing in the torture chamber beneath the seminary with her eyes squeezed tightly shut. Hail to my broken nation and its hard-hearted people. I should never have left you. There is no joy without you. For I missed a priceless beauty hidden underneath all that dust and cruelty.

Samiha, Samiha: my queen, my hope. I was wrong to desert you.

A scream echoed through the chamber, interrupting the litany of Jedda's thoughts. She opened her eyes to gaze at the Nurian youth chained to the back of the room. Sweat ran down Pallas' neck, glinting in the torchlight. His breath came in gasps after the screaming. He stared past her, beyond her, unrecognising. It humbled her to see how stubbornly he clung to life. She yearned to reach out and crush those hardwood links about his wrists and ankles like bread, crumbling them in her hands. She wished vehemently for fire and ruin to fall upon the head of the one who caused him pain. Pallas had already received a visit from the seminary inquisitors that evening, making a full confession of his activities in Argos city. Despite this he now suffered a further indignity, worse than torture in Jedda's opinion.

She could not bear to see the smirk of satisfaction on Wick's face as he stood before the Nurian lad, the picture of bullying confidence. Her fellow acolyte had only dared approach the prisoner because Pallas was weak and manacled to the wall. Wick had strutted up to him and grasped a handful of his hair, holding him up as if he were a lifeless doll; with his other thumb he had pressed a gleaming rod of *orah* into Pallas' forehead, his gaze locking with his victim's in a silent struggle. Jedda hardly existed beside the two youths. She was grateful to be ignored. She closed her eyes again; this was not the knowledge she had sought at the seminary. She was not here in this chamber. She was anywhere but here.

It was Lace who had insisted she be present at Pallas' punishment. The Envoy had her on probation, she knew, monitoring her from afar with the *orah*-clock. It was the night before the Kion's execution and the seminary was on high alert. Someone — a Lantrian spy, according to rumour — had in the past few hours broken into the bell tower to communicate with Samiha and absconded with some of the prisoner's writings. Although Jedda had not participated in the *orah* ritual conducted by the Envoy and his puppet, Saint, in which they sought out and eventually arrested the interloper, she could guess who it was. She was proud of Tymon, even if he stood no chance against the seminary.

She herself had been held hostage ever since Lace had caught her outside the bell tower that afternoon, her every movement controlled and watched. She too was a prisoner, though her chains were of a more subtle variety than those of poor Pallas. The Envoy had sent her here tonight to ram home the point, she supposed. Pallas was an untaught Grafter with no means of defending himself. It was her fault he was being subjected to such treatment: she had been the one to divert Tymon's attention at the temple, while her master struck his blow against the weaker target. It had been the last task she performed for Lace and one that caused her to boil with shame. She had never wanted the Freeholder to suffer like this. She turned away, unable to watch as Wick sucked the life and power from his victim. They had already wiped the young man's memory. Why were they dead set on destroying his mind as well?

'Because the memory blocks I put in at the temple were impermanent. He would have returned to normal in a few days, Jedda.'

She flinched as the familiar voice answered her unspoken thoughts, her shrinking gaze alighting on the black-coated figure in the doorway. The Envoy was one step ahead of her, as always, his teeth bared in a mirthless smile. There was no shutting her eyes on him.

'We have to do this, you realise,' he said, strolling into the room. 'We're at war. We cannot be seen as being weak or treating our enemies indulgently. You should participate: it would be good for you. That's why I asked you to come here.'

'I can't do that,' she answered hoarsely. 'You'll have to forgive me, sir.'

'Well then, watch and learn,' snapped her master, coming to stand by Wick. 'Your colleague here is doing wonderfully.'

'You're wrong not to try it, you know,' said Wick, leering over his shoulder at her. 'This is amazing. This is Power: all the rest is just child's play.'

As he spoke, Pallas screamed again. The strength had left the prisoner's limbs, and he sagged in his manacles, his face working. Wick was obliged to hold him steady, propping him up with one arm wrapped around his chest. It was an oddly tender pose seen from without. But there was nothing gentle in Wick's expression. He jammed the *orah* into Pallas' forehead, his face exultant.

'I can feel it,' he murmured. 'Feel his strength running into me. It's all mine.' Jedda glared at him in revulsion.

The Envoy shrugged off her disapproval. 'You disappoint me, Jedda,' he sighed. 'I was hoping to find in you an apprentice worthy of my attention, a strong mind willing to accept the rigours and challenges of absolute freedom. Instead, you're still shackled to your old ideas. You cannot decide which way to run. You remain a wavering, guilt-ridden slave. You may go if you desire. We have no need of weaklings here.'

Jedda knew better than to respond to his taunts. The Envoy's disappointment meant little to her; the glimpse of terrifying knowledge in Samiha's eyes had put paid to his paltry talk of power. She did not know who or what the Kion was and she no longer cared. All she knew was that compared with her queen, Lace was nothing. The so-called freedom he offered her was no better than dust and ashes. She had truly left her master's service when she fled in awe and confusion from the bell tower that day, to endure his spiteful threats on the temple buttress. She waited now only for the Kion's execution, knowing it would be the inevitable end to her career at the seminary. It would be both the death knell to her hopes and a final liberation: after that, there would be nothing to keep her in the city. Her master would either have to turn her loose, or put her out of her misery by killing her, too.

He had released her for the moment, at least. His last words had given her leave to quit this scene of infamy. As she turned to go, however, Pallas spoke. The whispered, painful words were addressed to Wick, but left an indelible mark on Jedda's soul.

'You're Eaten,' the Freeholder gasped out. 'Eaten from the inside. I see it coming through. Reaching the surface. Not long now. Burnt and Eaten.'

'What does he mean?' Wick asked the Envoy, with a frown.

'Ignore him,' said Lace dismissively. He inspected Pallas, peering at him with cold curiosity, as if he were a rare species of butterfly. 'His mind has been tampered with. No wonder he was so open with us. Who knows where this fool ran into a practitioner of the old arts. He's as good as an idiot already.'

Even as he spoke, Pallas' body stiffened in a last spasm and went limp. Jedda shook off the horrified torpor that had taken hold of her and strode towards the chamber door. But Lace was too quick for her. Although he had himself dismissed her, he sprang forward as she tried to leave, grasping her right elbow.

'Be careful what you choose to do, young lady,' he hissed in her ear. His eyes were flat and dark, untouched by the lantern light. 'If you turn away from me now, you'll suffer the consequences. I'll not forgive another transgression.'

She shrank from him, unable to answer. He fixed her a moment longer with his dead eyes before letting go of her arm and stepping aside with deliberate calm. She dodged past him into the corridor.

'Then you shall be cursed,' he called after her, slowly and clearly. 'Cursed to injure all who help you, to destroy all those you love. Cursed to See yourself for what you truly are. Be careful.'

His words clutched at her heels and made her stumble. She did not look back but ran up the steps leading to the College proper, her pulse hammering.

'Abomination,' Lace said under his breath, as Jedda's lanky figure disappeared from view. Then he shut his mouth with a snap. It was all the same to him if the turncoat turned again. She was still his, after all, bound to him by the very power he had given her. She would not easily escape her cage.

He returned to Wick's side. The acolyte held Pallas loosely; his eyes had a faraway look, and he did not appear to have noticed Jedda's departure. 'It's just like you told me, sir,' he said to Lace, his voice thick and slurred. 'The uninitiated are nothing. Nothing but worms and decay. I see that now.'

'You're better than they are,' replied the Envoy, nodding. 'You're superior.'

But Wick did not respond. He allowed the inert body of Pallas to slip from his arms, hanging limply from its chains, and knelt down on the floor, holding on to the wall for support, as if drunk. His head lolled back and his eyes were half-closed, his lips stretched into a smile of beatitude as he basked in the heady intoxication of stolen energy.

Lace regarded him with grim sobriety. 'Enjoy yourself, acolyte,' he said. 'But don't wander too far. Remember, we're expected to do our duty on the quays tomorrow morning. And shut down that connection after you're finished — permanently.'

It was done, it was over. Her Kion was gone: the moment of pain and liberation was at hand. Jedda stumbled out of the door at the base of the bell tower into a world made ghostly white by snow. White, the colour of oblivion, drifted down to shroud the city and its inhabitants. White, the colour of the mists that had swallowed Samiha's figure as she tumbled through the uncanopied emptiness. White as the clouds of the Storm through which her delicate body must have spiralled down, down, down to the Tree knew what bloody end.

Jedda wandered down the stairs from the temple buttress to the snow-lined streets, hardly caring where her feet took her. After quitting the torture chamber the evening before, she had spent a sleepless night in her quarters, counting down the hours to Samiha's execution. The next day, when the Kion had been taken to the quays and the priests had rung their fateful bells, Jedda slipped into the unlocked tower and spent that anguished hour weeping over Samiha's empty desk. She had risen and left the building when she heard the dim cries of triumph echoing out from the air-harbour, and spun loose from the seminary like an arrow shot wild. Lace might kill her whenever he liked. Nothing else was left.

But Lace did not kill her, and the snowfall eased.

After a while her aimless drifting through the city brought her face to face with the hordes of spectators returning from the air-harbour. She blinked at them through her tears, feeling the prick of hatred. These people had taken her Kion away, lapped up her death like a Tree-cat laps milk. It was all just entertainment to them: they did not care whether Samiha was a heretic or a truth-teller, guilty or innocent. The only thing that mattered was the thrill of the ride. They talked now of miracles as Jedda pushed by them on the main thoroughfare, of visions of angels above the temple dome and a boy burnt from head to toe by invisible fire. There was no end to their nonsense and perversity.

Jedda walked more quickly, her despair replaced by a steadily mounting fury. They all deserved punishment, she thought. Each and every one of these Tree-forsaken Argosians, down to the last squealing infant. Maybe it was worth staying alive, thumbing her nose at the seminary as Tymon had done, to see that day. She mouthed half-uttered invectives as she shoved her way through the throng. People turned to stare at her. She dashed her tears away with the back of her hand and barrelled past a sentry at the city gates, ignoring the man's officious query. From the expression of shock on his face she realised that the Seeming that had hidden her femininity in public had been stripped away, as part of the Envoy's curse. From now on she would appear exactly as she was: a woman and a Nurian, a pariah in Argos, just as Lace had promised. She walked swiftly along the emptying air-harbour quays with her green acolyte's cloak and hood drawn close about her. She did not wait to see if the guard was pursuing her but hurried towards the main ramp out of the town, sliding on the icy boards of the dock.

The Envoy might curse her but she would go on. She would do her best to survive. He would doubtless have her followed and murdered; she would probably expire on that ice-bound day, or perhaps the day after. But it was worth attempting to escape, if only as a last act of defiance. She fled Argos city without another thought, as if the place were caught in the grip of a plague.

PART ONE
ABOVE

Far from you, I wander lost
Tattered, searching through the dust
In desperate hope that I may find
A hint, a remnant left behind
Of you.
— Samiha Saman

I

The South Road was a faint wriggling line, no more
than a scratch on the face of the World Tree. Mile
after grey mile it traced the circumference of that
colossal wall. League upon league it wound its way
laboriously around the trunk perimeter. It was
pounded by the elements for there was little shelter
on the exposed ledge, no place to hide between the
sheer bark face on one side and the West Chasm on
the other. A person or vehicle travelling along that
perilous path, either forwards or backwards, either
north or south, was forced to crawl between two
extremes, hard up against oblivion. Few attempted
such a journey in the depths of winter, and during the
three days that Tymon sat crouched in the rattling
prison cart beside Verlain, hugging his cold-numbed
limbs to his chest, the vehicle did not pass a single
voyager. There was barely a bird in the fog-filled skies.
A snowstorm on the first evening had caused the
wagon to be half-buried in a drift. It had to be dug out
the next day by the cursing drivers, who evidently
would much rather have left their two charges behind
to expire in the cold. And Tymon might well have
expired on that journey, had it not been for the steady
presence at the back of his mind. The Oracle stayed
with him, her voice sustaining him in his darkest
hours.

The journey was a slow torture of starvation for him. The soldiers driving the cart had decided he did not need even the dry hunks of bread that had been his fare in the city jail, and gave him nothing to eat at all. He would have died of thirst had he not been able to painstakingly collect snowflakes through the bars in his cupped hands, licking the melted liquid from his palms. By the third day he was too weak and dispirited to move, slumped on the right-hand side of the shuddering cage with his weary eyes fixed on the fog of the West Chasm. He seemed at every moment to see the figure of Samiha etched against that blank whiteness, as he had last seen her on the execution dock. He imagined again and again that appalling moment he had turned away from, as she stepped into the empty air to tumble headlong into the space below. How long had it taken her to fall to her death? What had passed through her mind from that first horrid moment to the last? According to legend, a person's lungs burst on entry into the Storm; people died in the falling, so they said, the rush of air being too fast to breathe.

But despite reliving that moment in his memory time and again, he found himself unable to believe that Samiha was really gone. She had been too alive, too intensely present in his life to depart from it now. Her flame had burned the brightest of anyone he had known and could not be so easily snuffed out. She was not like his companion in the cart. For Verlain, it seemed, had finally given up on his muddled and vaporous existence, sputtering out like a spent candle. The body of Tymon's former employer lay sprawled on the floor of the cage, its skin gradually turning a livid greenish-yellow as the days went by. The soldiers turned a deaf ear to the young man's pleas, leaving him to travel in the company of the corpse. By the time they reached their destination, a military outpost fifty miles south of Argos city, the priest's stink had acquired the final sweetness of death.

The camp at Hayman's Point consisted of no more than a cluster of dingy buildings huddled at the bottom of a tear-shaped crevice in the trunk, the remains of an old bark tumour two hundred feet high and as many deep. But the cleft was less than half that distance across, the gully narrowing to a claustrophobic slit at the top. In past years the outpost had all but closed down during the winter months, the troops either deployed elsewhere or confined for a cheerless time in the drab huts on the floor of the gully. Now, however, the place crawled with newfound activity.

Tymon, already exhausted by the voyage in the cart, found his relief at reaching journey's end replaced by a quick-growing dismay. The road winding down the side of the cleft offered a good view of the camp in the watery evening sunlight, and he could see that recent constructions had multiplied in the gully like fungus. Enclosed corrals like those for livestock extended alongside the soldiers' huts. His heart sank when he realised that the pens were occupied by people: small figures sat huddled on the straw floor of the enclosures. They wore grey tunics, but the Argosians had not bothered to manacle them. There was nowhere for the Nurians to go.

'You can see when a civilisation has reached the point of putrefaction. It begins to prey on others to keep itself going.' The voice in Tymon's head jerked him awake from his half-starved stupor. 'The priests of Argos speak of signs and portents of the End Times, as if they were part of some great cosmic plan,' continued the familiar tones of the Oracle, dryly. 'The truth is, they're already dead.'

'They're copying the Lantrians,' muttered Tymon, gazing out in horror at the vision reminiscent of the slave pens in Cherk Harbour. 'I didn't realise there were so many. Pilgrims, I mean. They've brought so many!'

Indeed, there were far more people at Hayman's Point than could be warranted by a single tithe-ship arriving in spring. The Saint had increased his revenue from the colonies, though he obviously felt no need to transport the pilgrims to the capital more than once a year. It was enough to bring the usual number to the Sacrifice, a dozen or so; the rest, the scores that now sat in the pens at Hayman's Point, would simply be shipped off to plantations in the west and south.

The Nurians in the nearest enclosure glanced up warily as the prison vehicle halted by the door. Tymon estimated the number of people inside this one pen as thirty or forty, perhaps more. They were mostly youths his age or even younger. The two drivers of the cart opened the door of his cage and thrust him unceremoniously out of one prison and into another. The gate of the pilgrims' enclosure slammed on his heels and the vehicle rolled away, carrying its corpse. Tymon stood unmoving in the mixture of straw and dirty slush on the floor of the pen, for he was too weak to walk. He swayed on his feet before the group of Nurians. He wondered how they would react to an Argosian in their midst.

'The Sap help me,' he breathed.

'Don't worry. It will,' replied the Oracle gently.

Grey figures detached themselves from the group and approached him even as he fell. One caught him about the waist and guided him to the far side of the enclosure where there was a rudimentary shelter, a hut with a thatched roof. He was eased onto the bare floorboards. A rough bowl of rainwater was placed in his hands and he was given a piece of dry bread to suck on. He felt as though he had never tasted anything so good in his life. His hosts, two youths about a year younger than himself, spoke to him in Nurian and asked him his name. He responded haltingly. His efforts provoked wry comments and laughter, and he realised that they had taken him for a dark-skinned tribesman from the north fringes of the Eastern Canopy, one who spoke his own dialect, as they did in Farhang. He did not disabuse them.

He learned from the Nurians that most of the members of this particular group had been brought a week ago to the base, though some had been there longer. His two benefactors were brothers named Aidon and Aybram. They did not know their final destination, only that they would probably be separated when the overseers of various major plantations arrived to inspect them. They had sold their freedom in order to help their aging parents, a sacrifice they mentioned in passing, modestly, as if it were a small thing. They both hoped to work in vine-fields and not in a hardwood mine.

The next inspection at which workers would be chosen by the various overseers was due to occur in a day or two. Until then, Tymon was advised to rest, for obviously weak or sickening pilgrims were sent straight to the south mines, where they would not survive for long. Aidon and Aybram were under no illusion as to the characters of their Argosian masters. They warned Tymon not to rely on his native looks and clothes in order to escape. The soldiers at the base considered any fugitive fair game; he would be hunted down and slaughtered as sport. The tithe-pilgrims were under legal contract, their services paid for. The soldiers took this as a licence to kill, maim and dispose of them as they saw fit.

Tymon, in any case, was incapable of attempting a getaway that evening. He was still weak from the effects of starvation and his ankle was only just beginning to mend. Although the strange burns he had suffered to his arm and back in the fight with Wick had healed to a degree, the muscles were still stiff on that side and difficult to move. The brush with the Veil had left the skin on his right palm a dull red colour like a birthmark. He told his fellow pilgrims that he had been transferred to the base from another farm, for he doubted they would react well to knowing his true origins.

Night was rapidly approaching and the snow had started to fall with redoubled force, quenching the brief evening light. Tymon took the brothers' advice and curled up in a corner of the crowded, smelly hut, pressed against the back of another man for warmth. He was simply glad to be out of the wind and under a proper roof again. He closed his eyes.

'Oracle,' he whispered under his breath.

'I am here.'

'I don't see how we're supposed to get out of this one.'

'My advice is to sit tight,' she replied. 'The immediate future is vague. It could go in several different directions. Never fear: every path arrives at the desired goal. In terms of the Tree of Being, you're moving into the Letter of Union. All roads lead home.'

He knew he would regain his freedom, and soon: she had promised him that much, during their journey in the cart. He was destined to play a vital role in combating the Envoy. Tymon was grateful for his teacher's reassurances, for he might have lost hope completely without them. But for the moment the Oracle's help was more inspirational than practical. She could not tell him how exactly he was to escape the life of a slave. He stifled a sigh.

'It's frustrating,' he said. 'I want to contact Oren.

I want to know what Pallas and the Jays are doing, and See all these things for myself.'

Before she could answer, the man lying behind him groaned out a curse, telling him to be quiet if he didn't want a blacker eye than he already had. Tymon waited a few moments before speaking to the Oracle again.

'Are you sure we can't do a Reading yet?' he muttered.

'Be patient,' she said. 'We're not far enough from Argos city. The Envoy is watching you. He will draw you into the Veil if you attempt a trance, just as Wick drew you in that day on the dock. As you well know your encounter with the acolyte almost ended in disaster. Do not take on the master. You've had two lucky escapes from Eblas so far. Remember that his power is now reinforced a hundredfold, for he has the use of the *orah*-clock.'

It was the priests' dalliance with the ancient artefact, the Oracle had explained to Tymon, that drew the Sap, and therefore disproportionate power and influence to Argos. This was the vortex of life and light he had Seen hovering above the town like a cloud of flame, on the day of Samiha's execution. The general heightening of the Grafter's power in Argos city was so great that it had caused him to perceive his connection to Jedda with his naked eyes. The whole affair was no more than fodder for the Envoy, as the Oracle had noted. Lace bathed in the glut of energy produced by the *orah*-clock, sucking it off his associates. They had no clue that they would pay sooner or later for their greed, for there were limits to human power, checks and balances that would inevitably be redressed. One nation, one people, could not prevail forever, at the expense of all others.

'There is no one to stop him now,' the Oracle continued softly.

Tymon fell silent in the darkened hut, thinking of his experiences in Argos city. He remembered the flaming figure on the execution dock, so bright that he had imagined she would melt the very snow at her feet, so beautiful that he could hardly bear to tear his eyes away —

'No.' The Oracle's voice interrupted his thoughts, answering his unspoken desire before he could articulate it. 'You want to find a ghost with the help of the Reading.' Her tone was sharp. 'You want to contact Samiha in the world beyond death. The answer is no.'

Tymon shifted his tired limbs; the man behind him had mercifully fallen asleep and was snoring. 'Why not, *Ama?*' he asked. He had not really expected his desires to meet with the Oracle's approval, but wished to know why such comfort was to be denied. 'Isn't that one of the things Grafters do? Speak with the dead?'

'That's a myth. Grafters don't speak to the dead. Or at least, only very rarely. It's forbidden. The reason is simple. If we Saw our loved ones, truly Saw where they are and how they are, we'd forget our task in this world and want to be with them.'

'What about Ash?' he objected. 'I've talked to him without forgetting anything.'

'You talked to one of the Born who wished to help you. He took the form of someone you respected and would listen to, the fifth Focal of Marak. It is the Born who are the gardeners of this world of being. They speak to us and guide us. His own form would have shocked you unnecessarily: he found one easier for you to See.'

Tymon absorbed this belated revelation. 'So Grafters only talk to the Born.'

'Yes. And to each other, obviously.'

'And I'll never — see her again,' he breathed after

a moment, with dull resignation. He could not pronounce Samiha's name.

The Oracle's tone was warm, comforting. 'Of course you will,' she replied. 'We're always reunited with those who love us, in the world hereafter. For now you must be strong and patient. If you are, you will achieve a great victory. You must think of the requirements of the living, not of the dead.'

Tymon frowned in the darkness, feeling his sleeping companion snore and twitch at his back. He had no guarantee, other than the Oracle's promises, of any 'world hereafter'. He had not Seen ghosts after all: he had Seen creatures from the world of the Sap, Beings whose power he could only begin to guess at and whose motivations were equally obscure. He did not doubt the Oracle's good intentions but knew well enough that her 'hereafter' might mean any number of things unpalatable to him — some vague conjoining of energies in the Sap, a bloodless, faceless substitute for love. He had to admit that her explanations made sense, however. Why would he have Seen the spirit of Ash, but not those of Solis, Laska or Lai? Why would he not have Seen Samiha? He had begun to suspect that many of the things he had taken for granted about the Grafting were untrue, or true in a different way from what he had expected. He did not like the thought of powerful Beings manipulating him from another world.

'What do they want?' he murmured. 'The Born, I mean? Why do they garden?'

'Because that's their function. That's what the Born are born to do, if you like. They tend the fields of eternity. But they don't manipulate humans, even so. You're free to make your own choices.'

'How much of what I'm thinking do you actually hear?' he asked, raising his voice, somewhat piqued. 'Is there anything private at all?'

A snort interrupted the snores of Tymon's bedfellow, who turned around abruptly to punch him in the back. 'I give you private!' snapped the awakened Nurian. 'Y *maza Sav*! If you continue to hiss snake-tongue in my ear, you can freeze through night alone, *nordi*! *Mi-putar*!'

The pilgrim's grumbling deteriorated into a string of curses. The Oracle's soft laughter echoed in Tymon's ears.

'I hear most of it because you don't know how to hide it from me. But I do withdraw from time to time, as you may have noticed. I'm not interested in listening to your unchecked thoughts all night and day. It's like standing in a crowded marketplace with five different fruit-sellers bawling out their wares — deafening.'

He did not talk more to her after that, succumbing to deep weariness. But just as he was drifting off to sleep he remembered Jedda's claims in Argos city, that the Born cultivated human beings. He thought of the rolling expanse of grass outside the Tree of Being which he had witnessed briefly during his Reading with the Oracle, and the other tangled plants he had glimpsed from afar, stretching between loam and sky. Other Trees. Other universes. *The fields of eternity*.

Was there some truth mixed in with the Envoy's lies? he wondered. Nurture could have a selfish motive. Were all the millions who lived and died some form of fodder or crop for the Born? His teacher did not appear to subscribe to such a view, but Tymon could not help a niggling twist of doubt. He trusted the Oracle, but was she herself duped? If his mental visitor could hear these ruminations even as she heard his other thoughts, however, she made no comment. He drifted off to sleep, puzzling over his vision of Samiha in that strange world beyond time and space, the sight of her at one with the Tree of

Being. No other trance-form he had encountered had resembled it. The Oracle had told him that Samiha's fate was linked to the fate of all. And now she was gone; he would no longer find her there, among the branches of the Tree. Perhaps he would never find her anywhere again.

The next day Tymon awoke to the harsh sound of a horn-blast, and limped out of the hut to join the other Nurians near the gate of the enclosure. His fellow inmates were throwing themselves eagerly upon a heap of food the guards had dumped over the fence. Surprisingly, there was enough to go around, and not all of it was bad: some barley-bread only a day or two old, whole vine-fruits and even dried strips of what might have been shillee's meat, as hard as leather. The Argosians did not want their chattel to starve. But the Nurians were obliged to squabble with each other over the pile and rummage underfoot for scraps like beasts. It was a demeaning sight that caused Tymon to grind his teeth in anger, though he found himself sifting through the straw like everyone else, to satisfy his hunger. Aidon told him this was the one meal provided by the soldiers, and that he should take enough to last him for the rest of the day. Tymon recognised this form of treatment and knew its underlying purpose. He remembered the Bread-Giving in Argos city, the rituals of so-called charity designed to underscore the difference between those who had and those who had not. The pilgrims were considered less than human, and the Argosians were not about to let them forget it.

'Be careful,' cautioned the Oracle as he bent down to retrieve his portion of the food from the floor of the enclosure. 'You are starting to think of your countrymen as irredeemable monsters.'

'They are,' he muttered. 'They murder what's right and true, and reward cruelty. They're as bad as the Envoy. They deserve him. Soulless brutes.'

'What about Bolas? And Masha, and Nell, and all the other good people you've met in your home town?'

'It's not my home town any more,' blurted Tymon, sitting down on the straw with a thump.

'Where is not home town?' asked Aidon, from nearby. He stared curiously at Tymon but there was distrust in his eyes.

'Farhang,' gabbled Tymon, cursing himself for speaking to the Oracle aloud. 'I thought of going there once to ask for asylum. But I went to Marak instead and kept less than quality company, I'm afraid. I woke up one morning on a tithe-ship. I don't remember signing anything,' he added, as doubt flickered across the face of his companion.

'These things happen, *nami*,' observed Aidon. But his expression remained cool. Suspicion lingered.

They had no further opportunity to speak; at that moment another horn blasted out, a dissonant wail from the lookout post further up the side of the rift. Soon the reason for the signal became visible. Three medium-sized dirigibles were descending towards the base, flat-bottomed farmers' barges used to transport goods around the Central Canopy. The overseers had arrived early at their appointment.

The men in charge of choosing workers for the plantations did not waste time in beginning their task. As the three vessels docked on the short jetty near the mouth of the rift, a division of soldiers arrived at the pilgrims' enclosure to escort them to meet their new masters. The troops stationed at Hayman's Point were a vicious crew, bristling with weapons Tymon had never seen, or even imagined possible, in Argos city. They had ordinary spears and crossbows, but also savage-looking spiked clubs at their belts and short whips equipped with barbs. This time they placed hardwood fetters on the prisoners' ankles, so that the Nurians were obliged to walk in small, shuffling steps, one behind the other. Tymon was thrust along with the others into a tiny pen by the side of the dock. He and his fellows were pressed together like beasts at market.

From this holding area the pilgrims were released one by one. Their manacles were removed and they were paraded on the dock before the three Argosian overseers and the lieutenant of the base. The plantation men were evidently well used to their work. They insisted on inspecting the teeth of the workers, peered into the whites of their eyes and required their clothes to be removed so that they might note any sign of disease or deformity. They complained loudly to the lieutenant about the shoddy quality of the merchandise; they claimed that half their purchases died after a few months on the job, and that they were being delivered substandard goods. If a particular pilgrim was chosen by an overseer, he was immediately loaded onto one of the ships. If he did not pass muster, he was returned to the pen with the others, as inferior stock. No money exchanged hands: the plantation owners had all paid the seminary in advance, in Argos city, acquiring a licence for a certain number of workers.

Tymon hunched his shoulders as he waited in line for the inspection. He was hot with shame and anger at the behaviour of his countrymen, prickling with it even on the cold winter's morning. It was doubly hard to be near the back of the queue and obliged to watch almost everyone else paraded onto the dock before him. Only Aidon, his brother and a few others remained standing with him as the inspection dragged on. The soldiers jeered at the workers while they stripped down in the freezing wind, jabbing at them with the hafts of their spears. Fury pulsed through Tymon's veins, and Samiha's *orah*-pendant, long forgotten under the collar of his tunic, glowed with an answering warmth.

'Calm down,' said the Oracle. 'You're right to be angry, but calm down. You're only one. They are many.'

'Why don't they do something about it?' he hissed to her. 'Why don't the pilgrims resist? They could take on those guards if they worked together.'

But he guessed, even as he breathed his frustration, at the many reasons why they did not resist: at their isolation, their loss of heart, their awareness of the long and impossible journey home. It was nearing his turn to exit the pen. The Oracle remained silent as a soldier stumped up to him, undid his fetters and propelled him onto the dock with a shove.

'Off you go, traitor,' he jeered at Tymon. 'Time to get your just deserts. You're no Argosian now.'

No Argosian now. The words sizzled through the air to fill a sudden and complete silence. Tymon caught a glimpse of Aidon's expression as he stepped onto the dock, saw the hatred that closed down like a shutter over the youth's face. He felt the collective gaze of the Nurians bore into his back. He no longer cared about the overseers murmuring to each other in surprise, eyeing him doubtfully. His just deserts were lying in wait behind him, in the pen. Death would find him if he returned to the pilgrims' enclosure. Death would stalk him on any plantation where those workers shared his company. The sneering soldier had seen to that. He swallowed dryly.

'What's all this nonsense?' asked one of the overseers, a burly man with an abundant beard, gesturing towards Tymon. 'We do not pay to take on traitors. He should be executed in Argos city, not sent to us.' His colleagues nodded in agreement.

'He's young and healthy,' shrugged the lieutenant.

'He'll work well once he's broken in, I assure you. It's a shame to waste good muscle like this. He's been well fed all his life, not like those poor scraps back there.'

He strode up to Tymon and yanked at the laces on his tunic. 'Get your kit off, idiot,' he snarled in the young man's ear. 'Save yourself, if you have an ounce of wit.'

Tymon stood like a lump on the dock. He could not take off his clothes. He was still too proud, too unused to such treatment, to bow down in the face of overwhelming odds. He did not move despite the Oracle's warning not to be a fool. The lieutenant turned with a sigh to one of his hulking guards. The man barely needed prompting: he raised his barbed whip and advanced. There was no further alert, no chance for Tymon to reconsider his decision. The weight of the whip hit his left ear; the barbs raked across his cheek, sending a lightning-shock of pain through him. The strike made his head reel and he staggered sideways. The other soldiers on the dock burst into laughter.

'The traitor can't hear orders,' one hooted. 'He's deaf.'

'Open up his ears with the whip,' howled another.

'Take off your clothes, fool,' rapped out the lieutenant. 'Or suffer the consequences.'

Tymon did not respond. The blow to his head seemed to have rooted him to the dock. Even had he wanted to move, he would not have been able to do so now. A sticky trickle of blood ran down his left cheek, and he felt for a fleeting moment that he was back in the arena in Sheb, face to face with Caro. The lieutenant nodded to another one of his men, who strode forward and ripped the flimsy Jay tunic from Tymon's back. Before he could open his mouth to protest, the second soldier had forced him to kneel beside a mooring post. The man secured Tymon's hands about the short pillar with a belt, then glanced up in query at his superior officer.

'Thirty-five,' announced the lieutenant resignedly. He turned away.

'*Sav vay*,' the Oracle whispered, aghast, as the first guard lifted up his whip again.

'One!' barked out his colleague by the mooring post.

The soldier brought the whip down on Tymon's back with a resounding crack. A breath of shock escaped the young man's lips and tears leapt to his eyes. He blinked furiously and knelt with his cheek pressed against the rough surface of the post, resolved to not make a sound throughout the flogging. He gritted his teeth as the next blow came, followed by another, and then another; each strike was announced by his captors before ripping into his flesh like a searing fire. At the eighth blow a stifled moan escaped Tymon's lips and by the tenth he screamed aloud, unable to keep his pledge. He did not know how he would be able to bear thirty-five. He bent over the dock-boards, gasping.

'Keep the faith,' murmured the Oracle sadly, in the depths of his mind. 'Keep the faith, Tymon.'

He hardly heard her. The whip was louder. Eleven, twelve, thirteen, it cried: there was no difference between the soldier's announcement and the blow that followed. Words shredded his skin as he knelt on the planks made slippery with his own blood. The morning sun had intensified, a blinding beam on the boardwalk immediately ahead of him. In a delirium of pain he fancied he saw a form in the light, the figure of a woman. He could not make out her features. She stretched out her hands to him, palm-upwards. In each hand she cupped a leaf, and on each leaf shone a letter traced in fire, the Letter of Union.

'*Fear neither darkness nor defeat.*' He knew the voice

belonged to the shining figure, though he did not see her lips move.

'I shall not fear,' he said. He recalled having heard or read similar words somewhere before. Fourteen, fifteen, cried the whip.

'You'll fear, alright,' snarled the soldiers gathered about him, jostling each other. They smelled of acrid sweat. 'We'll see to that.'

'*Forget the quarrel between happiness and sorrow,*' cried the vision, bleeding light.

'Forget the quarrel,' Tymon mumbled in answer.

'Shut up!' shouted the shadowy soldiers. They had lost their individuality and their blurred faces — the same traits, endlessly repeated — were flattened, eyeless things with yapping mouth-holes. 'Shut up and eat dust, traitor!'

Sixteen, seventeen, cried the whip. Even as the faces of the soldiers melted into each other the woman became more recognisable, her features visible to Tymon in fits and starts between the raking blows on his back. He saw the delicate curve of her mouth, the tangled locks of her hair, details intimately familiar to him.

'*That you and I again might meet,*' said Samiha, gazing sorrowfully down at him.

She looked as she used to in the old days, before the trial and the execution. She stood a moment on the dock before him, her hair a shining river of flame, reciting the words from her last testament. He remembered it now. He had glimpsed the lines in his brief perusal of the paper bundle, the night he had hidden from the guards in the Jays' pavilion. But this was different. This was poetry. She finished the verse as he swayed, gasping beneath the soldier's blows.

'*In the heart, where all divisions cease.*'

Eighteen, nineteen, shrieked the whip. Tymon strained to keep sight of his love. But the vision was already dissolving, bleeding into sunlight. Sun and soldiers meshed together, and the voices on the dock became a faraway buzz. Twenty, wailed the whip in a faraway lament, while the taunts and whistles of the soldiers faded to oblivion.

He must have fainted, then, and been carried away to another location, for when he awoke, he was lying on his stomach in a dark place with his head twisted to the right and his cheek pressed to the floor. The vision of Samiha was gone. He did not know if the full sentence of thirty-five lashes had been carried out, or waived due to his infirmity; his left ear throbbed and his back was a searing mesh of agony. He heard the snap of sails and the faint discharge of ether from above, the telltale song of a dirigible.

'Where am I?' he croaked, though he had already guessed the answer.

'You are in a ship belonging to Master Lovage. You belong to Master Lovage now. We all do.'

Tymon blinked as his eyes adjusted to the gloom. He was in a long, stinking chamber in the bowels of a dirigible, lit only by the dim light filtering through a grille in the ceiling. There was a person sitting beside him. A hulking, ginger-haired youth with a wide gap between his front teeth, a Nurian pilgrim. He was tall and heavyset, his round face betraying a slightly simple earnestness as he bent over Tymon.

'They tell me you're an evil, lying Argosian,' declared the stranger solemnly. 'We're all of us evil here, of course, which is why we're being sent to Master Lovage. He's for the hard cases. But you must be a piece of work, because they —' he jerked his head towards the other pilgrims slumped against the wall of the hold — 'won't go near you.' He peered at Tymon's back. 'What did you do? Why did the masters beat you?'

Tymon squinted at the blurry faces ranged behind

the Nurian lad, not caring at this point what they thought of him. Other questions preoccupied his mind. The Oracle had told him it was impossible to speak with ghosts. And yet he had Seen Samiha. He had Seen Samiha! Had he Seen her?

'I didn't obey,' he said to the ginger boy. 'I was stupid.'

'You won't be stupid again,' observed the pilgrim lad, matter-of-factly. 'I'm called Zero, by the way. Because I have zero good in me. Here, have some water.' He retrieved a dusty gourd from the floor and helped Tymon drink, holding up his head till the drops trickled down his parched throat. 'I don't mind that you're evil,' he confided. 'Evil folks are nicer than good ones. Good people beat you. I think everyone should be evil. That way no one would ever get hurt.'

2

The Lantrian resettler ships had cut a vengeful swathe of destruction through the Eastern Canopy after the unsuccessful raid on Sheb, attacking villages and homesteads throughout the southern half of the Domains. They no longer held back from provoking the Argosians, going so far as to attack two outposts with a colonial presence as well as the usual Nurian targets. The profits from this satisfying venture had gone some way to assuaging that first, incomprehensible loss on the Freehold. They had returned to Cherk Harbour to find that the intelligence passed on by their superiors in the New East Company had been correct: Argos was now at war with Lantria. The pirates' raids were a cause of national celebration. But these unlikely heroes did not return home to the South Canopy at once. They stayed in Cherk Harbour, awaiting further instructions from their shadowy leader. The Reaper had not emerged from his cabin on the resettler ship *Aurora* for days.

Curses, filth without end poured from the mouth of the madman tied to the bed in the pirate chief's quarters. The lunatic who was ostensibly the Reaper strained against the cords that bound him to his bunk, causing the bed frame to creak and groan dangerously. He was a large man, possessed of great brute strength. The restraints stopped him from clawing the skin off his own face with his long nails, although the red gouges on his cheeks testified to the fact that he had, on previous occasions, attained his goal. The cords also prevented him from lunging out at his companion, who sat still and watchful on the chair by his bedside.

Gowron regarded with cold patience the sick man who played host to his master. He remained unmoved when the other eviscerated him with the only weapon remaining to him: his furious, blistering words, spat out from a perpetually red and gaping mouth. The Reaper's eyes were as wide as a panicked animal's, bloodshot and rolling. Gowron waited until the shuddering of the bed died down and the sweating bulk upon it grew still. Slowly, the lunatic's mouth closed. The wild light left his eyes and they became veiled and fathomless, the eyes of the Envoy.

'Hello, Gowron,' remarked Lace, through the Reaper's lips.

'Greetings, sir.' The priest rose from his chair and swiftly undid the restraints on the bed, helping his master to sit up. 'It's a pleasure to have you back.'

'For the last time, my friend. The Reaper has outlived his usefulness. The Company can do without us both, for a while: I'll be needing you back in Argos city.'

Gowron permitted himself a conniving leer. 'Running short of reliable acolytes, sir?'

The Envoy gazed at him a moment, his expression inscrutable, then nodded. 'She didn't work out.'

'I guessed that might happen, if you don't mind my saying so. The chit had her nose stuck way up in the air.'

'I don't mind you saying it, no.' Lace beckoned him closer, laying a hairy hand on Gowron's shoulder to heave himself up from the bed. 'The Nurry girl was bound to be a gamble.'

'What will you do to her? To punish her for leaving, I mean?'

The ex-priest's question tripped out a fraction too eagerly. The Reaper raised a black eyebrow. 'I was going to give her back to you, eventually,' he drawled. 'But now I really should do something for our poor, foolish Wick. I trust he has learned his lesson. I hope you don't mind giving the girl up this time, Gowron. There will be more, I assure you.'

'Of course not, sir.'

Gowron dropped his gaze obsequiously, but his eyes glittered under the lids as he watched the Envoy in the Reaper's form. The pirate chief stumped over to a sideboard, retrieving ink, a hardwood pen and a sheet of smooth pulp paper from within. He leaned on the top of the sideboard to scrawl a short note.

'Tahu will take over the resettler fleet, under the Company's direction of course,' he said, as the sharp nib of the plume scratched over the paper, leaving a trail of brown. 'Company headquarters are to move to Cherk Harbour for the moment — Lantria is no longer a reliable base. I'm sure the Governor will be delighted. I want you to return to Argos as soon as possible. Get that slinking rat, Yago, to drop you off in Marak, then find a freighter to take you home. I want you back before the new month is out. I'm sending you on a mission of my own: you'll be using that machine you confiscated from the Freeholders.'

The Envoy signed and folded up the note, securing it with the pirate chief's hardwood seal, leaving the folded paper on the sideboard.

'Where will I be going, sir?' asked Gowron politely.

'I can't tell you that right now,' replied Lace. 'But I will say this: your journey will bring you much closer to my Masters. Consider yourself privileged.'

This news seemed to discomfit rather than please Gowron. His smile faded but he bowed stiffly in acknowledgment.

'That's right,' said Lace, who seemed to relish his acolyte's unease. He stepped close to Gowron, breathing over him. 'I'm giving you an opportunity beyond your wildest dreams, worth more than any Nurry girl, I promise you. You'll be performing a task for the true Lords of this world. If you prove yourself worthy, you'll be taken into their confidence.'

Gowron swallowed nervously. 'I'll be up to par, sir,' he said.

'I'm glad. My Masters do not tolerate failure,' rasped the Envoy. He continued to fix his acolyte from under his bristling brows. 'Now. It's time to perform your last service for the Reaper.' He held out the hardwood pen with a peremptory gesture.

Gowron took it, hesitating. 'Are you absolutely sure, sir?'

'Do it when I tell you to, you fool.'

Gowron tightened his fist about the pen and licked his lips spasmodically. Then, with a swift, practised thrust, he plunged the sharp point of the pen deep into the Reaper's jugular vein.

The pirate chief crumpled to his knees on the floor of the cabin, his eyes still fixed on the priest. Blood spilled down his neck and soaked into his shirt, bubbling from his lips. Gowron watched his master's host for the Exchange topple face down, collapsing in a vast and silent heap on the floor. He bent and slipped the pen into the Reaper's hand, closing his fingers about the shaft so that the murder would seem a suicide. As the pool of red expanded beneath the dead host's body, he turned and quit the cabin, slowly mounting the steps to the deck.

The *Aurora* sat basking in the winter sun in the Cherk Harbour docks. The morning was fresh and bright after the stuffy darkness of the cabin, and Gowron stood at the deck-rail a few moments, breathing in lungfuls of air. Then he descended the gangplank and made his way down the length of the dock, towards the second largest vessel in the resettlement fleet. Tahu's ship was already primed for departure.

There was silence in the Reaper's cabin. It took a while to separate from the Exchange; the Envoy's consciousness gradually disengaged from the madman's death and pulled away, contemplative. It was a relief to be free of the stench of humanity, to be whole and pure at last. For a moment the roving spirit of Eblas hung in the foggy, intermediate state outside the Exchange, neither housed in the Reaper's mind nor in the half-real construct known as Father Lace. He was reluctant to return to that false body in Argos city, tired of inhabiting those scraps of physicality pulled together with energy siphoned off from his acolytes. He wished for something more. His form in the trance was a thing of light rather than shadow. It stretched tall, craning upwards through the fog. One of the Born should not have to sully himself with such dross, he thought, in a burst of bitter longing. One such as he, who had been there to greet the Tree of Life when it broke the surface of eternity —

Eblas.

The name was a chain about his neck, weighing him down, yanking him back like a leash. He could not refuse the call and fell, heavy as a corpse, to the bottom of creation. His form lost all its beauty and became hunched and knotted as it struck the floor of the Veil. The headless Beast scrambled up on all fours, claws slithering on the ice. Its mouth gaped like a wound between its shoulder blades.

'Masters?' it yelped in surprise, to the avian shadows ranged about it.

'Eblas. Eblas,' they whispered, one after another. Their towering wings rustled and blotted out the faint stars of the prison-world. 'Eblas, you have failed us.'

'How can that be?' protested the Beast. 'I exist only to serve you, great ones! Even now I return from an Exchange, that filthy tortuous immersion in human excrement, so as to better set in motion our plans against Matrya. All I do, I do to promote your interests, to honour you —'

'The half-caste abomination the humans name Kion,' croaked one of the bird-kings, his head tilted sideways to blink at Eblas in one-eyed fury, 'is still alive. Her existence offends us.'

'But I did exactly as you desired!' objected the Beast-that-was-Lace, bewilderment colouring its voice. 'It can hardly be called a life, Lords. Her spirit is caught between the worlds, her body imprisoned even as you asked —'

'We do not speak of that paltry physical existence,' said another of the Masters, stretching out his neck in disdain. 'Her thoughts are alive. Her words run amok among the humans: one of their Grafters has saved them. You have not silenced her. We hear echoes of her even here — even here.'

The accusation ended on a note of pain. The other Masters stirred and groaned in agreement, stamping their heavy talons on the ice, making the floor of the Veil shake with their harsh cries. The Beast cringed before them.

'Such incompetence!' screeched a third. 'To allow the testament of an incarnated Born to reach an audience! She will now live forever, and not in the way that we seek. Her ideas will take root and flourish.'

'But no one knows if she's telling the truth,' whined the Beast. 'We will circulate false documents to confuse the population. No one will know the difference —'

'Fool,' interrupted the first Master. 'The proof is in the words themselves. They will stand the test of time. They will endure.'

'Your decisions,' snarled the second, 'have been a little flawed lately, wouldn't you say, Eblas? Consider your choices for acolytes: a murderer, with the appetites of a mindless animal; the priest, an addict — dead now, of course; a whining, crippled boy-child without the good sense to know how to help himself. Trash, all of them. Your last, the girl, could have been something. And yet you let her go.'

'I haven't let her go,' muttered Eblas sullenly. 'She still has the pendant. She belongs to us.'

'Another gamble,' said the third bird-king, looming over the Beast. 'And what about the young Grafter, Tymon? How could you send him out of your sphere of influence? Did it not occur to you that he might do more damage? He has irrevocably altered the prophecies in Argos.'

'The change was so minute as to be completely unimportant!' protested the Beast, trembling with fury even as it cowered. 'A shade of grey, a single letter in the story! What difference does an atom's movement make?'

'The difference between success and failure,' snapped one of the Masters who had not yet spoken. 'The difference between desire and repulsion, dark and light. Or have you forgotten the First Laws, Eblas? It takes but a single atom to change the attraction of an entire world.'

He shuffled forward, beak gaping, to place one of his great claws about the cowering Beast. The Master did not dig his talons into Eblas, but let them rest about him on the ice like the curved bars of a cage, a reminder of potentially crushing force. Eblas shivered at the mention of the 'First Laws' but did not answer, crouching in the shadow of the giant talons.

'Luckily, some semblance of victory may yet be achieved, at least over the span of a few generations,' resumed the first of the Masters. 'We are taking over supervision of your projects. We will no longer allow you to blunder through your mandate, missing every opportunity.'

'We give you one last chance to prove yourself,' added the second. 'The omens are favourable for the Oracle's death for the first time in eight hundred years: do not miss this chance. Find the Prophecy of the Seed — there should be a copy of it in the humans' library, if they have not completely lost sight of the truth. Use the *abjat*, and the Reader you gave your strutting little Saint, to calculate the exact location of Matrya's physical form. Even you should be able to do that.'

The bird-shadows spoke in quick succession now, stretching down their necks to hiss derisively at the Beast trapped in its cage.

'The Eastern Grafters must not be allowed to frustrate our plans. You will keep them in check while we supervise the search for the body.'

'Your human minions will answer to us.'

'Hopefully they will not botch their task as miserably as you have yours.'

The Master who had held the Beast in his talons withdrew his clawed foot at last, and reared up to his full height, beating his shadowy wings. 'Be gone, Eblas,' he shrieked. 'And do not fail us again.'

'Be gone,' echoed the other Masters. 'Be gone!'

The wind from their dark feathers whipped across the icy surface of the Veil, raising a crystalline vapour that swirled and eddied about the grovelling Eblas. The Beast backed away on its belly, growling softly in obeisance. Then, with a flick of its own curved claw, it ripped a hole in the gloomy fabric of the prison world, slipped through the gap and was gone. The bright edges of the tear sucked shut behind it.

There was a moment of silence as the last glittering crystals drifted to the floor of the Veil. The dead air promised numb peace: the stars shone brighter through the hunched silhouettes of the Masters. But before oblivion could creep over them again, the one that had confined Eblas bestirred himself.

'That dog grows presumptuous,' he said.

'It mocks us,' hissed the first Master, nodding in agreement. 'It sucks on our influence, thinking it is indispensable to us.'

'Might Eblas not remember what else lies in the chamber of the Seed?' asked the third, craning his neck worriedly up at the stars. 'Might our servant not seek to gain power over us by its means?'

'Indeed, my Lords,' answered the one who had held Eblas in the cage of his claws, blinking a malevolent eye at his associates. 'That is a danger. Perhaps we should find ourselves another slave. One easier to control.'

The rest of the Masters muttered in accord, shifting from foot to foot on the ice, feathers rustling. 'But who?' asked the first. 'We have only these human worms to choose from. Which one will do for our purpose? The one named Gowron? The young cripple — Wick?'

His companion had no lips with which to smile, but cackled with raucous satisfaction. 'Neither, my Lords. Without direct control, we shall be forever pleasing and propitiating the worms, which is tedious. There exists another possibility we have not yet discussed: the Exchange. I believe I may have found a way of bypassing the cursed laws that bind us.'

A few hours later, a similar rustling and crackling could be heard in the seminary archives, where a figure as hunched and brooding as the Masters squatted on the floor of the chamber, bending over a storage crate. The Envoy, back in the form of Father Lace, rifled through the contents of the box by the light of a flickering basket lantern. A draught from the open door caused the flame to gutter; a few paces away, his companion in the chamber, Father Fallow, shuffled half-heartedly through a heap of scrolls on a shelf. Lace ignored him. The Saint was of little use in his current endeavour, but he had been obliged to involve him in his research, as only Fallow held the key to the innermost archives. A faint hiss reminiscent of his Masters escaped the Envoy's lips, a breath of frustration.

For it all to come to this — to this! he ruminated. He had been sidelined, relegated to the post of research assistant in this repository of mortal dust. He, Eblas, a child of eternity! His efforts were taken for granted, his contributions dismissed. He gritted his teeth as he pulled another box out from a shelf. He knew very well that his Masters were seeking to replace him, deciding even now which acolyte they would use as their lackey, as if a human worm could ever supplant one of the Born. It was a paltry recompense for centuries of loyal service, an insult to be used in such a manner by beings long past their prime — beings whose experience had become so divorced from reality that they could no longer tell truth from lies, light from fire, faithfulness from treachery.

A plague upon them, decided Lace as he rummaged impatiently through the loose parchments. He would not be shrugged off. The Seed Prophecies were here somewhere, and he was determined to find them. He would gain ascendancy once more. Oh, his Masters would be gracious, cringing before him soon. He knew of just the means to convince them. The Envoy kicked aside the second crate with a snort of contempt. He had not forgotten what legendary source of power lay

41

hidden along with Matrya's body. He would find her, and then he would be the one to control the Key.

'Are you sure these old liturgies are in the archives?' grumbled Fallow, still picking in a desultory fashion at the pile of scrolls on the shelf. 'They're pretty obscure. I've never read them, to be honest.'

'I already consulted the *orah*-clock — the result was quite clear,' said Lace flatly. 'The verses are here at the seminary.'

'I still don't see why you're wasting your time with the Nonnians,' shrugged Fallow. 'The sect was composed of drug-addled misfits, everyone knows that. They wrote complete nonsense.'

Lace lifted weary eyes towards the man he had helped reach the apex of human power and achievement in Argos city: this petty, unimaginative Saint.

'Do you remember Juno and Lyla?' he asked. Fallow stared at him blankly in the shivering lantern-light. 'The fable of the mystic seeker,' he continued, sighing. 'The lover looks everywhere for his beloved, even in the most unlikely of places. According to the theory, if what you have lost is precious enough, you will search for it everywhere. Even among the dust and dross. That way you don't risk missing it.'

What had possessed him to bring up that particular story? the Envoy wondered to himself, a moment after he had spoken. He had not thought of the tale of the mad lover for what felt like a lifetime, and frowned in sudden misgiving, remembering that the story had been one of Matrya's favourites, a maudlin fable she used to instruct her human followers. Was he being influenced against his will? Even such inconsequential yarns could be dangerous. He resolved not to mention Juno and Lyla again.

But he need not have worried about any susceptibility to the truth on Fallow's part; the Saint was as blind to the implications of mystic love as he was to the everyday kind.

'You certainly go for the archaic yarns, don't you,' he replied to Lace, a little sulkily. 'Alright. So we're looking everywhere for a precious thing. What's so great about the Nonnians that you'd ask me to spend an afternoon rooting for them in the dust?'

'The verses contain clues to finding a powerful Grafting artefact,' said the Envoy. 'A relic of the Old Times, one your seminary Explorers did not bring back with them from their journeys. It is called the World Key.'

Fallow sneezed violently; the mildewed air of the archives did not agree with him. He retrieved an embroidered green handkerchief from his pocket and blew his nose with the blast of a foghorn. 'Let me guess,' he snuffled. 'This artefact opens a door to another world?'

'It opens a stable door to the Veil, among other things. It allows the user to enter without the Grafter's trance, protecting him from all harm and entrapment.'

'Fantastic,' Fallow snorted. 'Though why would we want to do that? You've told me enough times that the Veil is no more than a prison.'

'Precisely, Holiness.' Lace regarded him evenly. 'The one who controls the Key can use it to force others into the Veil — like a more powerful version of that Explorer artefact we were never able to recover, the trance-chair. Imagine being able to lock your enemies bodily in a state that is neither life nor death, with no chance of them waking up. No more dungeons, no more torture chambers: those who disagree with you are simply Veiled. They are invited to leave this world. Their return is dependent on your good pleasure.'

'Interesting,' conceded the Dean. 'But how do you explain that I've never heard of this World Key? Surely an artefact as important as that would be mentioned in our holiest texts, our most sacred writings, and not in some fantasist's ramblings?'

'Not if the Council had decided to suppress the knowledge,' said Lace, shoving aside his crate and rising to join Fallow at the shelf. 'As far as one can suppress anything while Grafters are around, of course. The Nonnians were a collection of fools and dreamers, yes. But they happened to have a few moments of lucidity. They are the only Argosian prophets who ever spoke of returning to the World Below, for example.'

Fallow rolled his eyes. 'I rest my case. There was a great deal of bellweed going into jar-pipes at the time.'

'An idea,' added the Envoy sharply, picking up and inspecting the scrolls Fallow had abandoned, 'which you know very well has some basis in theology and history. The Nonnians were systematically discredited for a reason, Holiness. Do not be so unwise as to believe your own faction's lies. Those dreamers knew something — something the Council at that time did not want repeated.' He ran his square-tipped finger along the dusty crates, musing aloud. 'The World Key is one of the greatest buried secrets of this institution, a truth so fearful that it was hidden not only from the masses of the people but from the Fathers themselves. A knowledge deliberately discarded by those who took the secret to their final rest ...'

'If they didn't want it, why would we?' said Fallow peevishly, his nose embedded in his handkerchief.

Lace turned to stare at him. 'Can you really believe that, after all you've seen?' he asked, incredulous. 'A commoner, a man in the street might say as much. I thought we understood each other when I first repaired the *orah*-clock for you, all those years ago. There's one truth for the masses, and another for the elite that guides them. I thought you wished to be part of the elite.'

'There's no need to be condescending,' sniffed the

Dean. 'I understand your point. The *orah*-clock has been a great boon to me. But I'm a man of action, Lace, and it irks me to be forever chasing after a so-called glorious past. We have a military strategy to figure out. Our plans for Nur are still in abeyance, and our policy for Lantria needs implementation. I'm tired of these minor prophecies: I want to go for the big stakes, and that means war. I can't help feeling it's time to "cast out the old and bring in the new".'

The Envoy's face was expressionless, his eyes shadowed in the lamplight as he surveyed the Saint. 'Remember what I am, Holiness,' he breathed. 'I am "the old". And I have no intention of being "cast out".'

He continued to stare at Fallow until the Dean twisted his handkerchief into a nervous ball and shoved it back into the pocket of his habit.

'I didn't mean it that way, of course,' he said hurriedly. 'I have the utmost respect for your judgment, my friend. I just meant, do you really need me to do this, right now? I have a meeting with Admiral Greenly before the afternoon temple service —'

'Naturally. You should go to your meeting.' Lace cut him off with a wave of the hand, releasing him from his deadly gaze. 'These minor prophecies, as you call them, contain more truth than a roomful of your military strategies. But you don't have to be here, no. Go plan your war. When you run into trouble, and want some of the power of the old world to help you conquer the new, we'll talk again.'

'I always appreciate your help,' protested Fallow. 'I respect the old ways. But I have to be the new Lawgiver too, you know.'

'Oh, I know,' said the Envoy. 'Was I not the one who suggested it?'

'I'll check on you again after the service,' called Fallow, hardly hearing the reply as he hurried away. He paused at the door, glancing back at his colleague. 'Are you sure you don't want one of the boys to help you out with this Key business? I know it's hard to find someone trustworthy, what with one of your acolytes in hospital and the other — he was a peculiar fellow, wasn't he? — off on that whimsical retreat of his. What a time to leave. Anyway, I could try to find a fifth-year student for you, Ambien might be able to recommend —'

'I'll be fine,' interrupted Lace. 'I'll see you later, Holiness. Don't worry about me.'

As Fallow's steps retreated in the corridor outside, the Envoy turned his attention back to the shelf. He was surrounded by abject fools, he thought. But that was to be expected among humans. Besides, he preferred to work alone. He did not want his activities too closely monitored by the Dean, who would in any case come crawling back to him soon enough.

He began to go methodically through each crate, rummaging among the crumbling parchments and ancient relics, reflecting as he did so on the ironies of mortal existence. Possessed of a priceless secret, these creatures left it to rot in storage, or dismissed it as the ravings of a madman. Those few who appreciated its significance were too frightened to make use of it, preferring ignorance and safety to the challenges of knowledge. They truly were worms, thought Lace, locked in their pupae-like experience and blind to all else. They were not worthy of the sublime. So much the better: it would belong to him alone. The Nonnians would lead him to the Oracle, and the Oracle would lead him to the Key.

His Masters, he knew, were well aware of this second treasure hidden in the Oracle's resting place, this ultimate secret within the secret. They had not seen fit to mention it when they raked him over in the Veil, of course. They did not want him to be the one to discover it. The mysterious artefact had remained hidden for millennia, already relegated to the status of fable when the first human civilisations flourished in the Tree. It was more ancient than the Ancients, older than the Old Ones. It was a type of machine, according to legend, an intricate device like the *orah*-clocks but far more subtle in its workings. It tuned itself to the mind of its possessor, becoming one with him. He who discovered the Key would wield great power. But there were other privileges it conferred, besides access to the Veil.

Lace had not told Fallow why the World Key was so important to him, never mentioning that it might be used to call those in the Veil back to this physical universe, as well as to send prisoners there. The Key would give his Masters limited access to the world of the living. Although the sentence that bound them to the Veil could not be wholly contravened, such dregs of liberty might prove attractive, after a long period of imprisonment. And if he, Eblas, were the one to claim the Key, it would be a liberty accorded and controlled by him alone.

After an hour or so of rifling through the crates, the candle in the lantern burned low. Father Lace replaced it with another from the store in his jacket pocket, and continued his inspection of the crates piled on the archives shelves. At long last, his search revealed a box shoved behind two others, marked with a circular green symbol. The paint was so faded by time as to be almost invisible, but Lace immediately pounced on it with a hiss of triumph. It contained at first glance only various articles of yellowed clothing, ancient leather-soled slippers and a squashed skullcap, the effects of some forgotten saint. The Envoy tore out the clothes and flung the slippers away from him, lifting up a crackling pile of vellum from the base of the box.

'They wrote it on the skin of living beings,' he murmured aloud, caressing the translucent sheets. 'It was too precious a secret to confide to bark and pulp.'

A moment after, however, he frowned. There were only a few pages left in the box, too few. He flipped through the sheets of parchment to the end, then back again. Sections of the text were missing. Not all the liturgies were present. He groaned aloud in frustration.

Perhaps it was only the draught from the door of the archives, but at that instant, the Envoy felt a soft stirring of air on the back of his neck, like a human breath. He spun about on his heel, gripped by the uneasy sense that someone was watching him. But no one stood in the doorway of the chamber. The use of the *orah*-clock might provoke just such an effect, he remembered. Was the Dean trying clumsily to spy on him, after having feigned disinterest in his efforts? Or, worse still, was this the prick of his Masters' eyes, peering at him from within the Veil? As he looked back towards the shelf, the sensation returned, stronger this time, a warning prickle on the back of his neck. The spy was close, physical. He could have sworn there was a face peeping out from behind the crates. And it was not the Dean's. His fingers darted out to grab at the impudent watcher; he retrieved a mask, empty-eyed and painted with white enamel. The movement of the boxes had caused it to slip out of a loosely fastened bag of black velvet at the very back of the shelf.

Standing alone in the archives chamber, the Envoy gave a dry bark of laughter. Where the enamel had chipped slightly at the edges of the object, he glimpsed the telltale gleam of *orah*. Here was a pretty surprise, and a welcome one, too. He had not expected to find more Explorer artefacts in the archives. This one had evidently been overlooked by the catalogue clerks. He put the mask gently back in its bag and set it on the table in the middle of the room. Then he turned back to the crates piled on the shelves and continued his search. By the time the Dean came back into the archives to visit him, three hours later, he had gone through every single box, and was sitting on a stool by the table, his head in his hands.

'No luck?' asked Fallow, approaching him with careful solicitude.

'I found some of them,' answered Lace. 'The liturgies are incomplete.'

'Too bad.' The Dean peered curiously at the sheets on the table beside the Envoy. 'If you say we've forgotten why they're important, we may be in trouble. This place hasn't been properly inventoried for years, and vellum is expensive: I've known scribes to rub the ink off old sheets and use them again ... Would there be copies in the main library? We might check the stacks upstairs and cross reference "key" with the words "Nonnian" and "world" —'

'I already checked,' interrupted the Envoy, moodily hunched under his black coat. 'The Council's misinformation has worked beautifully: nobody mentions the Nonnians except in passing. Besides, partial copies are useless. The liturgies contain the coordinates to the World Key, but you need all the pages, all the writing, to figure it out. It's a code. You'd have to apply the *abjat* system on the verses: the numerological alphabet of the Ancients, if you recall —'

'Number-magic?' Fallow raised an eyebrow. 'Why didn't you say so to begin with? I know where your Nonnians are. We put all that *abjat* stuff in the novices' prayer room, to encourage the students' use of mathematics. I had no idea those code games were what you were after. Come along, I'll show you where they are. Hidden in plain sight, of course. I'm glad I

49

can make up for leaving you alone in this place all afternoon.'

He placed a companionable hand on Lace's shoulder, and the latter suffered himself to be led out of the archives chamber, the roll of vellum and the white mask in its velvet bag bundled under his arm.

He might have known, the Envoy reflected numbly, as he traipsed up the stairs after Fallow. The humans had relegated their most weighty secrets to mere child's play, using one of the mystic keys to the universe to help the pimpled sons of Argosian burghers improve their grasp of basic arithmetic. Not even his Masters had guessed how far humanity had sunk into ignorance, oblivious of the ancient ways; they had expected the priests to keep the Seed Prophecies safe. The Fathers accused demons from the Storm of tempting their flock into heedlessness, but Lace was beginning to think they achieved that objective very well on their own.

Fallow helped him retrieve the Nonnian liturgies in their moth-eaten bindings from deep inside one of the stacks at the back of the study room, and left him to read the vellum sheets, making some further excuse for leaving to which Lace paid no attention. He barely looked up as Fallow melted out of the room, poring over the light script that had faded with time to a watery grey. The author of the liturgies was anonymous; the question of his identity never troubled Lace. As far as he was concerned, the nameless mystic had fulfilled the whole point of his brief life in writing these verses. The prophecies themselves were nonsense, existing only to house the code within. He could already sense the pattern beneath the phrases, the repetition of certain words like musical notes. It would not take him long to decipher the coordinates of the World Key.

When afternoon drew to a close and student voices

began to echo in the quadrangle outside, Lace collected up all the vellum sheets into a binder, tucked it under his arm and left the prayer room. He had assured himself that the liturgies were complete and that his computations would be correct. It only remained for him to do the actual calculations, and since Gowron was not due back in Argos city for another three weeks, there was plenty of time for that. There remained one more task for him to accomplish, before he began organising the expedition his Masters expected him to undertake.

The Envoy stepped out of the library building and strode onto the College quadrangle. His tread echoed in the chill air of the winter's evening. The sky visible in slices through the trellis of branches above was a startling blue, the colour of wild flowers or parrots' plumage. The towering, snowbound leaf-forests gleamed with hoar frost. But Lace did not pause to admire the beauty surrounding him. He made directly for the College infirmary and mounted the steps to the private wing reserved for the professors, entering a room closed off by a green curtain. A youth sat on the bed at the back of the room, gazing out of the window at the students laughing in the quadrangle below. He did not look around as Lace came in.

'They told me you had your bandages taken off today,' said the Envoy, rattling the curtain shut behind him. 'So. How's my favourite acolyte?'

Wick still did not turn around. He was fully dressed and evidently able to move about, but the skin on his hands and neck was a dangerous purplish red. The colour of pain, thought Lace. The young acolyte's voice when he answered was tight and husky.

'I want to die,' he whispered.

'That won't do!' remarked the Envoy, sitting down on the bed. He tried to look at Wick's face, but the

51

youth would have none of it and twisted away. 'You're a winner,' announced Lace with false cheerfulness, in an attempt to raise his spirits. 'Winners don't give in. They're sometimes down, but never out.'

'Do winners look like this?' blurted out his companion, low and fierce.

He did turn towards Lace then, showing the whole ruin of his face. The injuries he had sustained on the day of Samiha's execution, when he was caught in the inexorably closing door of the Veil, had been translated with painful accuracy to his physical body. There was nothing left of the smooth-cheeked boy who had taken orders at the seminary. Wick's flesh was raw, his lips and eyelids consumed as if by a disease, his bland, childish roundness gone forever. He trembled as he spoke and his red-rimmed eyes were awash with tears.

'No one will ever love something that looks like this,' he said in a choked whisper, jabbing a finger at his scarred features. He bowed his head, his shoulders heaving.

'Now, now,' murmured the Envoy. He attempted to pat Wick on the back, but snatched his hand back hastily as the other cringed in pain. 'It's hard at the moment, but I promise you're going to come through this, and come through it strong. Think of the one who did this to you. Would you like Tymon to see you so defeated?'

'I'll kill him,' snarled Wick, looking up again immediately. 'I'll make him suffer for what he's done.'

'There you go,' replied Lace heartily. 'Focus on your anger. Use it to recover. You'll have your revenge.'

'The girl, too,' grated Wick. 'Jedda: you said she was gone when you visited the other day. Well, she should have been there with me on the dock, and helped. I want to make her feel like I do now. Raw. Eaten. Pecked to death.'

The Envoy's smile broadened. 'We might just be able to do that,' he said. 'Meanwhile, I have a present for you. This will make you feel better, I think.'

He put the prophecies in their binder down on the bed, and retrieved the velvet bag, which he had slipped into the pocket of his coat. 'It's no ordinary disguise, of course,' he said, drawing out the mask. 'It's made of *orah* under the paint.'

He did not give it to Wick at once, but instead placed it over his own face. Wick gasped in amazement as the mask slowly faded away and became transparent, showing only his master's familiar features.

'Another treasure plundered by our friends the Explorers,' Lace said, removing the mask again and handing it to Wick. 'I thought this one had been lost, actually. It was called "Hadron's mirror", back in the day. With a little concentration you can use it to look like anyone, but I imagine you'll be wanting to appear unscarred from time to time. Just a word of warning,' he added, as Wick turned the artefact over in his hands, inspecting it wonderingly. 'Don't use it for extended periods. If you must wear it for a whole day, or two, take it off for an equivalent amount of time afterwards. Otherwise the Seeming will lose potency — and you'll have other problems, besides.'

He rose from the bed, retrieving the binder. 'When you're ready, Wick, you may join me on the bell tower. Tonight, if you're feeling up to it. I have some chastisement in store for our troublesome Grafter friends. I need your help to achieve it.'

'Thank you, sir,' murmured Wick hoarsely, holding the mask against his chest. 'Thank you for everything.'

'All part of the service,' laughed Lace. 'What sort of mentor would I be if I didn't help my students? You and I are excellent allies, Wick. This unfortunate business will only bring us closer together, you'll see.'

He turned and stalked out of the infirmary, leaving the youth cradling the mask. He had not told Wick the other name that had been given to that infamous relic in days gone by, when it had been developed by a rogue practitioner of the subtle arts now known as sorcery. Even the humans had their master criminals, and this one had used the mask to escape the law of the Ancients, at least for a while. He had also given a pet name to his creation, calling his subatomic particle-warping device — his 'SAP'-warp — 'Sweet Oblivion', and wearing it until it drove him to his grave.

It was nearing midnight when the Envoy and his acolyte stood together in the arched alcove at the summit of the bell tower, gazing out over the moonlit city far below, a descending jumble of darkened rooftops and crooked chimney pots. There were only a few twinkling lamps visible at this late hour, as the inhabitants had already locked their doors and drawn their curtains against the encroaching night. Above the two standing in the tower alcove, the great, curved mass of the bells hung silent.

Wick's breath rose in chill clouds in the darkness. He shivered, the wind biting the newly healed scars on his cheeks as he surveyed the familiar spectacle of the town lying beneath him. Argos city had been his home since birth, the theatre of a thousand boyhood triumphs and frustrations. But now he was a stranger in his own country, cut off from the joys and cares of ordinary citizens, no longer even associating with his fellow lordlings in the upper echelons of society. He had given all that up to be the Envoy's acolyte, choosing the lonely road to power. The price was worth it, he told himself, shoring up his determination against the bitter night. For was he not possessed of the fundamental secrets of existence? He waited deferentially for his master to begin their next ritual, hunching his shoulders beneath his heavy winter cloak.

The Envoy waited for the time to be exactly right. Each hour of the day had its own occult significance, dependent upon the position of the sun and stars. The workings of space and time were not without meaning, for there were periods when the force humans called 'Sap' flowed more freely and the generating power of the universe was easier to predict or control. No stargazer's diagram or leaf-watcher's chart, no merely human system of divination had ever come close to correctly mapping those mighty ebbs and flows. Only the all-encompassing science practised by the Born, the science that was both logic and belief, experiment and intuition, had ever been capable of navigating its complexity. It was a profound and robust knowledge now abandoned in this world, replaced by the maudlin dabblings of sorcerers and the Grafters' blind, unquestioning faith.

Lace despised both, of course, though he kept his disgust well hidden from his mortal allies. He despised all things human, their clumsy, unripe attempts at understanding. But he was obliged to make use of the tools at his disposal; the sentence placed upon him left him no other choice. He had been forcibly severed from the Sap, the creative power of the universe, and reduced to beggary, his consciousness starved of all but the absolute minimum of energy. The bounty lavished so freely upon this physical world was denied him. The unpleasant truth was that a single spark of the smokeless flame burning in the heart of even the most stupid human being was brighter, warmer, stronger than anything still smouldering in the ashy soul of the Special Envoy of the First Born.

Although he would never tell Wick so, Lace needed a human accomplice to perform the slightest ritual involving the Sap. It was a grinding insult, a slap in the face, but he would not let that stop him. After a grim moment passed watching the frost-bound city, he came to stand behind his acolyte, placing his hands on Wick's shoulders and turning him inexorably towards the east. Those with the Sight were conduits, attracted like the points of the Ancients' compasses towards an inner north. Like the *orah*, they were irresistibly drawn to the world of their origins, the esoteric world of the Tree of Being.

'Weakness be strength,' the Envoy muttered. He could not keep an edge of bitterness from his voice.

There was an energy in anger, a power in bitterness. It was a debased and unstable force, but it had its uses. His acolyte was seething with both emotions, overflowing with bitter pride and furious injury. They had already marked him and would eventually consume him. But for now, Wick's hurt and rage were excellent tools for the Envoy. The garbled 'words of welcome' were hardly spoken before the youth flung back his head and jerked loose from his master's grip, falling to his knees on the floor of the alcove. Wick was gasping, his body racked with spasms. After retching violently for a few moments, his mouth opened and he vomited up a gluey mass of black feathers. A jagged wing forced its way between his teeth, followed by a jabbing beak. Even as he groaned and retched again, a bird-like creature clawed its way out of his mouth and hopped onto the floor with a single, raucous cry.

The creature's eyes were blind, two milky-white knobs on either side of its matted head. A vile stench rose from its body. It seemed more a mockery of a bird than the real thing, a travesty of ill-fitting bones and viscous feathers. Wick stared at it in stunned silence as it gave another hoarse cry and flapped heavily into the air, blundering through one of the arched apertures of the alcove. But the horror was not yet over. After a few moments the spasms shook the acolyte again and he bent over, moaning. Another head, another filthy beak thrust its way through his lips. A second matted nightmare emerged and flapped off into the night.

'How many?' groaned Wick, holding his belly and collapsing on the floor as the seizures wracked his body.

'As many as it takes,' replied Lace coolly. 'As many as need be to find our two troublesome friends, and bring our curses home to roost. That's what you want, isn't it?'

Wick nodded through a nauseous mouthful of feathers, and doubled up on the floor of the alcove in pain.

3

Time was hard to quantify in the dirigible's hold, as the only natural light shone through chinks in the trapdoor in the ceiling. Twice daily it was opened to allow a trough of slops to be lowered or hauled up as necessary. No one extended a ladder into the space below. As far as Tymon could tell from the alternating light and dark glimpsed through the chinks, he spent almost a week lying on the filthy floor of the hold before he was even able to move. The wounds on his back slowly closed over and healed, but his left ear remained dull and filled with a faraway ringing. Whether due to the gloom or some combination of pain and disorientation from the blow to his head, he could neither see nor hear properly. His vision was shot through by trails of drifting colour, bright orange and pink, as if a bright and unruly dawn had invaded the bowels of the ship. He tried to ignore the persistent illusion, and spent much of his time sleeping, finding more often than not when he awoke that he was being attended to by the boy named Zero. He was very lucky, the Nurian lad informed him with a snaggletoothed grin, that his cuts were healing so cleanly. People sometimes lost their lives after a flogging, as hungry spirits tried to enter their bodies through their wounds, causing a fever. Their blood turned yellow and they died, the ginger-haired boy announced cheerily.

Tymon learned from his eccentric new friend that the Lovage ship had arrived while he lay unconscious at Hayman's Point, picking him up along with the other workers rejected by the overseers. There was a worse fate, apparently, than being sent to a Tree-mine; Zero referred to their current destination as a 'death plantation', an outfit near the south fringes of the canopy where unwanted labourers were simply worked until they dropped. His fellow rejects were a tired and dispirited bunch, with the notable exception of this ginger-haired lad.

Tymon gathered that Zero was an orphan like himself, native to Marak city and sold to the priests a year ago by his one surviving family member, a feckless uncle. The Nurian boy bore no grudge against this relative, however, and accepted his fate with cheerful optimism. His topsy-turvy philosophy of good and evil appeared to have given him infinite hope, for he maintained that the more evil someone was, the better his chances of survival. The two of them were evil enough to escape any fate, he declared to Tymon. Zero's attentions undoubtedly saved the young man's life, for despite their loathing of 'lying Argosians', the other Nurians did not finish Tymon off while he lay helpless on the floor of the hold. They allowed Zero to minister to him unhindered, as if they considered the Marak youth sacred in his simplicity, and were loath to thwart him. It was thanks to him that Tymon was given his fair share of the scraps sent down by the ship's guards and slowly recovered his strength; Zero's unstinting kindness won his gratitude and, over the course of the following days, a firm friendship developed between the two youths.

There were some subjects, however, that Tymon could not raise in front of his companion. In fact, he had to wait for Zero's absence before he felt free even to consider them himself. But as soon as he was able to do so, he questioned the Oracle regarding his vision.

'I Saw Samiha,' he whispered to the floorboards some time after his first awakening, when Zero had left him alone in the fetid darkness. 'I Saw a vision of her during the flogging, *Ama*. What does it mean?'

'I don't know,' responded the voice in his head. The Oracle's tone was cautionary. 'Be careful, Tymon. That sort of harsh punishment is known to produce altered mental states. Your vision could have been a hallucination, nothing more.'

'So you don't think it was real?' His heart sank. 'Only a sort of fever dream?'

'I told you, I don't know,' she answered. 'I hear your thoughts, but do not See what you See. Perhaps you had a real vision. Perhaps not. Be careful, in any case.'

'What if it was real?' he insisted. 'If I can't see ghosts, what could it have been?' A marvellous idea dawned on him. 'Is she still alive, *Ama*?' he gasped, half-lifting his head from the floor, despite the pain.

'There is a slim chance, I suppose. I doubt it.' The Oracle sighed. 'My instinct is to tell you to put all this out of your mind, Tymon. To consider such possibilities while you can do nothing to verify them will only make you miserable. It's easy to become wrapped up in dreams when you have lost so much. Focus on the present. I suggest you worry about staying alive yourself.'

Tymon was obliged to swallow his disappointment and accept the fact that he would not be able to resolve the matter to his satisfaction, at least for now. He could not launch a trance surrounded by the Nurian prisoners, or search for traces of Samiha in the Tree of Being while he was in the hold of this ship; he was obliged to wait, frustratingly, until he was out of other peoples' observation and, most importantly, beyond the Envoy's reach. The point of his liberation from the latter was hard to gauge, for it was a mystical rather than mundane state and linked, according to the Oracle, to the sphere of influence generated by the *orah*-clock. The Envoy's power waxed and waned with the time of year and the position of the stars, in a strange amalgam of physical science and sorcery. Tymon had no idea how that sphere of influence was calculated, and could only do as his teacher had advised for the time being, concentrating on recovery.

Indeed, recovery was his one remaining hope, for he knew no allowances would be made for an injured worker on the Lovage farm. The pilgrims in the hold may have left him in peace because they knew, with bleak practicality, that punishment would find him soon enough in the death plantation. He took some comfort from the fact that neither Aidon nor Aybram were among the unlucky ones on the ship: the brothers had been kind to him, and he had no wish to see them suffer.

As the journey wore on, and Tymon gradually recovered from his flogging, the hours no longer bled into each other in a formless haze of pain. After a week on the dirigible, his back had healed well enough to allow him to stand up and move about. Although stray lights still bedevilled his vision, and the ringing in his left ear did not diminish, he was able to take short walks up and down the hold, leaning on Zero's arm. Recovery came none too soon, for he calculated that the ship must have reached the southern borders of the canopy by now. And still the Oracle gave him no practical insight as to how he would escape the Lovage plantation. She was frequently absent from his mind; when she returned, she encouraged and exhorted him as always, but did not tell him what he so desperately wanted to hear.

'You'll never be free, if you go on like this,' the Oracle informed him one morning, the eighth after his ordeal at Hayman's Point.

He had been shuffling down the length of the hold at Zero's side, mentally calculating their probable distance from Argos city for the third time that day. Despite his teacher's warnings, he could not help thinking about Samiha at every waking moment: he waited impatiently for the time when he would be far enough from the Envoy and able to launch a Reading. Perhaps the other Focals would be able to give him some clue about his vision, he thought.

'You'll always be susceptible to Eblas while you're wrapped up in your desires,' continued the Oracle. 'You aren't focusing on the present, like I told you to.'

'It's hard,' he mumbled. 'The present is pain. Can't a man have some hope?'

'I never hope,' announced Zero, at his elbow. 'Hope is for good people. Evil people do not hope. We hold on.' And he gripped tightly onto Tymon as he swayed.

'I like this one,' said the Oracle, amusement colouring her voice. 'Keep him close, he has a lot of sense. If you hold on to any hope, let it be him.'

'I'm holding,' Tymon protested, in answer to both of them. 'But I do need something to look forward to, you know.'

'Well, don't make it the Kion,' advised the Oracle. 'Your love for her is your greatest weakness. You were freer when you thought her gone for good, which I feel obliged to warn you is most probably the case.'

How can you be certain? he cried silently. *Even you admit that the future can be vague, that prophecies can change. How do you know she isn't there?* She did not answer him: she never answered his thoughts when it did not suit her. But he was not about to let her wriggle out of a response this time.

'If Samiha were alive, wouldn't you See her?' he muttered later, when Zero had left him alone in his corner of the hold. 'You Read the future differently from most Grafters: you're always in the trance. The Envoy can't hurt you, not really. Don't you sense her in the Tree of Being?'

'Oh yes,' said the Oracle. 'But not in the way you mean. She is there because her influence is there. Her testament will travel far and wide, thanks to you. That's one of your greatest triumphs and you should be happy about it.'

He bowed his head over his knees and remained silent, not happy in the least.

'Tymon, I must tell you something,' she continued. Her voice had become anxious: she sounded, if possible, harried. 'Remember, on the way out of Cherk Harbour, I spoke to you about the Envoy and his people.' He nodded, forgetting that she could not see him. 'Well, the powers that Eblas serves are still very much in existence and more than a match for me. They were banished to the Veil long ago, after the war that tore apart the Born, or the First Born as they were called at the time. Normally, the Envoy's Masters are not able to access the physical world even to the extent their lackey does, for they are bound by a harsher sentence. But they have other abilities. They can enter this world through our dreams, when they find a weakness. They are also capable of attacking me when they rouse themselves sufficiently. They are doing so right now.'

'What?' Tymon blurted. He was shocked out of his self-pity. 'The Masters are attacking you? Are you alright?'

'I can hold my own,' she said steadily. 'But I need you to be strong. I need you to focus. If I am detained you must be able to go on alone, do you understand? You cannot let yourself be distracted.'

'I won't,' he promised. The thought of losing her to some struggle he could not fathom was sobering. 'You can rest easy about me, *Ama*. I won't be stupid.'

But his teacher had made one of her periodic exits, abandoning him.

He pondered her words in his heart, in the gloom of the hold, under the scrutiny of the suspicious Nurians and accompanied by the babbling Zero. What had she meant, about being attacked, detained? How was it possible for him to go on alone? He had no answer to these questions and could only wait, anxious, for her return. Later, when the empty food trough had been withdrawn and the prisoners had huddled in their various corners of the hold, he felt her abruptly present in his mind again.

'It's happening sooner than I expected,' she announced, without preamble.

'What is?'

Despite his anxieties, Tymon had begun to fall asleep in his corner when her voice shook him awake again. He guessed by the diminishing light in the trapdoor that afternoon had given way to evening, and blinked groggily through the scraps of colour clinging to his vision. 'What's happening?' he repeated, wondering nervously if the Envoy's Masters were about to attack him, too. Nearby, Zero snored softly, his large body curled up like a Tree-bear by the wall.

'We're reaching a point of confluence, a point in the Tree of Being where many Leaf Letters intersect,' replied the Oracle. 'I call it a "knot". Events are going to speed up. Keep your wits about you.'

Tymon shook himself fully awake. 'Is the future clear to you again, then?'

'The future is always clear to me, but it's also always changing. Knots are dangerous but predictable moments, necessary crossing places. They occur no matter what path we take. Points of prophecy, if you will.'

'What do you See this time?' he asked, trying to rub the skeins of colour out of his eyes.

'An attack on this ship at noon tomorrow. The Lantrians are retaliating against Argosian manoeuvres in the South Canopy. I thought it would take place on the farm in a couple of days' time, but it seems set to happen sooner.' Her voice in his head, unlike the sounds in his shattered ear, was crisp, clear and unequivocal. 'This is your opportunity to escape. Regain your energy as soon as possible. You must at all costs be able to walk unaided when the attack occurs.'

He considered this sudden glut of information. The Oracle could be very precise when she wanted to be. 'What about the Masters?' he asked. 'Have they let you be?'

'For now,' she answered. And suddenly her voice was soft. 'Did you miss me while I was gone, child?'

'Yes,' he said, to his own surprise.

'Then I will do my best to stay,' she replied. 'Rest: every hour counts. You'll have need of your strength in the morning.'

He drifted to sleep then, rocked in the cradle of her silence. But it was still dark in the hold when she roused him again, her voice urgent.

'Tymon!'

'Yes?' He pushed himself up on his elbow rather too quickly, then grimaced as the brusque movement chafed his back.

'The Lantrian raid!' she cried. 'It's happening now. I swear by the Sap, they cannot wait to exterminate each other.' Her tone was exasperated.

They were interrupted by a dim shout from above, the muffled cry of the lookout. There was the thud of running feet on the deck and an alarm horn gave three sharp blasts.

'Damn their impatience,' breathed the Oracle.

Tymon rose shakily to his feet, clinging to the wall of the hold. The pilgrims who had woken at the sound of the horn gazed anxiously up at the locked trapdoor, the whites of their eyes glinting in the darkness. Then a terrific jolt and jerk of the ship almost knocked Tymon to his knees again, and there was a sickening crunch, as if the dirigible had crashed headlong into a branch.

'God's vengeance against the wicked,' yelped Zero, waking belatedly, his eyes round with terror.

'Get back!' ordered the Oracle, as Tymon stumbled and clutched at the wall again. 'There's going to be an explosion!'

And even as she spoke, Tymon Saw it. For an instant, her prediction hung visible before him: the timbers of the hull shivering under his hand, buckling, replaced by a perilous circle of expanding fire. The vision blinded him and he could no longer make out his ordinary surroundings. He staggered backwards in a black fog, grabbing what he hoped was Zero's sleeve and pulling the lad away with him as another massive jolt shook the ship. The darkness of the hold was replaced by brilliant light; a gust of hot air hit Tymon in the face and he fell to the floor, rolling away from the wall. The blindness lifted from his eyes, and he gazed in consternation at the spot where he had just been standing. The fiery ring was there, utterly real this time and accompanied by a shockwave of heat and light. The hull had disintegrated, leaving a circular opening punched clear through to the exterior of the ship. Beyond the hole, he could make out the chill grey silhouettes of the leaf-forests where the dirigible had been moored for the night, though as yet no Lantrian ship. Long tongues of fire licked through the gap and into the hold. Zero clung to his arm like a child as the pilgrims screamed and scrambled over each other to escape the flames.

'It seems the enemy have their own supply of new weaponry,' remarked the Oracle. 'That would explain the over-eagerness to attack, perhaps.'

'Blast-poison!' Zero blurted out, staring at the hole. 'Devil's work!'

'Not devils. People,' answered Tymon grimly. 'We don't need devils to do our dirty work, Zero. Both Argosians and Lantrians have blast-poison now. But a plantation ship won't be equipped to defend itself. We're in trouble.'

He turned aside, addressing the Oracle in an undertone as Zero gawped at the flaming gap in the side of the ship. 'What next, *Ama?*'

'It's all clear now,' she replied gloomily. 'Nothing destroys free will more thoroughly than war. The whole damned knot is predictable down to a hair's breadth. Stay sharp and do exactly as I say.'

She told him to wait a little longer where he was and to be ready to move at her signal. He kept hold of Zero's arm to prevent him from wandering off and remained crouched on the floor. Several pilgrims were attempting to reach the trapdoor, climbing on each other's shoulders to form a ladder of bodies. The man at the top called and pounded against the hatch, but his voice was lost, or perhaps ignored, in the shouting from above. The ceiling shook as people ran across the deck. Some of the remaining Nurians ventured to the edge of the hole caused by the explosion, in an attempt to escape their trap. But flames still crackled greedily about the opening and it was impossible to get a firm grip on the side of the ship. The dirigible was moored too far from any horizontal branch to allow the prisoners to jump to safety. Another rending crash went through the vessel, and a part of the ceiling collapsed on the unfortunate pilgrims by the gap. A dark form passed over the leaf-forests outside.

'Now,' commanded the Oracle suddenly. 'To the hole. You're going to jump.'

Tymon lost no time in stumbling forwards, dragging the shambling Zero after him. 'Where to?' he gasped to the Oracle, peering through the circle of wavering flames, his eyes stinging from the smoke.

She did not need to answer, for there below them was the Lantrian warship, a sleek vessel rising up through the leaf-forests parallel to the Argosian barge. The dark shape he had seen crossing the leaf-forests was one of the ether balloons. Near the stern of the enemy ship, Tymon made out the bulky form of a catapult surrounded by the hurrying figures of the crew. There was a small window of opportunity, a few seconds to leap down onto the deck of the other vessel before anything worse happened. He hesitated.

'What are you waiting for?' asked the Oracle anxiously.

He turned towards the other Nurians in the hold, still frantically trying to break their way out of the trapdoor. 'You have to jump!' he called to them. 'It's the only way!'

They did not answer. They barely looked at him. The deck of the Lantrian ship was now almost level with the gap. 'There's another ship below us!' he shouted desperately. 'You can make it if you try!'

But his fellow prisoners were deaf to the warning. At last, heeding the Oracle's urgent cry, he clutched Zero's arm and stepped out, pulling the Nurian boy after him. Out of the gap, into the air, falling into emptiness just as Samiha had fallen.

A moment later, they were both rolling on the deck of the Lantrian ship. Tymon picked himself up before Zero, his back smarting and his eyesight inexplicably restored, though his ear still rang. The trails of colour and light that had troubled him were gone. All too clearly, he beheld the white faces of the Nurians staring at him through the gap in the gutted hold of the plantation ship: a frozen image of disbelief, then dawning realisation and accusation, as though Tymon were the one who had done this to them. The Lantrian vessel drifted up and past, sliding out of reach. Somewhere to the left, an order was given, and the deadly catapult snapped again. Tymon turned away in horror as the entire side of the Argosian barge disintegrated in a sheet of flame.

Within moments, he and Zero were seized by the Lantrian soldiers, who marched them both down to the hold of the warship. The interior of the vessel smelled of dried hemp and Tree-pitch, a welcome change from the bowels of the farm-barge. The brig was evidently not designed to take many prisoners, though it had a hardwood storage locker equipped with a sturdy barred door. When the soldiers had left them there and clattered back up the ladder to the deck, Tymon sat for a while crouched in darkness, unable to speak. It was the Oracle who broke the silence.

'Don't feel bad,' she reassured him. 'You tried to warn them.'

'They wouldn't listen,' he whispered.

'You're going to have to get used to this sort of thing, you know. No one ever listens to prophets.'

The shock of their getaway appeared to have struck Zero dumb. The Nurian lad sat gazing fixedly at Tymon; after a while, he simply lay down on the floor of their cage in a helpless heap and closed his eyes. When no one arrived to question them or to bring more prisoners to the brig, Tymon did the same. The sounds of the attack above receded. There were no further explosions, and he could only assume that the Argosian ship had been destroyed. He did not ask the Oracle more about her 'knot' of events, or speculate as to how the Lantrians might have come by their weapons. He was too sad, too weary to care what happened next. He stretched himself out on the floor beside Zero and slipped into blessed oblivion.

How long he slept, he did not know, but it must have been several hours. When his eyes blinked open again, he saw rays of midday sun filtering through the open trapdoor of the hold. Through the hatch, he caught a raucous echo of laughter, sailors talking loudly in Lantrian on the deck. He could not for the moment distinguish the foreign words clearly, or scrape together the concentration to remember his language lessons at the seminary. Zero was standing by the locker bars, gazing up at the hatch door. When he saw that Tymon was awake, his face broke into a slow smile.

'You have powerful friends,' he said, coming to squat down beside Tymon.

'What do you mean?' asked Tymon, perplexed.

'Spirits.' The youth nodded meaningfully. 'Powerful, evil ones. You speak to them; I've seen you. They warned you about the attack, didn't they?'

'It's a form of explanation, I suppose,' noted the Oracle, from the background. 'And perhaps the most expedient, for now.'

Tymon grimaced and shrugged, making an allowance for Zero's statement.

'I thought so,' murmured the Nurian lad in satisfaction. 'Anyway, I wanted to say: thanks for helping.'

'It's nothing.' Tymon sat up, feeling the multiple stabbing points of pain in his back. 'I owe you my life. Of course I'd try to save you.'

'No, not just that,' said Zero. 'Thank you, because my evil had almost run out. I didn't want to leave the other pilgrims. You made me leave, and live. Otherwise, I'd have given in.'

Tymon winced again, both at the truth in the statement and the discomfort in his own body. 'Try not to think about it,' he said gently. He could not bear to.

The Marak boy rocked on his heels, considering him with his head to one side. 'Well, here's where we are then,' he observed. 'I hope your spirits help us again. I don't know much about Lantrians but I'm willing to bet they're honourable folks, right? Good, honourable and kind, just like our great *Argosi* masters. Nothing to choose between them. We're in trouble, right?'

'Oh yes, he's insightful,' chortled the Oracle. 'A rare treasure, this one. Pity he doesn't have the Sight: I'd have made a fine Grafter of him.'

'I'm sure the Lantrians think they're very honourable indeed,' said Tymon to Zero, smiling. 'But you're right. I'm afraid we've jumped from the pot straight into the fire.'

'We'll need to look out for each other,' declared his friend. 'Make sure each other's evil stays up to scratch.'

'Don't worry,' answered Tymon. 'I'll be looking out for you, Zero, I promise.'

They crossed into the South Canopy and arrived in the Lantrian mining concern of Chal that same evening, though they were only told the name as they were herded out of the warship and onto the bridge that served as an extended dock for the settlement. The two bored soldiers who accompanied them clearly considered the job of moving prisoners to be far beneath them; they grumbled all the way as they thrust their charges down the boardwalk, with a swiftness born of impatience.

Tymon glanced about him, as he was pushed along, in an attempt to take in his surroundings. The hardwood bridge spanned a natural crater in a colossal hollow branch. The rift that had split the vertical limb was

71

roughly a quarter of a mile across, while the great branch itself was at least twice as large as any Tymon had ever seen. Innumerable subsidiary branches extended out from this central column, filling the whole area about it with a fretwork of interlocking twigs and leaves. He had no doubt that it was one of the primary supports of the Lantrian leaf-table, one of the struts extending from the Tree trunk to support the entire South Canopy. And it was largely hollow.

Tymon found it quite daunting to march on thin planks over unimaginable depths. The fissure below the bridge plunged so deep that its bottom was lost in darkness. The walls of that interior crater, he saw in the distance, were dotted with winding roads and scaffolding, tiny human constructions leading down to the bottom of the mine-shaft. For this was not only a primal branch of the Lantrian canopy, but one of its principal sources of wealth. Hardwood was being mined in the depths of the great limb. Tymon gave an involuntary shudder as he followed his new captors, overcome by vertigo; the Lantrians evidently had no qualms about excavating deep into the very heart of their world.

Everything about Chal was oversized, grander in scale than he was used to. Dirigibles of all shapes and sizes were moored at the sides of the dock-bridge, from slow-moving barges loaded with hardwood to merchant greatships of the best quality. With sinking spirits, he glimpsed several of the sleek resettlement ships he had come to know and dread in Cherk Harbour. Although the guards prodded him on at a cracking pace, it seemed to take forever to walk across the acres of planks to the buildings on the far side, a row of colourful constructions bathed in the rays of the setting sun. He wondered gloomily what life awaited them there.

The custom house, when they finally reached it, proved to be a grandiose three-storey affair, painted a pale pink and lined with columns and windows. Lantrians with their distinctive flowing robes and shaven heads scurried in and out like ants in a ceaseless round of activity. Tymon's guards plunged inside with the rest, pushing their charges along crowded corridors and up stairwells echoing with the sound of feet, past scribes overloaded with scrolls and merchants arrayed in improbably ornate wooden collars. Tymon remembered the odious Governor in Cherk Harbour, with his clicking earlobes; the richer the Lantrian merchant, apparently, the larger the earrings and the collar. About him were all the trappings of wealth and industry, sophistication and cynicism a great nation would possess. He realised, with a rueful twinge, that he had fulfilled another childhood hope in visiting his dream destination of Lantria. The reality of the place, as well as the circumstances of his arrival, left something to be desired.

The guards did not halt until they reached the top floor of the building. There, they thrust the two prisoners ahead of them through a pair of large straw-screen doors marked with a word in Lantrian that Tymon recognised as 'Personnel'. Moving through the custom house, he had begun to recall his foreign language lessons at the seminary, piecing together fragments of overheard conversation and deciphering the writing on signs. He imagined that he and Zero would now be assigned their official duties in the mine, and braced himself for unpleasant news.

The long room they entered was filled with cramped desks and busily scratching scribes. Most wore the scanty loincloths common to the Lantrian underclass, with a few concessions to weather in the form of cloaks and tunics. One man seated near the entrance rose to meet them. Tymon thought at first that he was an official of some importance, judging by his white robe and headdress. But he carried a carved hardwood tablet about his neck, rather than a collar. Upon it Tymon made out the words 'This slave is the property of Dayan Hordannan IV'.

'Slaves managing slaves,' the Oracle mused. 'A whole nation made up of captives, some of whom rise to enjoy the material privileges of their masters. I've always found these people very peculiar.'

'May I help you?' the man asked the soldiers, in his own tongue. Tymon turned his good ear towards his captors so as to better understand the exchange.

'Two Nurian survivors picked up during a raid on an Argosian farm vessel,' answered one of the guards, over-officiously. 'They fall in the Hordannan preserve.'

The clerk retrieved an enormous bark-bound register from one side of his desk and heaved it open, the leaves crackling. He did not hurry in his task but turned the pages slowly, one by one, as the soldiers fidgeted with impatience.

'Former names?' the clerk finally asked.

He did not glance at Tymon and Zero as he dipped his quill-tip in ink, poised over the blank page to write. Tymon did not grasp that the booming words were being addressed to him, until he realised that the question had been asked in Argosian. He snapped to attention as the man looked up at him with a raised eyebrow.

'My name is Tymon!' he exclaimed belatedly. He patted Zero's arm: the Marak lad's shoulder was too high to reach. 'And this is Zero, sir.'

The clerk scratched a few marks on his book. 'You're both Hordannan now,' he remarked. 'There are no other names here.'

He continued to write in silence. Tymon could not

read the script from where he stood, and waited with trepidation. But the clerk appeared to enjoy having them hang on his every word, perhaps in retaliation against the soldiers. One of the guards snorted with suppressed frustration.

'The assignation,' the slave-clerk resumed mildly, after an excruciating pause, 'will be Third Regiment. A moment more, if you please,' he added, as the guards spun smartly about, preparing to leave the room with the prisoners. The clerk fixed his level gaze on Tymon. 'You're no Nurry,' he drawled, in Lantrian. 'And you speak our language.'

A hush descended on the room and the sound of scratching pens ceased. Tymon heard a muffled sound of whispering through the ringing in his ear. A few of the scribes nearby glanced slyly at him.

'I'm Argosian,' he mumbled in the foreign tongue, dredging up the words learned long ago. 'I studied Lantrian in school. A little bit.'

The clerk strolled out from behind his desk. He was a short man and overweight, but carried himself with dignity, coming forward to peer closely at Tymon's face.

'That wound on your ear,' he said, as the soldiers puffed and shuffled with impatience at the delay. 'Does it prevent you from hearing on one side?'

Tymon nodded, embarrassed. He was about to say that he had no problem on the other side, when the clerk interrupted him. 'That's fine,' he said. 'That'll do just fine.' He turned briskly to the guards. 'That one's Third Regiment,' he said, jabbing a finger at Zero to differentiate him from Tymon. 'This one is House.'

Tymon stared in anguish as his friend was dragged away by the guards. He had broken his promise to look after Zero already: they had been assigned to entirely different locations. The Nurian boy gave him a terrified grin as he was propelled out of the office.

'You're lucky,' continued the clerk, to Tymon. 'You happen to fulfil the requirements of our glorious master, Lord Dayan, who wishes to procure for himself a secretary fluent in Argosian. I presume you are able to read and write in your native tongue, as well as understand ours?'

Tymon nodded dumbly again, still gazing at the doors as they swung shut behind the guards. The office scribes returned to their copies as if all were now back to normal, a thicket of scratching pens and rustling leaves adding to the crackle in his ear.

'Good,' said the slave-clerk. He took Tymon by the elbow, and steered him out of another, smaller, exit on the far side of the room, pushing him down a narrow back staircase. 'You're a seminary lad, that's clear. I don't know how you came to be in the hold of a plantation barge, but I suspect it had something to do with crossing your superiors at home, no? Well, I have some advice for you, choirboy. You'd better listen up, no matter how deaf you are. Snap out of whatever doldrums you're in: that's an indulgence you can no longer afford. You're about to be given a reprieve your Nurian friend can never hope for.'

'That's sound advice,' added the Oracle quietly, as they wove once more through the labyrinthine corridors of the customs building. 'A House position will allow you to survive long enough to help Zero. Don't jeopardise your position by trying to escape immediately. That time will come. We're far enough from Argos city now to perform a Reading: tonight, we'll be able to contact the Focals.'

A Reading! Hope mixed in equal parts with anxiety in Tymon's heart as he suffered the clerk to lead him out of the building, and away from the docks. He wondered how he would be able to help his friend. Though he had no doubt that the Oracle was right, it galled him deeply to abandon Zero, even for a little while. And he was not at all reassured by the clerk's observations, walking along the road by the perimeter of the branch-crater.

'Don't last more than a month down there, most of 'em,' the Lantrian sighed, as they passed the start of the main ramp, spiralling down into the mine.

Tymon peered into the yawning chasm by the side of the road with misgiving. There was no sign of Zero or the guards on the ramp, lit faintly by the last dregs of evening sun.

'The Lord stipulated that he wished to have a secretary he could trust implicitly,' the nameless clerk continued. 'Deafness is the ultimate discretion, of course. From now on, you must learn to hear only what the Lord wishes you to hear. Do you know why?'

Tymon shook his head, miserably silent as they walked on.

'Well then, I have a few more words of advice for you. Give me your good ear.'

The clerk seemed to be taking a particular pleasure in informing Tymon's ignorance; the young man could not tell whether it was because he hated all Argosians and wished to see him humiliated, or because he genuinely wanted to help him survive the mine. The little Lantrian stopped in the road and faced him, his arms folded across his chest.

'You should know, of course, that as a slave, you aren't truly human,' he said. 'You don't have a soul, according to Lantrian law. You'd better get used to that or you won't survive here. But most of all —' he lowered his voice, glancing briefly about him to make sure no one was close by — 'you should be aware of one very simple fact. Chal produces hardwood. It also, on occasion, produces corewood. Have you heard of core, choirboy?'

The whispered word rustled in Tymon's good ear, a term distantly familiar to him. He remembered the glittering rings adorning the fingers of Governor Omni Salassi, and the tales he had heard during his student days of the fossilised nuggets extracted from the depths of the Lantrian mines.

'Core is the great wealth of Chal and its most dangerous secret,' murmured the clerk, still fixing Tymon with his bright knowing look. 'Slaves have lost their fingers after touching it. They have lost their tongues after speaking about it. You are lucky to have given up your ears already. I suggest you put aside all thoughts of your old existence, and concentrate on serving your new master, so that you may one day enjoy a life of relative health and prosperity.'

He said no more after that, but turned and continued down the road, with Tymon trudging silently behind. Even the Oracle made no further commentary, as if the subject had been adequately covered. The echoes in the young man's bad ear diminished as the cries and bustle of the docks faded behind them. The peripheral road was well constructed, smooth and edged by two low walls of bark-brick. It swept in a wide arc around the crater, then turned abruptly to the left and plunged through a thick stand of twigs, hugging the base of one of the secondary branches at the summit of the mine-limb. As they rounded a corner and emerged from the twigs, their destination became visible. A stately mansion of bark-brick stood at the foot of the secondary branch, near the mine but sufficiently aloof from it, overlooking the leaf-forests southwards. It was surrounded by a high wall topped with cruel-looking spikes, and could be accessed only by an immense hardwood gate, the bars carved to form curling vines about two letters of Lantrian script — a 'D' on one side and an 'H' on the other.

'Even the master is a prisoner,' said the Oracle, breaking her long silence, a curious note of satisfaction in her voice.

Tymon was about to whisper a reply, when a sound rose up from within the gates that froze the blood in his veins. A growling, snarling cacophony emerged from Lord Dayan's house, the like of which he had not heard since he confronted the Beast-that-was-Lace. Two terrifying bundles of dark fur and sharp teeth shot across the compound and threw themselves against the gate, causing it to shudder. The growling and barking continued as the creatures jumped and snapped through the bars. Tymon stared at them in horror and began to back away. He was arrested by the clerk's quiet laughter.

'Relax, choirboy,' chuckled the Lantrian, drawing out a key from a purse at his belt and inserting it into a padlock. 'You've never seen a Tree-dog before, hey? Well, show some spirit. These two respond to your strength of mind. If they sense fear or threatening behaviour, they'll tear you limb from limb.'

With these less than reassuring words he swung the gate wide. The two furious bolts of canine energy charged out and leapt upon Tymon, who fell down on the dust with a cry.

4

Jedda hardly cared where she was going in that first despairing dash out of Argos city. All directions were equal to her grief. She had climbed up the main ramp from the town without pausing for breath, turning left and northwards where the road levelled out on the sheer wall of the trunk. The North Road, as it was called from that point, cut straight across the face of the Tree like a wound, following the gradual curve of the trunk. She had vaguely imagined that in choosing that direction she might avoid any possible encounters with troops bound for the war in Lantria. In actual fact, the north and south routes were equally dangerous, the exposed ledges inhospitable to a weary traveller in winter.

Personal danger did not matter much to Jedda, however. She did not consider anything besides her desire to put distance between herself and Lace. Her Kion was gone, and she had wrecked her own choices, moreover; there was nowhere left to go but away. She stumbled blindly along the road for about ten miles in this manner in the waning afternoon light, sometimes weeping, sometimes bemoaning her fate aloud. Only when twilight fell over the canopy, the ever-green leaves hidden under a coat of frost, did she stop to consider her situation more clearly. The thought that she had quit the city with nothing but the clothes on her back, in the dead of winter and without provisions, almost caused her to laugh aloud at the bitter irony. The Envoy did not need to have her followed or killed. The Argosian winter would take care of the upstart foreign acolyte without him needing to lift a finger. Hunger and exposure would fulfil his curse.

And yet, in some ways, the weather was a blessing. It had kept her isolated from prying eyes. She had passed only two travellers on the road that day: one a dour herdsman, who had seemed as loath to speak with her as she to him when he brushed by her with his troop of shillees, making for Argos city, and the other a farmer moving in the opposite direction, in a cart pulled by two herd-beasts. This second character had been returning home from the festivities in town and rather the worse for wear, judging by the jaunty holiday hat he wore pulled down over his bloodshot eyes. He had peered in bleary astonishment at Jedda's cloak of priestly green and the incongruously feminine figure beneath, as he overtook her on the icy road. When he had asked her whether she needed a ride, she shook her head mutely and waved him on; he would have a tale to tell his fellows later about the peculiar effects of wine. She had little hope that the stolid inhabitants of the Central Canopy would open their hearts or doors to her in cold sobriety. Her only chance now, she knew, was to creep into their holdings under cover of darkness, to find shelter in their hay-barns or steal food from their stores.

But although the drunk farmer's homestead could not have been far off, she found no traces of it before evening fell. Or perhaps she had missed that doubtful haven in the fog that rolled through the branches at the close of day. The mist clung to the twigs, muffling sound and light. She paused on the road and listened anxiously. Not a bird sang in the dripping thickets.

The heat of her furious march dissipated, and the cold began to seep into her bones.

She realised she had no choice but to make the best of a night out in the open, on an empty stomach, and found the only shelter she could in the failing light: a shallow crevice on the trunk-wall to her right. Seated with her back to the bark, she tried to light a fire on the floor of the hollow by rubbing two slivers of bark together. It was a technique that had served her well enough in the dry Eastern Canopy, but here, in the wet and cold, her efforts were fruitless. Her belly grumbled and she could not stop shaking; it had become a matter of life or death, she knew, to find that farmer's keep and something to eat the next day. Wrapping herself in withered grasses and moss ripped out from the trunk, she curled up on the hard bark and passed a relentlessly uncomfortable night.

The following morning, she arose early and carried on, walking slower this time, kicking through the grey slush that covered the road. It was hard going on the high, exposed ledge, and slippery where pools of ice had formed on the surface. There were places where the bark had eroded because of poor maintenance and the edges had crumbled away; once, she came perilously close to falling where a fissure had formed, and a whole section of the road yawned wide. She had to inch her way across a narrow passage by the trunk-wall, before she regained a firm foothold on the other side. The sight in the spaces below and to her left filled her with foreboding, for thick clouds rolled through the West Chasm. The canopy was plunged in a green gloom and the skies above were shrouded in a glowering grey: there would be snow again before the day was out, and plenty of it. There was still no sign of the drunk farmer's holding, which she decided that she must have missed in the fog. She pressed on, hoping for another habitation.

But before long, her steps faltered, and she came to a halt once more. She had been overcome by a tingling sensation in her belly, and it was not hunger. It was the Grafters' twining connection; there was no mistaking it. She was gripped by the sudden conviction that Tymon was also on the road, and travelling south.

Jedda had always felt her connection to her fellow Grafter as a visceral reaction. No mere vision, it was a wave of emotion, a hook in her belly that pulled her inexorably towards Tymon. The feeling ebbed and flowed, changing its character from day to day. Sometimes it was no more than a whisper, hardly present at all. Or it could be an overwhelming rush, almost an ache of proximity. The call that summoned her now was powerful. Her twining partner was travelling in the opposite direction from her. She had already turned and begun to stumble back towards Argos city before she forced herself to stop again, torn between warring impulses.

'Fool,' she hissed aloud, her breath smoking the chill air.

How could she have left the town without thinking of Tymon? She knew he had been taken prisoner the night before the execution, sentenced to banishment: she was the only one who could help him. This was her duty, she told herself fiercely. This was what remained for her to accomplish since she had failed her queen. All was not lost, not yet. She could still be the friend she should have been. The Sap-connection tugged her eagerly on, as if in response to this desire. Conquering her reluctance to approach Lace, her dread of re-entering the environs of Argos city, she walked on, doggedly retracing her steps of the day before.

As she hastened towards the twining call, she peered anxiously into the West Chasm, now on her right, at the roiling grey clouds visible through a screen of leaf-forests.

Snow would be her immediate enemy, rather than her former master. Indeed, it was not long before the first flakes settled on her cheeks. The soft kiss of the snow caused her to break into a jogging run, desperate to put the miles behind her before the fall grew too thick. She guessed that the priests had sentenced Tymon to labour on one of their accursed plantations and sent him away on a prison cart, as there were no tithe-ships currently docked in Argos city. She still had a chance of catching up with the slow-moving vehicle that night, if she hurried, and some hope of coming to the prisoner's rescue, for she possessed the *orah*-pendant and the ability to dominate her enemies. She hoped that talent would be enough to help both Tymon and herself.

At length, however, the increasing snowstorm forced her to slow her pace. The weather as well as her own physical weakness mocked both her powers and her plans. By late afternoon, when she again passed the intersection that led down to Argos city, there was a white blanket a foot deep on the road and she was reeling with hunger. As evening approached, the drifting flakes multiplied, and the wind became a driving wet gale that left even the good seminary cloak sodden. Jedda was numb with cold, lacking sensation in her fingers and toes, giddy from starvation. Surely the prison vehicle would stop in this weather, she thought. Surely the soldiers would seek a spot to camp for the night, hunkering down under canvas to wait out the storm. She struggled on through the deepening drifts, scanning the whirling flakes ahead for the humped shape of a cart. Gradually, the grey of the road became indistinguishable from the grey of the West Chasm beside it, the whirling eddies spinning madly over both. Jedda clung to the trunk-wall on her left for a guide.

She almost cried out with relief when she saw the

gleam of lantern light ahead, thinking that this must be the cart, at last. She left the trunk-wall in her haste to reach the flickering point of yellow in the whirlwind; it was a fatal mistake. After a few paces, she felt the surface beneath her feet shift and slide treacherously, and realised in horror that she had stepped through a drift overhanging the Chasm. She lurched into thin air with a gasp, her arms flailing wildly. Down, down.

The fall through blind emptiness was both terrifying and short. An instant later, she hit something soft that gave way beneath her, and slid off the dark mass to plunge headfirst into yet more snow. At first, she thought her fall had been arrested by snow-covered leaves, and that she had tumbled into a twig-thicket miraculously close to the edge of the road. *O Ever-Green, o giver of life*, she thought gratefully. The Central Canopy did not lose its leaves in winter. But the substance supporting the snow was not solid, and sank with a muffled tearing noise beneath her weight. And the light was still there, dancing incomprehensibly above her and to the left. In the time it took for Jedda to imagine her bones scattered to the four winds, she heard a final rending tear of fabric, and fell through the sinking barrier in a shower of snow.

She crashed down onto the floor of a large tent, in a pool of lamplight. There were shouts, the sound of a child crying hysterically, and a few cheers and whistles: curious faces crowded around her as she rolled on the floor, winded. It took her a moment to place the colourful clothing and odd accents of the people. They were Jays. She had fallen onto a Jay dirigible. She had tumbled through the vessel's ether sacks and torn a hole in the roof of a large pavilion.

'What have we here?' asked a voice in Argosian. 'A white angel, wearing the colours of a priest? Did your wings blow off in the storm, angel?'

One of the Jays, a young man with a curved nose like a falcon's beak, bent over her where she lay, holding his hand out to her. His eyes, too, were bright and hawk-like, fixing her inquisitively as he helped her up from the floor. She realised to her dismay that her hood was off and her identity plain to see for all those gathered in the tent.

'You've made a hole in our roof,' said a woman at the young man's side.

She spoke in a quiet, matter-of-fact tone, but her face, Jedda noticed, was disfigured by a savage scar. The Nurian girl would not have found the sight so terrible to behold, perhaps, if she had not been so weary, and shaken by her fall. She glanced instinctively away from the ugly wound, then blushed crimson, realising her revulsion was far too obvious. She forced herself to look back at the Jay woman, but her head spun with fatigue. Even had she been strong enough to use her powers, the people in the tent were too many to take on all together.

'I'm sorry,' she mumbled in answer to both the man and the woman. 'I stole these clothes. I'm on the run. I fell off the road. Please help me.'

The garbled plea drew a round of laughter from the watchers and the faces in the circle relaxed. The child who had been so shocked by Jedda's arrival stopped sobbing and stared at her, cradled in his mother's arms.

'You're lucky we're Jays,' observed the scarred woman. 'When Heaven sends us visitors, we show hospitality.' She turned to her hawk-nosed companion. 'Our angel looks half-frozen,' she said. 'Why don't you find her something to eat, Anise, and a bed for the night?'

It was only outside the tent, as the Jay man led her through the swirling snow towards another, smaller, barge lashed to the side of the main dirigible, that Jedda remembered her visit to the docks in Argos city.

Belatedly, she recognised the striped pavilion in the dancing light of the storm-lanterns. She was aboard the very same convoy on which she had met Tymon and Pallas. She did not recall the Jays themselves, for she had not observed them closely on that occasion, seeking to remain unseen. But the name, Anise, rang faint alarm bells in her memory.

The realisation caused her to clutch the deck-rail between the two barges with misgiving. She did not know what, if anything, Tymon had told his travelling companions about her. It seemed that her deliverance might only lead to further trouble. When the man called Anise turned to ask her why she waited, she answered that it was nothing, that she was tired. She could barely meet his eye.

The Jays made good on their promises of food and bed that night. She was given what she could have sworn was the very same pallet in the sleeping tent occupied by Tymon, though her suspicions on the subject did not prevent her from throwing herself down on the thin mattress after ravenously consuming a meal of dried fruit, asleep almost before her head hit the pillow. In her exhaustion, she slumbered as deeply as a child, without concern for the future. But the next day her unease about the troupe returned.

She rose late, around mid-morning, and made her way to the main barge just before the three ships broke moorings. The roof of the striped pavilion had already been nimbly patched together, as Jedda could see from the outside, but Anise and the scarred woman were nowhere to be seen. She lingered a few moments on deck to watch the ship drift up above the twig-tips in the brilliant sunlight. The snowstorm was over, the canopy cloaked in glittering white. That treacherous beauty, Jedda knew, hid chasms and dangers without end. She remembered the near catastrophe of her slip the night before, and thought again of Samiha, plummeting through the snow clouds into the Western Chasm. Was there any chance of surviving such a fall? And what was to become of Tymon now? She could still feel the twining connection, a steady tug to the south, and longed to follow him.

But to her frustration, the main barge swung slowly around in the morning sunlight and turned in the wrong direction — northwards. Jedda tried to contain her impatience, hurrying into the pavilion in search of either Anise or his female companion, for she guessed those two were leaders of the troupe. She yearned to tell her hosts of her twining with Tymon, to ask them to go after him. To speak of the connection directly, however, would invite troublesome questions she did not yet know how to answer. She floundered through the door-flap and was relieved to find Anise and the scarred woman in the tent. A small group of Jays was installed on the floor of the pavilion, or on the lightwood bleachers left out as furniture.

'Why don't you travel south?' Jedda burst out to Anise, without preamble.

He had been busy writing in a log book, seated on one of the benches, and did not answer her at once, but glanced up at her with a curious expression. It was only when the silence stretched rather uncomfortably between them, and the woman nursing the baby Jedda had frightened the night before stood up and left the tent, that the Nurian girl realised she must have sounded unspeakably rude, as well as ridiculous to her hosts.

'Not that it matters to me,' she added hastily. 'I'm happy to go wherever you go. I just thought Jays went south during the winter. I had a lovely night, by the way. I'm so grateful to you all for helping me.'

She bit her lip to stop herself from gabbling like a fool, and hid her embarrassment by snatching up a hunk of bread and shillee's cheese from the communal breakfast tray in one corner. Her food in hand, she sat down beside Anise. The young Jay smiled faintly up at her from his notes.

'To go south would embroil us unnecessarily in the Saint's war,' he explained. 'We're heading up north, to Jay Haven, this year.'

He turned back to his log book then, as if the matter were closed. His scarred companion briefly introduced herself as 'Jocaste', then spread out an ancient and tattered map of the Central Canopy on the floor and squatted over it, plotting their course with the aid of a sextant. Jedda struggled to maintain her calm. She wanted to beg and plead with them to turn around.

'Oh, I would have thought it was easy enough to avoid the war,' she said brightly to Anise, between mouthfuls of cheese. 'The Lantrian leaf-line is ages away. Don't you want to get to better weather?'

She considered the enigmatic pair, wondering if she should simply admit to knowing Tymon and deal with the consequences. Part of her, a surprisingly strong part, was tempted to make a clean breast of all her crimes and start afresh with these people. But another instinct held her back, a tried and trusted reliance on secrecy. The Jays had so far studiously avoided asking her name or how she came to be fleeing from Argos city. In fact, the few members of the troupe apart from Anise and Jocaste who had been present when she entered the tent had already melted away like ghosts, and without speaking a word to her. Whether deliberately or not, she had been left alone with Anise and Jocaste. The atmosphere in the pavilion had begun to make Jedda deeply uncomfortable. She crammed the rest of her barley-bread into her mouth.

'Why are you so keen on going south?' murmured Anise, apparently engrossed in his log book.

'I'll be honest with you. A friend — a friend of mine is in trouble,' she stammered. 'He's been sent out of town in a prison cart. I wondered if you might help me to find him. You'd easily catch up with him in your ships.'

'So,' he replied slowly. 'You'd put us all in danger again, when we've already stuck out our necks to help you? You'd ask us to risk our lives in order to pick up another one of your dirty louse friends?'

Jocaste grunted in soft agreement from where she sat on the floor. 'First we get raked over coals by the city guard for harbouring dissidents,' she said. 'Then we pay out all our profits in bribes — profits that should have gone to buying new sails. And now you want us to take on more fugitives? What do we look like, a louse delivery service?'

Jedda stared at them both, at a loss as to how to respond. Did they really believe what they were saying? That Nurians were insects, unclean?

'Because that's how you must think of them, after all,' resumed Anise, never taking his eyes away from his book. His tone had grown scathing. 'Your countrymen: you must think they are vermin. You must believe what the priests say about them. Otherwise why would you betray your own people?'

There was utter silence in the tent. Anise still did not look up, but Jocaste had lifted her eyes to glare at Jedda. The bread stuck like a dry lump in the Nurian girl's throat. The Jays knew exactly who she was, she thought, panicking. They had recognised her right from the beginning. They had only extended their mercy to her for one night, perhaps the better to punish her the following day. Now the truth would be known.

'Did Tymon tell you that?' she asked, miserable.

'Ah, so you admit to knowing Tymon,' said Jocaste dryly. 'That's a start. Tell me: did it bother you that he, a stranger, was loyal to your people, while you were not?'

Her ugly scar was livid as she spoke, and her eyes blazed. Jedda felt that gaze ripping into her, laying her defences low. She rose unsteadily to her feet, scattering crumbs.

'You can stop judging me now,' she said. 'I know what I've done wrong. I don't need an Argosian to tell me.' Anise never once turned around or looked up from his book: she felt the insult keenly.

'Not just any Argosian, a Jay,' corrected Jocaste. 'But I'm curious. If you regret listening to the priests, why wait until you were out of the city to do something about it? Why not help Tymon, or even the Kion, while you still could?'

The last part of the phrase was like a mortal blow to Jedda. She hung her head in shame. 'I tried,' she whispered. 'The Kion wouldn't come with me.'

Anise and Jocaste exchanged astonished glances. 'Please,' Jedda begged. 'Have you never realised you made the wrong decision? Are you so perfect?'

She addressed her question to Jocaste. It seemed to her that the Jay girl would understand her, even if Anise did not. She would know the truth when she heard it, Jedda thought, with a stab of insight, because she knew herself.

'Far from it,' said the scarred woman softly.

'So, what happens now?' Jedda's throat had grown tight. She stood helplessly before the other two, wringing her hands with unconscious anxiety. But they did not even look at her. 'What are you going to do with me?'

She had meant the question to be a challenge. It came out as a broken murmur.

'Do with you?' Anise echoed, surprised. He finally faced her, putting down his pen and his book for the first time since the conversation began. 'Why should we do anything with you? We're not responsible for you, Jedda. Yes, we know what you've done. But we aren't priests. You can't ask us for punishment or absolution.'

He reminded Jedda of the Oracle in his pitiless equanimity. 'Will you at least help him?' she pleaded with the two Jays. 'Will you help Tymon?'

'We want nothing more than to help Tymon,' answered Jocaste. Despite her harsh intensity, she appeared less eager than Anise to judge and condemn. 'And we are. You asked if we'd ever made mistakes. We have: many, believe me. This is our absolution. We're carrying out Tymon's wishes by travelling north. He would not have wanted us to follow him into danger.'

'Why?' Jedda almost groaned. 'Alright, don't help me, I don't care about myself. But why not go after him? Why would he want you to go in the opposite direction? What kind of absolution is that?'

The two Jays looked at each other again. 'She'd find out sooner or later,' Anise remarked, as if in reply to an unheard question.

'Find out what?' cried Jedda. 'What's going on here?'

For an answer Anise rose and walked to a locker set into the floor on the other side of the pavilion. Jedda squinted to see what he was doing. He flipped open the lid and retrieved a bundle from the shallow trough beneath; her heart leapt and shuddered in her chest before she knew what he was carrying. He returned and laid a sheaf of paper in her trembling hands. The sheets were of varying quality, from smooth pulp to brittle beaten straw, all covered in a swift, flowing Argosian script.

'Who wrote this?' breathed Jedda. 'How did you get it?'

'I think you know the answers to those questions,' Anise replied. 'Go on. Read. You'll understand what our mission is, and why we don't go after Tymon.'

Jedda said no more, but sank down on the bleacher with the bundle in her lap, as Jocaste returned to her maps and Anise took up his log book once more. Cradling the sheaf of disparate papers, the Nurian girl scanned the first lines of the crackling page. Samiha's handwriting stared up at her, immediately recognisable. This was the text she had seen the Kion write in the room beneath the bells, the testament that had mysteriously disappeared the night before the execution. Tymon must have taken it: he must, against all hope, have managed to hide it with the Jays. No longer impatient at the thought of reading such a work, Jedda drank in the words on the page like clear water.

Already, it grows hard for me to remember. There is nothing, there was never anything but this hold, this ship. Sheb, Marak: all are gone. Place is gone. Time has no meaning. I hear sailors shouting to each other above deck, their voices like the cry of babies. My certainties evaporate with each furlong of empty air. I am not what they say I am. I am neither heretic nor queen. I am not even the girl from Hatha. The wind snatched away my old face and I have not yet seen the new. I have begun writing because I hope to catch a glimpse of it in these pages.

The testament was written to Tymon. It was an account of all that had happened to Samiha since she left Sheb, up to and including the trial in Argos city. It was more than that, thought Jedda: it was a conversation, a debate with an invisible friend, and a frank and open confession. The Kion addressed the young man who had briefly shared her life, telling him all that she had felt and thought in those weeks leading up to her death. It read on occasion like a private letter between two lovers, though it was clear from the text that Samiha had expected her words to be shared. Jedda blushed from time to time as she sat in the Jays' pavilion that morning, devouring the papers without pause.

It was not what was actually said that caused her pulse to race. It was the tone of the whole, the emotion of it that set her nerves tingling and brought a lump to her throat. She found herself wishing forlornly for someone to speak to her in the way Samiha spoke to Tymon. She would have liked to be the one the Kion addressed in the darkness of the tithe-ship's hold, or in the room beneath the bells — the faithful one who was always in the prisoner's heart, even at the bleakest of times. But she was not. She was barely mentioned in the papers as someone who had been duped by the priests. The passing reference was worse than a condemnation. Samiha never once dwelled on her treachery or blamed her for her abandonment of the Oracle in Cherk Harbour. She did not breathe a word of Jedda's botched attempt to rescue her, the day before the execution. The overall impression the girl was left with on completing the reading was of burning embarrassment and shame. She had been judged and found wanting. Samiha's silence regarding her was an act of mercy.

Jedda was not the sort to let matters rest there, however. She finished reading the papers in one sitting; when she was done, she returned to the beginning and started again. She had read it the first time as herself, as Jedhartha Aditi, cringing at every memory the tale provoked. On the second reading, she laid aside her shared history with the Kion and actually studied the testament. Samiha's account not only dealt with the past and present of her incarceration: it actively courted the future. There were times when she spoke of her hopes for Nur and even for Argos, cautioning Tymon against the problems she saw arising as the two nations inevitably went to war. By the end of her second perusal, Jedda realised the testament was precisely that — a statement of belief, an assessment of behaviour. It made no bones of criticising the seminary while at the same time challenging Nurian rebels on their use of violence.

Jedda pored over it, curled up on the uninviting bleacher in the draughty pavilion, long after Jocaste had finished plotting their course and Anise had laid aside his notebook, rising to carry out other duties. She was still reading the testament when the Jays moored their ships among the icy upper twigs and met in the main tent for lunch, stamping their feet and warming their hands over the hardwood stove. And she continued to be absorbed in the Kion's words throughout that afternoon, until the barges returned below the leaf-line to pass the night in more sheltered regions of the Tree. By the time the travellers had gathered for supper in the pavilion, she had finished her third reading of the testament from start to finish, and could barely contain her excitement. For she knew, then, that it was a rousing call for change.

'It's a prophecy!' she exclaimed to Anise, hurrying up to him as soon as he entered the tent. 'It's not just the past. It's the future!'

'Exactly.' He steered her gently towards the empty space at the centre of the tent where the Jays were seating themselves in a loose circle. 'You see now why we must tell the Kion's tale to the world. That is our mission.'

'Maybe,' said Jedda, frowning, as she knelt down on the bare floorboards. 'But I do believe we need to go after Tymon first. He should read this: there's no way he could have done so before he gave it to you. It's for him. He's at the centre of it all somehow — the Kion says so.'

The last members of the troupe were now entering the pavilion, bearing the food for the evening meal.

It had been prepared on one of the smaller barges and brought to the main tent on wide communal platters. Jocaste sat herself down on the other side of Anise and, to Jedda's relief, smiled briefly at her. But Anise only shook his head in answer.

'The Kion speaks to all of us,' he cautioned. 'I know this sort of prose style. Half the epics I learned off by heart as a child were written in the confessional mode. This is how Saint Loa and Saint Usala wrote, as if speaking to a dear friend. Samiha isn't just talking to Tymon: she is talking to each and every one of us.'

'But he's to meet her *in the heart of the world*,' protested Jedda.

'We will all meet the Kion in our hearts, if we truly live by her words.'

Jedda frowned again, uneasy with this glib answer. 'What if there's more to it?' she objected. 'I'm sure you're right, it's also for the rest of us, but couldn't it be primarily addressed to him?'

'What for?' asked Anise in surprise. 'If the prophecies were about him, I'd agree with you. But they aren't. They are about Nur and Argos in general. Why cover topics that concern everyone, if you're addressing your work to one person?'

Jedda racked her brains for a means of expressing what she suspected without coming across as mad, or else undermining the Kion, which she no longer wished to do. Samiha was a Born, but had chosen to hide that fact for reasons Jedda was dimly beginning to guess at. She had a plan, a reality that went beyond the human one. Complexity rather than simplicity was likely to be the rule here, Jedda surmised; the testament contained many truths nested together, each one fitting into the next without negating the one before. Samiha was speaking to all, but also to one. She had made public as well as private predictions in her testament. And she was able to do this, to find the balance between seeming contradictions, precisely because she was a Born. It was harder, however, to explain such notions to Anise. Jedda found herself reluctant to give away the secret of the Kion's true nature: it would only cause others to doubt her motives.

'If I weren't a Grafter, I might agree with you,' she said carefully. 'I might think it was all symbolic. But I know people like Tymon really do walk in other worlds. There might be a place he can find Samiha — a place we can't go — don't you see?'

'I see that you care deeply for Tymon,' observed Anise, smiling in his turn.

He indicated that she should help herself to the food on the steaming plates set before them. The meal consisted of lentils cooked in a bewildering variety of ways, served with large pieces of flatbread. There were no spoons or forks. Everyone dipped their fingers in bowls of rainwater passed around the circle, then used torn sections of bread to scoop up the lentils directly from the dish. Jedda was more than happy to follow the Jays' lead, for she had had no more than a few mouthfuls at lunch. This manner of dining reminded her, with an unexpected pang of homesickness, of Nurian customs. It was a welcome change from the stuffy formality of the seminary.

'If you care for him, then hear this,' continued Anise, as they ate. 'He did not keep the testament, because he knew he was always going to be hunted down by the priests. The words of the Kion are more important than any one person's life. The testament must survive and reach its audience. It would not do so if we rushed off after him, and were caught and imprisoned ourselves.'

'Believe me,' put in Jocaste, 'Anise and I have had this very conversation several times over the past few days. I for one took a great deal of convincing before I was ready to give up the idea of a chase. But he's right, Jedda. Our priority now is the testament. We can't run the risk of losing it.'

Jedda unhappily digested this fact with her lentils. She could not see why she and a few others might not travel south in one of the smaller barges, while the others went north and kept the papers safe. But Anise seemed immovable in his convictions, stubbornly refusing to countenance even the slightest change in course. Jedda wondered what could render a man so sure about anything: her own heart was never at peace, always doubting itself. She almost envied him his certainties.

As the meal went on, she gave up attempting to argue the point, and sat in silent thought, considering her rather reduced options. She might travel north with the Jays until a better opportunity presented itself. Or she might strike out on her own — a hazardous affair in winter, as she had seen on her first doomed attempt to leave Argos city. Even if she succeeded against all odds in catching up with Tymon, it would only be to carry out her original plan of a rescue. He would never have access to more of the testament than what her own verbal summary, inevitably incomplete, could provide. She might copy out the papers for him, but that would take days; with each passing day the chance of finding him on the South Road diminished. The whole affair was frustrating in the extreme.

She was so lost in her ruminations that she never saw the others clearing away the empty bowls and platters at the end of the meal, or noticed when they drew together again in a tight knot about the stove in the far corner of the pavilion. Night was deep outside when the cold roused her from her reverie, and she looked up to find herself isolated on the tent floor.

Someone was singing in a low, crooning voice, in a dialect unfamiliar to her. One of the youths by the stove was playing a melancholy tune on a stringed instrument, a traditional Jay air, from what Jedda could tell. She approached the people huddled about the glowing, crackling fire in its pot-bellied range — the one point of heat and light in the icy pavilion — and watched from the sidelines as the Jay boy finished one song, then launched into another, in Argosian. This time, she recognised the words.

Ye are the wind that carries forth the flame.

Before you, cities crumble, hearts are changed.

The lines were from Samiha's testament. The musician had modified them slightly to fit his meter, and the words that had been addressed to Tymon now sounded like a rousing hymn. Other voices chimed in as he continued, and soon most of the Jays were chanting Samiha's verses. Jedda scrutinised her companions in the pavilion with surprise. They sang earnestly, as if delivering one of the primary liturgies of the Tree. Her gaze came to rest on Anise, sitting cross-legged on the floor beside Jocaste; his eyes were closed and his expression full of joy as he held on to his scarred partner's hand. Even Jocaste sang the words of the testament in her low, rasping voice. The pair suddenly reminded Jedda of Oren and Noni. The Jays evidently believed in Samiha as one might believe in the prophets of old. She was not only an inspirational leader to them, but a divine figure, to be venerated as a living representative of the Sap. They had made a religion out of her.

Jedda shivered. She distrusted religions, whether of the East or West. As far as she was concerned, they turned the vibrant reality of the Grafting into a dead thing locked up in books or, worse, promoted the cult-like worship of individuals. She had objected to the

Saffids' idolisation of Tymon and privately deplored Fallow's claim to be the return of Saint Loa. This new obsession of the Jays' was just as dangerous, as far as she was concerned. Although she had seen the absolute knowledge in Samiha's eyes, the irrefutable evidence of her identity, that reality did not have to translate into temple hymns and rituals, in her opinion.

If Samiha had wished to be venerated, Jedda thought, she would have declared herself openly. She would have caused all Argos city to fall at her feet. The Kion had been an Awakened Born, after all, operating at the end of her life without the strictures placed on outcasts such as Lace. Jedda had read the secret histories in the seminary library: she knew of the ancient war that had forever sundered Samiha's kind, and torn apart the worlds. In those days, the Born had held absolute sway over their human vassals. God had possessed a human face. It was a story the seminary had been at pains to conceal and forget. But Samiha clearly did not wish to be seen as anything other than a mortal woman. She had wanted her words to be read and pondered, debated and discussed, not accepted without question.

And that, Jedda reflected, was exactly what Anise had omitted to do. No wonder he refused to countenance any interference with what he took to be his divinely appointed task. The testament was Holy Writ to him: there was no room for discussion or interpretation. He would never accept that it was a personal message. If it were that, his new convictions would come crashing down about his ears. Jedda did not wait to hear more, but rose quietly and left the group by the stove. She slipped out of the main pavilion and sought the relative quiet and chill of her sleeping tent, where only the young mother remained with her infant, singing the boy softly to sleep.

Stretched on her pallet, the Grafter girl thought again of the words addressed to Tymon, the words that had been interpreted by Anise as a divine injunction to all.

I pass the torch on to you now, my love. Fly fast and free, for you are my messenger. You are the wind that carries the flame. My story has the power to change hearts; it will cause armies to fall and cities to crumble. It will be the scourge of the priests of Argos. Do not allow your desires to blind you to the importance of your task: you will either set the world alight, or be consumed yourself. This is the Year of Fire, the beginning and the end. You can be either.

There was no doubt about it. The testament was a personal message to her friend and fellow student. And it was more than that, Jedda realised, sitting bolt upright on her rumpled bed, gripped by misgiving. It was a warning.

The moon had risen above the frosty leaf-forests when Jedda stepped over the prone forms of her companions, and left the sleeping tent. The three barges had been lashed together for the night; she slipped over the deck-rails onto the main vessel, as silent as a Tree-cat. Inside the striped pavilion, the hardwood stove in the corner was extinguished and the temperature had plummeted. She trembled spasmodically under her cloak as she hurried to the storage locker in the floor, squatting over the hatch. The hardwood mechanism of the combination lock was intricate, but this did not deter her. It had been enough for her to see Anise open it once: she had memorised his exact movements, and now reproduced them, turning the dials on the device to the required positions. It was something she had always been good at, a slightly heightened power of observation, the ability to remember visual details. She did not think of the talent as having anything to do with her Grafter power.

After a moment the lock clicked open beneath her fingers. The space under the deck-boards was crammed with maps and navigational paraphernalia, and what looked like old travel journals, a set of valuable antique books. It was an unusual collection for a band of travelling entertainers, and might have caused Jedda to wonder how and why they had come upon such treasures, had she been in the mood for contemplation. She was not. One idea occupied her mind. She rifled through the contents of the storage locker, and lifted out the bundle of variegated paper covered in Samiha's flowing script. She jumped to her feet, clutching the bundle to her chest, as a soft sound echoed from the doorway, a hiss of intaken breath.

'I was hoping you wouldn't betray my trust, Jedda. I watched and waited, but I still hoped.'

Anise had followed her to the pavilion. Jedda's heart sank as the Jay left the shadow of the doorway and walked towards her; she had hoped to make her escape with the testament without confrontation. Now there would be reproaches, recriminations. She must not waver, she thought. There was no time left for doubt. Already the twining link with Tymon had grown thin and stretched: soon, she would lose him completely.

'You don't need to do this,' said Anise earnestly. 'We'll make you a copy, if you're so keen on having one.'

Jedda shook her head. 'It's too late for that. It would take too long to get it to Tymon, don't you see? I have to find him before he leaves the South Road. Please, Anise: even if you can't help, don't try to stop me.'

Instinctively, she had reached up with her free hand to the *orah*-pendant at her neck, kneading it under her collar in a nervous reflex. Anise stopped opposite her, his expression sorrowful.

'I thought you would understand when you read it,'

he sighed, breathing white into the cold air of the tent. 'It isn't Tymon who needs to hear the Kion's words. Why don't you see that?'

'Let's just say we agree to disagree,' she growled. 'Anise, I will do my best to get the testament back to you when I've helped Tymon. But for now, I have to take it. Please don't make a fuss, and let me pass.'

But he did not let her pass, and continued to hover between her and the door, frowning. 'Jedda. Be reasonable. What purpose does stealing serve?'

He reached forward, grasping her by the arm that held the papers. It was an error that was to be his undoing. Her frustration leapt up like a flame at his touch; here was another man who was trying to force his will upon her, she thought. Here was another bully. The pendant at her neck glowed hot in response to her outrage. The *orah*-power flowed through her without her consciously deciding to use it, latching onto Anise like a hook. He made no move to resist at first, gazing stupidly at her. She did not have to concentrate hard to drain him of his vital energy. The act was easy, a natural extension of her anger. The Sap from his body coursed through her in a giddy torrent of heat.

'You dare speak of stealing?' she snapped, as he belatedly struggled against her, then sank to his knees. 'After all you've taken from me?'

'Taken from you?' he murmured in perplexity as he slumped to the floor.

'My innocence!' she blurted out. 'My soul. My queen —'

She choked, the sob in her throat swelling to a cough that hacked through her accusations. She blinked her eyes. She had been so sure for an instant, convinced beyond a doubt that it was the Envoy who blocked her path to the door, stymieing her plans, as always. Her anger had been directed towards him. Now the fog over her vision lifted, and she saw that it was Anise who lay at her feet. The river of Sap abruptly shut off, leaving her achingly cold. The silence in the pavilion was broken by her gasping breath. She had attacked Anise: poor, luckless Anise. Her shock gave way to panic, and she backed away from the body on the floor, the testament pressed against her. She had committed a terrible crime against a person who had tried to help her.

The thought caused her to stop in her tracks, appalled. The Envoy's curse! It had faded from her thoughts of late, replaced by Samiha's invigorating words and her desire to rescue Tymon. She passed a shaking hand over her forehead and stared in horror at the Jay man sprawled on the floor. She had been a fool to think Lace would let her go without a fight. Now, she was a murderer. She was no better than Wick — worse in fact, for the Jays had saved her from the snowstorm and taken her in. Gowron's sneering prediction to her, long ago on the way to Argos city, echoed in her memory.

You will think back to this day and understand. This is all there is to his instruction.

'No,' she moaned, backing away again through the door of the pavilion. 'No.'

Stumbling in her haste, she climbed over the deck-rail of the main dirigible and dropped to the snowy surface of the branch a few feet below. She paused an anxious moment to stare up at the three barges moored among the twigs. The moon shone ghostly white, glinting on her pale hair as on the snow. Jedda turned and jogged down the icy slope of the branch, disappearing at last beneath the gloom of the leaf-forests.

High above, a swift shadow passed over the moon,

followed by another. Two winged forms wheeled high above the twig-tops. Bird-like, but unnaturally large and silent, they criss-crossed the night sky in the wake of the Nurian girl, doubling repeatedly over the moon's bright disc.

5

Lord Dayan treated his dogs like his children, saving choice titbits for them from the dinner table and fawning over them as they lolled on the carpeted floors of the mansion, exposing their foolish bellies to the air. They had pelts the colour of charred wood flecked with white; Dayan maintained they were thoroughbreds of a breed now almost unknown in the Tree. He would whip a slave he suspected of mistreating them, or even bringing them their meat too late in the evening. But the familial tie between man and dogs went beyond mere companionship, extending to a physical likeness. Both the Lord and his animals possessed the same ice-blue, hungry eyes, paler than those of the Saffid, the ferocious gaze of born killers. And Tymon knew, from the start of his tenure at the House, that he must avoid angering either if he valued his life.

He began his duties as Dayan's secretary and personal valet the day after his arrival in Chal. The smiling clerk was evidently an old hand at managing affairs in the Lord's House. After rescuing Tymon from the Tree-dogs with no more than a clipped command to the two animals, he had led the young man into the mansion by a back door, installing him in a small but perfectly adequate sleeping alcove behind the kitchen stove. After that, the knowing little scribe had bidden Tymon farewell, leaving to speak with Lord Dayan regarding his employment. Although Tymon never learned how that first interview transpired, it appeared his tenure at the House had been assured, for he awoke in his alcove early the next morning with the cook already bellowing in his blocked ear, telling him to shift his lazy Argosian rump and take the master his breakfast.

The cook, Ystafa, proved to be essentially harmless beneath his bluster. All the burly Lantrian required of Tymon was the ability to wait at the master's table without dropping a plate. Besides him, there were three other slaves residing permanently at the House: the gardener, a dour youth inaptly named Sun, who kept the margoose pens and smelled of margoose dung, and two giggling scullery maids, Talua and Daria, who performed the housework.

To Tymon's great relief, Lord Dayan's personal servants were not required to keep the dress code reserved for most Lantrian bondsmen. The House slaves wore serviceable white shirts and black surcoats over loose-fitting trousers, and there was a thankful dearth of loincloths at the mansion. The girls — both tolerably pretty, though they dissolved into childish laughter whenever Tymon tried to speak to them — wore their hair long, and Ystafa, though bald, sported a magnificent moustache. Tymon himself was given a tablet similar to the clerk's to hang about his neck and was told that to remove it would earn him thirty lashes of the whip, and thirty more with each subsequent infraction. His designation officially became 'Hordannan five-hundred-and-twenty-two', though the Lord's servants still privately called each other by their given names. They accepted their lot with the same calm fatalism shown by the Nurian pilgrims who came to Argos city. For years, Tymon had thought of it as mindless subservience; now, he knew better. It was simply a desire for survival.

He found his situation difficult to adjust to, though not in the way he had expected. It was true that he enjoyed a level of comfort at the House that he had not known for weeks. He was given as much to eat as he wanted, and had the whole kitchen to himself once his fellows retired to their attic rooms for the night. But he was keenly aware that he was part of a pampered minority. The mineworkers, he was told, had a very different existence — one few survived for long. Every House slave lived in fear of being sent down to the mine. It was the threat that hung over them all, and kept life at the mansion profoundly peaceful. It was also Zero's everyday reality, as Tymon knew to his distress. He felt his only legitimate reason for staying at the House was to organise Zero's rescue. But to do that successfully, he needed help.

He took advantage of the opportunity, on that first evening, after the scribe had left to speak with Dayan, to launch a Grafter's trance. As the curling tendrils of the Tree of Being sprang up about him in the shadowy kitchen, he called out to the Focals in the world of the Sap, sensing their connection, their twining with him. They responded almost at once, doubtless engaged in a Reading of their own. This time, there was no painful merging with the Tree of Being: the Focals' shimmering forms surrounded Tymon even as they had on board the Jay dirigible, appearing as floating ghosts in the bright space between the branches. When they wordlessly embraced Tymon, one after another, their touch was a soft, electric burr. Their long-awaited reunion was both joyous and sad. Sad, because it was the first time they had seen each other since Samiha's execution, the first time they could share their grief; joyous because this time, Tymon did not enter the trance alone.

'Someone is with you,' said Oren, after the initial

greetings were over, pulling back and peering into his face.

'Yes, there's a visitor.' Noni scrutinised him eagerly, while the two younger Focals crowded behind her, agog. 'We all feel it.' Her eyes widened with hope. '*Ama?*'

There was a pause as Tymon struggled with the wonder of it. For he felt it, too: the sensation of another person occupying the same space as he did, a presence far closer and more intimate than any voice in his head. He sensed the Oracle like a heat brimming up inside him.

'May I?' she asked politely, inside his mind.

He realised she could only speak through him, even here, in the trance. 'Of course,' he answered aloud, aware that the Focals desperately wished to hear from their teacher directly.

The experience was overwhelming. It was nothing like the Reading in Farhang, when he had been caused to recite the Oracle's testament. Then, he had spat out her message in fear and pain, resisting all the way. Now, he felt her presence like a wash of tangible light, and was filled with awe. He had had no idea of the extent of his teacher's power. His trance-form grew bright and hot with her, brimming with the Sap. The red scars of the Veil, inflicted when he had fought Wick and still visible now, shone with a particularly bright light. His shimmering limbs were no longer his own to control; when his mouth opened, it was the Oracle who spoke.

The words were in Nurian. She spoke to the Focals, as far as Tymon could tell, of the events in Argos city and their journey to Hayman's Point. She recounted all that had befallen him there — described the terror Tymon had endured at the hands of the soldiers and praised his courage in such glowing terms, indeed, that he wilted with embarrassment to hear it. While she conversed he could not say a word, though he remained intact and very much himself, an observer in his own mind. When she had finished recounting their arrival in Chal, she switched back to Argosian to make a final announcement.

'We are on the brink of great changes,' she told the Focals. 'We are moving into the Letter of Union, where all things become whole. Even our enemies enter this state, though they do not know it. Masks and lies will fall away or else become the only reality. The Reaper is dead — the Envoy has chosen to discard his puppet.'

This piece of news caused a flurry of discussion among the Focals, as they debated the implications of Lace's withdrawal and its likely effect on the resettlers. After a while the Oracle gently interrupted them. The timbre of her voice passed through Tymon like a soft summer breeze.

'The main lesson we should draw from this is that Eblas has no further use for Lantria or its politics,' she said. 'We should be concentrating on other matters. I fear he will now transfer his sights eastwards, and wage a war on two fronts, both inner and outer. There will doubtless be a physical attack on the Freeholds at some point, which Gardan and her allies are doing their best to prepare for. But I am more worried about his plans for you. If he has divested himself of the Reaper, it is to better concentrate on annihilating Grafters. I suggest you discuss your plans for defence, and consider those who cannot yet defend themselves.'

'The fledglings,' Noni agreed. 'The young Grafters must be protected.' As she said it, Tymon remembered Pallas with a stab of compunction.

'Most importantly, they should be taught how to protect themselves,' replied the Oracle quietly. 'But you know best how to achieve that. I will leave you now to talk freely with Tymon. You have much to say to each other.'

She departed with a final, fond farewell to the Focals. Her withdrawal, the ebbing of that tremendous power, left Tymon feeling as light and dry as a dead leaf. The sensation was not unpleasant.

'Well,' he sighed to his friends. 'That was something.'

'Something not many experience,' said Oren. 'You have changed much, *Syon*, since we see you last.'

He reached out and took hold of Tymon's shimmering right hand in the trance, turning it over to inspect the marks on the palm. 'You are blessed,' he continued, gazing a moment at the battle scars before letting Tymon go with a grave smile. 'You have lost love, but gained something else. Strength. *Beni*.'

The reference to Samiha caused Tymon another pang. He could not help asking his friends, then, what they thought of his vision at Hayman's Point, an episode the Oracle had mentioned but not described in detail. But even after hearing the tale in full, his fellow Grafters simply repeated what their teacher had said — that the glimpse of the Kion was most probably a hallucination due to pain. Tymon hid his disappointment and plunged into a discussion of the minutiae of goings-on in Farhang. He found out that Galliano was in fine spirits, and busy producing a fleet of air-chariots for the united Freeholds as part of their defensive preparations. Oren promised to send one of the new machines to Chal to pick Tymon up, along with his friend Zero.

'What about Pallas, Masha and Bolas?' Tymon enquired anxiously. 'Could you find out what's become of them for me? Read them? The Oracle advised me not to try on my own.'

'It's difficult to access people living within the Envoy's sphere of influence,' answered Noni. 'We could and will try to find your two Argosian friends. But I'm afraid we've already looked for Pallas, without success.

We're sorry, Tymon: he's not in the Tree of Being. We think the priests killed him.'

'No!' Tymon cried in horror. 'That can't be. The Oracle said we'd meet again!'

'Maybe she meant in the next life.'

'No,' he muttered again, miserable. 'I was sure she meant this one ...'

'*Syon*,' Ara reminded him softly. 'This is war with Envoy. We all lose much. Not even Oracle can save all. Mata and myself lost all family, long ago.' His twin nodded, sombre. 'We must be strong.'

'Eblas has new powers,' said Oren. 'Or else old ones have awoken. *Ama* is right: our enemy has become strong. Never have we been so blind during Reading. All Argos is beneath his cloud.'

'Take heart,' Noni told Tymon, in an attempt to comfort him. 'Wherever Pallas is now, our enemies can do no more to him. We should focus on the people we can help. Your part in all this is to stay alive until we reach you. Don't rake yourself over coals for the ones you weren't able to save.'

Tymon left the conversation with his worries reawakened rather than set to rest, perturbed by the fact that the Oracle had said no word to him about Pallas. Indeed, she had told him that 'what was broken shall be mended', allowing him to think he would see his friend again. She knew very well he did not seek those meetings in the 'world hereafter': why had she not mentioned the danger?

'Because I didn't know for sure what had happened,' she answered, responding to his unspoken thoughts as soon as his eyes blinked open in the shadowy kitchen alcove. 'Because the others don't know either, not really. They're just guessing. Pallas has disappeared. It could mean he's dead, or it could mean something else.'

'Like what?' he muttered aloud in the darkness. 'Trust me, *Ama*. Tell me these sorts of things. I need to know.'

'Very well,' sighed the Oracle. 'A disappearance in the Tree of Being can have different causes. Most obviously there is the death of the individual. The branch is gone and the Sap no longer flows there. But other factors can cause a temporary disappearance. The Sap can be stymied, or diverted away from an area, clouding the vision of the Focals. With regards to Pallas, we can only wait and see.'

She paused, then continued almost to herself: 'Sometimes, I disappear. But I'm not gone, not really. There will always be an Oracle.'

Tymon was torn between anxiety and annoyance. Was she referring to the possibility of another attack? Why did she not simply trust him with the facts? Her cool rationalisations left him floundering. 'It seems lately that whenever I ask the Sap something, I'm given the same answer,' he grumbled. '*Wait.*'

'Maybe the message is being repeated because you refuse to listen to it,' said the Oracle. 'In any case we have our orders, soldier. You are to live. You are to survive. You are to get out of here in one piece, so we can return to Farhang and tackle the Envoy properly. All together.'

Tymon was grateful to her for that last qualifier, at least. But there still remained a long and frustrating period before the air-chariot would come for them. He would be obliged to endure life as a House slave — with the knowledge that poor Zero was enduring the mine — for another fortnight, the time it would take for a new air-chariot to be completed and sent from Farhang to Lantria. The existing ones were in constant use and could not be spared. Indeed, it was fortunate that he had chosen that first evening to speak to the

Focals, for he found in the days that followed that he did not have much time to consecrate to the Grafting. He was kept occupied by Lord Dayan for most of the day, and allowed to return to his alcove only late at night, when he was thoroughly exhausted.

His talents as a half-deaf scribe were quickly recognised and exploited by the Lord, who had him present at every one of his business meetings. Dayan conducted his office work in the conservatory, a room fronted by translucent panels of sap and bathed from morning to evening in a soft orange glow. There, the proprietor of the mine would converse with a stream of clients in his leisurely, nasal drawl, his blue gaze wandering vaguely about the room and his long body draped over his chair, as if the last thing on his mind were business. He never wore the ubiquitous Lantrian collars, apparently feeling no need to reinforce his status by that means. The two Tree-dogs lay stretched out beneath his desk, their menacing glare fixed either on Tymon or on the nervous visitors perched on the Lord's opulent divans.

A languid character with the inborn elegance of his set, Dayan hid a remorseless intelligence behind his front of boredom. As far as Tymon could tell, he always secured the better end of any deal. His clients held him in awe, paying their obsequious respects to him before negotiating over the price of hardwood. The war with Argos did not appear to affect business dealings between the two countries at all; several of the merchants who visited Dayan were of Argosian origin, though they took care to arrive in Chal by way of the Eastern Domains. They often bemoaned the hostilities as being bad for business, before settling down to haggle over the hardwood that would be used to build their nations' respective battle fleets. It was shocking to Tymon, despite his own distaste for the Saint's warmongering, to see how little the very rich of either canopy exhibited in the way of patriotism.

He soon found that the importance of a visitor could be gauged by where the Lord asked him to sit, and by extension how much of the conversation Tymon was allowed to hear. If Dayan wished his secretary to take notes during the meeting, he would be invited to occupy a stool on the left of the desk. If it were expedient that a scribe be seen to be present but actually oblivious to the exchange, the Lord would place him to the right, with his good ear turned uselessly to the wall. Sometimes, the merchants began to haggle over the price of corewood; on these occasions, Tymon was invariably transferred to his deaf post. The conversation between the Lord and his guest would descend into an echoing murmur as the young man crouched on his stool, his sheaf of bark-paper idle on his knees and his heart as heavy as one of the beams cut from Dayan's mine.

For despite the Oracle's predictions, despite all of Oren's staunch promises, he felt that his time was ultimately wasted at the House. His entire motivation for enduring the Lord and his cronies was in order to help Zero, but as time went on, he saw no means of doing so. Days passed before he was even able to visit his friend, as the regiments of workers laboured, ate and slept in the depths of the shaft, far from the mansion. Finally, on the fifth day after his arrival in Chal, he was accorded the task of delivering a set of scrolls to the chief overseer in the mine, a man named Gul. It was just the excuse he had been waiting for, a chance to at least ascertain Zero's living conditions for himself, even if he could do nothing immediately to help his friend.

It was late morning when Tymon set off down the ramp into the crater. The journey took longer than he had expected. He walked for at least half an hour, descending ever deeper into the hollow branch; the rough planks of the ramp were plunged in shadow long before he reached the bottom. At last, he discerned the bobbing points of the workers' torches in the dark heart of the crater, stars in that interior night. A faint sound of hammering rose up from the depths, growing louder as he reached the end of the ramp and struck out across a circular arena of chipped and gouged wood. He stumbled on as best he could in the gloomy twilight of the mine, following the faraway twinkling light of the torches. The hacking sound became a ceaseless thudding, reminiscent of Galliano's first steam-contraption built in Argos city. It was a sound, Tymon thought, that should only be made by a machine.

His first sight of the mine proper was of a group of makeshift huts, quarters for the Hordannan slaves. They appeared to be deserted: the Nurians had already climbed into the deeper pit at the centre of the shaft, to begin their work. It was from this lower level that the thudding came. Tymon approached the pit and peered over the edge. The torches he had glimpsed from above had been set about the perimeter of the cavity, as well as in orderly rows across its floor. Figures bent and straightened in the flickering light — bent and straightened without cease, bringing their axes down in unison, their silhouettes black against the glow of the torches. They worked in gangs of twelve chained together at the ankle, hacking out sections of hardwood into long beams. Their rhythm never changed or faltered. If an individual member of a gang paused to catch his breath, a burlier silhouette stepped up from the sidelines and cracked a whip over his back. Once, perhaps twice the cruel thong came down, until the weary worker resumed his task.

Tymon shuddered at the memory of pain, his

shoulders tightening instinctively. He had no choice but to shove his scrolls under his arm and descend one of the long ladders leaning against the sides of the hole, making his way towards the nearest overseer. He scanned the faces of the Nurians he passed, wincing at each overheard crack of the whips; the mineworkers were all gaunt, defeated creatures, never once meeting his gaze. He could not see Zero among them.

The burly overseer, for his part, gave Tymon a long and level stare when he was asked for the whereabouts of his chief, directing the young Argosian to the other side of the pit. Tymon assumed that his accent had given him away as a foreigner and hurried off, babbling his thanks before he could be questioned further. Not one of the workers looked up as he passed the heaving rows of backs. Halfway across the mine-floor he had to bite hard on his lip in order to avoid crying out with joy, for he had caught sight of Zero's familiar ginger-cropped head, the last in line in one of the gangs. The Marak lad was stripped to the waist, his body sweating in the gloom as he lifted the heavy axe and brought it down again. He wore no mere tablet about his neck to indicate his bond to Lord Dayan: instead, Tymon noticed with a stab of outrage, a freshly made brand marked the youth's right arm, similar to those used on Argosian herd-beasts. It was a florid 'H' like the one on the mansion gate, followed by the number five hundred and twenty-three, the burn still bright red and weeping as it healed. Zero's face was set in an expression of placid endurance.

Mindful of the overseers' whips, Tymon waited until the guard standing closest to them had turned his back before approaching his friend. As he sidled closer, trying to appear nonchalant, he was greeted by a soft whoop of triumph from Zero. The Nurian boy let his axe drop and crouched on the floor of the pit, pulling

Tymon down beside him. The workers may not have been quite as defeated as Tymon had feared, for the other gang-members never stopped or glanced in their direction, but continued to strike the beam in silent solidarity, providing cover for their conversation.

'Thank the Tree you're alive,' were the first words uttered by Zero.

'Me?' Tymon replied, almost falling over in his surprise. 'I'm fine! It's you I'm concerned about. This place — what they've done to you —' he winced as his gaze fell on the weeping brand-wound on his friend's arm — 'they're worse than devils in Hell. Do they feed you properly at least?'

Zero gave an answering grimace and shrugged his shoulders.

'I'll find a way to get you better stuff,' Tymon assured him. 'There's no shortage of victuals at the House.' He dropped his voice to a hoarse whisper. 'You've only got to stick it out for another week and a bit, Zero. My friends are coming for us. When do these chains come off? Do you go free at night?'

He examined the hardwood ring about the lad's ankle. It was smooth with years of use, but the chafing had already left a sore mark on his skin. The workers' fetters were as tough as the beams they painstakingly shaped. Zero's ring was the only one in his gang that possessed a lock. The other six were connected to it with a long thin rod, making movement away from the group impossible.

'The chains come off, but then we're shut up in the huts by these good people,' said Zero. 'Better still, there are guards everywhere. You can't get near the ramp. These friends of yours — do they bring ships?'

'Flying machines small and fast enough to come right down here and scoop you up. We just have to get you out of that hut.'

'I'll talk to the others. They'll come up with a way.' The Marak boy gave a conspiratorial wink. 'I hope your friends have enough machines. There are lots of decent, evil people down here who need our help.'

Tymon felt a twinge of compunction through his amusement; Zero's topsy-turvy ideas, as well as his generosity of spirit, were still intact, despite all that he had suffered. But the remark also caused Tymon to wilt with shame, for he had not even thought of freeing the other mineworkers.

'The air-chariot's only for us,' he said ruefully. 'The Freeholders can only send one — I'm sorry, that's all they can spare. We have to sort out a time, at night, when you can get away —'

Zero shook his head in the gloom of the pit. 'No, no!' he interrupted. 'We can't leave these people behind.'

'We have no choice,' mumbled Tymon.

Zero was asking him to perform an impossible task, he thought: there was no way to free the hundreds of mineworkers. He began to feel heavy and hopeless again, as he glanced up at the man standing closest to them. The Nurian was a skeleton of a creature, pounding faithfully away at the beam as they talked. Tymon wondered how much of their conversation he could hear.

'We do have a choice, Lord,' protested Zero. 'They've been expecting you. Don't disappoint them.'

'Expecting me? But you couldn't have known ...' Tymon frowned. 'Why are you calling me "Lord"?' he asked, assailed by a swift suspicion.

Zero wordlessly pointed out three members of a neighbouring work-gang. They were younger than many of the other slaves, Tymon saw. They had spotted him, and were glancing over their shoulders as they worked, their hollow faces burning with hope. Then he noticed the excessively pale tint of their skin, and the whitish colour of their hair under a layer of red wood-dust. The Saffid! He did not remember these particular souls from the slum in Cherk Harbour, but would have recognised their trademark fervour anywhere.

'The Tree help us,' he breathed, both glad to see members of the tribe alive and paradoxically struck with terror at the added responsibility. 'Tell me. Is there a woman named Dawn here?'

Zero nodded. 'They kept her for the guards to begin with, but she's too sick to do that work now. She told me all about you. You're the return of Saint Loa, saviour of Nur. Why didn't you say so before?'

'The guards?' A faint groan escaped Tymon's lips. 'How many of the Saffid are in the mine, Zero?'

'The older ones like Jan are gone, except Dawn. Nightside told me about twenty are left, spread out in different regiments.'

'Nightside, too?' muttered Tymon. 'Where's Dawn? Is she in one of the huts?'

'Number seven. Back the way you came, Lord.'

'Please, Zero, don't call me "Lord".' Tymon glanced over his shoulder, towards the shacks at the edge of the pit. 'I'm not what the Saffid think I am, though I wish I were. Then at least I could help ...'

He realised at that moment, with a lurch of panic, that the overseer had become aware of their exchange and was striding towards them, his face a storm cloud. There was no time to explain Dawn's fixations to Zero.

'Guard's coming,' he warned, jumping to his feet. 'I'll try to sort something out for the Saffid. But I can't make any promises, Zero.'

The Nurian boy scrambled up after him, and applied his axe to the beam as quickly as he could. But the overseer was already upon them.

'What d'you think you're doing, talking to the

workers, House-scum?' he boomed to Tymon. 'D'you want a lick of this, too?'

He raised his whip, laying two brutal strokes into Zero's back. The lad gasped with pain but carried on working. For Tymon, witnessing his friend's suffering was worse than any punishment the guard might have inflicted on him. His body went cold, then hot, the scars on his back aching with sympathetic pain. The overseer was a slave himself, of course, his old burns visible on his sinewy arm.

'It wasn't his fault,' said Tymon, glaring at him. 'I was just asking him how to find the chief.'

'Well, find this,' jeered the other. He shook the end of the whip under Tymon's nose. 'We don't talk to the help, my uppity little House friend. Lucky for you the Lord's a softy, or I'd tattoo my number on your high-and-mighty rump. Chief's over on the south side. Move, Sir Five-Two-Two!'

The last command was accompanied by a kick aimed at his back. Tymon scurried away, hot-faced, his scrolls jammed under one arm. When his delivery to the chief was accomplished, he made his way back across the pit, taking care to walk on the opposite end to Zero's overseer. On its southern side, the work-pit stretched all the way to the crater wall, and Tymon passed several tunnel-mouths leading down to a deeper level of the mine. He did not tarry, his eye trained warily on the guards posted at intervals around the workers. He was seething with suppressed rage.

'You said nothing about this, either,' he accused the Oracle, when he was out of earshot of the overseers. 'Pallas I can understand — maybe. But you should have mentioned the Saffid.'

'Why talk about something you'd find out all too soon on your own?' she sighed. 'It's not as if you could get down to the mine any earlier.'

'That's not the point!' he muttered, incensed. 'The point is I need to know things like this. You See all the time, you say. You should warn me. I can't necessarily guess what to look for in the Reading.'

'You can't, that's true, but it doesn't occur to you not to ask at all,' she said mildly. 'Never once have you allowed the Sap to show you what it wills. I guarantee you'd See all you needed that way.'

He was defeated by this line of reasoning, chewing on his frustration in silence as he clambered up a ladder on the far side of the pit. Although he was aware that the Oracle could read him transparently, he did not communicate his feelings aloud as he made for the huddle of sleeping huts. There were no confounded guards there, thank goodness.

'You're not really angry with me, are you?' his teacher observed, after a moment.

'No,' he admitted through clenched teeth.

'It's true. What people do to each other is worse than hell.'

'Yes,' he replied, brusque with her in his misery.

He could hardly speak at all. He burned with outrage at the thought of Nightside and Zero, branded like kine, and Dawn forced to serve the abominable appetites of the mine-guards. He strode in hot silence through the slave quarters, squinting to see the faded numbers painted on the sides of the huts and keeping a wary eye out for any more overseers. He consigned them cordially to any hell that might exist.

'Take heart,' murmured the Oracle in answer to his unspoken turmoil. 'I suspect this particular hell has a crack or two. Your coming here is a small thing, a hairline fracture. But even the smallest things can start an avalanche.'

Hut number seven was a dilapidated shack standing at the far side of the group of buildings. Tymon tapped on the door; it swung open at his touch.

'Dawn? Are you there?' he called softly into the gloom.

There was a faint scraping from within the hut, like the movement of grasses bending and sighing against each other. 'I knew you would come, Lord.'

Dawn's voice was faint, its tone of fervent conviction immediately recognisable. As Tymon felt his way into the deeper gloom of the shack, past the threadbare pallets jammed together on the floor, he made out the pale face of the Saffid girl lying near the back wall. Dawn was stretched out on a blanket, her form pitifully thin. She tried to sit up as he arrived, but was unable to do more than raise her head.

'Rest easy,' he begged, kneeling down and pushing her gently back on the blanket. 'Don't move on my account. You need to save your strength.'

For he could see as his vision adjusted to the darkness that her face was now covered in the telltale lesions, her body wasted away by the Saffids' version of the Slow Death. Her eyes glinted with feverish joy.

'You bring me strength, Lord,' she told him.

He dared not contradict her beliefs, with her laid out before him like this, in the final stages of her illness. He took her hand and held it in his own, no longer squeamish about the lesions that encrusted her skin. If he could have taken the mysterious sickness upon himself at that moment, curing her, he would have done so. It was with difficulty that he dredged up what he hoped would be the right words.

'I'm going to contact the Focals again,' he told her. 'I'm going to ask them to send as many machines as they can from the Freehold. Even if we can't get all the mineworkers out, we'll still do something for the Saffid, I promise.'

'I know you will,' she said. 'You will rescue them. You will get them out. I have faith.' Neither of them mentioned the fact that for her, rescue came too late.

'Tymon,' murmured the Oracle in the recesses of his mind, 'I would like to speak to Dawn, but I can't use your body outside the trance. Would you mind giving her the message?'

'Of course,' he answered aloud, in surprise. 'Dawn, I have to tell you that little Lai finally died after we left Cherk Harbour,' he explained to the sick woman, whose eyes widened at the implications of such news. '*Ama's* here with me, now, though it's not a full Exchange. She has a message for you.'

Dawn's face lit up with joy. She tried to struggle up again before sinking down on her bed, her gaze burning into Tymon as he tried to understand the Oracle and speak simultaneously.

'The time you have been waiting for so eagerly has arrived,' he said, repeating after his teacher. 'Your people will be free. There is a long road to travel before they reach redemption. The Sign will help you as any good person would, but do not expect him to do more for now. He has not yet passed the test.' He frowned: the Oracle's words seemed to both play along with Dawn's obsession and undercut it. He was given no chance to object, however. 'You will leave this place in a few days under his protection,' he continued, as the phrases succeeded each other relentlessly in his head. 'After that you will be free. He should be able to guide the Saffid to a safe haven, a place where they will live in peace until the Promised Time. Is that all?'

In his confusion he had spoken his own question aloud at the end of her speech. 'That's all for now,' the Oracle answered quietly. 'You should leave her, Tymon. Let her rest, or she won't last long enough to see the escape.'

His teacher's promises seemed to be enough for Dawn. A smile of beatitude had stretched over her bloodless lips, as if Tymon had just handed her the key to Paradise. When he bid her farewell until their next meeting and arose, she barely nodded to him. But her eyes remained fixed on him as he picked his way towards the door of the hut.

Luckily, none of the mine-guards were to be seen outside. Tymon hastened away from the huts and across the shaft, filled with brooding anxiety for his friends as he mounted the ramp that wound up the sides of the crater. Even blanketed by a layer of cloud and leaves, the winter daylight when he reached the top was almost blinding.

6

Tymon could not help bemoaning the fact for a second time, on his way back to the mansion, that the Oracle had not told him about the Saffid. His teacher's answer was more brusque on this occasion than it had been when he first made these objections.

'You must learn to See for yourself,' she warned him, as they walked along the perimeter road to the House. 'I cannot always be your keeper. You must learn to rely on the Sap for what you need to know, and not only on me. There will be times when I cannot help you: there will be times when you must help me instead.'

There was a severity in her tone that struck his conscience like a gong. She disappeared after that, much to his chagrin, and he wondered whether she was engaged in another of her mysterious struggles with the Envoy's Masters. He could not even begin to imagine how those contests were played out. Did they take place in the Veil? How was his teacher able to defend herself against Beings of such power? Was she in serious danger when she spoke of needing his help, or was it merely her way of encouraging his independence? He had not questioned the Oracle on these subjects before, partly because other matters had preoccupied him, and partly out of a sense of pride and discretion. He had learned through experience that his teacher would only trust him with information when she considered him ready for it, refusing to answer a question she thought was inappropriate. Up till now, such behaviour had simply annoyed him. This time, however, he was troubled by her absence, sensing a danger there that had nothing to do with evasion.

She did not revisit him all that afternoon. On his return to the House, he was set to work sorting through the Lord's correspondence in the conservatory, while his employer stepped out for a stroll. Dayan required his secretary to file his letters away in a special cabinet equipped with alphabetised drawers, for he was as punctilious regarding his business transactions as he was about the feeding and grooming of his dogs. The task was deadly dull for Tymon, and would have been made much lighter by the Oracle's return. But the hours passed and still she did not come.

In her absence, Tymon felt dismally alone. Sitting on the floor of the conservatory and leafing through the sheets of serviceable bark-rag and smooth pulp paper, he fell to thinking of his vision again, of the figure on the dock at Hayman's Point. Although he had been warned not to dwell on the subject, he had been unable to dismiss Samiha from his mind since his arrival in Chal. He speculated whether the glimpse of her had been some form of Sending, rather than a mere hallucination: a real, if brief, communication with her. He yearned secretly for it to happen to him again. His heart raced whenever the dismal winter weather was broken by a fine spell, and rays of light penetrated the leaf-forests; he stared at sunbeams, hoping against hope to see the shining figure. He never confided his obsessions to the Oracle, due in part to an obscure sense of shame. When she was with him, he was able to put the idea out of his mind, as she had advised. But when she left him to his own devices, as she had this afternoon, the image of Samiha returned to haunt him.

He had classified about half a box of letters, reflecting gloomily on his lost love, when he came upon a missive bearing the seal of the *New East Trading Company*. He stared at the words scrawled near the top of the page, by the blot of broken wax. They were like a hook dragging him back to bleak reality. Even the thought of Samiha faded away. This New East Trading Company had been the one mentioned by the merchant, Yago, in Cherk Harbour, the company connected to the Reaper. This was the business arm of the infamous resettler fleet. Ultimately, he realised with a jolt, it was Lord Dayan and those like him who were responsible for what had happened to Laska. Tymon had not forgotten the betrayal of his old friend. He stood by the cabinet, blinking down in shock at the sheet of paper in his hands.

He had been taken in by Lord Dayan's façade of dilettantism. He had considered his employer to be a self-centred drone, who never changed the conditions in the mine simply because they profited him. But Dayan was one of those who created the conditions in the first place. The letter, Tymon read in mounting fury, was addressed to the Company's honourable shareholders. It mentioned the need to transfer operation headquarters to Cherk Harbour, either due to 'unfortunate events' or 'an unfortunate illness' in the South Canopy — his grasp of Lantrian was not quite sufficient to tell the difference. Such steps were necessary, apparently, in order to ensure smooth business operations in the future, and a steady flow of 'merchandise'. Tymon could have balled up the paper and stuffed it down his employer's throat.

'A Grafter does not seek revenge,' said the Oracle, abruptly present in his mind again. She delivered her moral refrain with an edge of weariness, like the words of a song repeated once too often.

'Are you alright, *Ama?*' he murmured in the silence of the conservatory. 'I was worried about you.'

'The Masters harry me in their attempts to break out of the Veil — but yes, I am well enough,' she answered. 'I have not seen my charges so restless in a long while.'

'Can't we do anything to help you?' he asked, forcing himself to tear his eyes away from the letter. 'The Focals, I mean?'

'So,' she said, and he could hear the smile in her voice, 'you're beginning to identify yourself with them, aren't you? That's good. Actually, it's a balm to my heart and the best thing you can do for me. Work with the Focals. Keep vigilant. Stay unified. And for heaven's sake, forget this toad of a mine-owner. He isn't worth your anger.'

'It's hard to forget what I'm doing here,' protested Tymon. 'I'm helping him fill his resettler ships.'

'Ah, you're doing a lot more than that, unfortunately,' she replied. 'Lord Dayan is involved in every piece of dirty business the South and Eastern Canopies have to offer. He traffics in slaves. He controls the trade in core. Lately, he has paid an Argosian priest to sell him the secret of blast-poison, and is busily turning himself into the greatest arms merchant in the Four Canopies. He deals with all whom Argos chooses to ignore. After the attack on Sheb, the seminary abandoned their relations with the Nurian rebels. Now Caro and his proxies have taken to buying their supplies from Dayan. The Lord sends them blast-poison in exchange for shipments of *som*.'

'What?' Tymon almost laughed aloud at the bizarre juxtaposition. 'The Nurian rebels have ties with slavers? How does Caro justify that?'

'He calls it "pragmatism".'

'Do Oren and the others know this?'

'They know, because they are deeply concerned with the fate of the Freeholds, and the fate of the Freeholds is interwoven with that of the rebels. The two go hand in hand.'

'So strange,' mused Tymon. 'Caro hated me so much. And now he's willing to deal with Dayan.'

'He hated you because you had nothing to offer him,' observed the Oracle. 'People like Caro have been around since the beginning of time and I daresay will be around till the end of it. They actually think they're doing good, you know.'

The way she spoke of passing eons so matter-of-factly, as if worlds were born and died in the blink of an eye, made Tymon remember the Born.

'You said the Envoy's Masters were your charges,' he remarked curiously. He wanted at least a few more answers to his questions. 'Why, *Ama*? They aren't your responsibility, surely?'

'But they are, Tymon. I am the gatekeeper. They are hammering at the gate. I am the lock. They are searching for the Key. So it has been for a great many years.'

But he wanted a precise, not a poetic, response. 'How many exactly?' he asked, his pulse quickening.

This was one of the points she had never clarified to his satisfaction. She had never told him how long she had carried out her responsibility as Oracle, inhabiting host after host in her capacity as guardian. Something told him that it was a considerable amount of time.

'Yes,' she said softly. 'Far too long. And you're right about another thing: I don't wish to talk about it. Tell me more about that letter in your hands. I believe it's the important thing to focus on at the moment.'

When he had recounted the gist of the letter, she gave a grunt of derision. 'He knows, then,' she sighed. 'He has made arrangements.'

'Who, *Ama*? The Envoy? He knows what?'

'You're a sharp one.' She chuckled. 'The Envoy knows his affairs will be better served if the Company works out of Cherk Harbour. He made provision for that evidently, before abandoning the Reaper. I wonder how the decision went down. I doubt people like Dayan were happy about it.'

'I can't believe I have to work for that devil,' snorted Tymon. He gave the Company letter a disdainful flick of his thumb and forefinger. 'For this pack of devils who bring misery to everyone —'

'Beware of names,' said the Oracle, interrupting. 'They define us if we let them. You're thinking of your employer as less than human, just as you were beginning to do with your fellow Argosians. It's a dangerous habit.'

'But Dayan is a devil!' he objected. 'Only a monster would do what he does —'

'Tymon,' she admonished. 'This is essential for you to understand. No matter what Dayan does — no matter what he does to your friends, to poor people like Dawn and her fellow workers — it is essential that you recognise him as your own flesh and blood. There will be no end to this business, ever, if you can't see that. One day, your sort will triumph over his sort, and he'll be the one working in the mine instead of you. And so it will go, round and round, unless you stop the whole thing. Now!'

Tymon said nothing. He had never heard his teacher speak so strongly: her usual equanimity, her dry detachment had vanished, and her voice was full of emotion. Even so, he still could not bring himself to say anything remotely positive about Dayan. So he kept his mouth shut.

'Remember what you learned in Argos city,' she resumed in a quieter tone. 'The Tree contains all things. Happiness and sorrow. Dark and light. A Grafter accepts that and carries on. We cannot See every end.'

Forget the quarrel between happiness and sorrow. The words of his vision returned unbidden to Tymon's mind. He shivered. 'So, what do I do then?' he said. 'Here I am, working for Lord Not-The-Devil, digging out shiny baubles from the heart of the world so that fat governors can wear them on their fingers. I hate it. Give me some hope that my time here will not only result in horror and misery.'

'Don't forget the governors' wives and concubines, sitting at home in Lant city,' replied the Oracle. 'They're generally the ones with an insatiable appetite for corewood. But there is hope, Tymon. You're in a unique position to help your friends here. And I don't just mean the Saffid, I mean the Focals. There are things they don't See, things they rely on you to tell them. As I say, they are preoccupied with the Freeholds, and so other factors escape them. Allow the Sap to take you to places you cannot conceive of beforehand. Seek out new questions, instead of always wanting answers to the old ones.'

He did not have occasion to reply. At that instant, voices echoed in the corridor outside the conservatory. Lord Dayan was addressing a visitor on his way back to the office. Tymon hastily shoved the Company letter into the appropriate slot in the cabinet. As he did so, his nerves were set jangling by a sound he had come to dread: the low, menacing growl of the Lord's dogs.

His first terror of the Tree-dogs had long since passed, and he no longer thought of their superficial resemblance to the Beast-that-was-Lace. He even pitied the brutes, for he saw that they had been inbred to the point of torture. Their breathing was laboured, their snouts too short and their mouths perpetually agape. But they still represented a serious threat to his safety. The animals had never taken a liking to him, their jittery temperaments upset by this newcomer in their closed world; their hackles rose whenever they saw him, as if they sensed his unspoken aversion to their master. He had not noticed them entering the room this time, their padded feet making no noise on the thick weave-mat, and rose slowly to his feet, turning around.

The dogs crouched before him on the carpet, their jaws open and slavering, blue eyes shot with bloody hate.

'Good grief, not again. Ablash. Gaw. Heel, boys.'

Dayan's command, spoken in Argosian, rang out from the doorway. The aristocrat often addressed Tymon in his own tongue; the dogs, for their part, did not seem to mind the difference. They stopped growling as the Lord ambled into the room, his hands thrust into the pockets of his soft grey trousers, the picture of easy elegance. Dayan wore his greying hair cut long, in defiance of Lantrian convention. At a whistle from him, the dogs trotted over to sniff his boots, transformed into panting sycophants.

'What do you do to them?' he asked Tymon with a light laugh. 'I've never seen them object to anyone else like this.' He bent down to pat the heads of his furred sentries.

Tymon remained where he stood and bowed stiffly to his employer, reluctant to approach the dogs. The Lord spoke to him with polite camaraderie, as if he were a friend and equal; it made Tymon unspeakably uncomfortable. 'Careful,' cautioned the Oracle, a soft breath in his ear. 'Don't let him see your dislike. It's bad enough that the dogs do.'

'I swear I didn't do anything, sir,' said Tymon. He decided on an attempt at humour to disguise his unease. 'Maybe they hate me for leaving the seminary,' he joked. 'They say animals can smell out a traitor.'

Just then, the Lord's companion, whom Tymon had heard speaking in the hall, entered the conservatory. A tall, muscular man, the newcomer had his scalp clean-shaven in the Lantrian style and sported the sleeveless leather jerkin of a sailor. He did not in any way resemble the fussy, collared merchants who had visited Dayan on previous occasions. His eyes, when he returned Tymon's astonished gaze, were edged with ferocious-looking black ash. The joke about traitors fell completely flat in the silence that followed.

'Aha, the resettler,' murmured the Oracle. 'I was wondering when he'd appear on the scene. He's the Company's man in Cherk Harbour, Tymon. Let's hope he doesn't make the connection between the young foreigner he was hunting there, and the young foreigner standing in front of him here.'

'So, traitor,' remarked the visitor at last, in his drawling brand of Argosian, as he considered Tymon from head to foot. 'You were a seminary lad. How interesting.'

Tymon tried to smile, failed, and buried his discomfort in another bow. Dayan flung himself into his office chair with his usual carelessness, while the dogs padded under the table to flop at his feet.

'Captain Tahu here has recently returned from Cherk Harbour,' the Lord threw out, with a yawn. 'You may stay with us, Tymon, and take notes when I ask you to. Tahu, do make yourself comfortable, my old man.'

Dayan affected broad-mindedness by referring to his servants by their personal names. In the present circumstances, Tymon would rather he had been addressed by his number, or by the belittling term 'boy', as he had been at the seminary, for he would have liked to remain unnamed. When his employer indicated that he should bring his stool to the right side of the desk — his deaf post — his unease only deepened. Tahu's rough garb belied his importance, then; Dayan did not wish Tymon to hear their discussion. The young man silently cursed his disability, for he suspected that the information he would be missing might have served the Focals.

'Not really,' said the Oracle, responding to his thoughts. 'They'll talk about deliveries to Caro, I suspect. There's something else going on here, however, something important ... I haven't quite put my finger on it yet ...'

Her voice trailed off. Tahu's ash-edged scrutiny did not leave Tymon, but he did as he was bidden by Dayan, and sat down on one of the divans, his leather-clad bulk incongruous on the embroidered upholstery. 'Tymon,' he repeated, rolling the name over his tongue, as if testing its flavour. 'Tell me, Tymon. Have you ever travelled to the Eastern Canopy?'

The question sent a shiver down Tymon's spine. 'He suspects now,' warned the Oracle. 'He does not know. Be circumspect, but do not lie: this one is a hound himself, sniffing out falsehood.'

'Yes.' Tymon hovered on the right side of the desk, but remained standing to answer Tahu, in a show of respect. He would not in any case have heard what the other was saying, had he sat down with his face turned to the window. 'I was sent to do my indenture in Marak. I ran away and tried to get home again, but they caught me.'

He had given the most abridged answer he could think of while keeping to the truth. 'Well done,' murmured the Oracle. 'Enough and not too much. But we still have a problem. If only I could figure out what it was!'

'We should get to work,' put in Dayan impatiently. 'Sit, Tymon. I'll ask you to help in a minute.'

Tahu was evidently dissatisfied with Tymon's answer, but felt obliged to comply with his Lord's wishes. He remained silent, his lips pursed and his eyes lingering on the young man as he lowered himself onto his stool.

Tymon could not help speculating how much the Company man had seen of the debacle in Cherk Harbour, and whether he had been personally involved in Laska's arrest. It was all he could do to avoid returning the resettler's gaze with gloomy hatred. He half-faced the window, as Dayan required, turning his deaf ear to his companions. When the Lord resumed speaking, Tymon could tell that the conversation was in Lantrian, but his position plunged the rest of the dialogue into a ringing confusion.

Left to himself in the void of deafness, he stared through the orange panes at Dayan's garden terraces, brooding over the irony of Nurian rebels having ties with the slavers. How could Caro sleep at night, after indulging in so much bloody pragmatism? As the Lord and his thug continued to talk, Tymon's thoughts wandered from his old Nurian opponent back to Laska again, remembering how much the Freeholders had loved their brusque but fair-minded captain. Only Gardan was left now, he thought, to keep that spirit of leadership alive. After a while, as the conversation in Lantrian dragged on, he noticed distractedly that another storm was brewing outside. He gazed up in distaste at the oddly coloured clouds churning in the spaces between the leaves, giving an involuntary shudder as the carefully tended flowers and neatly clipped shrubs on the terraces began to toss and heave in the rising wind. Although the South Canopy with its low altitudes had milder weather than either Argos or Nur, he found the wet, windy Lantrian winter distinctly unpleasant.

'I don't like it either,' said the Oracle, through the muffled echo of the Lord's voice. 'This weather is tricky. Everything changes in the blink of an eye … It's all illusion, no substance.'

Even Tymon's deaf ear registered the grinding sound

of the divan's legs at that moment, scraping on the floor as the meeting drew to a close. He turned around to see Tahu rising from his seat.

'It will be done, Lord,' the resettler declared. 'You can rely on me.'

'I know,' smiled Dayan. 'That's why I chose you for this job, my friend. You have your instructions. Good speed on your return to Cherk.'

Tahu bowed, his ashen gaze sliding towards Tymon one last time. Then he turned and strode from the room. When he was gone, Dayan beckoned the young man back to the other side of the desk. The dogs stirred and snuffled as Tymon wearily repositioned his stool again. Their master leaned back in his chair, his expression thoughtful as he scrutinised his secretary.

'I suppose you're wondering what all that was about,' he said.

'Yes, sir,' admitted Tymon.

'I have a few business deals in the Eastern Canopy that I do not wish to publicise. But I'm glad you met Tahu. This brings me round to a subject I have been wanting to broach with you for some time.'

'Oho,' muttered the Oracle. 'It's coming. This one is hatching a plan.'

The Lord stretched out even farther in his chair, as lanky and languid as his lolling dogs. 'Why did your masters really banish you from the seminary, Tymon?' he asked, drawling out the question.

'Like I say, sir, I ran away from my indenture,' answered Tymon warily. 'I had some contact with Nurian Freeholders. They declared me a traitor.'

Dayan shrugged. 'Yes, yes, all very interesting, I'm sure. But not quite enough to justify the punishment you received … they had a special reason to hate you, did they not? To send you to the harshest pilgrim camp in the Central Canopy, where the soldiers in charge would do things like that to you.' He indicated Tymon's shredded ear.

Tymon was at a loss as to how to answer. 'A devious little scheme from a devious little mind,' noted the Oracle from the background, somewhat unhelpfully.

At last the Lord spoke again. 'Undo your shirt collar,' he said.

Although various swift objections to this request passed through Tymon's mind, he did not need the Oracle's warning to put them aside this time. His experience at Hayman's Point had taught him not to value outward dignity above the inner kind. He kept his face neutral and undid the buttons at his neck. As he did so, Samiha's pendant, lying for so long next to his skin, slipped over his shirtfront, next to the slave's identification plaque.

'So,' murmured the Lord triumphantly.

He leaned forward and brought his face close to Tymon's, taking hold of the little pendant. He obviously considered his houseboy to be a passive object, to touch or not as he pleased. He inspected the *orah* greedily, rubbing a thumb and forefinger over the bright inlay.

'It's true then,' he breathed. 'You are an acolyte of the Old Order.'

'Of course,' said the Oracle, her voice full of relief. 'The Lord knows about the Grafting. Don't worry, Tymon, we'll be able to use this to our advantage.'

'The Old Order?' echoed Tymon, feeling far happier as his employer withdrew his hand and settled back in his chair again.

'You have another name for it,' answered Dayan. 'But occult Lantrian scripture is formal on the subject. Those who wear *ashk* — the "substance of shining tears", to translate literally — are seers who can predict the future. Your masters in Argos could not have borne

138

any opposition from an acolyte initiated into their deepest secrets. Does that about cover what happened to you?'

'Maybe,' said Tymon. Despite the Oracle's assurances, Dayan's interest in the Grafting struck him as positively disturbing.

'Oh, you know very well it does,' smiled the aristocrat. 'We both know that the prophets were not merely pious teachers concerned with promoting a system of ethics. They were powerful practitioners of an art still extant in the world — an art that is the secret of the seminary's power. Am I not right, Tymon the Grafter?'

The young man stared at him apprehensively. 'And if you are?' he asked. 'What happens then?'

'Then,' replied the Lord, his smile becoming unctuous, 'you and I may enter into an agreement.'

He did not immediately elaborate on what such an agreement might entail, however, and creaked back in his seat, pressing the ends of his fingers together and contemplating Tymon.

'That's not anywhere near the whole of it, though,' mused the Oracle, her tone preoccupied. 'There's something else going on, something besides the Lord's little plan ... If I could only See ...'

'Do you know why we bring Nurians to work in the mines?' Dayan asked abruptly.

Tymon's back stiffened. 'No, sir,' he mumbled.

'For the same reason as Argosians bring them to their plantations,' said the aristocrat, without missing a beat. 'The Nurries aren't like us, of course. They can't take care of themselves: they need someone to organise them, to put them to work properly. It could, and should, be a mutually beneficial arrangement. The Eastern Canopy was in a shocking state before the Argosians went in, you know. I personally deplore the war between our two great nations.' He rapped his finger decisively on the desk. 'But you, Tymon, are different from the other slaves. You have a soul. That's why I am willing to enter into an agreement with you. You will use your powers to answer a question for me. In return, I'll free you as an act of mercy. You'll be given passage to Lant city. Thereafter you may do as you like.'

Another gust of wind shook the window. The dogs at Dayan's feet stirred and pricked up their ears. Tymon was torn between hope and disgust at the Lord's insinuations. He would have appreciated the Oracle's input at that moment, but she seemed suddenly preoccupied by the weather.

'I'll be damned if I can See in these shadows,' she sighed, as sun and cloud conducted a swift contest in the sky above the terraced gardens.

Tymon ignored her grumblings. He was prepared to hear the mine-owner out; the hope that had taken hold of him was not for himself.

'I might be able to help you,' he said cautiously. 'But not in exchange for my own freedom. I'd like to ask for something else, sir.'

'And what would that be?'

'There are a few people in your mine I call friends. That's another reason the priests hated me: I have Nurian friends. Free them instead of me.'

One of the dogs — Tymon guessed it was Gaw — began to emit a high-pitched whine, raising its head to stare through the window at the tossing leaf-tips. Dayan raised a well-mannered eyebrow at his request.

'I see that you genuinely care for these pathetic creatures,' he said. 'Such indulgence is foolish. Be that as it may, I might be disposed to agree to your demands. But an act of mercy that covers several individuals is difficult to justify. I would have to have sufficient motivation for my actions, especially if we're talking about mineworkers.' He rose from his chair and strolled to the window, peering up at the slivers of overcast sky visible through the leaves. 'I need an excuse I can sell to my personnel managers, out there in the real world.'

'I hate being blind,' complained the Oracle, in the depths of Tymon's mind. 'It's always a bad sign for what comes next.'

She did not seem to be following the conversation with Dayan at all. Tymon felt a twinge of annoyance. He was on his own in his negotiations. He cast about for some cold, business-like logic the Lantrian might accept.

'My friends are mostly too sick to work, or too young to be really productive,' he said. 'All but one are members of the Saffid tribe. They suffer from an accelerated version of the Slow Death. You'll only get a few years out of them anyway.'

The dogs had evidently seen something they considered a threat in the garden. Both of the animals were now sitting up beneath the desk, growling at the faraway clouds. Tymon squinted in the same direction, at the leaf-tossed, orange-tinted sky. He glimpsed a flock of birds circling high above the mansion. There was definitely a thunderstorm coming, he thought.

Dayan shrugged again. 'The average life of a slave is two years in the mine,' he said, without turning from the window. 'I'm sorry to say that even the Slow Death makes no difference to productivity.'

'Did you just see birds outside?' asked the Oracle, with sudden interest. But Tymon was too keen to argue with Dayan to answer.

'Then do it as an investment in your future,' he persisted to the Lord. 'I'll stay here and help you as long as you like.' He meant it, too: he would have been

141

willing to forgo the Freeholders' rescue himself, if Dawn, Zero and the others were able to leave the mine without harassment. 'I'll be your resident Grafter,' he said.

'Something's wrong,' gasped the Oracle.

The distress in her voice gave Tymon pause at last. *What's the matter?* he asked her silently. He glanced about him, but everything in the room seemed normal, apart from the dogs. They were still emitting their foolish noises, staring at the far-off circling specks. *Is it the birds?* he enquired.

But his teacher did not respond. Dayan's blue eyes glinted with cold satisfaction as he finally turned around to face Tymon.

'That's more like it,' he said. 'You're learning how to survive here, I see. You just might have garnered yourself a deal, my good fellow.'

He rubbed his fingers together languidly. Tymon was reminded of the Sap-siphoning Doctor, Jocaste's dead father; Dayan was a parasite of a different sort. It was the kind of correlation he would have expected the Oracle to make, but she gave no further sign. In fact, she appeared to have exited his consciousness, once again. Tymon was left with the hollow sense of having failed her.

He was about to rise from the stool in deference to his employer, preoccupied by the Oracle's disappearance, when the Lord waved him down.

'You can have the rest of the evening off,' he announced. 'You must conduct a holy trance to answer my question, no? Well, my demand is simple. I wish to know how a certain person is plotting to kill me. Not if, because I know he will, but how. You have just met the person in question.'

'Tahu?' asked Tymon, taken aback.

'Yes,' said the Lord calmly. 'My death would put him

in a prime position in our Company. I want you to find out precisely how and when he will strike. That is the price of your friends' freedom. Conduct the trance right here, if you like: I will give instructions to the staff to leave this room undisturbed tonight. Ablash, Gaw.'

He whistled through his teeth, causing the Tree-dogs to scramble out from under the desk, panting. They no longer seemed in any way concerned by the window. When Tymon glanced at the sky again, he saw that the birds had gone.

'We leave you to your mysteries,' said Dayan. 'Depending on how I like your answer, I will free some or all of your friends. I hope for your sake — and theirs — that I like it well.' Without waiting for a reply, he marched out of the room, followed by the obedient shadows of his hounds. The panelled doors clicked shut behind him.

'*Ama?*' Tymon whispered, as soon as he was on his own. But the space at the back of his mind remained disturbingly empty.

The whole episode left him feeling ill at ease. The Oracle's last words were particularly troubling, and he berated himself for being so involved with the Lord's proposition that he had ignored her at that critical moment. What would she have advised him to do? How would she have counselled him to respond to Dayan?

He told himself that there was nothing for it, given his situation, but to try to do as he had been told. Striking a deal with the mine-owner would allow him to free Zero and the others with the least amount of trouble; he might arrange to have the released slaves left at a certain location outside the mine, which he would then communicate to the Focals in the trance. If he could manage it, he would escape himself and join them as a final snub to the Lord. But he was willing to stay behind if it ensured the Saffids' safety. Having settled this point to his satisfaction, he rose from the stool and installed himself on the weave-mat on the floor of the conservatory, leaning his back against the divan where Tahu had been sitting a few minutes before. Whatever dangers the Oracle was facing in the world of the Veil, he thought, he might at least assure himself that he was carrying out her mandate in the physical one, by protecting the Saffid.

'In weakness find strength,' he murmured, gazing out of the window at the fading daylight.

Whether because of his fears for the Oracle, however, or some deep-seated reluctance to help Dayan, strength did not come to him on this occasion. Every time he attempted to clear his mind, he remembered his teacher's final words, and lost the thread of his concentration. *Something's wrong*, she had said. *Something's wrong*. He shut his eyes and forced himself to think of his employer's question, the Lord's calm certainty about Tahu's intentions. *Not if, but how.* But the harder Tymon tried to hold on to the image of the resettler, the further the trance seemed to slip from his grasp. Despite his recent strides in the craft, it was as grindingly difficult to launch the Reading now as it had been the first time he tried it. Part of the problem, he knew, was that he secretly wished Tahu every success in his bloody endeavour. The empty minutes marched by fruitlessly as he sat there on the mat. After what seemed an age, the hour-candle Dayan caused to be regularly replaced in a wall-bracket sputtered and went out. The young man rose to light a second one, then returned to his post on the floor. For a long time, nothing further happened.

Finally, he opened his eyes, knowing he would never attain the trance in his current state. He had to calm himself down, for the sake of Zero and Dawn, and all those who depended on him. In an effort to distract himself, he allowed his eyes to wander over the design on the silk weave-mat on the floor of the conservatory. It depicted a stylised tree, a classic Nurian motif he had seen many times during his journeys in the Eastern Canopy, though this was the finest specimen he had ever come across. A variety of animals was woven through the pattern of leaves and twigs, with cunning attention to detail. Bird, snake, monkey, cat ... he had always wondered why shillees and margeese were not included in the traditional designs. In Lord Dayan's carpet, there was a creature he had not encountered before — an imaginary animal, a bird with a woman's head. It sat perched on the very top of the tree, its features reminding him oddly of Samiha.

At that moment, he recalled his love as she had been on the Freehold, a young wife and companion. The memory was overpowering and he almost groaned aloud. He was overcome by physical longing for her, as if his body were now in mourning, separate from his mind. He would have faced another flogging if he were sure it would conjure up her image again. Even a hallucination was better than nothing. He bent his hot forehead to his knees, despairing.

When he looked up again, he was standing on the brink of the mine-crater.

The trance had taken him by surprise. This time, the shift between states was instantaneous: there was no tangle of greenery filled with Leaf Letters, no merging with the Sap in the Tree of Being. He had stepped directly into a vision and found himself gazing into the vapour-filled shaft, at the scaffolds and ramps clinging to its sides. They seemed even more fragile and precarious than before, the work of ants. The dock-bridge and customs buildings, about a mile off to his right, were as ephemeral as gossamer. He realised that he had not been focusing on Tahu. He had missed his opportunity to answer Dayan's question. This was a vision controlled by the Sap.

Just as the thought crossed his mind, a tremor went through the bark.

The mine was about to collapse. The insight arrived without warning, an absolute certainty, like the knowledge gained in a dream. The Sap had brought him to a juncture of extreme danger. He had nothing to fear from a simple Grafting vision, of course: he was not in the Veil. But this Reading was visceral. The prospect of a cave-in, of being buried alive under a heap of bark, terrified him. He stood rooted to the spot at the edge of the crater as the bark beneath him shuddered again. The movement was stronger this time, a shivering, rolling shake, as if the branch supporting the mine were an enormous animal waking up from sleep. The dim sound of tearing timber echoed from the shaft and a blast of warm air hit his face. He looked anxiously towards the dock buildings, remembering the nameless scribe who had helped him on his arrival. He knew, then, that the little clerk would die.

A scene of devastation met his eyes. The struts supporting the dock-bridge had begun to sway from side to side, causing the long walk of suspended planks to buckle between them. Dirigible barges were breaking loose from their moorings, dragged into each other by the crumpling bridge, and cracking like eggs. A faint cacophony of human voices rose up from the customs buildings. Tymon watched in horror as huge chunks of bark broke off the sides of the crater, to slide down into the mine with a ruinous crash. The supporting branch beneath shook with repeated tremors, and the chain of planks on the bridge flipped upwards, turning inside out. Dirigibles spun off it like beads from a broken necklace.

'The end of the world,' said a cheerful voice, as if this were the best news imaginable.

Tymon spun around to find his old friend Ash standing on his other side. The illusion of Ash, he corrected himself, remembering what the Oracle had told him. He had never Seen a ghost in his visions, only the Born. This one, who was smiling pleasantly at him, did not even possess the fifth Focal's trademark scar. How could he have possibly mistaken this ethereal Being for the poor man from Marak?

'Who are you?' he asked, curt in his surprise. 'Why do you take the form of Ash? What do you want from me?' The Born's gaze was piercing, even as the dead Focal's had been. In that they were identical.

'I often worked with the one you name, when he was alive,' said the Being who had borrowed the form of Ash. He did not seem to care that the bark they were standing on had begun to tremble, a forewarning of collapse. 'I want nothing from you. I am here to help.'

'Then please tell me what to do,' said Tymon. He fought off the panicky urge to run. 'When does this happen? Should I warn Dayan?'

The Born glanced up at the far-off disc of the sun shining through the leaf-forests, as if it could show him the exact hour and date of the apocalypse. 'This happens tomorrow,' he answered. 'At half-past noon, or thereabouts. Yes, I would warn everyone, if I were you.'

'Tomorrow?' repeated Tymon, aghast. 'But the air-chariots won't have arrived by then! The Saffid will be trapped down there!'

'Many people will be trapped down there.'

'Why didn't the Oracle mention this?' said Tymon in dismay. 'She must have known! Why did she let me go on thinking that I could save them?'

The Born raised an eyebrow, laconic. 'You wish to be considered a full-fledged Grafter, and yet you continually rely on others to do the hard work,' he replied. 'Your teacher told you to See for yourself. Now you do.'

'How can you be so calm, when everyone's going to die?' protested Tymon, rounding on him in frustration. 'If you really wanted to help, you'd show more heart!'

'A heart,' said his companion mildly, 'is a place where love grows. Tend your own, instead of worrying about others.'

With that, he turned his back on Tymon and began walking away towards the dock buildings, oblivious to the widening cracks in the bark. The young man hurried after him, battling annoyance and a sense of urgency in equal measure.

'No!' he called out, his voice hoarse. 'You can't do this. You can't show me this, then walk away. It doesn't matter how good or bad I am, or whether I'm worthy. It's the people down there who matter — Dawn, Zero, Nightside and all the others. You have to tell me how to get them to safety!'

The Being resembling Ash glanced at him then, but did not stop walking. 'You should ask the Sap to guide you,' he said. 'Do what you think is right.'

'You're just washing your hands of us!' shouted Tymon, overcome with emotion. He was gasping with the effort required to follow the Born, stumbling and staggering over the shaking bark. 'You know the answers already!' he cried to the other's back. 'You could tell me! You have all that power, but you don't use it to help people, not really. You just slip in and out of the world like it's a game — like it doesn't matter! I don't even know your real name!'

At that, the Born halted and faced him. He did not answer Tymon immediately, surveying him with steady equanimity. The young man lost his balance and fell to his knees as another violent tremor rocked the branch. The crash and smash of falling bark grew deafening.

The axis of the world seemed to him to be shifting: the leaf-forests to the south were inching upwards as the supporting limb beneath them gradually toppled over. The Born remained aloof, untouched by the surrounding ruin.

'Fair enough,' he said at last. 'My name is Ashekiel. And this is no game. It does matter to me. Very much.'

Tymon shrugged off these vague declarations. Part of him, a corner of lucidity, wondered why he was directing all his anger and frustration at the Born. His friends' suffering was not Ashekiel's fault. But the sight of the immortal creature, standing there untouched while the world fell apart, irked him in a way he could not articulate. He was forced to grovel at Ashekiel's feet, clinging to the bark as the branch toppled ever farther and the lip of the crater became a crumbling slope. And yet the Born did nothing to help, or to stop him from sliding towards the brink. Tymon peered over his shoulder at the gaping hole behind him. For some reason the heart of the mine had grown bright, full of roiling white vapours.

'The Oracle would have helped us,' he cried to Ashekiel. 'She cared about the Saffid.' Then he bit his lip, remembering the circumstances of his teacher's disappearance with a stab of remorse. 'You could at least tell me if she's alright,' he finished lamely.

'Matrya,' sighed Ashekiel, 'will endure for as long as those with whom she does battle. And she would have answered you as I do. Have you not realised by now that your teacher is one of the Born? We are one, she and I.'

Tymon pondered this revelation from his perilous position on the crater's edge. To his own surprise, the answer did not disturb him. He realised he had suspected the Oracle's true identity for a while. Only a Born could See the future continuously, after all. Only a Born would have the strength to combat the Masters in the Veil. He did not mind what his teacher was: he knew her well enough to be assured of her priorities.

'Then why don't you help us, as she would have done?' he said.

The Born's bright gaze bored into Tymon. 'Even as you demand one thing, your heart clamours for another,' he replied softly. 'You are not thinking of your friends in the mine, are you?'

It was all too true. Another question had suddenly consumed Tymon, even as he heard the Oracle's identity confirmed. 'What about Samiha?' he blurted out. 'Was she one of you, too — a Born?'

Ashekiel's smile betrayed a glimmer of satisfaction. 'She was what she was,' he said. 'And she is what she is. She has both natures.'

'You mean she's still alive? She survived the fall?' Excitement almost choked Tymon. 'You have to tell me!' he begged. He tried to get up again, but could not balance upright on the tilting bark.

'Do you wish to help the Kion, or your friends in the mine?' asked Ashekiel.

Tymon stared at him, astounded. Born or not, this Being was nothing like either the Oracle or Samiha. Those two would never have given him so cruel a choice. He drew himself up on the shuddering slope, and replied with as much dignity as he could muster.

'I want to help the people in the mine, of course,' he answered. 'It's what *Ama* would have wished.'

'So be it,' said Ashekiel. 'In that case, hear this. If you wish to save them, all of them, then you must go down.'

Tymon glanced instinctively over his shoulder again, at the cloudy crater. In his vision, it was the Storm that lay at the heart of the mine, a well of clouds. But daylight came from within the hole, filtering upwards, as if the sun were inside the mine-shaft itself. It made no sense.

Even as he frowned at the light in confusion, the branch toppled too far, and he finally lost his grip on the bark. With a last panicked glance at the immovable Ashekiel, Tymon slid down the slope and tumbled over the brink of the shaft, clawing at empty air. He fell backwards even as Samiha had done — down, down, down into the Void. The Storm opened its cloudy jaws to receive him; the world trembled, whirled and broke apart, and the vision of the mine disintegrated.

Matrya rose to her feet from where she had been knocked down on the icy floor of the Veil, wrenched out of physical space to face her enemies again. The seven giants loomed around her in an unbroken ring, menacing silhouettes in the gloom of the prison world, their features barely defined.

'So, you choose to appear in human form, Matrya,' sneered one. Something like a crown was faintly outlined on his head; the folds of shadow about him recalled a kingly cloak. 'Even here, you're one of them.'

'And I see that you have practically forgotten what form is,' she replied tartly, drawing herself up — an ordinary, middle-aged woman in a shimmering black dress, defiantly small before the Masters' hulking menace.

The shadow-kings stirred with anger, their cloaks becoming hunched and thick like wings. There was a glint of curved claws on the ice beneath their robes.

'You took our seed-forms from us,' hissed another. 'You stole our natural bodies. Now, we use other shapes. Better ones.'

All semblance of ancient majesty dropped from the figures gathered about Matrya, and they became monstrously avian, clawed and grotesque, stretching out their scrawny necks to gloat over their prey.

'We'll soon peck you to shreds, whatever form you choose,' croaked the one who had first spoken, fixing an unblinking eye on the Oracle. 'We'll tear your filthy spirit apart. And by the time we're through with you here, our servants will have done the same to your body, in the world of the living. You're finished, Matrya.'

'Finished, finished,' echoed the others in a cackling round of laughter, shuffling forward on the ice and unfurling their great wings to blot out the stars.

The Oracle did not answer, but held up her right hand. Out of it grew a narrow beam of light that seemed to slice through the murky darkness of the Veil. She raised the light, blade-like in her palm as the bird-kings advanced, calm and ready for battle.

7

The image of Anise lying at her feet remained etched in Jedda's mind as she slithered down the face of the icy branch, leaving the Jay vessels behind. The moon disappeared behind high clouds and she blundered on in the darkness beneath the leaves. It seemed to her that she had never stopped moving, walking, fleeing across the length and breadth of the Tree since the day of the Kion's execution. She crawled down the branch-slope for almost two miles before she was able to leap into a stand of twigs on an adjacent limb; there, she alighted in a snowdrift which turned out to be covering a deep knothole or gap, and sank into the soft wet snow to her chest, desperately holding Samiha's papers up over her head to protect them. It took a heart-stopping few minutes to scramble to a firmer position. The new limb was no easier to navigate than the first, covered in dense twig-thickets through which she blindly stumbled, and by the end of the night she was exhausted, aching and wet through from slipping to her knees, getting up and slipping again. She had travelled only about four miles from the convoy's position as the crow would fly, but covered easily three times that distance in her winding journey. The face of the Jay youth on the floor of the pavilion hovered accusingly in her memory throughout. His eyes had been open and staring, the pupils dilated to a yawning black. She was in no doubt that she had killed him.

Abomination.

That was what the Envoy had called her, and she was beginning to believe it. It occurred to her that every one of her recent associates — Samiha, Laska, Tymon, Pallas and now Anise — had come off the worse for meeting her. Even little Lai, the Oracle's host, had suffered at her hands, she thought miserably. All through her apprenticeship with Lace, she had shrunk from contemplating the consequences of her actions in Cherk Harbour and their disastrous effects on the Saffid child. Although she had heard that the Oracle had resurfaced at least once more in the Veil, she had no way of learning what had truly happened to Lai. When she had agreed to switch sides, she had not realised how summarily Gowron would deal with the Oracle's little host. As far as she knew, an innocent had been murdered as a direct result of her decisions.

It was an agonising knowledge, which she had buried at first under layers of self-justification, furiously blaming her teacher for any harm that had come to Lai. The Oracle had been aware of the risks to a host in a time of war. And yet she had chosen to inhabit the mind of a child, with the typical cold calculation of her kind. For a while, Jedda had even managed to convince herself that Matrya had chosen that host on purpose, in a cynical bid for self-preservation. The little girl's death was a necessary evil, according to such logic, the final sacrifice required to bring an end to all needless sacrifice. It was a theory that held only while Jedda believed the Envoy's cause to be superior to that of the Oracle. Now that she was disabused of that fact, her justifications crumbled and she was overwhelmed with horror at what she had done. She had made all the wrong choices from the beginning. Maybe she truly was an abomination, she thought — a curse to those who helped her, even as the Envoy said. She certainly left a trail of death and destruction in her wake.

After several hours of wandering up and down the pathless branches, occupied by such dismal speculation, she came upon an isolated terrace-farm and was able to rest for the night in a barn stocked with root vegetables and animal feed. She knew better than to rely on that shelter for long, however, and left the terraces again at sunrise, her pockets stuffed with the life-saving tubers. She followed the farmer's track up to the higher regions of the canopy, finding to her relief that it joined a small but serviceable branch-road headed south and east among the close-growing twigs. She guessed this path would lead to other settlements and perhaps eventually link up with the South Road. The twining connection with Tymon still tingled faintly in her belly, reassuring her that he had not passed completely beyond her reach. The mission to help her fellow Grafter had taken on paramount importance; she clung to it like a lifeline, as if saving him were the only means to save herself. She rejected the misgiving in her heart which suggested, almost in the Envoy's mocking tones, that in seeking to rescue Tymon, she would only bring her curse down on him, too.

About halfway through the morning, her journey was interrupted by the sound of wheels approaching from behind. Wary now of meeting anyone, she hid in the twig-stands by the road and watched as a covered wagon pulled by a single snorting herd-beast rolled by on the lines of parallel planks. The peasant driving the vehicle was bundled in shawls and blankets from head to foot; only his shrewd eyes were visible over the folds, peering out from under a wide-brimmed hat. The encounter made Jedda feel exposed, and she realised that it would be safer for her to travel by night. So she found a crevice among the twigs large enough to hide inside, and passed the rest of the day snatching intermittent rounds of sleep, wrapped once more in the dry grasses for warmth.

When evening came, she rose and pressed on in the freezing darkness. The Argosian winter proved to be the main obstacle to her progress, as she had feared: her feet and fingers grew numb after barely an hour, a dangerous prelude to frostbite. She was able to stuff her boots with the readily available dried grass but the rest of her remained achingly cold, even under the thick seminary cloak of shillie-wool. After some thought, she took the sheets of Samiha's testament and packed them carefully inside her undergarments, padding the bulky paper close to her skin. The solution both protected the testament and made it easier to carry, giving her a much-needed layer of warmth.

As night wore on, the full moon broke loose from the clouds to shine on the snowy planks of the road, lighting the way. Jedda stumbled forward, half-asleep, her mind as sluggish as her limbs. The journey seemed endless. She had always been on this road, groping through this snowy gloom, this moonlit silence. Only the Envoy's mocking whisper echoed in her memory, chilling her heart even as the sharp wind chilled her body. *Abomination*, it repeated time and time again. *Abomination*. But Jedda's wits were honed for survival. Even in her dismal state, her attention was caught at length by a strange sight far above, a moving shape flitting over the full disc of the moon. It was swiftly followed by another. Jedda blinked upwards in confusion, wondering what creatures flew at this late hour. They were too big to be bats. Were they birds? They wheeled through the canopy, descending ever closer over the leaf-thickets, silent as drifting clouds.

At that moment, as she walked along the road

planks with her head thrown back, frowning at the sky, someone grabbed her from behind. Her arms were twisted and pinned against her back, and she was unable to move. She felt the cold nudge of a hardwood blade against her throat.

'Not another step, moonlight traveller,' hissed a muffled voice in her ear, speaking in Argosian. 'Or your night-walks end with this one.'

A second shadow detached itself from the twigs by the road and darted up to Jedda, rifling through the pockets of her cloak and patting her legs and torso with practised ease. This individual's face was wrapped in a thick scarf so that only the eyes were visible, glinting over the fabric. Jedda realised, with a contradictory surge of relief, that she had been accosted by nothing more terrible than a pair of highway robbers. Unfortunately for them, she was carrying nothing of monetary value.

'Breadroot,' remarked the second thief bemusedly, withdrawing one of the tubers from Jedda's pockets. From the tenor of his voice, he was a young lad. 'It's a girl,' he added as his hands passed over the relevant parts of her anatomy.

'Well, well,' observed the muffled voice from behind Jedda. 'What a surprise.'

Her attacker released her, and she was free to turn around and scrutinise her adversary. She did so calmly, for the threat of violence no longer troubled her. She knew, after what had happened to Anise, that she was far more dangerous to others than they were to her; and though she was ashamed of it, she could not deny that the thought gave her a certain furtive satisfaction. The figure standing before her was engulfed in a voluminous shawl wrapped tightly about the nose and throat, and wore a long cloak and wide-brimmed hat. Jedda recognised the silhouette. It belonged to the peasant who had passed her the day before in the cart.

'You're not the least bit frightened, are you?' murmured her muffled interlocutor, unwinding the shawl. 'If I were a young woman, walking alone at night in these remote parts, I'd be a little more wary.' The shawl dropped down and the thief's face was exposed: it was smiling, mischievously handsome, and female.

'Oh, wait.' The highwaywoman shook out a cascade of dark curls from under the hat. 'I am one,' she noted with a grin.

'Shall we stick her?' asked the boy who had made the search. He had loosened his own scarf to reveal a sullen, acne-pocked countenance, perhaps a year or two younger than Jedda. 'She ain't got nothing.'

'Patience, Lud,' admonished his companion. Her black eyes lingered appreciatively on Jedda. 'We have quite a specimen here. It's a treasure in itself. Look at the colour of it. See how bright and soft it is.'

She circled around the Nurian girl like a prowling Tree-cat, gazing at her with frank admiration from both the front and back, and peering at her face under the hood. Jedda stared back warily and kept still, deciding for the moment to allow events to unfold as they would. If the thieves intended to kill her, or 'stick' her, as the boy named Lud had termed it, they would have done so already, she reasoned. The highwaywoman wanted something else. Though ragged and tinged with grime, this extraordinary creature exuded an energetic carelessness, an air of owning the whole world. She reached up and playfully pushed the hood off Jedda's head so that the fair Nurian locks glinted in the moonlight.

'Shiny,' breathed the thief-woman.

'A runaway pilgrim,' sneered Lud. 'Who cares?'

'There are no female pilgrims,' said his companion. She winked rakishly at Jedda. 'Are there, my beauty?'

Jedda conceded this point with a cautious smile and shrug. There could be any number of reasons why the bandit had decided to spare her. Not all were advantageous.

'Oh, you're good,' chortled the black-eyed thief. 'Now I have to know more. I can't resist.'

She offered Jedda her arm, as gallant as a young Argosian lord, though it was clear she had never set foot in any civilised region of the Central Canopy. She might have been about nineteen; certainly she was young enough to be a sister to Jedda. 'I hope you'll forgive our earlier misunderstanding,' she declared. 'I'd like to hear where you pinched that Tree-preacher's cloak. Come and visit with me and my merry band tonight.'

'Merry bat-shit,' swore Lud. 'Don't bring this one home, Varana. Please.'

The woman ignored him. 'Do come,' she appealed prettily, when Jedda did not move. She indicated the dusting of frost on the seminary cloak. 'You can't deny you need our help. We don't care if you're Nurian. Free food and a bed for the night — no grief, I promise. Breadroot gets dreary after a while, doesn't it? You can go on your way in the morning. Or tomorrow night, if you prefer. Whenever you like.'

'Do I have a choice?' asked Jedda.

When the woman shrugged and smiled in her turn, Jedda slowly accepted the proffered arm. There was something attractive about Varana, a tearaway charm that made her forget for the time being that the highwaywoman had recently been holding a knife to her throat. To resist the invitation would mean calling on the power of the *orah*-pendant, which Jedda wished to do only as a last resort. She allowed herself to be drawn off the road and into the leaf-thickets.

'What's your name?' Varana queried, as they walked.

'June,' said Jedda unthinkingly, then bit her lip, wondering what had possessed her to choose her dead sister's name.

'June. That's lovely.'

'Shit,' groaned the pockmarked boy again, stumping after them. 'Another one of your lame stray bawds. I'm sick of this shit.'

'Watch your foul mouth, Lud,' said the highway-woman.

The boy did not respond, kicking at the snow with his boots as they passed between the twigs. 'Shit,' he repeated to himself, after a while.

Jedda glanced up at the pale orb of the moon glinting through the serried leaves. There was now no sign of the wheeling avian shapes above.

They walked on for about a quarter of a mile before coming to the basin-like hollow in the bark where the bandits had made their camp. The rest of Varana's 'merry band' consisted of two decidedly morose-looking men sitting hunched over a glowing fire on the floor of the hollow. Behind them, Jedda glimpsed the covered cart with its herd-beast patiently chewing dried moss. The animal had evidently been coaxed up to the hollow from another point on the road.

One of those sitting by the fire, a taciturn fellow with stooped shoulders whom Jedda later learned was named Ambrose, barely glanced up as they arrived. His companion, however — a short, barrel-chested fellow — leapt to his feet, tense as a spring and overwrought, his ginger-coloured eyebrows bristling at the sight of Varana's new guest. Jedda had noticed some time ago that Argosians were not as homogenous a people as they imagined themselves to be: there were fair-skinned individuals among them, people with green eyes and reddish hair, even as there were darker, Argosian-looking people in the East. The squat little man looked outwardly like a Nurian, though from the shocked invective that spewed from his mouth she suspected he would have taken great umbrage at that comparison.

'She's with me,' answered Varana imperturbably, fending off the other's objections. 'No, I haven't lost my tiny female mind. Yes, she's a runaway. No, I don't care. Why do I bother with her? Have you no eyes? Shoot, meet June. June, meet Shoot. He's a prize fool.'

'Yes, I got eyes,' spat the red-haired Argosian, the two green and globular organs in question almost popping out of his head in outrage. 'I see a damned-to-root problem, is what I see. I see trouble. I see you only thinking about yourself, as usual.'

'Live with it,' drawled the highwaywoman. 'June is staying for as long as she likes. You'll all be nice to her, please.'

The stooped man, the last member of the band, had not moved from his position by the fire bowl. He gazed without particular interest at Jedda and continued warming himself in front of the crackling flames, rubbing his knuckles together.

'We need to get closer to Ethis,' he remarked. 'Three empty nights, Varana. This can't go on.'

'Agreed,' Varana said, interrupting as the red-haired Shoot tried to protest again. 'Ethis will have better pickings. It's worth the risk. We'll turn south tomorrow.' She cocked her head at Jedda. 'Does that suit you?' she asked solicitously.

'South is fine,' replied Jedda. 'I was heading that way myself.'

'Listen to hoity-toity,' growled the red-haired man. 'Looks like a priest, talks like a priest. Who trained this monkey?'

'Oh, do shut up,' sighed Varana, rolling her eyes.

Lud squatted down by the fire next to the stooped man and warmed himself at the flames. 'Ape-shit,' he remarked meditatively, to no one in particular.

Shoot subsided onto the bark beside the placidly chewing herd-beast, muttering a string of curses.

'Come on,' said Varana to Jedda. She took her by the hand and drew her towards the covered cart. 'Leave these dull folks to themselves. I want to hear the story of the pilgrim and the priest.'

She pulled Jedda up the small folding ladder that led into the back of the cart. The vehicle turned out to be a sleeping wagon, complete with rumpled bedding spread out on every inch of available floor space. There was even a hammock strung from the hardwood hoops supporting the canvas roof. Varana took down a basket lantern and a box of firesticks from a shelf, coaxed a flame to life in the lamp and hung it from a hook, filling the vehicle with a sputtering orange glow.

'My friends are idiots,' she observed to Jedda after a moment, installing herself cross-legged on a bed at the back of the wagon. 'They've plenty of brawn, but barely half a brain between them, I'm afraid. Ignore them.'

She rummaged under the pillow to retrieve a small pipe and a bag of jar-weed, and patted the covers beside her, inviting Jedda to sit down. Cautious as ever, the Nurian girl knelt down on the bed. She shook her head when Varana offered the lit pipe. It was a great relief to be out of the icy wind.

'The world is full of idiots,' Varana said comfortably, blowing a smoke ring up towards the lamp. 'Tree-preachers most of all. Tell me how you nabbed that cloak.'

But she did not allow Jedda to speak, despite the fact that she had asked three times to hear her story. Instead, she laid aside her pipe, reaching out a languid hand to caress Jedda's cheek. Then she hooked her arm about the Nurian girl's waist and drew her close.

'I love it that you're not afraid,' she murmured, before planting a kiss on Jedda's mouth.

And because the night was cold, and everyone she

had ever cared about was either dead or far away, Jedda let her do it.

The decision to yield to Varana bought her three days of grace, during which the covered wagon with its lacklustre occupants rolled south along the branch-roads, inching into more inhabited regions of the canopy. On the first morning they passed a small settlement, a collection of ten bark-brick huts huddled together in a horizontal knothole. Every one of the inhabitants, as far as Jedda could tell, was equipped with a broom, rake or hay-fork. The villagers watched suspiciously from their doorways as Varana drove the wagon through the centre of the knothole and wound out and up the road along the crest of the limb. No one hailed or greeted them, though the highwaywoman tipped her hat politely to the peasants, her disdain hidden safely behind her shawl. They gazed back at her with the dull abhorrence of the settled for those who travel.

Jedda never left the relative security of the vehicle until nightfall. During the day, she dozed on Varana's bed, or peered from behind the canvas at the changing Treescape outside the wagon. She thought of Anise as they jolted in silence along the branch-roads, and of Pallas, and Tymon; after a while, the faces of the young men became blurred and indistinct in her mind. Like her, the other members of the thieves' band only emerged from their berths in the evenings, when they came to a halt. The two men and the pockmarked boy pointedly ignored Jedda, though they sat only a few feet from her in the rattling cart. She learned not to ask her fellow travellers questions or indeed to make any form of conversation at all, for she knew that she would only get a stare and a shrug in answer. Shoot simply turned his back to her when she spoke.

At night she hovered on the fringes of the group by the campfire, listening to the bandits argue about where next to mount their operations. The group was running dangerously low on winter food stocks, which consisted mostly of dried fruit, winter tubers and the occasional piece of fresh game. But the canopy had remained locked in a deep frost over the past week and the snowy world seemed entirely empty of life. To make matters worse, there had been no travellers to accost, no 'pickings' for the bandits for days, and everyone was in the very worst of tempers.

By Jedda's second evening in the company of the thieves, they were reduced to finishing off her stock of breadroot. She sat on a twig-stump some distance from the fire and listened to the others trading insults, wondering if she would ever find Tymon again. The twining connection had dwindled to no more than a whisper in her belly, and she guessed that he was travelling by dirigible now, beyond her reach. She was cold, weary, and achingly lonely. Her encounters with Varana — short, sharp affairs conducted in the dubious privacy of the wagon — gave her little comfort. The thief-woman had hardly spoken to her after the first night; by the second, she had taken to ignoring Jedda almost as completely as the others. Her careful solicitude vanished, and the fictitious story of the pilgrim remained untold.

At dawn the next morning, following a night excursion of his own, Shoot brought a stolen child back to the wagon.

He said it came from a nearby farm, and that they should trade it back to its family in exchange for food. Varana lost her temper and accused him of being a gross liability to the band. It was not the cruelty of the kidnapping that provoked her fury, but the fact that they might easily be hunted down by the farmer in retaliation for the crime. She pointed out with scathing sarcasm that a man could run faster than their plodding herd-beast; worse still, a posse bent on revenge might hunt them down on a harvester's dirigible, cutting them off on the winding road long after they had quit the farm. Jedda crouched in the wagon on Varana's bed, listening to the two rage at each other outside. She stared at the boy kneeling in a shivering heap in the opposite corner of the sleeping cart.

He was about six years old, a rumpled, peaked little fellow with enormous brown eyes that seemed to take up his entire face. He said no word but returned her gaze in abject terror.

'I'm Jedda,' she whispered, in an attempt to comfort him. 'Don't worry, I'm not going to harm you. I don't want to be here, either.'

He did not answer. She had her doubts whether he had really heard her. Outside, the debate continued, with Ambrose suggesting that they give the boy a cautionary hiding and return him home before he was missed, under strict orders never to breathe a word of what had happened. Lud responded that the brat would squeal anyway, and that they should 'stick' him. Varana noted that this was his answer to most problems. Shoot told the others that they were behaving like squealing girls themselves, and that it came of having a woman for a chieftain, which provoked another shouting match with Varana. Jedda rose and went to sit on the other side of the cart, near the child but not too near, and studied him in the dim light seeping through the canvas walls.

'I find,' she said, 'that when I don't want to be somewhere, there are two ways out. Most of the time I escape to a place I call "the Quiet". It's in my mind, see. No one else can get in.'

She reached up and, at the back of her head, mimicked a little door opening and shutting with one hand. With the other she made a bird that stretched out its beak from the doorway to squawk and jabber at the boy, then pulled it in, slamming the door shut. After several rounds of making the squawking bird appear and disappear, the tiniest twitch of a smile appeared on the child's face. Ambrose had now joined forces with Lud to advocate the sad necessities of life; Shoot yelled at them all, and Varana yelled back.

'What's your name?' Jedda asked the boy.

After a further hesitation, he replied in a husky whisper: 'Issy.'

'Well, Issy, I must tell you the Quiet doesn't work every time,' said Jedda. 'Sometimes I have to use another way.' She carefully moved closer to him: he flinched but stayed put. 'When the others come in,' she murmured in his ear, 'I want you to do something for me. I want you to stay right where you are, until I tell you to move. Do exactly as I say, or the bad men will get you. When I tell you to run, go out through the flap at the front of the cart, over the driver's seat, understand? Run all the way home. Do you remember the way?'

He nodded wordlessly. 'Good,' she said. 'Remember, only move when I tell you to.'

The voices had died down outside. Jedda had barely finished speaking before the canvas flap at the back of the wagon was drawn aside, and Varana entered.

'Go outside,' she told Jedda perfunctorily.

The Nurian girl rose to her feet. 'You're not going to hurt him, I hope,' she said to Varana, glancing at the boy, who cowered in the corner behind her.

'Hurt him? Of course not.'

The thief-woman smiled with easy assurance, but Jedda's quick eye noted the gleam of the hardwood blade hidden in the palm of her right hand. 'I won't let you,' she said, moving between Varana and her quarry. 'I'm warning you.'

Varana gave a snort of derision. 'You, threatening me?' she scoffed. 'Don't make me laugh, doll. Stay away from business that doesn't concern you. Get outside, now.'

She kept her knife arm discreetly low, and tried to elbow past to reach Issy. But Jedda remained immovable. Her fingers, already hovering at her throat, closed over her *orah*-pendant at the same time as Varana attempted to shove her aside. The highwaywoman uttered an exclamation of annoyance.

'I'm so sorry, Varana,' Jedda murmured.

The flow of energy was immediate and over-whelming, far stronger than it had been with Anise. Varana's fingers cleaved to Jedda like glue even as she tried to push her out of the way, and the knife dropped with a clatter from her shaking right palm. She stared at Jedda in dumb amazement, before the strength abandoned her limbs and she toppled forward into the other girl's arms. Waves of the Sap-power passed over Jedda; she sank to her knees, almost losing herself in the giddy sensation. It was with difficulty that she kept her wits sufficiently to call out to Issy.

'Run,' she croaked. 'Run now, and don't stop for anything!'

The boy had been staring at her with round eyes. When she spoke, however, he jumped obediently up and scrambled through the flap at the front of the wagon that led to the high driver's seat. No sooner was he gone than the head and shoulders of Shoot appeared in the back entry, his mouth already open to ask a sarcastic question. The sneer died on his lips as he caught sight of Jedda kneeling among the scattered bedding with Varana slumped against her.

'What in hell's name is going on here?' he cried.

'Witch-shit,' murmured Lud, awestruck, peering through the canvas beside him.

Jedda saw Ambrose's face floating behind the other two through a shining fog. She did not know whether the cloud of Sap was visible to the others, but for her the wagon was filled with scintillating, darting flames. They streamed up from Varana, writhing through the air in a living torrent to pierce Jedda with unbearable sweetness. She could not let go of her victim or stop the flow. She did not want to. The stolen energy wiped away all the pain and remorse of the past few weeks, erasing sorrow. It was pure joy, pure forgetting.

She smiled drunkenly at the bandits when they overcame their surprise and leapt into the wagon, prying her loose from the unconscious Varana. She did not care that they shouted in her face, or when they set upon her in fury, kicking her out of the wagon. They continued to pummel her as she lay on the bark outside; she did not feel it. She lay smiling up at the leaves above while they stripped her of her outer garments, cloak and boots. They did no more to her, abandoning her with superstitious caution to die of exposure rather than at their hands, for they were terrified of her in spite of their fury. They seemed to fade away like a cloud of buzzing insects. The wagon was gone in the blink of an eye, and the leaf-forests were empty again. None of it had any importance for Jedda. There was only the Sap. It cradled her: it was her life, her truth, her paramour. *This was all there was to his instruction*, she remembered. Gowron had been right. The Envoy only had this one blinding insight to offer. And now that she had understood it, she wanted nothing else.

She came to her senses several hours later, when the setting sun stretched in dazzling *orah*-coloured bands through the twigs. She sat up on the frozen slush to find herself dressed in her underclothes, the pages of Samiha's testament crackling under the flannel. It was all the bandits had left her with — that, and the pendant about her neck. A dim echo of the Sap-flow still pulsed within her. Her body did not feel cold, nor was she hungry. She rose to her feet, teetering dangerously, and staggered out of the twig-thicket onto the road. There was no sound but that of her own footsteps in the quiet winter's evening. She continued southwards along the planks with an unsteady gait. Her instincts warned her to press on despite the afterglow that gave her strength, to reach a farm or holding where she might steal clothes and food. There would be a time, she knew, when the warmth of the Sap ran out.

That time came after midnight, when the waning moon had risen to shine through the leaves once more. The return to full normality was bleak. The cold cut Jedda's skin like a knife and she was overcome by the desire to weep. She forced herself grimly to carry on. At long last the road, which had been meandering in zigzag fashion towards the base of a steep branch, reached its lowest point and turned onto a more level limb. Jedda could see the path wriggling ahead of her along the crest of the branch, a white scar on the exposed bark. Neat vine-terraces had been cut into the slopes on either side and farm buildings were visible on the limb, about a mile off. The glimpse of the settlement came none too soon. Her body was racked with cold, shivering convulsively, her hands and feet entirely numb.

She had stumbled about half the distance to the farm when she realised what she was doing. Although she was cripplingly cold, she was not seeking shelter. Though starving, she was not looking for something to eat. What she wanted to do was to go into that farm in order to find someone else to drain of the Sap. The thought of food and clothes had evaporated, replaced by a more urgent need. She had been eager to feel that rush of power again, to quash another existence between her fingertips like a candle flame. The awareness of what she had been seeking caused her to stop short on the road in horrified dismay. The *orah* was addictive. Lace must have known she would abuse the pendant this way sooner or later, and be caught in its thrall; it was just as Gowron had said. She belonged to her master now, as thoroughly as if she had never left Argos city — as thoroughly as did Wick.

'No,' she whispered vehemently, her breath a curl of white on the night air. 'Not that. Not yet.'

A ragged sob, half-furious and half-agonising, escaped her lips as she turned and plunged into the line of vines to her left. These were bare and pruned back for winter on their frames, no more than stumps in their bed of loam. She did not pause at the edge of the first terrace but jumped down onto another field several feet below, the last before the sloping side of the branch turned vertical. At the end of that terrace she came to a slithering halt, teetering on the brink, dashing the tears from her eyes.

She would rather die than live in slavery. Was that not what she had promised herself, all those years ago, in the stinking canteen storeroom? The decision had given her the strength to pry open the window, tearing through the grating until her fingers bled. There was no way, none at all, that she would barter up that hard-won freedom and belong again to anyone, man or Born. Better to fall over the edge of the terrace and tumble down, down, down.

Like Samiha, who had belonged to no one but herself.

The thought sent an almost electric thrill through Jedda. In a single sweep, before she could change her mind, she tore the *orah* from the cord at her neck and flung it into the Void. Her heart seemed to leap after the pendant arcing over the precipitous edge of the branch. The moonlight caught the reflective trinket briefly as it fell, a slick white gleam, abruptly swallowed by darkness. After staring a long moment after it, she turned her back on the edge of the terrace, and retraced her steps slowly through the vine-frames.

She regretted her decision by the time she reached the road. The use of the *orah* may have been perilous, but it had also been her only means of defence. The night seemed to close in about her as she trudged on towards the farm, and she fought off a creeping sense of dread. The moonlight was strong enough to cast shadows through the rows of posts on the terraces, sending faint lines across the road, black and white and black again. Occasionally, the lines were sliced through by a shape that sped over Jedda's head. A black form flitted across the leaf-forests. She glanced up to see the wheeling birds again, or what passed for birds; they were closer this time, swooping down and round between the great arcs of the leaves. She hurried along the road in terror now, wiping away the last of her tears, the sound of wing beats in her ears.

All at once, something hit her between the shoulder blades then tumbled onto the road, causing her to spin around with a gasp. A clumsy avian shape sprawled before her, about the size of an ordinary crow; it recovered its balance and waddled towards her, both horrific and ridiculous. But a glance was enough to confirm that this was no natural bird of the Tree. Its feathers were a dull black in the moonlight, the matted down of a dead thing, and it moved in jerking hops, head sideways and beak agape. One putrid eye gleamed at Jedda, full of vile intent.

'His curses,' she breathed, her whole being thrilling with revulsion as she stared at the bird.

She had no doubt that the nightmarish thing had been conjured up by the Envoy, for she knew a powerful sorcerer might call forth his hatred in physical form to track down his unhappy victims. She could have laughed at her own naivety in thinking her former master would rely only on the *orah* to keep her in line. He had sent another grotesque gift to find her. Such psychic constructs were parodies of life, decomposing over time into the true matter from which they were formed. But they could be mortally dangerous, especially if they attacked in large numbers.

She glanced up at the sky to see her fears confirmed. Other dark shapes wheeled between the leaves. First one, then another, then the whole unnatural flock hurtled down in a flapping cloud towards Jedda, their wings carrying the stench of carrion. She screamed and beat them away as they blundered into her, turning to flee along the road with her arms cradling her head. But she could not outrun the creatures. No matter how many missed her and smashed onto the bark, there were always more on her shoulders, pecking at her head and at her eyes. Although their claws could not rake through the thick paper stuffed into her garments, they scored every available inch of bare skin, bloodying her arms, her hands, the back of her neck. She tried to fend them off, but only succeeded in shredding the flesh of her fingers on their beaks and claws.

Finally, she came to a halt and withdrew a roll of Samiha's paper from one of her sleeves, using it to ward off her assailants. That weapon was more effective, but the birds still came — wave after wave of them, smashing into her with mindless insistence. She withdrew a second roll of papers and used both hands to combat the creatures, retreating as she did so towards the farm buildings. If she could only find shelter, she thought desperately — some hole to shut herself up in — she might escape the horrific spell until she found a way to fight it.

Oddly, the attack served to strengthen her resolve to resist the Envoy. It banished, for a moment at least, her craving for the Sap. No longer did she waste time regretting her decision to forgo the *orah*. Instead, to give herself courage, she sang aloud the words she had read on the Jays' dirigible, the words she had heard her rescuers sing and the words she could see now, glinting in the moonlight on the rolls of paper.

Fear neither darkness nor defeat. Fear no loss, for you and I again shall meet.

She sang with a smile on her bloodied lips and a spark in her eye, beating off the carrion-birds as she walked step by step along the road.

When Anise awoke, he took a deep and shuddering breath, as if he were just remembering how to pull the air into his lungs. He lay on a mattress in the Jays' sleeping tent, his head cradled in Jocaste's lap. Morning light streamed through the open flap of the tent, shining full on the Jay girl's tear-streaked face as she peered anxiously down at him. She gave a gasp of relief as Anise opened his eyes.

'Oh, thank the Tree,' she said. 'We weren't sure you'd make it. You were so cold when they brought you in, Ani: so cold, I thought you were dead.'

He attempted to rise to a seated position, but she would not allow him to and pressed him back down on the mattress.

'Jedda?' he asked, the one name containing all of his enquiry.

'Disappeared,' answered Jocaste, her expression growing hard. 'We guessed she was the one who did this to you. Oh, just you wait till I get my hands on that witch. She'll be lucky to keep her worthless life —'

'No,' he interrupted hoarsely. 'Not revenge. Not what I want, Jo.'

She frowned over him. 'She can't be allowed to get away with it. She took the Testament. We're going after her. She has to get back to a branch-road at some point —'

He waved this away feebly. 'I know it off by heart. Testament, I mean. Can recopy it if you get ink and paper, Jo.'

'Nonsense,' she said firmly. 'You rest first. And you eat something: whatever that harridan's done to you, it's weakened you dangerously. Food first, and everything else after.'

She would not brook any argument, for he was barely coherent. She brought him some leftover soup and he submitted to be fed by her, in shallow spoonfuls. After the meal he lay back exhausted on his bed. But before long he roused himself again. Something was evidently troubling him, Jocaste thought with pity.

'I'm the one who's done a stupid thing, Jo,' he croaked. 'I should have given the Testament to Jedda in the first place. No, hear me out,' he said, when Jocaste tried to protest. 'She attacked me by accident. I don't think she meant to. She loved the Kion, in her own way: I should have recognised that. Instead, I kept on trying to make her love in my way, to force her into my mould. It doesn't work like that.'

He had been trying to keep his head raised but collapsed back on the pillow, fatigued by the effort. 'We all have our own road to travel,' he continued after a moment. 'Leave Jedda to find Tymon, if she can. We have something else to do.'

'What's that?' asked Jocaste, resignedly.

'Meeting Jedda made me realise something,' he whispered. 'No one owns the Testament. The Kion would have wanted her words to reach everyone. Everyone, Jo — that means Nurians, too. We have to take the Testament to Nur.'

'What?' Jocaste burst out. 'You can't be serious. We're risking our necks right here in the Central Canopy, harbouring the works of a convicted heretic, and you want to go and mix yourself up in the East? Ani, think about it. This is madness.'

'Sometimes the only logical course in a lunatic world is mad,' he said, his eyes drifting shut. 'The Kion had a legacy to give her own people. We're the only ones who can deliver it.'

There was silence between the two of them after that, broken by the occasional sound of the other Jays talking or whistling on the deck of the little dirigible. Jocaste bit her lip with worry as she looked down at her companion. His stubborn conviction seemed to have grown in direct proportion to his fragility. And yet she still yearned to make him happy, even if it was madness. When his eyes opened again and he smiled wearily up at her, she reached out and pushed the sweat-slicked hair away from his forehead.

'What about the others?' she said. 'Don't you think they should be consulted before we do something so drastic? A journey to the East would involve at least half the troupe.'

'Yes, we should ask,' he admitted bashfully. 'We shouldn't do anything against their wishes. Thank you for reminding me, Jo.'

'I sometimes wish,' she murmured to him, after a further pause, 'that you wouldn't fly so high the whole time. That you wouldn't be so … so …' Her voice trailed off as she searched for the words to articulate her thought.

'Idealistic?' he suggested.

'Far away from the people and things surrounding you, as if the only ideas that mattered were the big ones that affected the entire world.'

He chuckled at this, rueful. 'I have to fly high,' he told her. 'Remember what your father used to call me? The eagle.' His hand crept up to his chest, where the necklace of talons used to hang; it was no longer there, discarded since he had ceased catering to the Doctor's demands.

'My father said a lot of things,' replied Jocaste grimly. 'He was wrong about most of them, and he was wrong about you. He called you the eagle, because he thought you were a trained hunter who brought him his prey. But you're no ravager of innocents.'

'I still see the world from up high.' He gazed earnestly at her. 'And it's very plain to me, Jo, that there are patterns in it. Things don't happen randomly. We have the Testament — we still have it, I just need to write it out again — for a reason. We should honour that responsibility.'

'I'll help you do whatever you feel the need to do,' she answered in a rush, for there were tears in her eyes again. 'But Ani, it's only because I love you. The others in the troupe feel the same way. We put up with you, but you're a mystery to us all.'

'Well, life's a mystery.' He closed his eyes again, overcome by exhaustion. 'We'll copy out the Testament later. For now, we should do as you say and consult the others. We'll ask them to vote on the journey east: it's only fair. This is a big step.'

He slipped back into slumber then, as his partner continued to watch him. Since the attack, Jocaste thought in anguish, his skin had acquired a luminous transparency, as if all the youthful pith had been sucked out of him and replaced by pure light. It broke her heart.

8

The Reading did not end after Tymon fell into the Void. The vision shifted, and all at once he was slamming through branches, plummeting through the Tree of Being as a fledgling bird might plummet from its nest. He realised in horror that his trance-form had acquired a deadly weight, the same that had once sent him hurtling into the Veil, when he had fled Samiha's Tree-form. This time, however, arms reached out to catch him as he fell. The Focals were there with him in the trance, supporting him, forming a web of safety. At their touch, the heaviness drained from his limbs and he floated free in the bright world of the Sap.

'The mine,' he gasped to his friends, as soon as he had recovered his balance. 'It's going to collapse.'

He saw his anxiety mirrored in their eyes, but the first words out of Noni's mouth concerned the Oracle. 'Ama isn't with you,' she said, taking Tymon's hand in her own and peering into his face. 'And just when we Saw the curse of Eblas ... What happened?'

Even as she took his hand, Tymon was assailed by a brief vision, not his own. To his surprise, he glimpsed Jedda fighting off a flock of murderous crows that harried and tore at her with their talons. The Nurian girl was clearly exhausted, crouched on a branch-path in the dead of night, and beating off the creatures with her bloodied fists. Then the vision winked out and he found himself staring into Noni's shocked face again.

She let go of him abruptly, as if the touch of him burned; the others also released him, and he guessed from their reaction, as well as the rush of Sap-heat surging through him, that he had inadvertently traded his own Reading for theirs. Even as he had caught sight of Jedda beating off the murderous flock, the Focals had experienced his vision of the collapsing mine.

'Ashekiel!' gasped Ara, confirming Tymon's suspicion. His eyes were round with awe.

'The Angel,' added Mata, turning to the others in consternation. 'All will die, it's sure ... the Saffid, the mineworkers ... all of them.'

'Ashekiel only speaks to us at times of great trouble,' Oren clarified for Tymon's benefit. 'Ancients called him "Angel of Death". He is not evil, but brings warning of disaster. His presence means much ill.'

'And meanwhile, *Ama*'s gone,' Noni cried in distress. 'We have no guidance! Please tell us, Tymon. When did she go?'

'Just before I launched the trance,' he said sadly. 'She told me she was being attacked by the Masters. It's been happening for a while.'

As Noni hung her head, anguished by this news, Tymon blurted out his own questions. 'What's happening to Jedda?' he asked the other Focals. 'What were those bird things?' He had hardly thought of his fellow student in weeks, and was taken aback at this violent glimpse of her.

'Acolyte and master have had disagreement,' replied Oren. 'Envoy sent curses after Jedda, in form of evil birds. She will die soon, if she is not dead already.'

'Curses?' repeated Tymon uneasily.

But it was Noni who answered. 'Psychic constructs,' she sighed. 'They're only refuse held together with a sorcerer's energy, but they're deadly in large numbers.'

Tymon shuddered. To be torn to pieces by beak and claw was a fate he would wish on no one, not even Jedda. 'Well, I suppose we should be glad our enemies are fighting among themselves,' he said half-heartedly, and not without a pang of guilt. The Nurian girl's desperate cry still rang in his ears. It had sounded like a warning.

'Do not be glad about constructs,' cautioned Oren. 'Envoy can also send them after us. It is bad he has found power to create so many. Ashekiel warns us of more than just mine disaster, I fear.'

There was an anxious pause as the Focals considered the implications of the combined Reading. The shadow of Ashekiel's warning seemed to dim and darken even the serene spaces of the Sap-world. Tymon remembered his previous encounters with the creature he had taken for Ash: he had received his first visitation from the 'Angel of Death' in the arena in Sheb, prior to the Argosian attack. The second had occurred in the Tree-caves below the Freehold, just before Solis' murder; the third had taken place in a dream in Cherk Harbour, the morning of Laska's arrest. He vaguely remembered glimpsing his otherworldly visitor as he stumbled delirious with fever through the Eastern Canopy, prior to Lai's passing. And of course, he had met the Born when he stepped outside the Tree of Being. On that occasion, Ashekiel had been surprised to meet him, as if he were the visitation. But it did seem as if the 'Angel's' presence in every other instance presaged disaster.

'One thing I don't understand,' said Mata, breaking the silence. 'About *Ama*. Why now? Why do the Masters attack her now, with so much force?'

'Perhaps they are more awake than before …' suggested Oren doubtfully.

'That's not enough to explain it.' Noni shook her head. 'Mata's right. Remember what Wise Ash used to say? They've woken in the past, slept, and woken again. Yet we haven't seen this sort of sustained assault on the Oracle before, an assault able to silence her completely.'

'You're all talking as if this is a major disaster, and we'll never see her again,' protested Tymon. 'But she has been attacked, and returned several times since I've known her. Won't it be the same now?'

'Do you think it's the same?' asked Noni, giving him a piercing look.

The Focals gazed at him as one. He felt a rush of remorse: he knew that it was not the same at all. He remembered his last conversation with the Oracle before the trance, when she had complained of being blind. She had gasped for help, and been wrenched away in mid-sentence. He realised, with a pang, that she might never come back. He was too ashamed to openly admit to his friends how remiss he had been during that final exchange, how inattentive to their teacher.

'No,' he said to Noni, subdued.

'So, we need to figure out why,' she continued. 'We need to answer Mata's question.'

'Something is different,' said Ara.

'Something has changed,' added Mata.

Something's wrong. Tymon remembered the Oracle's cry.

'This is End Times,' Oren pointed out. 'Everything changes.'

'Including the Masters, I suppose.' Noni grimaced. 'Just our luck.'

'But why weren't they killed outright, back in the

day?' Tymon cried. 'The Masters, I mean,' he specified as the others stared at him. 'They just cause endless trouble and give the Envoy the power to do the same. Why weren't they executed after the war of the Born? Why allow this to happen?'

'You don't kill a Born,' said Noni, her expression resigned. 'The Born are world-architects, or rather world-gardeners, bound up with their creations. You can banish or imprison them, but not destroy them, unless you're willing to destroy all the worlds they've created. Which is a bit unfair, I think you'll agree.'

'Is there nothing we can do for the Oracle?' Tymon remembered the five gardeners he had glimpsed briefly outside the Tree of Being, patiently trimming the curling tendrils of space and time. It was a paradox he still could not quite grasp. 'Why doesn't Ashekiel help?' he asked. 'Are the Masters more powerful than he is?'

'Other Born don't involve themselves in our world,' answered Noni. '*Ama* was the only one who worked with us directly. That's what made her so special. We believe she'll prevail against the Masters. But who knows how long they can keep her distracted. We haven't the strength to face them in the Veil: we're on our own, for now.'

'But *Ama* wasn't the only one who worked here.' The words came tumbling out of Tymon's lips, unstoppable. 'You know as well as I do from what Ashekiel said: Samiha was a Born. If she's still alive, couldn't she help us? Couldn't she find the Oracle?'

The news of the Kion's true nature had been the one part of the Reading his fellow Grafters had not commented on, he realised belatedly. They had not been surprised at all. 'You knew about her, of course,' he finished, rather lamely. 'You tried to tell me before. I didn't listen.'

He remembered their refusal to treat Samiha just like any other person, their vague intimations that she was more than human. Bizarrely, it had been the Kion herself who protested her humanity, when he spoke to her in the bell tower. He wondered, mortified, why she had thought it necessary to lie to him. Had he been so unready to hear the truth?

'We didn't know she might still be alive,' Noni assured him. 'Just that her nature wasn't like our own. It's something Grafters learn when they're properly initiated into a Focal group. The vision does seem to indicate she's alive. But we have no way of contacting her directly. And we can't risk interfering with the work of a Born.'

'Which is why,' said Oren, with some exasperation, 'we do not Read Kion.'

'I didn't,' Tymon answered. 'Ashekiel just knew what I was thinking. It's clear from what he said that we're meant to know about Samiha. She might be trapped or hurt from her fall. She might need our help, as well as us needing hers.'

Even as he articulated the thought, it possessed him, urgent and all-engrossing. Samiha needed him. It was all he could do not to beg the others to let him Read the Kion then and there, to find out if she were in trouble.

'Maybe,' allowed Noni, as Oren remained silent. 'I promise you we'll look into it, Tymon. We can still allow the Sap to take us where we need to go. Others require our immediate attention, however. What of the mineworkers during the collapse? What of Jedda? Do we leave the traitor to reap what she has sown?'

Tymon hesitated. Despite the horror of Jedda's predicament, he was unwilling to worry over her while so many people he cared about were in need of assistance. Her welfare, after all that she had done — particularly to Pallas — simply did not compare with that of Zero and the Saffid. The Focals did not even know if their vision of her was past or future, whether her fate was sealed. He could tell, from the uncomfortable silence following Noni's question, that the others felt the same as he did.

'First things first,' he said, when no one else spoke up. 'If we try to help everybody at the same time, we'll do no good to anyone. The Reading seems to indicate there's a chance of saving the Saffid. I don't know how long I'll have left to warn them when I wake: probably only a few hours. The workers are chained together, so it won't be easy to escape. But we'll find a way.'

'Agreed,' said Noni, as Oren and the twins nodded in mute relief. 'We can at least help the mineworkers. Leave the mine-limb with as many as you can, Tymon, and find a way onto another branch. We'll have our pilots comb the canopy for you. I should ask Gardan, but I think we can spare four or five machines from the combined Freehold fleet. We've heard rumours of Argosian ships crossing the Gap, but we have speed on our side. You'll arrive back in Farhang long before anyone troubles us.'

'Thank you.' Tymon felt a wave of relief flood over him, too, the consciousness that now he could achieve something of real worth. Whatever else he had bungled that day, at least he had kept his promise to Dawn. 'The Saffid have no one to turn to but you,' he told the Focals gratefully. 'You're their only hope.'

'No,' replied Oren slowly, 'it is you who are their hope.'

'And their Witness,' smiled Ara.

'And their Saint,' grinned Mata.

'Don't you lot start with that nonsense too,' said Tymon. 'So, they have a few odd beliefs about me. Does that make them bad people?'

'We never said they were odd beliefs,' said Noni.

His companions' forms were growing faint, Tymon realised. The Reading was almost over. 'Just a minute,' he called to them. 'What about Samiha?'

'We talk on this again, friend,' Oren replied. 'Noni will speak to you when she arrives. For now, we work on saving miners.'

'So, I'm going there?' Tymon heard Noni ask her brother, as the images of the Focals faded away. 'That's new.'

'You are needed,' responded Oren's voice, lingering after his form winked out.

Only when his friends had disappeared completely, swallowed up by the glowing space of the Sap-world, did Tymon notice the subtle change in his surroundings. He did not know if it had already existed when he first fell through the branches of the Tree, following his vision of the mine collapse; he had barely glanced at the tangle of greenery about him while talking to the Focals, preoccupied by other matters. Once he was aware of it, however, the detail was hard to ignore. The Tree of Being was different.

The forest of tendrils around him had been overtaken by a single Leaf Letter. One branch pattern — a spiral loop curled in a closed circle — was echoed everywhere in the Tree, in larger and smaller variations, from the sturdiest limb to the most delicate new shoot. Wherever Tymon looked, he found Union, *Kamsala*, the beginning and the end. He wondered what it meant, and whether the Focals had noticed the phenomenon too, as they were bidding him farewell. In any case, they were gone, and he could not ask them about it. He could feel that he was leaving the trance-state himself, sucked inexorably towards his body. Esoteric questions would have to wait.

He did not wake up immediately. The lengthy double Reading must have given way to the oblivion of ordinary sleep, for there was an interval of dreamless dark, a period of forgetfulness before his eyes blinked open again. He awoke in the light of early morning to find himself sprawled, face down, on Dayan's conservatory carpet. The second hour-candle had burned out long ago, and sunlight was streaming through the orange sap-panes, a welcome sensation on Tymon's chilled skin. But it was the sound of the Tree-dogs barking outside that finally caused him to roll over and sit up. He felt stiff and sore, as if he had walked for miles, and he stretched his joints for a moment on the floor of the conservatory, shaking off the fog of slumber.

And then he remembered, with a thrill of excitement. *Samiha was alive.*

The thought was quickly followed by another, guilty one: Jedda, on the other hand, was probably dead. And with that, the rest of the Reading came flooding back to Tymon, and he jumped to his feet in a panic.

The mine collapse! If he did not warn the Saffid, everyone would be dead, and soon. He hastened to the window, peering out at the bright point of the sun twinkling through the leaf-forests, and calculated there were at least five hours left till noon, a precious period of grace in which to reach his friends and organise an evacuation. Hesitating no longer, he hurried out of the office and slipped down the back stairs to the servants' end of the House, wary of encountering Dayan or his dogs. He told himself he would warn even his perfidious employer about the collapse, all in good time; for the moment, he did not wish to engage in long-winded explanations. He made straight for the kitchen, where he found Ystafa making pan-fried griddle cakes for the Lord's breakfast.

'You're late,' snapped the cook, in Lantrian. No one at the House but Dayan pretended to be open-minded with regards to Argosians. 'You may be the Lord's pet, but that doesn't mean squat to me. You're still expected to wait at table.'

'Pet?' Tymon echoed wearily. 'As you will. But listen to me, Ystafa. I've something very important to tell you.' He attempted to catch the cook's eye as he bustled about the stove, but the other man avoided his gaze, evidently resentful of his status as the Lord's new favourite. Tymon was forced to follow him stomping about the kitchen as he carried out his tasks.

'Go out with the girls and Sun today,' he begged the bristling Lantrian. 'Make an excuse to get away from the House and the mine-shaft, around noon. Go mushroom-picking, or moss-gathering, or whatever keeps you out for a while. There's going to be a terrible accident in the mine.'

'What?' Ystafa finally swung round and glared at him, his brows knit. 'What are you talking about, Argosian fool? Isn't it enough that I have to put up with your infernal laziness? Enjoy your moment of glory, it won't last for long.'

'Just trust me. You don't want to be near the mine today.'

'Whatever you say, pet.'

Tymon exhaled with frustration, hurrying towards the back door of the kitchen. 'I'll try to remind you later,' he said.

'Hold on one moment.' Ystafa brandished the two griddle cakes on their hardwood platter. 'What about taking up the master's breakfast?'

'Lord's errand,' Tymon threw over his shoulder. 'Sorry, Ystafa.'

It was a lie that would be found out as soon as Dayan asked for him. He had no time to lose. He ducked out of the door into the courtyard beyond, the cook's frankly descriptive curses about the Lord and his pets singeing his ears.

To Tymon's relief, there was no sign of the Tree-dogs in the courtyard as he hurried to open the ornate mansion portals. Like the rest of Dayan's personal servants, he had been given the keys to the main gates on a knotted cord to keep in his pocket, as well as those for the stores and back kitchen door; the penalties for runaways were so severe that the comparatively cosseted House-workers never abused that privilege. He was further encouraged by the thought that it was early enough in the morning to expect to make the journey to the mine without encountering customs officers or guards, who would delay him with questions.

The weather was almost muggy after the rain and wind of the past few days; as he stepped out of the gates, locking them behind him, he saw that the yawning gap of the mine-crater was filled with warm fog and the sun was already burning through the condensation. *Alive, she's alive!* the bright beams of light seemed to sing, as he jogged down the road. *Samiha is alive!* Anything seemed possible after his vivid Reading. Despite the knowledge of impending danger, his thoughts soared, and he did not at first remark what had plummeted through the leaf-forests to his right, with a muffled thud.

He stopped with instinctive caution, squinting at the gleaming rain-washed twigs above, then at the foggy lip of the crater. Had someone thrown a shard of bark at him? Before he could locate the source of the sound, however, it was repeated. A dark shape dropped heavily onto the road in front of him. Tymon stared in alarm as a winged creature unfurled itself on the bark and hobbled towards him.

He recognised it immediately: it was one of the Envoy's 'curses', what Noni had called a 'psychic construct', like the creatures he had Seen attacking

Jedda in the Reading. He had never particularly liked birds, and the thing scrabbling on the bark before him stirred up a childhood dread of having his eyes pecked out. Now that he was able to inspect the creature more closely, he saw it resembled a corpse of a bird rather than a living one — or more precisely the component parts of several corpses, assembled together and brought to life by an amateur god. It was a travesty, a grotesque copy of a crow. Too late, he wished that he had asked the Focals more about the curses and how to combat them. The thing before him emitted a single raucous caw, lurched into the air and flapped directly at him.

Tymon cried out, throwing up his arms to protect his face as the construct alighted clumsily on his back. He could feel its weight, the claws digging through his coat, and a sharp smell of putrefaction filled his nostrils. Panic took hold of him and he lurched along the road, trying to beat the vile thing off. It took him a while to dislodge it, for he could barely bring himself to touch its stinking, matted feathers. He stumbled perilously close to the low wall at the edge of the mineshaft in his terror, before finally throwing the feathered horror away from him, onto the road. It took off again with a croak, blundering up to settle on the top of a nearby twig, still emitting its harsh cries.

Tymon eyed the hunched creature on the twig-tip, his fear prickling-hot. Its cries reminded him disquietingly of an alarm. Noni had said the curses attacked in numbers, he remembered, tilting up his head to search the sky over the mine. Chal was positioned in a well of light, and he could see the distant patches of blue through the upper canopy. He also saw, with a sinking heart, the funnel of dark specks gathering swiftly over the mine-crater, circling between the leaf-forests. They descended in response to their fellow's call, flapping ever closer. There were dozens of them. He began to hasten down the road towards the docks, his throat dry.

He had not gone ten paces before a heavy weight struck his back, knocking the breath out of him. It was no bird, however: someone large and heavy was grappling him from behind. A meaty hand was clamped across his mouth, and he felt the point of a hardwood knife prick his ribs.

'Not a sound,' breathed a man's voice in his ear, in guttural Argosian.

His assailant hooked an arm about his neck and dragged him bodily into a clump of twigs on the north side of the road, still holding the knife to his ribs. Tymon was thrust ahead of his captor, over the uneven growth at the base of the shafts; he could not turn to see his assailant's face. Although he craned up at the slivers of sky visible between the twigs, he could not see the birds, either, at least for now. The black specks had abruptly withdrawn, as if one attack precluded the other.

Deep among the thickets, his captor halted and twisted him about, shoving him against the trunk of a twig. Tymon found himself staring into Tahu's ash-lined eyes, the flat of the pirate's blade against his throat.

'Greetings, choirboy,' said the Lantrian resettler, baring his teeth. 'You and I are going to have a little talk.'

'What do you want?' gasped Tymon. 'I'm on an errand for the Lord —'

'I'm sure you are,' snapped the pirate. 'You and the Lord are mighty close. Too close for my liking, sorcerer.' Tahu gave a harsh laugh. 'Oh yes, I know what you are. Took me a while yesterday, but I remembered you and your uppity Freehold friends, in Cherk. The Governor was all over you lot, though I personally draw the line at courting lice.' He spat on the bark. 'I don't mind telling you, my boys and I took a great deal of pleasure in teaching that upstart Freehold judge his place.'

'I'm sure you did!' cried Tymon, a rush of rage getting the better of his good judgment. 'You and your "boys" beat Laska senseless and left him to die in a pile of garbage. That doesn't make you better than him — it makes you stinking cowards!'

Tahu leaned close to Tymon, pushing the knife-blade harder against his throat. His breath smelled of stale jar-weed.

'Nurians are garbage,' he hissed. 'I like to put things where they belong. I guess you belong on that pile too, since you like 'em so much, louse-lover.'

Tymon glared back at him in mute fury. Tahu considered him with his head to one side, his smile fading. 'But we're not here to talk about that,' he said. 'I've been waiting for you to set foot outside that precious House of yours since yesterday, so I can find out one thing. What's Dayan asking you to predict, hmm? Don't tell me he hasn't figured out what you are. I know all about our fine Lord's secret hobbies.'

His eyes glittered. Tymon swallowed uncomfortably against the knife, remembering the Oracle's warning. He should give this man enough, but not too much. 'You're right, Dayan asked for a prediction,' he admitted warily. 'It's about his business deals in the East. He wants to know if the rebels will betray him.'

Perhaps his dislike of the resettler made him sound as if he were lying unconvincingly; in any case, Tahu snorted with disbelief. 'I don't think so,' he sneered. 'I see I'm going to have to convince you of the seriousness of my request.'

He hooked his arm about Tymon's neck and, keeping the knife pressed to his ribs, continued to half-thrust, half-drag the young man through the twigs in the direction of the dock-bridge.

'Where are we going?' asked Tymon.

Tahu's voice grated in his good ear. 'You're coming aboard my vessel. Quietly. We're leaving for Cherk Harbour today. A fair few people there will be mighty eager to see you, choirboy.'

'No!' Tymon tried to stop his stumbling progress, then grunted with pain as the knife point pricked him. 'You can't take me away!' he pleaded in desperation, as Tahu shoved him on. 'I've had a Grafter's vision! The mine's going to collapse — I have to warn people!'

'How very convenient,' chuckled his captor. 'A major disaster threatens just when you need it. Try again, sorcerer.'

'This is real! I swear — it'll happen at half-past noon!'

'Then we're safe. The *Aurora* drops moorings an hour before that.'

Tymon stared at the vista before him in dismay. They had reached the last clump of twigs before the customs buildings, and stood on a little knot above the level of the road edging the mine-crater. The Lantrian pirate locked him in his harsh grip and peered cautiously through the twigs, scrutinising the dock area. The air-harbour bridge was already dotted with hurrying figures and the custom house bustled with activity.

'You walk on my right side all the way to the ship. You let me talk if anyone stops us,' ordered Tahu. He brandished the knife under Tymon's nose before replacing it in its sheath. 'If you try to run, I'll slit you in half.'

Tymon had little doubt that he would. Tahu's fingernails dug into his flesh as he led him down to the road in grim silence, turning to their right to make for the custom house. Tymon trudged along at the pirate's side, his pulse hammering, wondering how he was ever going to escape, to warn his friends. His eye drifted towards the start of the mine-ramp as he passed it on his left, wondering if he might make a dash into the crater. But he dared not attempt to break free of Tahu without some form of distraction; he knew the other's long stride would equal his in an instant. He would even have welcomed an attack from the Envoy's accursed birds, if they could have separated him from his jailor. But his airborne nemeses had disappeared; the swathe of sky above the crater remained empty and cloudless. The sun had by now burned the fog away and the weather was turning unseasonably warm. Tymon calculated with growing distress that it was past the eighth hour of morning.

As they approached the custom house and docks, his legs began to feel weighed down with tension. He could see no opportunity to break loose from Tahu and the enforced delay was excruciating. But just as they passed the front of the custom house, a loincloth-wearing boy burst out of a door ahead of them, laden with rolls of bark-paper up to his chin. He dodged past Tymon and Tahu without a second glance, heading for the dock-bridge, and at his heels emerged the nameless scribe Tymon had met on the day of his arrival.

'Greetings, Tahu,' observed the little clerk, in Lantrian. His eyes widened slightly as he registered Tymon, but he expressed no other sign of shock. 'Aren't you on your way out of Chal this morning?' he asked the resettler.

Tymon could feel the frustration seeping through the pirate's fingertips, clamped down on his arm. They were obliged to halt and converse politely with the chief clerk.

'We're on our way,' muttered Tahu. 'Late morning, I expect.'

Tymon gazed wordlessly at the scribe. He remembered his vision of the mine collapse and the inescapable knowledge that this man would die in just a few hours. He found himself regretting the clerk's death. The dryly observant Lantrian had been kind to him, to the extent possible in his situation. A host of inarticulate warnings and unsayable advice caught in Tymon's throat. He longed to tell the clerk to leave, to run, to flee the scene at once. He knew that it was useless: Tahu would never give him the chance to speak. Some part of his distress and desperation must have communicated itself to the scribe, however, for his eyes never left Tymon's as he answered Tahu.

'You'll want your final receipts done now, in that case,' he said softly. 'Follow me upstairs.' When Tahu tried to protest, the clerk held up a hand in polite insistence. 'No, no, it's no trouble at all, I'll see to it myself. You, Lord's boy —' he winked to Tymon — 'while you're waiting for us, why don't you go down to the stores on the first floor. The clothes the master sent you to collect are there. He wanted you to pick up the package from Lant, did he not?'

Tymon nodded dumbly. Somehow, the little man had known. Somehow, even as Tymon had ached to warn him of his danger, the scribe had read his plight at the hands of Tahu. The trumped-up errand to the stores was his chance to escape; for once, Lantrian bureaucracy had come to his rescue. He watched as the clerk took hold of the fuming pirate's elbow, pulling him inexorably into the custom house, already engaged in a patter of conversation. Tahu's face was livid with rage; he glared meaningfully over his shoulder at Tymon as he was pulled through the doorway, as if to say he would soon be after him. When they had disappeared, the young man turned and sped back along the road the way they had come, away from the docks. His mind hammered with the thought that the clerk had given up his life for him. The man who had saved him would not survive the morning.

The reprieve might just be enough to help his friends, however. Determined not to waste his opportunity, Tymon made directly for the one place Tahu would never think to look for him; the one place a House slave would avoid at all costs. He swerved purposefully to his right at the intersection leading to the mine and continued at a steady jog down the ramp into the crater. All seemed empty and quiet as he wound around the first great looping bend, descending ever deeper into the foggy shaft; even so, he felt uneasy, naked and exposed on the empty road. His steps slowed, and he glanced about him, belatedly aware of the danger threatening him now that Tahu was gone. Another enemy approached: he could feel in his very bones that he would not be left in peace to complete his descent into the mine.

He felt rather than saw the first flitting shadow darken the sky. A moment later, he peered upwards to see the evil specks circling above the mine-shaft again, a funnel of swiftly moving black. A single raucous cry echoed in the crater. Closer and closer the birds whirled above him, filling the air with the sound of their beating wings. Tymon broke into a run, sprinting down the ramp, but this time he was unable to escape.

The first construct hit his shoulder with a glancing blow, knocking him forward. Another swooped over his head an instant later, its claws raking his cheek. The creatures blundered into him in eerie silence, no longer emitting their cries. The smell of rot surrounded Tymon as he desperately fended off the attack, overcoming his disgust to strike at the birds with his bare hands. He tried to shelter his face beneath his coat, but the curses harried him continually, scrabbling through the folds of cloth until he retreated with his back to the wall of the crater, unable to advance and beating the clawed and feathered horrors away. He felt more angry than afraid, now, incensed at being prevented from reaching his friends when they needed him most. He had had enough of the Envoy's interference: he was tired of bowing to his enemy's continual harassment.

'Get off!' he shouted hoarsely to the birds. 'The Sap take you, all of you!'

He knew there was no such thing as a spell in the Grafting, no intrinsically powerful phrase that could help him do more than concentrate on the task at hand. But on this occasion, brimming as he was with righteous indignation, his outburst acted as a watchword might, ridding him of an unconscious barrier. His anger became focused, sharp, a channel: he was suddenly filled with the familiar heat of the Sap, overflowing with its power. The subtle flames were just visible to his waking eyes, running over his chest and down his arms. They accumulated in a well of energy in his right hand, the scarred hand that had pulled Wick out of the Veil. To his own surprise, the creatures swooping down on him abruptly veered away from his raised incandescent palm. One of the curses that had attempted to alight on his head now took off with a croak of dismay. The others wheeled and turned, breaking off the assault. They remained circling in the air above Tymon, but did not attack.

'That's right,' he muttered, eyeing them in triumph, the protective warmth of the Sap welling up inside him. 'Get lost. Scat.'

Then he remembered Samiha's words. *Fear neither darkness nor defeat.* There was a precious burning hope in his heart, the hope that she might yet be alive. While that hope remained, no shadow would stop him.

He wasted no further time on the birds but continued down the ramp, his mind occupied with the task ahead. Although the Sap-heat ebbed to a quiescent glow, Tymon could feel it within him, ready to be called upon when necessary. After a while, he glanced up to see that the mine-shaft was empty, filled only with drifting wisps of fog. The Envoy's curses were gone, as if they had never been.

There was no occasion to mull over his victory. Once he had reached the permanent dusk of the mine-floor, he made straight for the shacks near the central pit, seeking out Dawn's hut. The buildings were deserted and the workers' hammers echoed relentlessly in the lower section of the shaft. To his dismay, Tymon found no sign of the Saffid girl in her quarters; even her mattress had been stripped of its thin covering and lay empty. He quit the shack with a heavy heart, fearing that her illness had taken her before he could do anything to help her. He made his way to the central pit.

Crouched on the lip of the inner crater, he scrutinised the gangs of workers below in the hopes of identifying the people he knew. He could not make out Zero's large, red-haired frame anywhere, but pinpointed a dusty, pallid youth whom he thought might be Nightside in one of the closer gangs. When the nearest overseer had turned away to stroll along the north side of the pit, Tymon descended the ladder, keeping a wary eye on the whip-wielding guards dotted about the work-pit.

The youth he had picked out was definitely one of the Saffid: he could see the boy's white hair under a layer of dust and grime as he approached. The slaves in the gang lifted their axes and brought them down again, lifted them and brought them down. Tymon did not try to stop them, for he knew the lack of activity would draw unwanted attention, but stepped over to the Saffid boy, peering into his face as he worked. It was not Nightside, after all. Tymon did not recognise the lad, but it was clear that the other knew him, though he never broke his working rhythm. Up went his axe and down again, his gaze inquisitive as he glanced over his shoulder.

'You're in danger,' Tymon murmured in his ear. 'There's going to be a cave-in at the mine today. It's happening at half-past noon. You believe me, right?'

The Saffid boy nodded swiftly. The other gang-members stared sidelong at them both as the axes rose and fell. The long rod at their ankles prevented any one individual from acting alone, Tymon realised; they must all move at once, or drag each other down.

'Can you break loose from these fetters?' he asked the youth.

'If we jump guards,' answered the Saffid lad, as he toiled. 'Noon break. Should be possible if we try together.'

'Good idea.' Tymon breathed in relief. 'Once you're out of the mine, find the quickest way off this branch. Nurian dirigibles will be scouting the canopy for you. They'll pick you up in a few days' time, at worst. I'll spread the word to the others.'

He did not wait to attract the notice of the guards, but struck out across the pit towards the next gang. He spied another unfamiliar Saffid youth at work on the beam and halted beside him, whispering his warning once again, as well as the directive to attack the guards at noon. Although they had never spoken to each other before, the second boy accepted the prophecy with comparable calm to the first, exhibiting the same unquestioning trust. Indeed, Tymon began to be glad of the Saffids' peculiar beliefs, for it made an evacuation far easier. He did not have the energy to argue or persuade others of the danger at this point. He continued moving across the floor of the pit from gang to gang, speaking to the Saffid wherever he could, pushing his luck as far as it would go. He did not care now if the guards caught him. He was determined to get the message to as many people as possible.

His luck ran out after the fifth conversation. An overseer spotted him talking to the workers and hurried over with a shout; what in the name of the Tree's black heart did Tymon think he was doing, and what gave him the right to hold up production? The young man's rehashed excuse of seeking out the chief overseer did not win over this new adversary, a hulk of a fellow dressed in nothing but a leather thong, his slave's number tattooed proudly across his chest. The giant took hold of him by the scruff of his neck and dragged him bodily up a ladder to the huts, telling him that he would indeed see the chief, and enjoy explaining his pretty little houseboy's mission directly to him. Tymon was thrust into one of the larger buildings which he guessed was reserved for the guards, and shoved down on his knees on the floor, in front of Gul.

They would not believe him. He repeated, he pleaded that they must leave the mine, that only three hours remained before the cave-in. But they refused to countenance the possibility that he might be telling the truth. They took him for a spy; he was on a mission to subvert Lantria, they claimed. He had allowed himself to be captured and brought to Chal on some mission of mischief. Why else would he waste time talking to mineworkers? Their questioning of him was oddly perfunctory, however, even bored, as if they did not much care if Lantria were subverted, or were acting out their bullying roles simply because it was expected of them. They tied him to a chair in the guards' hut and split open his lip, but did not do much else. After several rounds of desultory interrogation, they left him alone in the one-room building. He was abandoned there a long and exasperating while. As the minutes ticked by and noon drew ever nearer, his only consolation was that Tahu would never think of looking for him here.

But he had underestimated the efficiency of the hierarchy governing the slaves of Chal. Someone must have been dispatched to the House to inform on him, for barely an hour later the door opened, and the Lord himself strode into the room. Behind him, the overseers crowded anxiously in the entrance; he slammed the door in their faces.

'Good morning,' he said to Tymon coldly.

'The mine —' began the young man, before Dayan cut him off.

'I suggest you consider what you're about to say to me with great care,' he snapped. 'You have one last chance to save your miserable, treacherous life. You can answer the question I put to you yesterday to my satisfaction. Or you may face the consequences. Speak.'

'I haven't been able to answer your question yet,' sighed Tymon. 'But it won't matter once you hear what I have to say. I had a vision —'

'Won't matter?' The Lantrian frowned. 'I should say it matters a great deal. It's all that matters right now.' He stepped closer, looming over Tymon in his chair, his expression hard. 'I have indulged you up till now,' he said, 'because I thought you might have something special to offer me. Because I believed in your powers. I was hoping very much that you would not disappoint me.'

At that, Tymon's patience deserted him. 'What's the use of powers,' he cried, 'if nobody listens to my predictions? You all just want to hear what you want to hear. Even if it means you'll die.'

The Lord gave a sarcastic laugh. 'You would have me believe this trumped-up crisis, this ridiculous story of a cave-in. I'm no fool, my fine little prophet. You were seen with Tahu this morning. And I have my own mystic abilities: I don't have to rely on standard reports to know which tunnels are safe, and which servants are turncoats.'

He rummaged in the pocket of his own coat and, before Tymon's astonished gaze, withdrew a small bag of green velvet, reaching into it to retrieve a fistful of what appeared to be painted shards of bark.

'You're a fraud, Tymon of Argos,' he said, stepping closer to Tymon's chair with the fistful of bark held high, as if it were precious. 'You weren't able to do as you were asked, and now you're scrabbling for a way out. Did you think I was nothing but an ignorant yokel you could impress with tales of doom and disaster?' He drew himself up, pride flashing in his eyes. 'I have made a study of all five schools of divination, I have been initiated into the Mystic Lodge and risen to the rank of Grand Master. You didn't know that, eh, novice? I'm no prophet myself, but I know when others have the true Power.'

Dayan bent down and shook the handful of shards beneath Tymon's nose, as if they proved his point. The pieces were carved to mimic the spear-shaped foliage of the World Tree, the young man saw, painted white and green. On the flat upper surface of each was a stylised rune he recognised immediately.

'The Letters are formal,' declared the Lord. 'There is no danger to the mine.'

'You think these are the Leaf Letters?' Tymon laughed in his surprise. 'That's superstitious trash. I've Seen the real Tree. Not this physical one, where we live, but the Tree of Being, in the world of the Sap. That's where the Letters are —'

Dayan abruptly struck him across the face with his hand, silencing him. Tymon's split lip left a smear of red on the mine-owner's palm.

'You've had your chance, and made your choice,' snarled the Lord, slipping the shards back into their pouch. 'I'm done with you.'

He turned and quit the hut, leaving the door open. Tymon heard him give the guards outside a perfunctory command in Lantrian. 'He's all yours,' he said, as he disappeared into the eternal twilight of the mine. 'Have fun.'

'What time is it?' Tymon asked the three overseers when they entered the hut.

The guards beat him, then. They beat him with the methodical brutality of those for whom violence is simply another language, a grammar made of sinews and bone. They told him, in this tactile language, that today was a day like any other day, and that seeing his pain lessened their own. They told him that they were real, not shadows to banish with a hope and a prayer, like the Envoy's birds. Their fists debated eloquently that some were born to rule while others suffered and died; they untied him so as to better kick him to the floor, in a final clincher to the argument. They did not tell him the time.

When Tymon was finally able to raise his aching head from the floor, he saw that the hut was empty. He realised he must have lost consciousness for a while, for he did not know when the guards had left him, and had not registered the cause of their departure. He had no idea how much time had passed. His whole body throbbed, the old wounds on his back torn open and bleeding afresh, but he could still move. As he staggered to his feet, swaying, he heard the far-off sound of a hardwood bell clanging an alarm, and remembered the slaves' revolt. It must be noon, or some time past the hour. The mine catastrophe would be upon them at any moment.

He tottered unsteadily out of the hut, clutching at the door jamb to keep from tumbling down the steps. There were no guards in sight: he guessed they had returned to the central pit, for a clamour of voices arose from that direction. He began limping away from the noise, towards the road out of the mine. His injuries prevented him from moving fast enough, however. He had not yet reached the ramp before the first faint tremor passed through the bark beneath his feet. It was followed by a sharper jolt. The collapse had begun!

Tymon broke into a run, ignoring the stabbing pain in his back and sides. But his shambling, awkward progress was unequal to the oncoming collapse. He had hardly stepped onto the foot of the ramp before the shaking of the branch became a continuous roll, almost knocking him to his knees on the planks. Behind him, the shouts and orders from the pit turned to cries of alarm; Tymon stared upwards, aghast, to see the top of the ramp begin to detach itself from the crater wall, a thin black tendril clearly visible against the bright circle of sky overhead. There was no escape, not this way at any rate.

Sections of torn planks from the ramp were already plummeting about his ears as he turned and lurched back across the floor of the shaft. Several figures, guards and workers both, dashed towards him from the direction of the huts, then stopped in consternation as they saw their path out of the mine cut off. Larger sections of the crater walls were falling down now with a screech and crash of timber, a sound Tymon remembered all too well from his vision. High above and to the north, the grand arc of the dock-bridge had begun to rock on its vast pillars.

He made his way back to the huts, for there was nowhere else to go. Some of the guards called to him as he passed, but he ignored them, and they did not follow him. He struggled on across the shaking floor of the mine, barely able to think in the continual din. Then, all at once, Zero was beside him, holding him up, shouting in his deaf ear. Tymon could not hear what he said, but allowed himself to be led towards the workers' pit. Everyone else was scrambling in the opposite direction, attempting to scale the sides of the collapsing crater, but Zero helped him descend a ladder, into the lower level of the mine. They staggered together in stops and starts towards the south side of the trench, across the shuddering wilderness of half-finished beams left behind by the workers. Tymon was relieved to see that none were chained to their posts, though he did not know what had become of them.

At last, to his joy, as they were nearing the south wall of the pit, he glimpsed a group of about twenty workers sheltering in one of the tunnels leading to the enclosed levels of the mine. Most were Saffid, though there were a few other Nurians there, too, waiting a short distance inside the tunnel-mouth. The side of the crater immediately above had already begun to groan and crack apart as Tymon and Zero reached the tunnel, the bark showing great rifts. The mine-passage was the best shelter they could hope for: its walls trembled, but held for the moment. When Tymon limped up to the group of workers, leaning heavily on Zero's arm, the first two Saffid boys he had spoken to that morning threw themselves on the trembling bark at his feet.

'You save us, Lord,' they cried.

'Oh, for the love of the Tree,' muttered Tymon. 'We're not through this yet.'

He pulled the youths up from the floor. It was not only the Saffid who gazed at him as if he were the answer to their prayers, however. Other mineworkers, ordinary Nurians and even two Lantrians, fixed ardent, awestruck eyes on him as they crouched in the gloom of the tunnel. They had heard about the Syon's prophecy and seen it fulfilled. Now they awaited his guidance. He swallowed dryly.

'Where's Nightside?' he asked. A moment's scrutiny was enough to confirm that his Saffid friend was not present.

'We haven't seen him.' Zero shook his head. 'I don't think he made it. He wasn't as evil as us, you know.' But as Tymon's face fell with disappointment, the Marak boy added, 'Dawn's here. The guards left her out to die this morning, but we found her. She's sleeping.'

He indicated a rough bier made of woven bark positioned further down the tunnel. It was comforting for Tymon to see the thin form bundled in a blanket upon it, though he doubted Dawn's sleep at this point in her illness was a great cause for joy.

'What now, Lord?' put in one of the youths who had thrown himself at Tymon's feet. 'How do we get out?'

The Saffid stood beside him, peering out of the tunnel-mouth, at the chaos on the floor of the shaft. The entire crater was crumbling away, Tymon realised. They did not have much more time; he could tell from the position of the leaf-forests far above that the gigantic limb had already begun to topple over.

'We can't stay here,' he answered. 'This whole branch is breaking off the trunk. It'll fall, who knows how far.'

'Where else is there?' objected Zero, glancing at the black interior of the tunnel.

If you want to save them, then you must go down. Ashekiel's words, forgotten in his haste to leave the mine, returned in a rush to Tymon. It was clear guidance. 'Into the tunnels,' he replied eagerly. 'Now. Everybody.' He turned towards the group of slaves huddled together in bewilderment, waiting for some miracle to save them. 'We need to go deeper into the mine,' he said. 'There's another exit. We can find it.'

He did not wait for an answer but, gripped by a sense of urgency, began limping down the pitch-dark corridor, feeling his way along the left-hand wall. Walking in complete darkness was not as difficult as he had feared: he had already accomplished a similar feat in the Tree-tunnels in Cherk Harbour, and this passage was easier to navigate, smooth-floored and wide enough for a wagon. Even with his injuries he was able to shuffle along at a moderate rate. Glancing back over his shoulder, he saw that the others were following him obediently. His last twilit vision was of two Saffid picking up Dawn's bier and joining the end of the advancing line. Then the cavalcade was swallowed up in impenetrable darkness. The mouth of the passage became a grey point behind them, then disappeared.

The tunnel must have been used to transport cartloads of timber mined from the deeper levels. It spiralled steadily down and to the right, deep into the heart of the vertical limb. As they hurried on through the gloom, the tremors of the great branch lessened about them. The sounds of collapsing planks and beams became more distant, and the cries and screams from the mine gradually faded away behind them. But the floor had begun to tilt beneath their feet as the branch continued its slow, ruinous descent through the canopy. The movement was more subtle as they raced towards the base of the limb, but still noticeable. Finally, after perhaps a quarter of an hour of blind stumbling, the wall to Tymon's left ended and the tunnel opened out into a wide, empty area. He stopped short, feeling the whisper of cool air against his face. He had not expected a choice of direction.

'What's this place?' he whispered to Zero as the Marak youth halted at his heels.

The darkness seemed to demand that they lower their voices. From far above and to the right came the echo of a vast and booming crash; Tymon guessed that the struts of the dock-bridge had finally given way.

'The entrance to the lowest levels,' his friend replied. 'I'll ask the others about it. Someone might know more.'

Tymon remembered the hall in the abandoned mine where he had stayed with Jedda and the Oracle. The equivalent in Chal would surely be far larger and contain several exits. He had no idea which one to take, however. He wondered if any of the Saffid had been there before, and if they might help him choose the right path. It was not long before the answering whisper reached him, back up the line. None of the members of the group had been inside the tunnels. All they could tell him was that this was where corewood was mined, a secretive, closely guarded enterprise. The core-guards had long since abandoned their posts and climbed out into the chaos of the collapsing mine, so there was no one else to ask. The workers' expectation was that the *Syon* continue to guide them simply by instinct. When Tymon suggested that Zero scout out the perimeter of the hall to find out how many exits there were, the Marak boy initially laughed.

'Talk to your spirits,' he responded, his candid voice full of confidence. 'They'll tell you where to go.'

Tymon thought of the Oracle with regret. He would have given much to have her guidance now. And then he remembered Ashekiel's reproach, that he continually relied on others to See for him. Though this was no time for a Grafter's trance, he had other means at his disposal.

'Listen, Zero,' he said carefully. He did not wish to dampen his friend's zeal too much, for he guessed he would have need of it. 'My spirits have left me for a while. They'll be back, but for now we need to go on as if we're on our own.'

After Zero had acceded to his request, Tymon leaned his hot cheek against one of the tunnel walls, feeling the dim rumour of destruction through the wood. The final wrenching crack that would snap the branch in two had not yet occurred, but they were still too close to the upper levels, too far from the safety of the main trunk.

'Sap help me,' he breathed.

He could have laughed at his predicament: that of a minor prophet who, having delivered his one reliable warning, was now required to lead his loyal followers out of further, unforeseen quandaries. They would not hear of him being as confused as they were, as ordinary and alone. Crouched there in the darkness of the mine, aching from the guards' beating, he found himself suddenly and incongruously preoccupied with the fate of the Lord's dogs. He wondered what had become of the foolish, innocent brutes, and whether they would die along with their horrendous master. A wave of dizziness washed over him; he rubbed his eyes.

It was an agonising interval before Zero returned. 'Three ways out,' he announced. 'The left is small, I think only a service tunnel. The middle one is wide and goes straight down. The right tunnel also goes down, but it turns.'

'Spiralling, like the one we just took,' sighed Tymon. 'Maybe that's the one that goes to the deepest levels. Let's try it. We might even reach the trunk.'

It was a bastard decision, neither entirely rational nor able to properly benefit from a Grafter's intuition, but he knew he must not hesitate. The other escapees were fidgeting behind him, murmuring to each other; the group needed him to choose quickly, even if the choice was wrong. Besides, the branch groaned ominously now on all sides, boding further trouble. The final collapse, when it broke at the base, would be all the more devastating for the delay. His mind made up, he called the others to their feet, leading them around the right-hand side of the hall to the spiral tunnel. They continued on, trudging ever deeper into the depths of the mine.

At first, it appeared he had made the correct choice. The passage plunged purposefully down into the branch-core, as if it were as eager as they to reach its goal. There were other tunnels, small openings their questing fingers passed on the walls, but these were minor by-ways. The main passage did not falter. The groaning and tearing of wood grew faint behind them, and the shuddering of the branch gradually stilled. As the floor began to feel level again beneath his feet, Tymon allowed himself to hope that they had indeed taken the vital turning into the main trunk, and were out of immediate danger. The air was not dead and stagnant in these lower passages, as he had worried it might be, but stirring with the promise of another, far-off exit.

An age went by, with only the shuffling steps of the workers and their muted conversation to break the silence. On and on in single file they walked, down into the black heart of the Tree. After a while, Tymon's body began to be racked with shivers, his weariness catching up with him at last. He had not eaten since the day before and the reopened wounds on his back were wet with blood, sticking to his undershirt. He bumped dizzily against the wall of the tunnel, causing Zero to reach out and steady him from behind with a whisper of concern.

'I'm fine,' Tymon muttered, brushing his friend away. 'Everyone else is just as tired as I am.'

He was furious with himself, now. He felt as if his body were a clumsy impediment, a liability after all he had been through. He had withstood the accursed birds — survived Tahu's machinations — even endured the brutality of the guards and not succumbed, only to be thwarted by his own physical weakness. He forced himself to take the next step, and the next. He began to feel suffocated by the claustrophobic darkness of the mine. If only it would end. If only they could reach an opening. The thought of Samiha, alive and waiting somewhere in the Tree while he wandered aimlessly through these tunnels, became excruciating. He had to get out!

'Just do it,' he mumbled aloud to himself as he stumbled on. 'Just damned-to-root do it.'

When the first chant echoed out behind him, he almost fell. The husky voices of the mineworkers were rising up in the darkness, one after another, blending into a ghostly melody. They sang to give themselves courage, to fend off the gloom. They sang, surprisingly, neither in Lantrian nor in Nurian, but in a language known to slaves in both countries, the 'twig-tongue' Tymon remembered from Marak.

Up to Heaven, take my feet, they crooned, their shuffling steps keeping time. *Those who dead lay down to sleep.*

Tymon straightened his back, kept his hand on the wall to his right and walked on, his companions' voices buoying him, pushing back the darkness.

Chain-men don't go lying down.
Walk me up to Heaven's crown.

So much for the slaves of Chal being legally soulless, thought Tymon. The workers had their own ideas about a heavenly reward.

But the songs could not keep the encroaching dark of the mine at bay for long, and soon even the dauntless workers of Chal sighed and fell silent. By now the passage had ceased its spiralling descent and ran straight, as far as Tymon could tell, though he could no longer guess the direction. He was just wearily considering the merits of calling for a halt and a much-needed rest, perhaps even attempting a Reading to determine their course, when he caught sight of a light ahead — a faint, pale flickering in the far reaches of the passage.

Daylight! he thought. An opening, an end to this unbearable hole. Panting with effort, he staggered towards it, leaning heavily on the right-hand wall. When Zero, hurrying behind him, asked him once more if he were well, his answer was barely audible.

'Don't you see it?' he muttered, his gaze fixed on the faraway glimmer.

As he neared his goal, however, his steps faltered and he frowned in perplexity. The light did not behave like an opening to the outside world. He realised with a shock that it was moving towards him. It wavered, a wandering white smudge in the blank darkness of the tunnel. He stopped short, causing Zero to blunder against him again.

'What is it, Lord?' whispered the Marak boy.

'My spirits,' said Tymon. His voice sounded thick and slow in his own ears. 'They're back. Come on. We're getting out of here.'

Before him walked the familiar vision of Samiha. He could See her now, clear as day, some distance down the tunnel. Her form was transparent, glowing with pale light, but otherwise she was as he remembered her in Sheb: a small, straight-backed figure, grave and beautiful, her long, shimmering hair braided down her back.

Giddy excitement took hold of him, and he forgot his aching limbs and tiredness as he hastened towards her. She gazed at him an instant, then turned and walked down the tunnel ahead. He followed her eagerly. A moment later, he saw her faraway form step into an opening on the right; he struggled to catch up with her, plunging into the side-passage only to see the glimmering figure still walking ahead of him, still some distance down the tunnel. It seemed to him that she glanced over her shoulder before continuing, as if to check that he was there. He hurried after her without a moment's hesitation, while Zero and the others pursued him as best they could, far behind.

9

Ephelius Gowron, born some fifty years ago in the slums of Argos city, the sole bastard son of a seminary tax collector and a laundry maid, disembarked once more in his native town on the nineteenth day of the month of Sunlight Return, four weeks after the Kion's trial. He had made the long voyage from the colonies on board two merchant dirigibles, first travelling to Marak, then catching a winter freighter back to the Mother Canopy. He looked almost respectable when he set foot on the air-harbour quays that morning; his hair and beard had been trimmed, his ancient priest's garb replaced by a sailor's double-breasted coat and boots. Only his eyes, peering with veiled disdain at his compatriots in the streets of the city, betrayed their old, murderous gleam. That hint of violence was no less dangerous for being officially sanctioned. He was ushered into the Saint's opulent office at the College after barely a word of questioning from the guards, for the men had been told to expect him. And although his subsequent report to Fallow might have amazed the Saint, it came as no surprise to the two other witnesses present at the meeting.

The Envoy, accompanied by an apparently restored and smooth-faced Wick, sat through Gowron's revelations about traitors within the ranks of the seminary without batting an eyelid. The evidence regarding one of the Fathers who had been caught selling state secrets to Lantria had been concocted by Lace himself, of course, and given to his acolyte in secret, well in advance. The only one in the room who had not yet heard the trumped-up tale of Rede's treachery was Fallow. After Gowron had finished his account, the Saint sat back in his chair, his expression frankly gleeful.

'That's terrible, terrible,' he observed, looking anything but upset. 'Father Rede, eh? Who'd have thought it. And the link to the East, too: my goodness. We'll nip this thing in the bud, my friends. What wonderful timing. I don't know what I'd do without you, Ephelius. You'll have your tenure at the seminary fully reinstated, of course. I'm grateful to you for your hard work.'

'It's my pleasure, Holiness,' smiled Gowron. 'I can't stand a traitor. I've made my mistakes in the past, but I'm still proud to be an Argosian and loyal to the Mother Canopy — not like these white-necks. They have no sense of honour.'

'Well, well,' Fallow ruminated. He rose, still rubbing his hands together. 'I suppose I ought to take care of this immediately. No sense in letting it linger, however much I deplore arresting a colleague. And there's all the other arrangements to make, too, the go-ahead to send to Admiral Greenly … Forgive me, all of you, if I hurry off. I'll see you later. This is a day of great achievements.'

Before quitting the room, however, the All-Father paused a moment to stand by Wick. 'Congratulations also on your rapid recovery, acolyte,' he added, patting the lad good-naturedly on the shoulder. 'A fine day on all counts.'

With that, he bustled out of the office, leaving the Envoy and his two co-conspirators gazing at each other across the hardwood desk.

'I'm impressed, too,' drawled Gowron, his eyes lingering curiously on Wick. 'Healing from an accident in the Veil is no mean feat. May I ask if there is some form of — ah — enhancement?'

Wick turned aside from his scrutiny, mumbling an incoherent reply.

'Wick's good health, however pleased we are to witness it, is not the issue here,' Lace reminded them dryly. 'I have some business for us to attend to while our Saint is occupied by his witch hunt. I summoned you back to Argos for a higher purpose, Gowron, if you recall. The Sap is finally moving in our favour. The time has come to rid ourselves of our greatest enemy.'

He waited for the announcement to sink in, then continued, lowering his voice. 'The time has come to move against Matrya. My Masters have already mounted a successful assault against our adversary in the Veil: it remains for us to destroy her physical form. I believe I have found the location of her birth-body. It was not hard to discover, once I had the right source material.'

He retrieved a wad of bark-paper covered in neat notes and calculations from an inner pocket of his waistcoat, smoothing the sheet out on the table. 'What lies at these coordinates is less certain. There will most probably be a sealed chamber, deep within the Tree, and there may also be secondary safeguards, locks or traps protecting the body.'

'Where is it?' asked Wick, swallowing nervously. 'Where is the —' he pulled one of the papers towards him, squinting at the transcription of what looked like poetry — '*the heart of the world, where East meets West?* What does that even mean, sir?'

'Nothing.' The Envoy shrugged. 'The coordinates were embedded in a set of nonsense verses. That they have remained hidden thus far is due to the shocking incompetence of the Council, rather than any effort on the part of our enemies. The cache won't be anywhere near the real heart of the world — that's deep in the World Tree's trunk and would take weeks to reach on foot, even if a tunnel could be found to take you there. My guess, according to these coordinates, is that Matrya's body lies at the base of the Tree, beneath the southern reaches of the Gap. Of course, the canopies merge below the clouds and it's all one trunk. East certainly does meet west in that sense. But the verses are without import. It's the numbers we need to remember.'

'Why did the Ancients write down the coordinates of the body in the first place, even in code form?' asked Wick. 'Wouldn't it be safer not to mention it at all, if they wanted to keep it a secret?'

The question was a reasonable one, as far as he could tell, but it seemed to rankle Lace. The Envoy glanced sharply up at him, a glint of suspicion in his eye, and did not immediately respond. Wick was left with the uncomfortable sense of having brought up an issue his master did not wish to discuss, yet again. Or perhaps Lace had not considered the problem in that light, and disliked being shown up. Wick never found out which, for at that point Gowron brushed aside the remark with one of his own.

'So we'll be able to cross the Storm safely, using this steam-driven machine from Cherk?' he enquired of the Envoy.

'Absolutely,' Lace replied. 'They are useful devices. Fallow was far too eager to destroy the first one we had.'

The eyeholes burned in Wick's mask as he listened to his companions. He was not overly concerned that his question had not been answered; his main aim in asking it had only been to appear intelligent, and engaged in the conversation. But the mention of

Galliano's air-chariot conjured up painful memories. He recalled how he had watched Tymon's humiliation on the knot outside the old man's workshop, the night the first machine was destroyed, and thought with a pang of his schoolfellow's adventuresome spirit, the foolish plan to cross the Storm. Nothing was ever simple, Wick ruminated. He had given up much to be where he was now, at the hub of power in the seminary. He quashed the troublesome memories with another, hurried query.

'What's it like in the World Below?' he gabbled to Lace. 'What's beneath the Tree? Are your Masters there?' Too late, he remembered this was another subject to avoid. The Envoy hated it when a human being mentioned his Masters.

The blood rushed to his face beneath the mask, causing the invisible scars to prickle; although he was not overly eager to depart on this mission to assassinate the Oracle of Nur, that journey paled in comparison with an encounter with the shadowy Powers he knew were directing the Envoy. He had been schooled enough to realise it was the Masters whom he should hold in awe and dread, and conversely anticipate meeting in the course of his career, as the key to his own success.

The Envoy fixed him with his steady, empty gaze, but did not lambaste him for his temerity. 'My Masters are in the Veil,' he answered shortly. 'For the time being, you will remain in this world, and travel to an ancient city named Kand, the ruins of which lie at the base of the Tree. There won't be much of it left by now. I expect you'll only see a pile of rubble, if that. It depends on the location of Matrya's body.'

'You mean …' Wick gaped, as realisation sank in. 'You're not coming with us, sir? Weren't you going to …?'

There was absolutely no change in the Envoy's

expression as his acolyte trailed off. 'No, I won't be with you,' he said. 'Other matters require my attention. I must make sure the Nurian Grafters are in no way able to See or impede our operations, among other things. I will be dealing with the eastern front.'

'Do you require regular progress reports?' Gowron asked.

'No ordinary missives will be necessary. We must conduct our affairs in the utmost secrecy, my friends. Rest assured, I will check on your progress with the *orah*-clock when my other duties permit.' Lace gave a small, frosty smile. 'And my Masters are taking a personal interest in your mission. I have little doubt they will also be overseeing your endeavours: I suggest you perform adequately.'

There was a pause as both acolytes mulled over this last chilling piece of information.

'Regarding the Freeholders' machine,' persisted Gowron, after a moment. 'Are you certain it can hold up to the winds? Half the Explorer ships that attempted this voyage were ripped to shreds under the Storm.'

'Even then, a century ago, some were not, though the winds were stronger,' replied Lace. 'Ah, the whole affair has been long forgotten — you Argosians are so good at forgetting. You'll have no trouble crossing the Storm in the air-chariot. We can't use it openly, of course: I've had it transferred to another location outside Argos city. You'll go from there.'

'And once we break into the chamber? Do you wish to have the body destroyed in any particular way?' Gowron enquired coolly.

Wick stared at him, aghast. But Lace remained unperturbed.

'Just kill her,' he said with a dismissive flick of his fingers. 'She won't be able to stop you. But there are dangerous artefacts — remnants of the Old Ones' sorcery, if you will — that have been sealed up with her. If you find anything in the chamber, in or around the body, you must bring it straight to me.'

His tone was careless as he said this, but there was no mistaking the greedy edge to his smile, which he turned on Wick at that moment. 'I warn you, do not seek to use or even handle anything you find for too long,' he added softly. 'It may be lethal to humans.'

'It's these Jays I don't understand,' Fallow complained, later on that evening, when the Saint and his Envoy walked together after dinner, down the candlelit corridors of the seminary. 'What's this ridiculous snippet of news I hear from Marak city? A group of jokers caught disseminating rebel tracts to the population? What are Argosian Jays doing in the colonies, anyway?'

It had been a satisfactory day on all accounts for Fallow. The business of apprehending Rede had been carried out and the traitor's links with Nurian rebels announced by crier in the city, as well as discussed at great length among the worthies of Argos seminary. The colonial professor had never been liked; he was the perfect whipping boy for all who wished to show themselves loyal to Saint and state. Rede provided, furthermore, the long-awaited excuse to go to war with the Nurian Freeholds. That was, indeed, where his main usefulness lay, and the reason Lace had offered up evidence of his trumped-up crimes to Fallow.

The Envoy threw his companion a shrewd, sidelong glance at the mention of the Jays. The presence of the performers in Marak city was indeed a perplexing question, one that had been niggling at Lace ever since the news had arrived by bird that afternoon, hot on Gowron's heels. It seemed that a group of Jays had been caught distributing rebel literature in the colony, as well as associating with the natives. They had been summarily arrested by the Marak authorities, who did not credit the incident with much importance, inserting it as a footnote in a long missive asking for more money. Lace had not expected Fallow to pick up on the true significance of the story, although it foreshadowed worrisome changes. A group of Jays found in the Domains, far from their normal air-routes, was simply an oddity. The fact that they had been associating of their own free will with the local population and distributing 'literature', on the other hand, was potentially disastrous.

But one glance of quick assessment reassured him that the Saint had mentioned the matter only as an afterthought. Fallow had merely been struck by the absurdity of it all, and had not realised it was precisely these ridiculous, unheard-of associations they had most to fear from, in the long run. Eventually, such floutings of convention would bring down the power of the seminary. Not yet, but soon enough. There was a ways to go before that happened, Lace thought to himself grimly: a century or two of meat left to gnaw on the old priests' bones. His task was to maintain the status quo at all costs, and bolster his own influence. When the seminary was of no further use to him, he would move on.

'Oh, I expect it's part of the blast-poison affair,' he told the Saint dismissively. 'They'll be messengers of some kind, pawns of Rede's, perhaps. In any case, the network is dead now that its head has been cut off. We needn't worry about the Jays.'

'Good,' said Fallow, satisfied as usual with the explanation that required the minimum effort. 'I was beginning to dread a colonial production of "The Seeker of Saman", with a Nurry slut singing soprano.'

He rolled his eyes as the Envoy gazed at him in blank incomprehension. 'The story you mentioned in the archives, remember?' he prompted.

Lace still did not react.

'Juno and Lyla. It's been made into an operetta, didn't you know?' resumed Fallow, exasperated. 'You really should get out more, my friend. It's all work, work, work with you, Lace: enjoy yourself a little!'

After receiving that piece of hackneyed advice, the Envoy took a rather stiff leave of Fallow, pleading fatigue, and fled the company of the All-Father. Lace may have been pulling the strings on his puppet Saint, but he occasionally balked at the hollow company he was obliged to keep. He stalked back along the corridors of the seminary to his own modest sleeping quarters, an acolyte's garret equipped with nothing but a single bed, and locked the door behind him, breathing a sigh of relief in the narrow peacefulness of his chamber.

It was just then, of course, that the leash from the Veil yanked tight once more, calling him home.

There was hardly a moment of the day or night that Lace did not feel the link to his Masters, the twining connection that pulled like a chain about his neck. He was tied to them, and they could call him imperiously into the prison world whenever they willed. They would be wanting to hear his plans for the Nurian Grafters, he knew, as well as news of the expedition below the Storm. They did not really need him to return to the Veil right now, but obliged him to make his reports in person, in order to press home a point. They were waiting for him to grovel to them, as usual. They loved to bring him to heel. Well, he thought, he might have to play the part of the cringing cur, but he stole meat from his Masters' table, when they had their backs turned.

He quelled his irritation and lay down on the bed, allowing his construct-body to fall into a stupor. This physical simulacrum he had put together with Wick's help lacked permanence, but was simpler to use than a human body. Once he ceased to hold himself to it, the headless Beast-that-was-Lace stepped out of his physical casing as easily as from a garment. Despite the Masters' yanking chain, Eblas stopped to bend a moment over the construct, snuffling at it with invisible nostrils.

Prisoners from the Veil could not normally access the material realm, and it had taken the combined power of the Masters to send the Envoy into the world, even as a half-real wraith. The scraps of physicality he possessed were unstable and had to be continually shored up, replacements scavenged from elsewhere. The current construct was growing frayed, decaying at the edges, and would have to be renewed before the acolytes left for the World Below. With that thought in mind, Eblas raised a barbed claw and rent open a passage to the Veil above the body, leaping through the fissure onto the icy surface of the prison world. He wished to be done with his report as quickly as possible, and return to complete his preparations. Behind him, the gaping tear between the dimensions slowly meshed shut.

The bird-kings were waiting for him. They sat in a hulking ring on the ice, almost as he had left them, vast winged shapes blotting out the stars. But although their invisible leash on him tightened, the Masters gave no immediate sign of noticing their servant's presence. Eblas wondered a moment, incredulously, whether they had fallen asleep on the spot after their last encounter, for their shapes seemed to have solidified, settling into black ice, their heavy-lidded eyes no more than gleaming slits in their heads. Then he realised they were preoccupied, not asleep, engaged in the unseen battle against Matrya from which he had been summarily excluded. They had probably trapped the Oracle's trance-form in a folding corner of the Veil dimension, a prison within the prison, assailing her spirit with their combined forces.

Such tactics could not keep a Being such as she confined forever, of course: the attack would only distract her long enough for the acolytes to reach her body. And that, Eblas swore, would be his victory alone. Although he needed them to fight their common enemy, the Masters would be required to loosen his leash when he retrieved the World Key. He crouched quiescent, a black lump on the floor of the Veil, outlined in faint starlight. It was a long, chilly wait before one of the bird-shapes stirred and blinked to life, shaking off glittering crystals of ice.

'Eblas,' whispered the imprisoned Born, in acknowledgment of him.

The Beast-that-was-Lace bowed, throwing itself down on its belly to make its obeisance. There would be time enough to work out personal plans of ascendency. For now, Eblas needed the Masters' help to combat Matrya, and he needed them strong.

Two days later, after an emergency court hearing in the temple Hall, Father Rede was pronounced guilty of treason and sentenced to hang by the neck on the city docks, as an example to all. Wick found himself on the crowded quays again, witnessing his second public execution in less than a month — his third, if he counted the sentence carried out on Pallas, in secret, in the seminary dungeons.

The thought of that dark tryst caused him to shiver with a combination of remembered ecstasy and self-disgust, and he wrapped his cloak tighter about him as he stood with the rest of the townsfolk in the chill morning fog. But it was not the cold that made him pull the seminary's green cloth protectively tight. He was, perhaps, a little too ready to see another man die, a little too hot and eager beneath the folds of his cloak. The Explorer mask kept him well hidden, veiling his conflicted emotions as well as his scars. The people on each side of him were oblivious to both his shame and excitement, craning their necks to catch a glimpse of the tiny figure on the execution quay.

Wick eyed his companions with contempt. They had no idea, he thought. They were unaware of what he could do, how intensely he could feel, the heights he could reach. For he was one of the elite who had learned the real secret of existence. He knew, despite the last rites delivered publicly to the condemned prisoner before the rope was placed about his neck, that there was no chastisement in another life, no Hell awaiting sinners after death. Heaven was right here, right now, in the sliver of *orah* about his neck.

And so was Hell. For he sensed he had grown dependent on that borrowed power, yearning day by day to revel in it again. But Lace would not allow it. He was not ready for a second dose of the Sap, his master had told him, rather coldly, following the debacle on the night before the Kion's execution. He had permitted himself to be carried away then, it was true, forgetting to shut down the connection to Pallas. The Nurian lad had lingered on in a reduced state for hours; Wick could not think of the transgression without a flush of embarrassment. He had let himself go — he had made a fool of himself. But he knew better now, and would never waste that precious rush again. Perhaps he was being sent away on this long and arduous trek beneath the Storm as punishment, he thought gloomily. He was not allowed to taste the Sap again until he had carried out his task. He was, moreover, to answer to Gowron on the journey, for Lace had placed that lowborn murderer in charge of their mission, a decision that enraged Wick. His master, he reflected bitterly, did nothing but hold him back.

The acolyte shuddered slightly as he watched the tiny figure of Rede twisting round and round on the rope beneath the execution quay. The condemned man had stopped kicking some time ago; there was only an involuntary jerk of his left heel visible now and then, to indicate the proximity of death. Wick wondered, in passing, why the Saint had not chosen this far more efficient method for the Kion's execution. Why had she been thrown alive into the Void, like the saints from the old stories, instead of being dispatched before the eyes of the crowd? But no one thought to consult Wick about such things. Neither the priests at the seminary, nor his own family, nor the Envoy had ever truly valued his judgment, he thought bitterly. His master stymied him at every turn.

He longed for a chance to make his mark, to answer to no one but himself. One day, he would show them all what he could do, he reflected. One day, through the power of the *orah*, he would come into his own. He dreamed of the Sap flowing through his limbs as he watched the demise of his half-remembered professor, caring nothing for the life that ended there beneath the quays. He could never have imagined the last image flickering through the mind of the dying man as he swayed in the breeze, never guessed at the remembered conversation with the heretic in the prison cell.

Rede died thinking of tiny blue flowers in the courtyard of an eastern city, far away.

The traitor's demise had ushered in a new epoch in

Argos city, or so the Saint claimed in his triumphant speech to those gathered on the air-harbour that day. The court had examined definitive proof of Rede's involvement with the Lantrians, yes, but also and by the same token established Lantria's involvement with Nurian rebels. This network of treachery included the Freeholders, who provided raw spice-fuel to the South even as Rede had provided information. All were conspiring together against the Mother Canopy; the enemies of Argos were linked in a foul web that extended from Cherk Harbour to Marak, Farhang and beyond.

It was time, Fallow declared, from his special podium — raised for the occasion of Samiha's execution and never demolished — to rid the Tree of this spreading disease. There would be an Eastern Crusade, he announced to the madly cheering crowd. An ultimatum had already been sent to the Freeholds: Argos would no longer tolerate such insults to its sovereignty. The Saint offered the people florid promises to 'cleanse the nests of rebellion and heresy with the fire of Truth'. The Nurians had lost their chance at repentance, he said: now, they would experience God's righteous wrath. The crowd cheered, and cheered again.

In the hours following this rousing speech, as celebrations occasioned by Fallow's announcement swept through the streets of Argos city, Gowron and Wick set sail from the air-harbour in a small farmer's dirigible requiring no crew but themselves. The official reason for their departure was to search for their absent fellow, the mysteriously vanished Jed. The foreign acolyte had disappeared during his retreat, it was said, feared to be lost in a snowstorm. His ostensible rescuers carried limited provisions and were due back in a fortnight if they found no trace of their companion.

The guards on the quays watched their departure with idle eyes. While their vessel was still visible from the air-harbour, Gowron took care to steer them westwards, over the Chasm. But once they were hidden by an outcrop in the leaf-forests, he turned the flat-bottomed barge to the south and east again.

The Freeholders' machine, recently embargoed from Cherk Harbour, had been transported to a military cache an hour's journey away. It sat draped in tarpaulin in the recesses of a wide Tree-cave, a natural hangar in the trunk five miles south of Argos city and some five hundred feet below, in the lower limits of the inhabitable canopy. There were no roads or terraced farms nearby and the face of the trunk stretched unbroken as far as the eye could see, a blank wall lost in mist. Gowron tethered the farmer's barge at the entrance to the cave and spent the rest of the afternoon exploring the workings of the air-chariot, filling it with the barrels of Treespice for fuel, and starting and stopping the propellers with a thud-thud-thud that tore open the foggy silence periodically. He wasted no words on Wick, who sat with his back against the bark wall of the cavity, watching him glumly.

Far from the theatre of his dreams on the docks that morning, the younger acolyte was in an execrable mood. It irked him to miss the city-wide celebrations of the crusade back in Argos: it would have been the first time he could have actually enjoyed his new face, and mingled in desirable company while wearing the mask. He had not bothered to don the artefact for the purposes of this journey, for there was no point in wasting it on Gowron. Besides, though he did not want to admit it to himself, the mask stung his skin when he wore it too long. He glowered at his fellow traveller through savage, red-rimmed eyes. But the Envoy's orders had been absolute: there was no time to waste.

They were to leave at once to retrieve the machine, and must depart no later than the following morning for the Storm. Their work, Lace had assured them, was more important than the launching of any crusade, though Wick was beginning to have his doubts on that score.

He was even beginning to doubt the Envoy's curses. When he had dared ask his master in private, before they embarked, whether the promised chastisement of Jedda and Tymon had been carried out, Lace had rounded on him with a snarl. The fulfilment of that promise depended entirely on how he completed this assignment, he had snapped. Kill the Oracle, retrieve any artefacts and bring them directly home, and his enemies would suffer the sweet humiliation he desired. Fail, and that reward would be withdrawn.

It was all the more irksome to Wick, in the circumstances, to witness how the Envoy lavished favours on Gowron. Lace had gone so far as to entrust the former criminal with a special, secret item to aid them in their endeavours. Gowron refused to reveal the contents of the small leather-bound package he kept with him at all times, in an interior pocket of his jacket. Wick burned with curiosity to know what it contained, but his companion never took off the jacket, not even to sleep. As evening approached and the temperature dropped in the cave, the youth bestirred himself with a martyr's sigh and began establishing their camp for the night. He pitched a tent at the back of the cavity and gathered a pile of loose bark shards to light a fire. When darkness made further navigational experiments impossible, Gowron returned to squat beside him at the flames, rubbing the palms of his hands together against the cold. He seemed brutishly satisfied with his exertions, so much so that he actually initiated a conversation with Wick.

'Ready to see Hell in the morning?' he grinned, with a too-familiar wink.

'As ready as I'll ever be,' replied Wick guardedly. He could not understand what the Envoy saw in this mindless thug: servicing a machine was certainly all Gowron would ever be good for.

'You should be happy,' remarked the older man. 'We have the chance of a lifetime here to advance our careers.'

Wick shrugged. 'If you call advancement to risk our necks,' he grumbled.

'What, don't you want to stick the Nurry Oracle, and see her silenced for good?' asked Gowron, still leering at Wick with his abominable familiarity.

The youth drew himself up, on his dignity. He was a gentleman's son, after all; the seminary may have blurred social boundaries, but did not banish them entirely. 'It's an assassin's job,' he said. 'I'd rather fight out in the open, like a man, and score a victory against the Nurry Grafters.'

'Child's play,' answered his companion. 'Nonsense. A diversion.'

'But that's what our master is doing,' protested Wick.

'Our master would much rather be here with us. Oh yes,' he continued, as Wick stared at him askance, 'we've got the sweet job, despite appearances. He always said he wanted to be the one to deal with the Oracle. And now he sends us off on our own. Doesn't it occur to you to ask why?'

'He said —' Wick began.

'Oh yes, I know, I know, busy, he has other things to do!' sneered Gowron.

He leaned towards the boy, his eyes lit by the crackling flames. 'I heard them talking, when they thought they were alone last night,' he whispered huskily. 'Him and the Saint. There's something buried in the chamber along with the body. It's called the World Key. I don't know what it is, but I know Fallow's keen on getting it. But the one who's really desperate is Lace. I could hear it in his voice. I've known our Envoy for many years, and very few things make him that desperate, I promise you. If he wants this Key so badly, you can be sure the Masters want it too.'

He fell silent, staring into the fire. Wick did not reply at once. It appeared the brute had some brains after all; the younger acolyte was torn between the desire to know more and the paranoia instilled by years of life at the seminary, compounded by an all too personal appreciation of Lace's methods. The Envoy could very well be watching them right now, with the aid of the *orah*-clock. This might be a test of loyalty.

'If he wants it so much, why doesn't he go after it himself?' he said to Gowron, after a moment.

'Aha.' The other gave his unpleasant leer. 'That's the bottom line, isn't it? I think he's out of favour. He's been told off. His Masters decided we should be the ones to do this — he didn't make that decision. They don't trust him. They want us to bring them this Key. All that nonsense Lace was spouting about not touching the things we find and taking any swag straight back to him ... Whatever the Key does, I can assure you it won't be lethal to humans.'

He said no more, refusing to advance any theory as to what the Key might be. But it seemed obvious enough to Wick that night, bedded down beside his unwanted companion, that if they truly wished to advance their careers, only one course of action remained to them.

The World Key, if they were lucky enough to obtain it, should never be returned to Lace at all. They should go over his head and take their prize to the Masters themselves, entering the Veil. The prospect caused

Wick's heart to beat wildly with fearful anticipation. For his insights did not end there. It was evident that he, Wick, should be the one to personally contact the Masters. He saw no pressing reason, stretched out beside the objectionably snoring Gowron, absolutely no reason at all why he should share credit for the discovery of such a treasure with anyone else. Once they had found the Oracle's body and fulfilled their mission, he would be far better off on his own. His fellow acolyte, if he were truly intelligent, would have come to a similar conclusion.

And with that thought, Wick found himself unable to sleep properly for the rest of the night. For now, he knew, he would have to fear for his life at the hands of Gowron.

10

Tymon followed the ghostly figure down the passage, his pain and doubt forgotten. He felt instinctively that the vision of Samiha was showing him the way out of the mine. He only desired one thing: to approach her, to see her, to speak with her again. A voice in his head warned him that that was more than one thing; in fact it was three. He ignored it. He hurried after his love, hoping against hope that she would wait for him.

But she did not. No matter how quickly he stumbled along on the uneven floor of the tunnel, she was always too fast for him. Over and over again, he thought he had almost reached her, only to find that she had walked swiftly into the gloom ahead. At last her form dwindled to a white speck and winked out. He struggled on in the dark, stubborn, desperate, until a sound penetrated his dulled ears. Zero gasped from far behind that they needed to rest at some point, and that Dawn was awake, asking for him.

It was hard for Tymon to delay the pursuit even for a short while, though he felt ashamed at having ignored the others' needs in his haste. He reluctantly agreed to a halt, and felt his way back along the narrow passage, down the line of travellers, until he came to Dawn's bier. He had to bend down close to hear her talk: her voice had grown extremely weak.

'Is *Ama* with you?' she whispered.

Her words caused him to wonder gloomily how his teacher was faring. He could not offer Dawn the comfort of speaking with the Oracle, now.

'I'm sorry,' he said. 'I haven't heard from her in a while.'

'No matter.' Dawn sighed. 'I worry for you, mostly. Do you know where you are going, *Syon*?'

'Don't worry about that,' he answered. 'We're getting out of here, all of us. I had another vision.'

'I believe,' she murmured. 'I believe you will take Saffid to safety. But I worry for you. Where are you going?'

Tymon winced in the gloom, aware that the sick woman was fading fast; she was beginning to repeat herself, her faculties waning. She would not last much longer, it was clear. A dangerously sweet smell, the forerunner of decay, arose from her body.

'We're all going together,' he replied gently. 'We're getting out, like I said.'

'No,' she insisted. 'No, you cannot get out. You're cold, too cold.'

He said no more, but took her icy hands in his and chafed them, full of pity, until she slipped away again into sleep. Then he returned to the head of the procession, restlessly awaiting the moment of departure. After a while, he could bear it no longer and begged his companions to rise, to make one final effort. He had become obsessed with the notion that they must find a way out of the mine before evening, though he could not tell whether the sensation was due to the vision of Samiha or some other, separate intuition. He seemed to hear a call, pulling him onwards. The workers did not argue with him, but bestirred themselves at his insistence. Though tired, they were still willing to accept his judgment. He could not help speculating as to how long it would last — how many hours of weary stumbling would eventually cause their faith in their 'Lord' to falter.

The by-way Samiha had taken was nothing like the tunnels Tymon had glimpsed at the start of their journey, lacking the smooth and serviceable layout of the passages at the core-mining level. This was an older tunnel by far, perhaps a natural, or semi-natural fissure in the Tree. The walls were rough and the floor given to sudden descents like oversized steps. The fugitives were obliged to creep forward at a snail's pace to avoid colliding with each other in the pitch dark. The Saffid began to sing again, softly, as if to alert each other to the distance between them. Despite his earlier impatience, Tymon was grateful for his companions' presence, especially since the vision of Samiha did not revisit him, leaving him forlorn in the darkness. His notion of time was reduced to the interval between the singers' breaths. He had no way of knowing how long they had been walking, only that the breaths had become numberless.

When the change came, he could hardly believe it, blinking as the gloom of the tunnel turned first to grey, then red. Only when the Saffid broke off their crooning song and called hoarsely to each other did he realise this was no further vision, but reality. The tunnel was coming to an end. The glowing reddish point of light remained static and docile as they approached, and the air was sweet against their faces. The passage widened, its roof opening out into a chimney, and the exit revealed a slit of glowing sky.

The evening seemed as bright as a conflagration to the exhausted people emerging from the mine. An awed hush fell over the members of the group as they walked out of the tunnel; they found themselves standing on a broad ledge extending out of a wall of bark. They had reached the main trunk, after all. It was backwards-leaning and broken at this point, scored with innumerable shelves and outcroppings like wandering roads. Before them lay a vast well of cloud, possibly an arm of the Eastern Gap itself. Long ribbons of mist trailed in thin wisps up the trunk-face and between outflung limbs of the Tree, beneath which the travellers could dimly make out layers of increasing density and blankets of ever thicker cloud. They were barely fifty feet above the topmost layers of the Storm, and must have been facing southeast, for the sun was setting behind them and to the right, the sky a riot of crimson and purple.

Tymon sank down to his knees on the ledge, the burst of energy that had sustained him thus far dissipating. Instead of the moment of triumph, of relief and gratitude he had expected to feel when they escaped the mine, he was utterly depleted and oddly discontented. The wide expanse of empty sky lay boundless before him, but he sensed himself to be imprisoned by that limitless horizon. He also felt dangerously exposed on the ledge, and shivered in the misty air. But the sensation that troubled him most, the thought he could not articulate to any of the others, was that by stepping out of the tunnels he had given up the chance of Seeing Samiha again. He felt instinctively that he was unlikely to witness the vision here, in the wide-open, outside world. He could not even fully admit to himself that he regretted leaving the mine for this reason — that he would have continued walking, stumbling through the darkness, just for the sake of that glimmering possibility ahead.

'She's gone, Lord,' observed Zero, squatting down beside him on the ledge. 'Dawn didn't make it.'

The words shook Tymon out of his reverie. In spite of his yearning for the vision, he knew where his current duty lay, felt keenly his responsibility to the

Saffid. He glanced over his shoulder at the body of the woman on the bier. He did not weep over Dawn's loss, for the moment: he was too tired, too anxious about where he would lead his charges in the trackless wilds of the canopy. The mineworkers did not loudly mourn their kinswoman, either, but sat beside her in silence, with their heads bowed. They had placed Dawn's body outside the tunnel, a little ways along the ledge, as if to give the corpse one last taste of sunlight and fresh air before she faced her funeral rites and plunged below the clouds — down, down, down. Somehow, Samiha had survived that same fall, Tymon thought distractedly. And now she had appeared to him, saved him from the mine. What did it all mean?

'She died happy,' Zero declared, as Tymon stared dismally at the bier. The Marak lad was optimistic even in the face of oblivion. 'Dawn always knew you'd get us out, Lord. Your spirits are powerful.'

Tymon found nothing to say to this. His aches and pains had returned tenfold since leaving the tunnels, and he shifted his shoulders uncomfortably under his coat. 'I suppose we ought to … I suppose we should find a place to camp …' he mumbled, squinting at the ledge that wandered down the Tree-face.

It looked navigable enough, eventually joining a projection as wide as a road in the trunk. But it was clear everyone needed a rest after their ordeals: they would travel no further that night.

Just as he spoke to Zero, however, another sound caused them both to glance up — first at the jumbled, broken wall of the trunk behind them, then again at the blood-red clouds. It was a noise that caused Tymon's pulse to quicken, a sound like the beating of a thousand hammers. His searching eyes spotted a black speck on the eastern horizon, gliding low over a rack of cloud. For an instant, he panicked. The dark shape conjured up the spectre of the Envoy's birds. What if the accursed flock had returned to plague him, now that he was in the open air? How would he be able to combat them in his present state of exhaustion? But the din that accompanied the approaching speck was familiar, and most welcome. It was the chop of an air-chariot's propellers.

'What is it?' breathed Zero, shrinking back against the trunk-face. 'What bird makes a sound like that? Is it evil?'

Tymon smiled at the Marak boy, his heart suddenly warmed. 'The priests in Argos always said so,' he replied. 'But it's only a sort of dirigible. These are my friends I told you about, who have created mechanical birds to help them travel fast.'

There was indeed something bird-like about the machine flying towards them. This air-chariot, evidently one of those newly built in Farhang, was different from the others Tymon had known, equipped with rigid wings that extended from its body and a propeller mounted on its nose. The Nurians must have journeyed through the night in order to reach him at this vital juncture. The coincidence was not lost on Tymon: Noni would be with the rescue mission, he knew, tracking him through the Grafting. But as he squinted at the bulbously avian shape of the air-chariot, his dismay returned. There was only one machine, after all. Had Oren not been able to send more, as he had promised? He stared at the lone transport, speechless with disappointment.

It was Zero who grasped the urgency of their predicament. 'Come on, everyone!' he called to the mineworkers, as they stood peering warily up at the noisy mechanical bird. 'It's the Freeholders! We have to signal them!'

He was right, Tymon realised. If they did not draw the attention of those in the air-chariot, it might fly over and miss them in the failing light, despite all of Noni's insights. Something in Zero's voice, a note of giddy hope perhaps, roused the refugees to one final effort. They stood up and spread out in single file along the ledge, shouting and waving their arms at the machine. Some took off their dusty slaves' tunics — a pale, pilgrim grey beneath the reddish wood dust — and flourished them in the air like ragged flags. There was a moment of anxiety as the air-chariot passed over, and disappeared above the leaf-forests. Then, the hammering grew louder and it reappeared, circling to the south. The fugitives cheered madly and waved their arms as the machine descended.

It bounced to a halt on the road-like plateau about forty feet below them, at the very brink of the Storm. As the propellers slowed and stopped, two figures jumped out of the hatch to salute the escapees from the mine. Tymon recognised Noni as she unwound the long travel garment covering her from head to foot. His companions lost no time in slipping and stumbling down the upper ledge to the point where it joined the plateau; Tymon followed more slowly, unable to walk without Zero's assistance. Behind him, the last two Saffid bore Dawn on her bier.

Noni caught up with Tymon before he stepped off the ledge, embracing him tightly. He could not remain unhappy for long in the face of that reunion: he found himself overcome by a delayed rush of emotion, wanting to weep because of Dawn, and Nightside, and everything that had happened, and simultaneously overcome with relief. Noni's gaze immediately took in his exhaustion, the blood seeping through the cloth of his tunic and the dead woman on the bier behind him. She relieved Zero of his duties, supporting Tymon as he hobbled towards the air-chariot. Her associate, a Farhang soldier Tymon did not know, was already distributing food and blankets to the rest of the party. The Freeholders had come well prepared.

'Don't worry that there's only one machine, for now,' Noni told Tymon as she helped him sit down just inside the air-chariot's hatch. 'We have three more scouting the surrounding area. I had a vision of your escape, but wasn't sure exactly where you'd come out. The other pilots will find us over the next day or so. We should head north, towards the Spur of Sails — that's the meeting point. I'm willing to bet this big ledge we're on will take us right there. Anyone who's wounded can travel on the *Dev*.' She scrutinised him, worried. 'Maybe you should,' she suggested.

Tymon nodded again, grateful that she had guessed his concerns and laid them to rest without him having to articulate a word. 'It was a disaster back at the mine,' he said. 'We were the lucky ones. According to my friend Zero — the grinning fellow over there — we lost maybe five of the Cherk group in total. Dawn and Nightside among them. A few others joined us who aren't Saffid. That's all we were able to get out, I'm afraid.'

'I think you've done tremendously.' She was looking at him with frank admiration. 'In my last Reading I Saw you battle the Envoy's curses. We should have warned you better — we were distracted by other matters. You've done remarkably well, all the same.'

'I did something else which you may not be so happy about.' He took a deep breath; there was no way he could avoid telling Noni about his vision. 'I Saw the Kion again, Noni, in the mine,' he said. 'She helped me. She led us all on the right path. Without her, we wouldn't be here.'

The Nurian girl's smile faded. She did not respond immediately, but rose and busied herself about the air-chariot, fetching him a blanket and a spare packet of food.

'I'm not going to pretend I'm happy about this,' she answered at length, when she had wrapped the covering about his shoulders. 'But you are here, it's true. We'll talk about how and why tomorrow. You should eat now, and get some sleep.'

He pushed away the piece of cheese and flatbread she offered him. 'You can't just dismiss this, Noni,' he objected. 'It's important. I think I understand, now. Samiha's out there, somewhere, still alive. Why else would she communicate with me? It's a Sending — it must be. She's probably hurt, and calling out to me in a trance.'

He spoke loudly, ignoring the people sitting on the bark close by, who glanced at him curiously.

'Hush,' murmured Noni. 'It's a Sending, yes. I promise we'll go into this in more depth tomorrow. Please don't mention the subject in public, Tymon. No one knows about the Kion but you and the Focals, and it should stay that way.'

'I don't see why,' he said.

But he allowed Noni to bully him into eating the bread and fruit, and accepted lying on a blanket on the floor of the air-chariot while she eased off the blood-encrusted tunic. She bit off a cry of outrage when she saw the wounds inflicted by the flogging, and the newer damage from his altercation with the mine-guards. For a long while, all she would utter was a venomous diatribe against tyrants and slavers from all Four Canopies, as she dressed his injuries with the familiar Nurian healing salve. When she had finished, she made Tymon sit up and wrapped him about the middle in a long bandage. At that point, he took the opportunity to broach the subject of Samiha again.

'When I had that vision of the Kion, I felt that I could do anything,' he said. 'I forgot I was hurt.' He fixed Noni with an earnest stare. 'It was as though I

239

were the one who had died and been brought to life again. I have to know what's happened to her and why she's trying to reach me. I have to, Noni.'

She pushed him firmly down on the blanket, pulling another cover over him. 'I understand,' she answered carefully. 'You love her.' But her gaze was troubled as she bent over him.

He could not long resist his fatigue, however hard he tried, and although he attempted to focus on Noni, her form grew blurred. 'Samiha's out there, somewhere,' he whispered. 'And I'm going to find her.'

And with that, he promptly lost consciousness, slipping into a much-needed slumber.

It was the dreamless sleep of healing, deep and complete. But just as he was beginning to resurface from the necessary oblivion, swimming towards the morning light like a tadpole in a Tree-pool, a brief vision came to him of the Oracle. He Saw his teacher as she had been in his Readings long ago, a mature woman dressed in robes of starry black. She was standing in a dark place, surrounded by a nimbus of light, and she was under attack: the shadows about her spawned monsters, clawed and feathered horrors that harried and raked her with their talons. Tymon was reminded not only of his own experiences with the Envoy's curses but also of Jedda's, glimpsed briefly in his last vision with the Focals. The shadows that attacked the Oracle were larger than the Envoy's constructs, made of voluminous shadow rather than decaying matter, but just as vicious. They harassed the Oracle relentlessly, bursting out of the darkness to swoop down on her face. She fought them off with a beam of searing light she wielded in her right hand, cutting them down again and again, though there were always more. Her left hand she held behind her, as if she hid something from the creatures.

The dream ended as Tymon blinked awake in his cocoon-like blankets. He had no doubt the vision was real and important, though there was something refractive about it, like a vista glimpsed through rain. He knew enough about the Sight now to realise that all visions were not equal. Some, especially those in his dreams, spoke to him obliquely, in symbols and metaphors. Not everything was as it seemed in the vision, though the basic fact that his teacher was under attack was in no doubt. He made up his mind to discuss the matter again with Noni, as soon as he arose.

Despite the sense of urgency in the dream, however, he lay an instant cradled in the grateful warmth that follows deep slumber, unwilling to rise. The sun was already high in the sky and streamed through the air-chariot's open hatch. Then a shudder passed through the floor of the machine, and the propellers began to thud.

'No!' cried Tymon, in sudden alarm.

He scrambled out of his nest of blankets, cursing as the movement wrenched his muscles, seized by the fear that the air-chariot was already whisking him away on its trip north. He did not want to go north. He had been overcome, as he lay in his bed, by the abrupt and complete conviction that Samiha had appeared in the mine precisely because he had been close to her there. He could only think that she was trapped somewhere deep inside the Tree, perhaps injured, perhaps lying helpless in a crevice. All other matters receded to the background, even his dream of the Oracle. He did not stop to consider that the mine in the South Canopy was far from the place where Samiha had actually fallen into the West Chasm, near Argos city. The answer to his problems seemed obvious in the morning sunlight. He must return to the mine and find her.

He rose and lurched past the surprised Farhang soldier at the machine's controls, almost throwing himself out of the hatch. He was wearing nothing on his chest but his bandages; the cold morning air took his breath away as he tumbled on the bark.

'What's wrong?' Noni was beside him in a flash, helping him up. 'What's happening, Tymon?'

The young man belatedly noticed one of the Saffid youths peering out from under the air-chariot, his curious face smudged with soot, and the camp paraphernalia still spread out over the bark ledge and glittering in the sunlight. It had only been a test run of the propellers, after all.

'I thought we were leaving,' he answered, apologetic. 'I'm not going north with you, Noni. I know what I have to do, now.'

'Which is?'

As there was evidently no emergency, Noni's reaction to this announcement was dry, her voice crisp. She surveyed him with her hands placed on her hips. She looked tired, he thought ruefully. He noticed the tents planted about the bark plateau and the remains of a cooking fire in the camp. She must have been working half the night, doing everything possible to make the fugitives feel comfortable; she would not appreciate what he was about to say. He was going to pass responsibility for the Saffid on to her.

'I have to go back into the mine and search for Samiha,' he answered, in a rush.

'Oh, for the love of the Tree.'

Noni reacted with more anger, or perhaps disappointment than he had anticipated, striding off to the edge of the plateau, her expression as grim as the Storm itself. The other people in the camp glanced up as she passed, surprised. Tymon began to follow her but thought better of it, grabbing his blanket from the machine before joining her on the ledge overlooking the clouds.

He was glad of the good shillee's wool against the chill wind that blew out of the Gap, as he peered into Noni's scowling face. She reminded him briefly of Samiha, then, as his love had been when he first met her in Argos city. There was some resemblance between the two girls after all — particularly when they were angry with him. But Noni had grown in the past few months, her frame solid and sensible compared with Samiha's thin, almost transparent form.

'I know you don't approve,' he began carefully, 'and that you think Samiha's life shouldn't be tampered with, because she's a Born —'

'It's not what I approve of that matters,' broke in Noni, lowering her voice so that they would not be overheard. 'It's just that we've been through all this before. Doesn't it seem rather familiar to you?' She gazed at him unhappily. 'How many times are you going to rush off to rescue the Kion? You did it once already, and it didn't work.'

It was Tymon's turn to feel annoyed. He had put up with this sort of needling from the woman he loved, but was beginning to tire of it from other quarters.

'Samiha was actually very grateful that I came to Argos,' he said, a little huffily. 'She called me her Witness. I don't know what that means, but I'm damned if I'm going to walk away from this. What do you expect from me? That I pass up the chance to help her, if she's alive? What kind of gutless coward do you think I am?'

'I don't say pass it up,' replied Noni. 'I say, be wise. Let's do this together. Come home: let the Focals guide you. The result will be to your advantage, I assure you.'

He shook his head. 'It would take too long. The trek to the Spur of Sails and then the trip to Farhang — days. What if she's in trouble and needs me now? She's down there, in the heart of the Tree, I know it. I have to go to her. You'll be fine to bring the others home without me.'

'Will we be fine?' she echoed, bitter. 'Does it ever occur to you that people might need you for tasks that aren't quite so glorious? It's not just getting the mineworkers to their new home. It's afterwards. Helping them settle. Defending them. The Focal group will always be incomplete without you, Tymon. We need our Fifth. There, I've said it. But you don't care about that. It's boring. You take what you need from us, food and medicine and transport, then you're off again to be a hero.'

'It's not like that,' he protested.

'There was something heroic to be done, actually,' she continued, her voice trembling with emotion. 'We were supposed to begin training young Grafters again. The best defence is offence. That's what the Oracle wanted you to do next; we were going to raise a mighty call in the world of the Sap and draw all those with the Sight to Farhang, for training. We can't do it properly without you. We need our Fifth.'

'I didn't know,' he said.

Then, he remembered that he had. The Oracle had mentioned the idea already in Chal, telling him that they would return to the Freehold and 'tackle the Envoy' together. She had furthermore cautioned them all on the subject of the defenceless Grafters during the conversation in the trance; the image of Jedda fighting off the abominable birds, alone and unaided, returned fleetingly to Tymon. He thrust it away, impatient. It was Samiha who needed him now.

'I'll be back as soon as I can,' he promised Noni. 'I see why you need my help. In the meantime, it's not as though you're completely alone —'

But she was already stamping off towards the

air-chariot, furious. She began to wrathfully pack up the camping equipment, slapping blankets together and shoving pots in bags as if they had committed some outrage against her. He watched her a moment, wondering at her continued refusal to help Samiha; the thought that she might be jealous crossed his mind. He could not remain angry with her after her last plea, however, and soon pursued her with the aim of making peace. As he did so, he found Zero plucking at his elbow, pulling him aside.

'We've been talking, Lord,' he said. 'Me and the others from the mine.'

'I'm not your Lord,' sighed Tymon, his eyes still on Noni.

'We want to say thanks for what you did. You stuck by us in Chal. You warned us. You did everything you could —'

'Of course I did!' interrupted Tymon, with an edge of impatience, turning to Zero. 'I couldn't just leave my friends there to die, could I? And some of you did die, in spite of everything,' he added, his heart softening at the sight of the Marak lad's wide, earnest countenance. 'So I let you down. I just wish Dawn and Nightside could be here.'

He picked out the Saffid woman's bier, lying beyond the air-chariot at the edge of the plateau. The body had been dressed for the inevitable funeral, wrapped in a spare cloak and bound with strips of flexible bark to the bier. Zero's gaze followed his.

'We're going to say the last goodbye to her soon,' resumed the Marak lad quietly. 'Like I say: because of everything you've done, we want it to be you. We want you to sing the Song of the Dead.'

'What?' Tymon blinked at his companion in confusion, the request finally sinking in. 'But it's women who always sing the Song. In Argos and in Nur.'

'We,' said Zero, nodding towards the other Saffid — the tribesmen had been staring at the two of them for a while, Tymon realised with a shiver — 'want you to sing it this time, with the girl from the Freehold.'

They would not be gainsaid. Once provisions for the journey had been divided up between those who were walking to the Spur of Sails, and the rest of the camping gear packed away in the air-chariot, the Saffid gathered around Noni and petitioned her in their own language. She did not make much of an objection, or indeed speak more than three words altogether to them. Tymon barely had the time to fetch himself a spare tunic from the air-chariot's stores and splash some cold water from a gourd over his face, before he was invited to stand by the bier, alongside the taciturn Noni. The Saffid watched him expectantly. This was indeed all he had left to give Dawn, he realised. He had not been able to do more for her.

He cleared his throat, and began haltingly to sing the words of the liturgy he had always heard, but never uttered. He sang in Argosian while Noni answered him in Nurian. As he did so, he remembered Nightside together with Dawn, the absence of one wrapped up in the fragile presence of the other. Despite their faults, he thought, they had been two of the most extraordinary people he had ever met. They had led lives of unmitigated disaster, and still managed to keep their faith. They had spread hope where there was none, created trust where there was nothing left to believe in but belief itself. He admired that capacity, even if he questioned its aims; he did not think he possessed the same strength.

After the Song was done, and he and Noni had moved a respectful distance from the body, two of Dawn's tribesmen lifted up the bier. It was light: Dawn's thin corpse was no burden at all. They slung her off the plateau and into the void beyond without difficulty, where she disappeared in an instant, erased by cloud. But the recollection of the Saffid girl and all she had suffered lingered in Tymon's mind.

'Why do they get sick?' he whispered to Noni, when the rest of the group had shuffled to the brink to peer after their lost companion. He asked her about the Saffid because he hardly dared speak to her of anything else; her mouth was still set with disapproval. 'Do the Focals believe in this curse nonsense too? Is it something like the Envoy's birds?'

'There are really no such things as curses,' Noni responded in a flat voice. 'Or magic. Sorcery, science, even the Grafting: it's all the same thing by different names, which is knowledge, arrived at by various means. We don't know what really happened to the Saffid, but my guess is that their ancestors ran afoul of a rogue Born. Those like the Masters had the power to afflict people over generations, twisting something inside them so they couldn't have healthy children. It's the power to make and unmake, and yes, in that sense it's like the birds. Have you ever wondered where we come from, Tymon, or why we resemble the Born to a degree?'

He shook his head. Noni almost resembled one of the Born herself, he thought; she had Ashekiel's implacable conviction.

'The old gods had human faces.' Her expression as she turned towards him now was no longer scowling, only sad. 'But it would be more accurate to say that we were made in their image, the image of the Born. Long ago. Our creators weren't perfect. Those who were truly good taught us the Grafting, so we could know and worship something better than themselves.'

Tymon frowned at the backs of the Saffid, gathered together in a knot and blinking down into the cloudy well after Dawn. He wanted to ask Noni why it was necessary to worship anything at all, why human beings could not learn to think independently, instead of blindly obeying some higher power, even the Sap. Samiha had never asked for his obeisance, Born or not. Suddenly, in the midst of his ruminations, he realised the Saffid had all turned to face him again. They shuffled towards him as one, silent as ever. Even those who were not members of the tribe, the ordinary Nurians or Lantrians, hung eagerly at the edges of the crowd, their eyes devouring him. It was a look he knew all too well, smacking of Dawn's fervent belief.

'Yes?' he asked them, wary.

'Lord,' began one of the youths, speaking for the group. Tymon recognised one of the boys he had first approached in the mine. 'We know you cannot stay with us. We know you have to go.'

'You do?' he mumbled, then remembered that he had made no effort to keep his announcement that morning a secret.

'We Saffid believe in you, Lord. You will return and cure us one day. We believe in prophecy.'

'Ah,' he answered miserably.

'Maybe it takes years. But we have faith.'

'The Sap help me,' he muttered under his breath.

'In meantime, we swear fealty.' The youth stepped forward, his eyes bright with gratitude. 'Hail, Lord. We are yours.'

He knelt on the bark before Tymon and, to his deep embarrassment, kissed the hem of his tunic.

'Hail, hail.'

The whisper went through the group like wind. One by one, the Saffid bowed and pledged their allegiance to him. Some touched Tymon's hand or his clothes, and some, to his horror, stretched themselves out on the bark to kiss his feet. He knew very well that he had done nothing so great that it might deserve adulation, and tried to remonstrate with them and pull them up, but they refused to listen. The fact that he was about to abandon them and resume his search for Samiha made the experience that much more unbearable. Through it all, Noni stood wordless at his side, neither participating in nor condemning the ritual. He grew hot in the face, and quite irritated with her when she did nothing to help him.

'Why do you put up with it?' he burst out in a loud whisper, when they had both retreated to the air-chariot to make their final preparations for departure. 'They shouldn't be treating me like this! Why do you let them?'

She appeared to have decided to accept, or at least tolerate, his decision to leave. She calmly handed him one of the Freeholders' small backpacks containing food rations and a blanket. 'You tried to stop them and couldn't,' she observed. 'What makes you think I'd have better luck? When people are determined in their prejudices, there is nothing one can do.'

He was annoyed by the inference that he was being as stubborn as the Saffid. 'You could tell them I'm just an ordinary Grafter like you!' he pointed out. 'We make predictions — that's what we do! I mean, if you want to train up a whole army of us, we can't be so unusual, right?'

'The Saffid wouldn't listen. It's not just the predictions. They believe you're special, more so than an ordinary Grafter. They need someone to follow and revere: it helps them carry on. They've had hard lives, as you've noticed.'

Tymon checked through the contents of the pack, snorting with irritation. He was thinking of the Saint's abominable posturing in Argos city. 'They shouldn't be following an ordinary person like this,' he said. 'They should learn to think for themselves.'

She pursed her lips. 'As you're doing right now.'

'What's that supposed to mean?' he asked, eyeing her.

'You know very well. Are you sure you're thinking for yourself, in deciding to go to the mine?'

'What else could I possibly be doing?'

She shrugged. 'A vision is a very personal revelation. So is a Sending. Do you know where yours came from, exactly? Are you sure they're legitimate messages?'

'I don't believe this!' His voice had risen with indignation; he lowered it, glancing over his shoulder at the open hatch. 'You're still questioning my vision of Samiha? Even when it led us out of the mine?'

'Yes.'

'What exactly do you think happened? That I hallucinated from fatigue, got lucky and somehow managed to miraculously choose the right passage out of a thousand?'

'I don't know,' she said. 'I'd know more if you consented to come back to the Freehold, and let the Focal group Read you.'

'Oh no, not that again,' he retorted in disgust. 'No thanks. I'd rather take a chance on my heart. It's pretty clear to me you lot Read what you want to Read.'

Even as he uttered the ugly words, he was suffused with shame. She looked so distressed that he regretted the outburst immediately.

'Is that really what you think of us?' she said with an expression of dismay.

But even though he had only spoken out of frustration, he could not bring himself to apologise. 'I just wish you'd have some faith in me,' he grumbled. 'I wish you'd give me your blessing, for once. It's like struggling against the wind, the whole time.'

'We have faith in you as a person. But you want more. You want the Focals to agree unreservedly with every choice you make. We can't do that.'

'Fine,' he snapped back in mounting fury. 'Don't.'

'Fine,' she repeated, as angry as he was now. 'Just so we understand each other.'

They finished their preparations in dismal, furious silence. It was a sour note to end on after the serenity of Dawn's funeral and the Saffids' displays of devotion, however misguided. Tymon felt wretched, but could not bring himself to try to make amends to Noni a second time. Less than a quarter of an hour later, he was bidding farewell to the mineworkers, wishing them fair weather for their journey to the Spur, and from there on to the Freehold.

The skies over the Gap looked set to grant his request. Although the wind was sharp, the late morning sun warmed his shoulders through the copious Farhang travelling cloak, and the blue immensity above was unbroken. There had been no sign of the dreaded birds since he exited the mine, and he was beginning to think that he had chased them away for good. Even the pain in his muscles had subsided to a dull and manageable ache. All would have been quite satisfactory, indeed, had it not been for the unhappiness he saw stamped on Noni's face. He told himself he could do nothing about that, and extended his hand to her in a last stiff courtesy before leaving. She shook it wordlessly.

It was with deep regret that he turned his back on her and trudged towards the ledge that led up to the tunnel. As he set foot on the narrow pathway, however, he realised that he was not alone. Zero had followed him.

'What is it, my friend?' he asked the lumbering young man.

When he had tried to say goodbye earlier, Zero had simply hung his head and refused to speak. He now looked sidelong at Tymon, like a child who catches an adult in a foolish act. 'You forgot,' he said, reproachful.

'Forgot what, Zero?'

'Forgot to ask me to come with you. So I'm reminding you.' The Marak lad stuck his chin out stubbornly. Tymon noted with relief that he did not call him 'Lord'.

'I promise you, Zero, you don't want to come with me,' he assured his friend. 'I'm going back into the mine. Into the dark.'

'I know. I'm not stupid. I got all the right stuff, torches and everything.' Zero indicated his own travel pack. 'You're the stupid one. You forgot to ask.'

Tymon stared at him in surprise. 'Alright,' he admitted. 'I might be the stupid one. Do you really want to do this?'

Zero rolled his eyes, as if he had enquired whether the sky was blue. 'You're doing it, aren't you?' he pointed out. 'We evil folks should help each other.'

Tymon nodded dazedly. How could one disagree with such striking logic? He continued up the ledge towards the fissure, followed by his friend. Below them, the others watched and waved. When he glanced down one last time before plunging into the tunnel, he could no longer spot Noni's red head among those in the group. She had already climbed into the machine and was lost from view.

It was then, too late, that he remembered his dream of the Oracle; he had never told Noni about it. But would she have listened? It seemed he always spent half his time arguing with his fellow Grafters. Maybe, he told himself sadly, he was better off on his own. He turned his back on the outside world and walked into the darkness of the mine.

Over that day and the night that followed, as celebrations for the Saint's Eastern Crusade took over Argos city, the temperature in the Central Canopy plummeted. The shift in weather was abrupt and cold, and frost descended like an icy shroud over the leaf-forests. A thick coat of white covered the leaves and twigs, causing bark to crack and split in the moonlight, and a white pall crept over the roads and terraces of the town, appearing in a brittle bloom on the rooftops.

The late-night revellers still celebrating in the streets hastened indoors, their eyebrows dusted with particles of frost. It was the most dramatic cold snap in living memory; people said the Tree itself was preparing for war.

The change caused a great deal of anxiety for the crew of the military vessel *Stormbringer*, already five days out of Argos city when the cold snap hit and about to enter the permanently frozen Upper Fringes. The dirigible had been dispatched in haste before Rede's arrest, the last of over fifty ships carrying troops to Marak city. The Saint, buoyed by the successes of his southern campaign, had decided to take his war games a step further. The Eastern Crusade had been planned long before Fallow's rousing announcement to the citizens of Argus, of course, and the bulk of the fleet already moved into position for a conflict weeks in the making. But the *Stormbringer* was also a messenger ship, bearing an edict from the Saint ordering Admiral Greenly to begin a wave of attacks against Nurian targets. It took a shortened route across the Tree in order to reach the Domains in time for the first planned offensive.

The Upper Passage was a secret held tightly by the Argosian military, for though the way through the canopy's icy crown was fraught with dangers, it more than halved the travelling time to Marak. In favourable weather, the *Stormbringer* could make the trip to the Domains as fast as a messenger bird, in about nine days. Favourable weather, however, was key. Sudden storms were known to bedevil the summit of the Tree, maelstroms of wind and hail no dirigible could survive. The sailors on the army vessel noted the frost on that fifth night with dread, fearing a return of the snowstorms that had battered the Central Canopy after the Kion's execution.

Their fears proved unfounded. By the next morning the clouds had lifted and the voyage through the snowy branches took place in brilliant sunlight. But even if the wind did not threaten, the ice did. The frozen twigs were laced with hanging icicles that sometimes reached the size of a man; they sparkled in the sunshine above the ship and could be deadly to the ether sacks. Apart from the occasional far-off crashes of loose ice, therefore, the silence on board the *Stormbringer* was complete. All on board watched anxiously as the captain steered the vessel through the treacherous forest of vertical blades. The sailors seemed equally frozen at their posts, hardly daring to carry out the tasks required to keep the ship on course, wheezing painfully in the thin air; the environment at the crown of the Tree was hostile to most life, the branches frostbitten and as shorn of their leaves as the Eastern Canopy. No one breathed, no one moved, as the ship slid through the white silence.

After the initial moments of awe at the sight of the ice-fields, the young soldiers travelling on the ship were sent below deck and issued with strict orders to remain there, for fear their noise might dislodge the deadly blades. They spent the time drinking barley-beer and throwing dice. The Saint's recruits were young and poor in the main, second sons without prospects at home, who had signed up for a military life in quest of regular food and pay. Such troops would have been sent in former times to man the colonial outposts; now, they were being sent to destroy the Freeholds.

It was a job that excited rather than perturbed the

young sons of Argus. Many had greeted the official announcement of the crusade with a rousing cheer, and an impromptu rendition of 'The Merry Bells'. Most agreed that this was a chance to prove their very recent entry into manhood and only a few seemed less than enthusiastic about being sent into active service before their training was complete.

But one of the soldiers did not sing at all, apparently caring little for his manhood. Bolas had received his conscription papers long before Rede's arrest, finding himself summoned to present himself at the *Stormbringer* within the hour, on pain of court martial. He had barely been given the time to bid farewell to his anguished family and friends, taking leave of the weeping Nell on the quays. His shocked sisters and his grief-stricken mother had bewailed this sudden turn of events, incomprehensible to them. But Bolas knew very well why he was being sent to the Eastern Canopy. He knew that in spite of Tymon's attempts to save him, his jail sentence in Argos city had merely been commuted, not revoked. He was paying the price now for all his childish delusions of free thought, and for having helped his friend. Fallow had waited patiently to exact his revenge, sending Bolas to serve in a war that filled him with dismay.

PART TWO
BELOW

And Saint Usala answered, 'This I believe.
The End is within. The Beginning is always.
We call up Jury, Judge and Witness,
And play executioner to ourselves.'

— Saint Usala the Green,
chapter nine, closing stanza

II

Wick hated flying. His first hour in the Freeholders' machine was spent crouched miserably on one of the passenger benches, bracing himself against the shuddering wall and wondering if he were going to vomit. He eyed Gowron at the controls with envy. His companion had the instincts of a born pilot, and sent the ugly vessel soaring out of the Tree-cave and up above the frost-bound leaves without a qualm. Gowron was endlessly impressed by the air-chariot's speed, remarking on the fact to Wick with wearying regularity over the course of their journey. At this rate, they would pass Ethis the next day, he announced triumphantly. The Saint was a fool to suppress this invention, according to Gowron: it would cost him his hold on power.

Wick could not have cared less about the Saint's power at this juncture. He attempted to ignore Gowron and kept his nose near the open window. The cold wind alleviated his nausea. They followed the instructions given them by their master before leaving Argos city, travelling south in a wide arc about the circumference of the trunk in order to avoid the inhospitably cold regions at the summit of the canopy. He wondered gloomily how his queasy stomach would fare once they began to negotiate the turbulence of the Gap.

It was past noon when he first glimpsed the specks wheeling over a hole in the canopy, slightly north and east of their route. Carrion birds, hundreds of them, circled in a funnel shape over some quarry on the branches below. Wick blinked at them, his nausea forgotten for a moment in his fascination. Then he straightened, gripping the edge of the window with whitened fingers.

'Turn left!' he cried to Gowron over the din of the propellers. 'You have to turn left! Now!'

'What are you talking about?' The other scowled at him over his shoulder. 'That'll take us back north!'

Wick quelled his unease as best he could, lurching up from the bench to join Gowron by the controls. 'Just a short distance,' he said, indicating the wheeling specks through the front viewport of the machine. 'I want to take a closer look at those birds. It'll hardly cost us any time, not at this speed.'

'The birds?' Gowron shouted back in surprise. 'Why?'

'They're curse constructs.' Wick only hesitated a moment before answering. 'The master and I — we sent them after Tymon and Jedda. I want to know which of the two they've found.'

'Are you sure they're not ordinary birds?'

'They're mine,' muttered Wick. He gave an involuntary shiver. 'I can feel it.'

The sensation was almost worse than the flight nausea: an uncomfortable slicing in the gut, as if he were being heaved out of himself, his innards stretched taut towards the creatures circling over the canopy. He leaned against the wall of the machine, clutching his stomach. His discomfort increased as Gowron steered the air-chariot towards the birds. His fellow acolyte laughed knowingly at his predicament.

'What does it feel like to be a pregnant woman?'

Gowron mocked. 'Chin up, darling. The worst will be over soon. I used to give birth to the master's babies, too. Just breathe and release.'

'Shut up,' groaned Wick. 'You're not helping.'

'Breathe and release,' chuckled his companion. 'Lie back and think of Argos.'

'Go to Hell!'

'Oh, we are, I assure you.'

They spiralled down over the hole in the canopy, descending into the well between the branches. As the machine approached, the birds separated and scattered, passing the air-chariot in a blizzard of flapping black, and Wick began to breathe more easily. By the time Gowron brought them down with by-now effortless skill on the back of a horizontal limb, the last of the curses had disappeared and the air-sick acolyte was able to disembark rather shakily from the machine, staggering through the ice and slush alongside his companion. They walked a short distance down the road that followed the crest of the branch, making for the bloodied human form they had spotted a few hundred yards away, huddled under a piece of canvas. Before they reached it, however, Wick stopped and withdrew the Envoy's mask from his cloak pocket, placing it over his face. Whichever of his two former associates lay sprawled there on the bark, he felt unable to confront such incursions from the past without the protective illusion of normalcy. Gowron raised a wry eyebrow at his action, but mercifully made no further comment.

The curses had found Jedda. She lay face down and unconscious in the slush, pecked raw by the attacking birds and half-rolled up in a canvas cover of the sort farmers used to protect vine-stumps from the frost. She had succumbed at last to exhaustion, it seemed, harried to breaking point by the creatures. This was how the 'constructs' wore down their intended targets, pursuing their quarry until fatigue and exposure did their worst. Although the cuts inflicted were not deep, infection, and most of all injury to the eyes, would eventually cause death to the victim. Jedda would probably not have survived had the attack not been interrupted. As it was, she was still alive, her breath a slight shudder between her shredded shoulder blades. Wick stood a moment over the torn body of the girl who had rejected him, feeling the thud of triumph in his veins.

'Happy now?' asked Gowron laconically.

'She betrayed me,' said Wick.

'I would have used her a little differently to get my own back,' yawned Gowron. He rubbed his arms; the weather was cold, despite the sunlight. 'But there's no accounting for tastes. Have you seen enough? Shall we go?'

When his fellow acolyte did not answer, he stamped his feet in the slush and turned away.

'Wait.' Wick frowned down at Jedda. 'You say you've done this before …'

'What, wasted time? Yes, ever since I met you,' snapped Gowron.

'No, I mean: given birth.' Wick winced. The sensation of movement beneath the mask was odd, as if the artefact had bound with and frozen the muscles in his face. 'How long do they last?' he continued. 'The curses, I mean? How long can we expect them to track her down?'

'Between the phases of a single moon, generally. After one cycle, they lose cohesion.'

'We sent them out about two and a half weeks ago,' mused Wick. 'So we have just under a fortnight left.'

'Left?' asked Gowron. 'For what?'

'To play with.' A slow smile spread over Wick's perfect features. Surely his master would not begrudge him this opportunity, even if he were spying on them with the *orah*-clock. And if Gowron was right, and Lace had been sidelined from involvement in their expedition, he might not be watching them at all.

Gowron glowered at him. 'What in hell are you talking about?'

Wick grinned. 'You said yourself you'd use her differently,' he said. 'So let's make this more interesting. Let's take her with us, and have some games. We can always turn her out again in a few days and watch her die.'

Her life, Jedda thought, had grown thunderous. The surface beneath her lifted and jerked, and there was a continual sound like the beating of a hammer or thresher in her ears. Death would have been a blessed silence in comparison with this reminder that she was still alive. It was deafening. She wished she could die.

As she struggled with consciousness, she found herself piecing together what had happened, sorting out the pieces of recent memory, though she yearned to simply let go of them and slip away. She had spent the past two weeks on the run, travelling mostly by night, stealing food from the farms and holdings she passed in order to survive. At first the desire for stolen *orah*-energy had been overwhelming, the lack of it a grinding misery. But as the days passed the sensation had ebbed and become less troublesome. Simple survival, and most of all the need to escape the Envoy's curses, had preoccupied her. She had lived from moment to moment and shelter to shelter, always harried by the infernal birds, unable to snatch more than an hour of broken sleep at a time or a mouthful of raw root to stave off hunger. On the few occasions she had found a secure bolt-hole to spend the night in — a dry rain-well, a rundown shed with a door that locked from the inside, a derelict bird-keep — she passed out for long periods, losing hours, perhaps days to oblivion. Time became warped in its passage. And even space seemed now to have left its normal parameters behind. Where in the Tree was she? And what was this unbearable pounding noise about her head? She had emerged from a period of forgiving blankness, but her final memory was not of finding refuge. She must have lost consciousness, she thought, during the last attack of the birds.

The curses had assailed her again while she was trying to cross a stretch of exposed road. It had been a savage onslaught, worse than the previous ones. She had tried to use a piece of canvas salvaged from a vine-field to protect herself, unable to fight off the curses any longer with rolls of parchment. And then — what? She must have fainted from pain and fatigue; the birds would have had her at their mercy. But that particular doom had been replaced by another, deafening one. Her eyes blinked open, wandered over the curved ceiling of a structure shuddering with the noise. She was lying on the floor of a vehicle. Her skin was covered in lesions, crawling with the bloody memory of beak and claw. Abruptly, she identified the thudding noise coming from above. The Freeholders' machine! She struggled up to a sitting position, almost shouting aloud with joy. She was safe!

But the hope that had flared briefly in her heart was snuffed out as her eyes focused on the figure before her, seated on one of the air-chariot's benches.

'How are you feeling, Jedda?' asked Wick solicitously.

She gazed at him in speechless dismay. The acolyte's words were as smooth as his face, but something hateful juddered beneath them, like the noise of the engine, causing her to shrink back. So this was the machine that had accompanied her on her first voyage to Argos city, the *Lyla*. And this was the boy she had watched suck the life out of Pallas, as if her countryman were a tender morsel to be feasted upon rather than a human being. She wanted to scream at Wick that she felt awful, thank you, and that his presence did nothing to improve matters, but a glance at who was manning the air-chariot's controls caused the retort to die on her lips. The sight of Gowron's familiar form dredged up a rush of unpleasant memories. The older acolyte seemed to feel her horrified gaze on him, for he glanced around, leering at her.

'Welcome back to the world of the living, doll,' he said. 'Lucky for you we dropped by, eh?'

She did not answer, not trusting herself to speak to Gowron just yet. These two would not have rescued her from the birds out of any humane motivation, she knew. The realisation that they could now be taking her straight back to Lace, after all she had endured, caused her heart to quail. Painfully, she manoeuvred her aching limbs up from the floor. The skin of her face, neck and hands was raw, scored by cruel marks. None of the wounds on its own was particularly deep or dangerous, but the sum total was torture. She installed herself gingerly on the bench opposite Wick.

'Are you taking me back to the seminary?' she asked the young acolyte.

'Oh no,' he assured her. 'The master's pretty angry with you — as you can probably guess.' He watched her intently as she shivered with pain and fatigue under her torn clothes. When she said nothing, he pressed on. 'He's the one who sent the birds, you know,' he added, with smug commiseration. 'If we go back he'll have you thrown in prison. Or worse.'

He waited again for a response, but Jedda still did not react, unable to summon up the right words in her fatigue. Wick cleared his throat and assumed an air of indifference. 'I was annoyed with you too, at first,' he said. 'But I figure you have to make your own choices. I don't believe in forcing people into anything.'

Gowron snorted with disbelieving laughter at this, as if Wick had said something particularly funny; the older acolyte even threw a wink at Jedda from his post at the controls, though he said no more.

Jedda remarked an involuntary spasm in Wick's expression. For a second time, it was as though something rippled beneath his skin, an unspoken intention. Now it betrayed irritation at his companion, rather than a hateful gloating over herself. There was more here than met the eye, she thought. The acolytes might be plotting some more personal revenge against her, perhaps as a prelude to delivering her to the Envoy; she could imagine, given Gowron's wink, what that revenge might entail.

'I don't think,' Wick continued, his tone hardening as he glared at Gowron, 'that it's right to make people do things they're not comfortable with.'

In spite of everything she had endured, Jedda was able to distinguish the note of jealousy that had crept into his voice. Was it possible that the two acolytes were in some form of competition with each other? It looked as if they had different opinions regarding her, a fact she might use to her advantage.

'That's very generous,' she said to Wick, carefully, when Gowron did not deign to make a reply, turning back to his controls. 'I'm in your debt.'

'I'm not someone,' Wick said with airy condescension, 'who imposes myself on other people. You should know that by now, Jedda.'

She did not say a word in answer to this. The statement was untrue, of course, and there was a smoothness in Wick's expression that she mistrusted instinctively. She had seen exactly how eager he had been to impose himself on Pallas. But she knew that salvation lay in diplomacy.

'Thank you both,' she said, deliberately including Gowron in the conversation. 'Those accursed birds have been following me for days. Longer, actually — weeks. You're very kind to risk the master's wrath for me.' There was nothing for it, she told herself, but to play the damsel in distress. 'I wouldn't have survived without you.'

'I warned you about him, if you recall,' sniggered Gowron. 'Mild as milk when he's happy, hard as nails when he's not. You got on his bad side.' He grinned over his shoulder at her again. 'Not something I recommend, sweetheart.'

'We're on a mission out east,' put in Wick. 'Well, south first, then east. We're travelling by the Fringes: the war's going well in Lantria, there's no danger from that point of view. You can come with us, if you like. We have no further quarrel with you.'

He picked up a map from the floor by Gowron's feet and busily perused it, as if he were the navigator on this expedition. But after a moment of squinting at the wriggling, concentric lines of Tree topography, he looked away, his expression queasy. He was air-sick, Jedda realised with faint amusement, through her own discomfort.

'To be honest, you don't have much choice,' he resumed, thrusting the map away from him impatiently. 'The curses will last another week, and they travel about as fast as we do. You won't be able to keep them off on your own, not in your condition.'

Jedda hunched her shoulders inside her torn clothes, feeling the pages of Samiha's testament crackling in the lining, and conscious of Wick's burning gaze. It had been the papers that had kept her alive in the cold, laid against her heart; they had also protected her against the birds when she lost consciousness, she was sure of it. Neither Wick nor Gowron appeared to have noticed the scraps stuffed into the lining of her undergarments. Or if they had, they thought them of no consequence, for none had been removed from her, as far as she could tell. Now the pages offered her protection of another sort, a private barrier against Wick's ogling. She crossed her arms over her breasts. She had a hard time concealing the loathing she felt towards the smiling acolyte, and did not immediately respond.

'Well, what do you say?' he prompted, spreading his hands expansively, a gesture of forgiveness that reminded her unpleasantly of Lace. 'I'm happy to let bygones be bygones, Jedda.'

Reluctant as she was to admit it, his assessment was entirely correct. She had no choice. She nodded in mute agreement, willing herself not to hiss out her hatred, determined to hide just how much pain she was in.

'Do you happen to have any healing ointment on board?' she asked after a moment, with as much nonchalance as she could muster.

They made their camp that night inside a shallow crater they found at the summit of a vertical branch, dead and lopped off at the crown. Jedda helped Wick clear the floor of the hollow and light a fire of bark shards, then crouched beside the two acolytes as evening fell, holding her hands close over the crackling flames. Warmth was a luxury she had not known since she left Varana's band. During the journey she had accepted food, medicine and a fresh set of outer clothing from Wick, who treated her with scrupulous if condescending courtesy. He had also offered her a new set of winter underclothes which she refused, reluctant to give up the ones lined with the testament. He had taken her reluctance to disrobe for modesty, and laughed. She made no effort to disabuse him, and kept the precious pages out of sight, next to her skin. They felt almost one with her now, a secret double hide.

Though she trembled with weariness, she knew she must not sleep that evening before scoring whatever advantage she could from Wick. She had not yet pinpointed the unease she sensed when speaking to him, nor the vulnerability she felt in him as he maintained their patter of conversation, but she knew that her survival depended on winning him to her side. She remained seated with him at the fire after they had eaten their meal, eyeing Gowron warily. The older man, she knew from unhappy experience, would not be so amenable to her. But to her relief, the ex-priest left her in peace that night, ignoring both of his fellow travellers in favour of a gourd of Nurian *kush*. It was not long before he was nodding in front of the fire.

'You say you're going east,' Jedda whispered to Wick, when Gowron rose to relieve himself a short way off, humming drunkenly. 'I wanted to know if you're crossing the Gap. I realise now that I don't belong here, in Argos. There's no point in pretending. I can't go back to the Freeholds, but I could start a new life somewhere else — a garrison town, maybe.'

Wick gazed at her fixedly in the firelight, smiling his infuriating smile. It was almost a perfect half-moon, she thought, obnoxious in its symmetry. 'Oh, we're not crossing the Gap, Jedda,' he said. 'We're going into it.'

'What?' she blurted, taken aback.

'Into it, under it, what you will.' He still smiled.

'You're going to the World Below?' asked Jedda in astonishment. 'In this machine? Why?'

'I can't tell you that. You're not an acolyte any more,' he answered with abominable smugness.

She scowled at her chapped knuckles, covered in the seminary's healing balm. The Envoy's willingness to engage in heretical activity ought not to surprise her, she thought. She had learned during her tenure at the seminary that the defunct Council had already sent Explorers to investigate the World Below, bringing back artefacts like the *orah*-clock that served the Dean so well. Their findings had been kept secret, ostensibly to protect the ordinary population.

She tried to remember what the Envoy had told her about the ancient civilisation that had once flourished beneath the Storm. Contrary to the seminary's more widely accepted teachings, it was loam, not the fiery Maelstrom of Hell, that lay at the foot of the Tree. There, the Old Ones, both human and Born, had long ago built great cities, all supported by loam. Jedda found the thought intriguing. What held up the loam? In any case, the cities had been destroyed millennia ago, razed by a war that shook the foundations of the world. In her imagination there was nothing left about the roots of the Tree but a pile of broken and blasted shards. There was only one reason to go to such a place.

'So,' she said to Wick, 'are there other artefacts of the Old Ones Lace wants to get his hands on, then?'

Wick did not answer, but simply gazed at her. Even when he pursed his lips with that knowing expression, she thought, he was still damnably smiling.

'Fine, don't tell me,' she muttered. 'I guess I'll see for myself.'

Gowron had not yet returned after completing his bodily functions. Jedda saw Wick's eyes flicker towards his fellow acolyte, staggering uncertainly with his legs apart on the far side of the hollow. The night sky was clear and the waning moon filtered feebly through the ice-bound leaves, casting strange geometrical shadows about them. As light and darkness passed across his face, the younger man appeared to come to some personal decision. He leaned close to Jedda, speaking with syrupy familiarity in her ear.

'I can't tell you about our mission, but I can do something else,' he said. 'Once we're done, I can drop you off in the Eastern Domains. Where exactly do you need to go?'

Jedda searched Wick's face, wondering if she could trust that smooth, bland expression. His eyes were rimmed with shifting dark in the firelight. 'Anywhere within a half-day's journey of the Central Canopy,' she said.

'No problem,' he replied. 'But you have to do something for me, first.'

'What?' she muttered, the many things he could ask her to do for him flitting in an unpleasant sequence through her head.

Wick did not answer that question at once, his smile disappearing into shadow. Instead, he reached out and almost dreamily traced the hollow at the base of her neck with his finger, just above the tunic collar. 'You've lost it,' he remarked.

It was a moment before she realised he was referring to the *orah*-pendant. 'Yes,' she said, too rapidly perhaps. But Gowron had turned back towards them now, reeling. 'It's gone. What do you want me to do?'

Wick sighed and withdrew his hand. 'The master didn't only send the birds after you, Jedda,' he admitted. 'Tymon's life is in danger, too. I regret that.' His smile had grown bitter as he surveyed Jedda, but there was an eagerness in his tone. 'You're still twined with him, right? From before?'

She was beginning to guess what he would ask her to do. A shiver of combined hope and fear passed through her. She nodded.

'In that case,' Wick breathed as Gowron stumbled nearer, 'I want you to tell me if you feel him. Tymon was sent to one of those big southern plantations where they use pilgrim labour. We'll be close enough for you to sense him. The curses won't take much longer to reach him: he'll be doomed, as you were. Together, we can help him.'

His words were urgent, hurried, their conversation brought to an abrupt end by Gowron slumping heavily down by the fire. Wick froze into silence as the other man gave a loud and unapologetic belch; he evidently did not wish to elaborate on his plans in his fellow acolyte's hearing. A short while later, he bid the others goodnight and withdrew discreetly to the sleeping tent. Jedda took the opportunity to excuse herself at the same time, fleeing Gowron's company to pass the night wrapped in blankets on the floor of the machine.

Although she surreptitiously barricaded the hatch from the inside with one of the provision packs, no one troubled her. Instead, her own preoccupations kept her awake for some time afterwards. Her heart quickened at the thought of finally finding and helping Tymon, even in these unlikely circumstances. But would she simply succeed in bringing down further troubles on his head? And were the acolytes actually going to *Lacuna*? How odd it was, she thought, that the place should come back to haunt her, now, after all these years.

For it was not only the Argosian priests who retained knowledge of a destination beneath the Storm. The mention of Wick's mission brought back painful memories for Jedda. Her father had often spoken of the second canopy beneath the clouds; it had been one of his favourite fantastical stories, the ones he told in the old days, before disaster struck their family. She remembered well the stories of the *abjat* philosophers, divine mathematicians who knew the true coordinates of Heaven and Hell and calculated significant dates from the prophetic verses. According to that system, each letter of scripture possessed its own associated number and significance. It was possible in this way to calculate the exact time of the end of the world, as well as other ritually important events. Alas for her father, Jedda thought bleakly. No *abjat* had foretold the utter annihilation of his own universe.

The next day, the party embarked on their journey early and travelled south again, flying high over the upper leaf-forests. It would take them between four and five days, Gowron announced, to make a half-circuit of the Central Canopy, and reach their destination near the southern marches of the Gap. Jedda sat silent in the air-chariot, ruminating over what Wick had told her the night before. Did he truly regret the Envoy's actions and wish to help Tymon? Or was he so pathetically involved in his own fantasies that he still dreamed of winning the young man over, after all he had done? She rather suspected the latter. She also suspected Wick was not above attempting to seduce her, too, with the promise of safety. He was assiduous in his attentions to her that day, so much so that Gowron took to glowering at them both and spitting in the wind. He laughed heartily when it flew back into their faces, snorting with derision whenever Wick offered Jedda some meaningless civility. 'Watch out he doesn't vomit in your lap,' he once growled.

The tension between the acolytes only increased after a second night encamped on the crest of a deserted limb. There was a battle of wills taking place between the two men, as Jedda had surmised, and she was certain now, with a sinking heart, that it had to do with her. Gowron, judging by his savage observations and increasingly snide comments, could not understand Wick's decision to treat her like any other member of the expedition. The older man's behaviour had not changed from the first moment he had addressed her on the floor of the air-chariot: she was 'doll', 'sweetheart' and 'Tree-pussy'. But while his intentions towards her were blatant, Wick stubbornly refused to allow him to abuse his power over their hostage. The young acolyte pursued his own agenda, and clearly had personal plans for Jedda that did not include Gowron at all. By the third day of travel, the two priests were barely speaking to each other, and the girl had to be careful to avoid being pulled apart between them. The hours dragged by wearily, surrounded by the thudding cacophony of the propellers.

They were now passing over regions entirely free from snow and frost, their circumnavigation of the Tree taking them ever lower, to warmer latitudes and milder climes. By the time they had, by Gowron's calculations, encircled half the circumference of the trunk beneath the Central Canopy, the great plantations that occupied the southern marches of Argos stretched out below them. Snake-like terraces wound along almost every horizontal limb; Jedda could see the wriggling parallel lines of vineyards and loam fields through the partial screen of leaves. This was where her countrymen toiled, she thought numbly. This was where the gangs of patient pilgrims worked off their contract with the seminary, enclosed in the paddy fields until they were the manure they were spreading, producing the staple foods they themselves were denied. And this was where the prisoners of Argos were sentenced to hard labour.

Perhaps it was such thoughts as these that distracted her; in any case, she was unable to feel Tymon close by. According to Wick's information, they must have been somewhere near the farm where the young Grafter served out his prison term. But the familiar twinge in Jedda's belly was gone. In vain did she search for any vestige of the connection with her twining partner: there was nothing. It was unclear whether this was because she had somehow lost her abilities, or because Tymon was further away than they thought, in a place Wick did not expect him to be. She began to fear that the loss of the *orah* had cost her even the powers she possessed before becoming the Envoy's apprentice. She was careful not to divulge her failure, however, sensing that Tymon was her best means of leverage with Wick, the only barrier that stood between her and Gowron's savagery. She remained vague in her reports, whispering in Wick's ear when the other acolyte's back was turned that it was difficult, in the confined space of the air-chariot and with Gowron's antagonism so close, to be sure of the Grafting connection.

On the third evening, their haven was a lonely, flat-topped stump surrounded by a lake of shifting cloud. They had brought the air-chariot down at the edge of the stretch of wilderness that preceded the Gap, where the plantations gave way to a tangle of untamed leaf-forests. The limbs about them were widely spaced, vertical clumps of leaves and twigs separated from the rest of the canopy by yawning holes; mist swirled unnervingly in the gaps. It was a gloomy place, threatening not only because of the palpable proximity of the Storm but also because Jedda faced the prospect of sharing her berth with her fellow travellers that night. For the first time since they had set out together, it was raining. The priests' tent was prone to flooding in harsh weather, and the men were better off inside the machine.

Jedda enjoyed no such guarantee, however. She lay bundled in blankets beneath one of the benches, as far from the others as possible and miserably sleepless, listening to the drops drumming on the ceiling of the machine. Wick, too, seemed to wish to be left alone that night: he lay at the cockpit end of the craft, his face turned to the wall, entirely cocooned in blankets. Only Gowron sat awake on the bench opposite Jedda, steadily consuming his gourd of *kush*. The drink put him in a foul temper, or perhaps he was furious to begin with; he would not relax, but shifted and muttered to himself on the bench, starting up from time to time with an oath before sitting down again, so that the Nurian girl froze with terror beneath her blankets. His eyes gleamed in the dim light seeping through the window-holes. More than once, she saw them dart towards her. She kept as still as she could in a pretence of sleep, tense and wary of every sound, deploring her helplessness. For she had thrown away the *orah*, her one means of defence, and become again the girl in the garrison town, the girl without power.

Exhaustion betrayed her at last, the price for weeks of homeless wandering. She must have fallen asleep; from one moment to the next, she felt a heavy weight on top of her. Strong arms dragged her out from under the bench and a hand was wrapped across her mouth, so that she could not cry out. She struggled against Gowron's grasp, his breath sour in her face. He did not speak. The moments became long, a single-minded tussle of weaker and stronger muscle, bone against bone. He used his weight to prevent her from rising, pinning her wrists together with one hand and rummaging with the other in his jerkin pocket. Jedda caught a fitful sparkle of *orah* as he withdrew the sliver she remembered all too well.

'What are you doing?' she heard Wick protesting from the other end of the air-chariot. 'We talked about this! She's mine! I decide when!'

'I'm sick of your damn game,' growled Gowron. 'I'm going to have some actual fun tonight.'

He cursed as Jedda jerked her head to one side

and prevented him from pressing the *orah* into her forehead. It was the same stub of the stuff he had used against her before she travelled to Argos, unmounted on any pendant. She thought in panic of his hold over her then; she remembered Pallas' fate in the seminary dungeons, and struggled against her opponent with renewed vigour.

'Stop it!' Wick's silhouette bent over them, trying ineffectually to pry Gowron loose from his prey. 'You're ruining everything, you damned fool!' he groaned in frustration.

Jedda whipped her head round out of Gowron's reach, pressing her cheek to the floor of the air-chariot as he attempted to subdue her again. The ex-priest pronounced a furious oath.

'Let go of me!' he hissed to Wick, for the younger acolyte continued to tug at his shoulder. 'I've had enough of your pussyfooting around, you damned ugly freak. If you don't have the stomach to be a man, go wait outside.'

Jedda could not help noticing, even as she struggled grimly against her assailant, that there was something odd about Wick's face peering down at them in the gloom of the air-chariot. It looked blackened and twisted, lacking its usual smug smoothness. His expression seemed real to her for the first time since he had rescued her from the birds' attack — no longer perfect, but resentful, wounded, human. He drew himself up at Gowron's last words, his hand creeping to his throat in a gesture Jedda recognised.

'Ugly freak, am I?' he snapped. 'Fine. You asked for it. *Get off her.*'

The last words were a sorcerer's command, reinforced by the use of Wick's own pendant. Somehow, Wick's power was greater than Gowron's, in this instance; perhaps by dint of using the *orah* first, he had temporarily achieved the upper hand over his companion. Gowron loosed his gasp on Jedda's wrists and stood up, compelled.

'You fool,' the older acolyte cried, incensed. 'We don't use the Power on one of our own. Do you think the master is going to stand for this? He Sees us: don't think he doesn't know what you do.'

'Then he also Sees you taking away what's mine,' said Wick. 'It's up to me to decide what happens to the girl. You have your perks on this job: I have mine.'

The two acolytes glared at each other, fuming, as Jedda scrambled up and backed away, moving as far from Gowron as she could in the cramped cabin. Let them argue over her, she thought fiercely. Let them tear each other to shreds, and she would finally be free.

But Gowron evidently did not wish to let the standoff degenerate into a fight. 'I'm not going to forget this,' he told Wick, mastering his anger. 'Later, after the real job is finished, you'll pay for what you've done tonight. You'll wish you'd never been born.'

With that he strode to the hatch, bursting out of the air-chariot and into the glistening, wet darkness. The rain had stopped, Jedda realised, shuddering in her corner. The half-healed gashes on her wrists smarted where Gowron had gripped her.

'Thank you,' she said to Wick.

But the youth had already hurried away, and was scrabbling among his blankets on the floor by the controls, searching for something. When he turned back, the moment of truth was gone. His expression was flawless again, unmarked by suffering and distinctly less appealing.

'That's fine,' he smiled. 'He won't be happy about this, though. Best you stay close to me from now on.'

She acquiesced, dragging her blankets over to his side of the cockpit. He did not seem interested in further intimacies, however, wrapping himself up in his cocoon once more and huddling next to the wall.

It was sunrise when Gowron returned to the air-chariot after spending the night outside, slamming through the hatch to awaken his fellow travellers. He did not say a word to the young people, but surveyed them both for a long, disdainful moment before moving to the small engine hatch in the floor, to light the machine's furnace. Jedda watched him cautiously over the edge of her blanket, but Gowron did not meet her eye again, his back resolutely turned as he carried out his tasks. He had the air-chariot up in the air before they served breakfast, and refused all food when it was offered to him.

The lapsed priest drank regularly from his gourd that day as he manned the controls of the machine. The *kush* did not affect his ability to steer, but the others remarked their increased speed as they hurtled over the furlongs of wild canopy before the Gap. When Wick tried to remonstrate with him, Gowron growled out such a string of oaths, almost barking like an animal in his rage, that the younger acolyte backed away and left him to his own devices. Wick in any case was clearly battling nausea again, and sat in wordless misery next to Jedda on the bench. By late morning they had reached the Gap, that vast horizon of emptiness where the wriggling green line of the canopy's Fringes met cloud. The Storm seemed pale and placid in the winter sunlight, but its vastness was oppressive. Gowron brought the air-chariot around to the south, checking the map for their position and all the time maintaining the same glowering silence. His companions were left to guess when he would take the fateful plunge below.

It was not long before he angled the nose of the machine downwards. Jedda watched through one of the air-chariot's round windows as the rolling cloud-carpet drew closer. It seemed impossible that they should not come up against a hidden barrier, a low branch or jutting portion of the trunk, concealed by that treacherous layer of mist. She found herself edging closer to Wick, seeking out any shred of human comfort in the face of the immensity. But the clouds, when they entered them, were oddly tranquil.

To pierce the Storm was to descend first and foremost into a dreamlike topography. The upper layers were filled with floating strands, fingers of trailing fog. About the air-chariot lay hummocks and dells, rifts and columns of twisting white and grey, solid-seeming from without but vanishing like smoke upon contact. For a brief spell, they flew through a forest of tendrils, in and out and in again, and it seemed that the clouds were tame, no different from empty air.

Then blankness took them, and they flew blind into the heart of the Storm.

The first bump of turbulence came as a surprise to Jedda. The air-pocket hit the craft like a series of thudding knocks, as if a giant were rapping on the hull in an effort to get in. She grabbed Wick's hand and, to her private shame, held on. The young acolyte did not prove much of a comfort in this instance, however. He seemed worse off than she was, leaning against the wall of the air-chariot; his face even in its smoothness was distinctly ill and green. Gowron stood hunched over the air-chariot's gear sticks, intent on maintaining their course. He had thankfully ceased taking swigs from his *kush* gourd.

The second pocket of turbulence sent both young passengers sprawling onto the floor. This time, the juddering did not cease. It continued as they scrambled up as best they could, hanging on to the bench. The air-chariot pitched and swayed. The provision packs loaded onto the air-chariot slid across the floor in jumps and starts, for nothing had been secured. After a moment, Wick doubled over and vomited under the bench. A twinge of nausea visited Jedda, too, but her sickness receded when she kept her face close to the rushing cold of the window. She fixed her gaze on the tapered nose of the craft, hurtling through patches of light and dark cloud.

Against all reason, she felt a wild stirring of joy. This was a good way to go, she thought. She preferred to die like this, at breakneck speed, with the wind in her hair, rather than be pecked to death by the Envoy's curses or suffocated under Gowron. If the Storm took her that day, she would be content. Words welled up inside her in response to her exultation, and she found herself whispering them aloud, to the wind.

I do not stumble at the door. Death is but a portal.

The seed cracks as it gives birth: who mourns the shell?

She had thought they were more of Samiha's poetry, that she was repeating a fragment of the Kion's testament to comfort herself, as she had many times before. But although some verses in the Kion's testament had the same joyfully defiant tone, she knew even as she spoke that this one was different. It was new. She shut her mouth with a snap, and gripped the edge of the air-chariot's bench in confusion. The words that had tumbled from her lips had not been her own, arriving without premeditation, as if dictated by an outside source.

There had been, for a brief moment, another person in her head, chanting.

12

Tymon had feared at first, trudging back down the gloomy mine-tunnel with Zero, that he would not find Samiha waiting for him, that the apparition would not guide him, and that they would be obliged to return to the sunlit world within a few days when their food stocks ran low. He could not in all conscience pursue a dream forever, not with the Marak boy following faithfully on his heels. Besides, he was still aware of the other responsibilities calling him — Noni's pleas for his return to the Freehold, and the Oracle's trust. But the vision of Samiha reappeared sooner than expected. After only a short march into the tunnels on that first day, the far-off figure was walking before him once more, a reassuring glimmer in the darkness. His heart leapt towards it, and he felt he was on the right path at last.

'Samiha!' he called hoarsely, hurrying forward with such eagerness that he quit the shaky circle of light emanating from Zero's torch. His companion cried out for him to wait, but he did not listen. 'Samiha!' he called again, stumbling after the vision.

But it did not pay him any heed, dwindling in the distance. After a while it winked out completely, and he was left in darkness, panting and clutching the wall, until Zero caught up with him again.

'Wait for the light, *Syon*,' his friend chided him in exasperation.

'She's here, Zero,' said Tymon. Despite losing the apparition, he felt filled with bright, febrile joy. 'I Saw her. The Kion. We're on the right track.'

'You saw your spirits?'

'Not exactly. Samiha's not dead — this is no ghost. It's what we Grafters call a Sending.'

'Sending.' Zero tried the word out, full of doubt. 'Anyway, don't leave the light, *Syon*. It's dangerous.'

Zero's incomprehension did nothing to dampen Tymon's enthusiasm. A feverish faith had been kindled in his heart; he pressed on, begging the other lad to walk faster, burning for a further glimpse of Samiha, for he felt that they had only to follow the direction the vision had taken for it to return. His devotion was rewarded perhaps two hours later, just as they reached the point where their side-passage intersected with the main route down into the mine. They had barely stepped out of the by-way before Tymon caught sight of the white figure once more, standing some distance down the tunnel. He hastened towards it, trembling with joy and calling out Samiha's name.

The vision hesitated before turning away. It seemed to Tymon now that his love did not See him properly, after all, but sensed him as a blind person would. Her face wore a listening expression as if she heard, rather than saw, him stumbling after her in the gloom. Again, she walked on and he hurried after, transported by the bliss he had felt on first finding her, unaware of the bandages he wore or the pull and strain of his sore muscles. Again, the vision winked out, but it was much closer this time when it disappeared. Before fading away, the figure turned once more and listened for the sound of footsteps behind, peering into the darkness.

Zero could not prevail on his companion to stop for lunch, and they continued on into the heart of the mine with Tymon always walking a few eager paces ahead. When Samiha appeared once more in the far reaches of the tunnel, she was standing still and facing him, her head cocked in the listening attitude. On this occasion, when he cried out her name, she looked up immediately, sensing him; her lips moved, as if speaking his name. He hesitated no longer but sprang forward, running full tilt into the dark with Zero's warning shout in his ears. To his joy, his vision did not turn away but waited for him, the shimmering figure casting a pale light on the walls of the tunnel. As he drew closer, Samiha appeared to focus on him, seeing him properly. She laughed and held out her arms, and he stumbled along the last few feet of the tunnel to stand before her. For a moment, he could not speak, gazing wonderingly into her face.

She looked like the girl he had left behind in Sheb. No longer the battered stranger he had glimpsed at the trial and execution, she was the woman he called his merry night-wife on the Freehold, long-haired and beautiful. The shimmering trance-form reflected a cherished, older reality. Her smile was like rain on his parched soul.

'Well done, my love,' she said to him. 'I was hoping I'd find you here.'

'You're alive!' He blurted out the obvious, his heart racing. 'I knew it, even at Hayman's Point!'

'Hayman's Point?' she echoed, as if she did not recognise the name. Even her slight frown was achingly familiar to him, nostalgic. 'Maybe. I've been trying to reach you for a while. I'm in a strange state, Tymon. I couldn't See you before now, but I knew you were there.'

'Tell me everything,' he begged. 'Where are you? What happened at the execution?'

'I'm not sure, I'm afraid.' She shook her head. 'I fell a long way, through empty clouds — and then, nothing.

It was like someone had switched off a light in my mind. I don't know where I am, exactly: I just know I'm not dead. I think my body must have been caught and imprisoned somehow. I was forced into a Grafter's trance, anyway, though I can't fully control it. This has to be part of the Envoy's plan. He has weakened me terribly. I sensed you were down here, in the mine. I think it's not far from where I'm being held.'

Tymon gazed longingly at the pale, flickering form hovering before him. The vision reaffirmed all his instincts. It seemed so ethereal and at the same time so familiar, so utterly real. This reunion was of course exhilarating, but also deeply comforting in a way he had not expected. Samiha was no otherworldly Being, despite her ephemeral form. She seemed to have no obvious powers belonging to one of the Born. The two of them spoke as they had spoken many times before, as if they had left Sheb only yesterday. His long-lost love was there in spirit, if not in body, and she needed him.

'I'm sure you've been imprisoned inside the Tree,' he gladly agreed. 'I say we explore the tunnels, until you feel we're getting close to your body. You should be able to sense that by how easy it is to do a Sending, right?'

She nodded as Zero jogged up to them, breathless. The Marak boy had been left far behind in Tymon's initial headlong sprint, and had only now managed to catch up with his friend, his torch held aloft and his childish face puckered in distress.

'I told you, it's dangerous to leave the light, *Syon*!' he protested, his voice full of hurt and concern.

'Who's this?' asked Samiha.

'This is Zero,' answered Tymon. 'He's helping me. The Kion is here,' he added for the benefit of the puzzled youth, who stared in consternation as Tymon

285

spoke to a patch of empty air. 'Right now, beside us. You can't see her, but she's here.'

He indicated the area where the softly glowing image of Samiha stood, gazing intently at Zero. 'The spirit?' asked the Nurian boy again, querulous, peering at a point slightly to the left of Samiha's ear. 'The dead have come to guide you?'

'No, I told you — she isn't dead. A Sending is just a way of journeying without a body.'

'I don't understand,' muttered Zero.

'Is he simple?' remarked Samiha with an edge of impatience.

Tymon winced at her use of the word. It was unlike her to be so blunt; the Kion knew the difference between lack of education and lack of brains in her compatriots. He put her reaction down to the stress of her state, and patted Zero's shoulder comfortingly.

'It's alright,' he told the boy. 'Just call it a spirit and don't worry. We've found her, that's what counts.'

'And we should get going, if we want to find my body,' put in the flickering form of Samiha. 'It's hard for me to maintain this state.'

Zero was still frowning as they turned and continued down the passage. 'I don't understand why she's not dead,' he qualified unhappily. But Tymon was too absorbed in his vision of Samiha to respond.

'How did you know the right way out of the mine, when I was here with the mineworkers?' he asked her. 'You saved us — we wouldn't have made it without you.'

She shrugged in embarrassment. 'I can't explain it, really. It's odd, being outside my body. I know certain things about you, things I wouldn't be able to know if we were just together physically. I understood you were in the mine with your friends, and I knew how to help you. But I couldn't See you properly. Now I can. I think it's because … because of love.' She smiled shyly at him. 'Your love is like a light for me in the darkness. It calls me and holds me together. I sometimes wonder if you didn't keep me alive.'

The pleasure of hearing her say it rippled through him. 'Maybe you're still alive because you're a Born,' he suggested, lowering his voice to be out of earshot of Zero, trudging patiently in the rear. 'You're different from us. More powerful. You can't really die, can you?'

'You know what I am?' she whispered, peering at him in curiosity.

'Yes. The Focals told me. Actually I guessed it before then.'

'And you don't mind?'

'Why would I mind? I'll love you whatever you are, Samiha. If you'll still have me, I'm the happiest man alive. I realised that during the trial. I was a fool in Sheb. You're mine, and I'm yours, and nothing will ever come between us.'

'Let's not speak of the trial,' she answered. 'Those were hard times.' But the smile lingered on her lips as she walked, weightless by his side.

He was almost floating on air himself, buoyed with joy. He hardly felt his fatigue or injuries any more; he felt as if nothing could hurt him now. One final comfort, however, eluded him. He could not help wishing he could throw his arms about Samiha, press her close as he used to do.

'It's most frustrating,' she murmured after a moment, echoing his thoughts. 'I want to hold your hand.'

'Why not try?' he asked, halting in the corridor.

He said it without premeditation, though the thought did give him a slight, surreptitious thrill. He did not really expect anything when he held up his hand, and Samiha reached out hesitantly to brush it with her fingers. But there was a very faint sensation when she touched his skin, an intimate burr, as if the touch came from within him. She held his gaze a moment, her own eyes growing wide with surprise.

'Well, we won't be getting very far with that,' he laughed in an effort to dispel the tension.

Then Zero caught up with them, mumbling a complaint about the speed of spirits, and the moment was over. They walked on in silence. Tymon's heart beat quickly, thumping against his chest. He could not forget that faraway, static touch.

'We're carrying provisions for a week,' he said to Samiha. 'More, if we stretch it. We can search a fair number of tunnels before then.'

'It won't be difficult,' she assured him. 'You're right. I think I can tell which way to go.'

They continued walking together down the main tunnel for several minutes, until Tymon saw that the passage was rapidly narrowing to a rough-hewn hole. They had reached the end of the mine-tunnel, encountering their first major hurdle on the journey. The way ahead was blocked. Before them stretched an undulating wall of wood, gouged out here and there by tools, the passage clogged with miners' utensils and carts. It looked as though the workers had left everything behind them in their hasty exit; Tymon's elation at being in the presence of Samiha was slightly dampened at the thought of the core-miners, who must have tried to escape by a different route from the one he had taken with the Saffid. They would have been safer staying inside the mine, he realised regretfully.

Samiha was adamant that the right direction was onwards, and deeper. 'Keep looking,' she beseeched Tymon. 'You're bound to find a hidden crevice somewhere, some access way.'

But there were no side-passages leading off the tunnel. The ceiling was low here, and the air was stale, lacking the promising movement of the upper levels. After searching the jagged end-wall with Zero's help for some minutes, and finding no sign of a continuing passage, Tymon began to lose patience.

'It's not in the mining levels,' the Samiha-vision insisted, urging him on. 'It's somewhere lower, older. There's something under here. Maybe another set of tunnels they don't know about in Chal —'

At that moment, her words were abruptly cut off, and Tymon found himself surrounded by darkness. Samiha had disappeared, unable, as he guessed, to maintain the Sending. In her absence his joy and energy ebbed. It was as if all his fatigue had caught up with him at once; he felt a moment of blank despair and noticed for the first time that Zero was drooping with exhaustion. He admonished himself for reacting like a fool, and paying so little attention to his faithful companion.

'Let's take a break,' he said to Zero. 'You must be as hungry as I am. If the Kion doesn't come back soon, I can do a Reading and figure out where to go from here.' He was sure Samiha would return when she was strong enough. Or when he was.

They sat with their backs against the gouged face of the end-wall and, opening one of the Freeholders' food packets, began to gobble down the food. But although they had not eaten for hours, the tried and trusted combination of dried fruit, bread and cured meat tasted strange and bitter to Tymon. He wondered if the Freeholders' food was tainted, though it had been only a few hours since they had bid farewell to Noni. He had meant to launch a trance after the meal to determine their best course, as well as keep his promise to the Focals. But he was either more tired than he thought, or else they had walked through the mine longer than he supposed, for after a lapse of time he found himself awakening from a nap he had never meant to take.

He sat up and stretched his joints, annoyed at himself for sleeping. His head ached dully, an unpleasant burning sensation in his temples. Zero's torch sputtered where they had left it, wedged between two upturned barrows. The Marak boy was slumped on the floor nearby, softly snoring. Tymon stared at him in a daze, feeling faintly sick.

'Bad air,' he suddenly gasped, jumping to his feet.

He could taste the acrid bitterness on his tongue, the dry, warning odour of stagnation. He realised there was not a single sap-soaked torch of the kind carried by Zero among all the paraphernalia cluttering the end of the passage. Nothing but candles could be used in the very deepest mines, he recalled belatedly, dredging up some forgotten piece of lore from his seminary lessons. Other light sources would use up the air and cause the workers to suffocate. The torch was slowly killing them.

He grabbed a piece of sacking from the floor and smothered the flame, so that the mine-passage was plunged in impenetrable gloom. Then, half-choking, he bent down over the spot where he remembered Zero lying, found his friend's shoulder and began to shake him awake.

'Spirits help us,' wheezed the Marak boy, when he finally understood Tymon's agitated explanations. 'We almost lost our evil again.'

The dousing of the torch certainly saved them from disaster. Tymon blamed himself for not thinking of contingencies, for Zero was clearly unable to do so. He could not rely on Samiha to warn him at every juncture, either, faced with her faulty Sending connection, though he did wonder at her selective powers of foresight. Her last words to him had been to persist, to keep looking right here, where they had almost died. He took a long, shuddering breath. In any case, the moment of danger had passed. After a while, he started to breathe more easily, though the acrid smell still lingered faintly in the air. He only regretted, crouched in the dark passage beside Zero, that he could not search for the workers' candles as substitutes for the torch, now that they were left in absolute gloom. When Samiha was with him, her trance-form shed enough light for Tymon at least to see by. But she was not always present.

Over the next few minutes, however, as he sat whispering to his friend in the tunnel, discussing their next stop, Tymon realised that his surroundings were not entirely obscured. He began to see faint points and threads of light in the wood-grain of the walls, unnoticed before. At first he blinked, thinking his eyes were playing tricks on him. Then he understood what he was seeing.

'Core!' he burst out to Zero. 'It's everywhere!'

They were surrounded by faint traces of the precious substance, the glittering, secret wealth of Chal. Pink and orange starlight bespeckled the walls and ceiling of the mine-tunnel, promising greater lodes beneath. Tymon could have laughed at the bitter irony: all of Lord Dayan's riches were useless to them now.

'The workers called it "fire of the deep",' said Zero. Tymon could see his friend's silhouette, faintly outlined against the gleaming core. 'Someone from the upper levels would have had his eyes put out for seeing this, *Syon*. It's a good thing there aren't any guards here.'

The thickest lodes of petrified sap stretched in diagonal bands down the end-wall, and were already half-picked out by the mineworkers' tools. They all led — flowed, thought Tymon — in a similar direction, descending in a sweeping arc towards the right-hand corner of the wall. He rose and followed them, tracing his finger along them, feeling his way past the obstacle course of invisible objects jumbled and heaped haphazardly on the tunnel floor. The bands ended in a soft swirl of colour. He pushed a heavy cart out of the way to better see the design they made when they converged.

But the pattern had been gouged out. A large beam had been removed from the wall at this point, evidently rich enough in core to merit being dug out in its entirety. The horizontal passage it created would have been wide enough to crawl through, had it led anywhere, but the space, Tymon saw in surprise, was no longer empty. It had been blocked by a beam of similar size, though slightly different in shape and lacking the telltale core-lodes. The end of the replacement beam stuck out a few inches from the wall, as if it had been shoved in hurriedly.

'I think I've found our lost passage,' he said to Zero, triumphant. And once again he felt a tingle of confirmation, vindicating his faith in the vision. Samiha had been right about the existence of other tunnels! He should never have doubted her.

The two youths worked the beam out gradually, first using their fingers, then prying the section loose with the hardwood tools they found scattered on the floor of the passage. Their eyes had become sufficiently attuned to the dim phosphorescence of the corewood to permit an educated guess as to what they were doing, though they stubbed their toes and pinched their fingers more than once in the process. The beam had not been meant to stay in as a permanent block, and after a sustained effort they were able to pull it loose with a shriek of splintered wood.

Light welled out of the empty passage beyond, accompanied by a fetid odour. The luminescence was so unexpected that Tymon and Zero stared at the pinkish glow in astonishment, before going down on their hands and knees to investigate the opening. The glow, so bright to them after near-total darkness, was in fact only a stronger pool of phosphorescence. As they crawled along the passage, dragging their packs behind them, the acrid smell Tymon had noticed earlier grew ever more sharp. The crawl-space came to an end and the passage opened out into a natural chamber in the Tree, a hollow bubble about fifteen feet in diameter with a smooth, slightly concave floor.

The walls of the chamber were a dazzling mass of core, scored with rivers of petrified Treesap. In the centre of the space lay a heap of bundled objects Tymon could not immediately identify: it was a pile of darkness, a dark lump within the circle of leaping orange. The acrid tang was now very strong, and he fought the impulse to gag.

He scrambled upright to find himself standing in the middle of a womb of pink and orange starlight. It was the remains of an ancient sap-sack, he realised in awe. The chamber was clearly part of the hollowed-out vascular system of the Tree, millennia old. He remembered similar tunnels beneath Sheb; this one had a similar, natural exit, a chute leading out of the wall opposite to plunge steeply downwards. There was less core in the floor than in the walls and ceiling, or else it had been obscured. The surface beneath his feet, Tymon noticed with growing unease, was stained dark.

'Syon,' murmured Zero in distress, at the same time as Tymon saw with prickling horror what was actually piled at the centre of the chamber.

Bodies lay heaped on top of each other on the floor. The core-glow glinted on their yellow hair and sun-starved skin. From what Tymon could tell, staring in dismay at the scene before him, about twenty Nurians had been brutally murdered in the chamber, their throats slit and their heads bashed in with hammers. And it had not happened long ago. The stink of blood and faecal matter filled the air, and there was a dry, day-old stain at his feet. The coreworkers must have been killed by their guards when the tremors started in the mines above, rather than being allowed to leave and seek safety. The cruelty of the action, the venality of the Lord's policies that maintained secrecy even in the face of total ruin, astounded Tymon. His stomach curdled and he looked away, telling himself that he should have expected such a thing. There was little satisfaction in the knowledge that neither the guards nor their master had in all probability escaped the mine collapse.

'I'm so sorry you had to see this,' whispered Samiha, at his side.

The vision was there again, a reassuring presence. He fixed his eyes on it instead of the murdered people, the sight of that luminous and familiar form assuaging his heart-sickness. Only Samiha could make sense of such brutality.

'I hate to say it, but I fear we can't stay here long,' she continued with a sigh. 'The Sending is growing more difficult for me every time, and we still have far to go.'

Tymon could not help feeling slightly shocked as she turned away from the bodies without another word, and walked to the mouth of the glittering, core-lined chute. As with her reaction to Zero, Samiha seemed to have lost her sensitivity to human suffering along with the use of her physical body. He told himself sternly that she was right, that their current mission should take precedence over all else, even the dead workers. Samiha, too, might slip through his fingers if he did not hurry. Roused by this thought, he nudged Zero towards the chute. But the Marak lad dragged his heels, lingering over the murdered Nurians with his head bowed.

'All too good,' he said. 'They were all too good.'

'I thought you used to say your countrymen were evil,' Tymon replied.

He spoke brusquely, because he felt ashamed: despite the reek of decomposition in the chamber, it seemed heartless as well as disrespectful to be abandoning the workers so soon. But they were beyond his help now. He could not even give them a proper funeral, sending their bodies into the Void.

'It's the living who need to be evil,' Zero answered sadly. 'The dead, *Syon*, have none of that left. All the evil has run out. They're done with life — or they're hungry.'

'Your friend,' put in Samiha, from her post by the chute, 'is a trove of interesting contradictions. But we really need to get going.'

'I know,' Tymon mumbled in answer to both of them. He tugged on Zero's arm until the boy reluctantly allowed himself to be led away.

'He's also a very sweet fellow,' Samiha added when they had joined her at the chute, as if she sensed Tymon's turmoil. 'I'm glad you brought him. He'll help us.'

'Do you have a better idea of where we're going now?' he asked her, as he ducked after her into the dark mouth of the exit.

'This passage links with another series of Tree-tunnels,' she said, her glow drifting ahead of him down the sloping, narrow tunnel.

The passage was about the height of a man, starting off level but quickly plunging downwards. After a moment Tymon was obliged to take his eyes off Samiha's glow and concentrate on the steeply sloping floor at his feet, lest his descent turn into a headlong slide. The grain of the wood was silky, treacherous.

'I think these hollow passages will take us all the way to my body, though it'll be a long journey.' Samiha's voice echoed ahead of him as he inched his way down the chute, followed by Zero. 'Days, maybe. It's somewhere deep down.'

'What happens when you can't do the Sending?' Tymon asked, slithering a little on the smooth floor. He had to brace his arms against the ceiling, which had steadily grown lower as they descended. 'Do you wake up and see where you are?'

'It's dark.' The answer drifted back. 'I could be awake, I don't know. There's darkness, and pain.'

'We'll get there as quickly as we can,' he assured her, overcome by remorse at this revelation. He craned his neck to see Zero, carefully negotiating the passage behind him. 'Won't we, Zero?'

'Yes, *Syon*,' said the youth obediently.

Tymon did not articulate the other concerns that now occurred to him in swift succession. Even if they were lucky enough to locate Samiha's body, he realised, they would still have to find a way to spirit her away from their enemies. It would be far harder to climb the smooth Tree-conduits than to slide down them, especially carrying her weak or injured body; they would have to find another way up, or out, of the Tree.

The ancient sap-course soon became a near-vertical chimney, steep and unbroken. Thankfully it also narrowed at that point, allowing the two youths to descend by pressing their backs against one wall, and bracing their legs against the other, using the regular ripples and ridges in the grain as toeholds. The vertical portion did not last long, and they emerged after perhaps a quarter of an hour of slow descent into a larger, more gently graded passage. Although the core lodes here were fewer, merely bespeckling the walls with points of light, Tymon was heartened to feel a steady flow of cold air on his face. He could See Samiha clearly again in front of him, her ghostly form throwing a faint glow on the walls and floor of the passageway. Zero risked lighting another torch, and their journey became easier, well lit and following the downward course of the conduit as it plumbed the depths of the Tree.

Cut off from sunlight, they could only guess at the lapse of time by the rate at which Zero's torch was consumed. One sap-soaked cord wound about the tip of the handle equalled an hour's worth of illumination, and in the course of their journey that afternoon they used up four of these, out of a store of thirty-six. It was Tymon who tired first on the long march. He had not realised that he was so fatigued; it must have been early evening outside when his bruised limbs simply buckled under him, and he knelt down on the floor of the sloping passage, unable to move. By then, the gradient of the conduit had grown steep again, and Zero declared the *Syon* unfit to negotiate another near-vertical descent. When Tymon was inclined to agree to his companion's demand for food and rest, Samiha assured them that the passage would be passable a little further on, and urged them to keep going. She possessed a Born's foreknowledge of details like the character of the passage, Tymon thought, but seemed oblivious of the merely human requirements of food, rest and breathable air. Again he put that down to her unusual out-of-body state, making excuses for her lack of empathy.

She had appeared and disappeared three times over the course of their journey that day, begging Tymon to hurry whenever she returned. Her body, she had told him, was weakening. Without it, the strength to perform a Sending waned and ultimate recovery slipped out of reach. He needed no other encouragement to press on, and only regretted his own infirmity, the frailty of his flesh compared with his intentions and desires. Now that he had stopped walking, he found that he was shaking with exhaustion. Once more, he did not have the stamina to launch a Grafter's trance, as Noni had asked him to do at the close of each day. He had no strength left to assure the Focals of his wellbeing. He pleaded with his love to be patient, if only for Zero's sake, and insisted when they ate the evening meal that the young lad take much of his own share, claiming to be too tired to digest it. After they had finished eating, he stretched himself out beside Zero to sleep on the floor of the Tree-tunnel, grimacing with pain.

'I think I can help you,' Samiha said, bending over him with a concerned expression, as he attempted to find a comfortable position. 'Sometimes I forget, nowadays. I forget what it means to be in a body, tired and hurt. But I can help you. The Sending is a permeable state. I can give you a little of my own energy: what use is it if I go on living and you expire here?'

Zero had already fallen sound asleep, curled up under his blanket on the hard, smooth floor of the passage as Samiha crouched beside Tymon.

'Don't be silly,' he murmured to her. 'You have barely enough to keep going yourself. A night of rest will do me just fine. Or whatever passes for a night. I doubt we'll know what time it is when we wake up.'

'I'm not being silly,' she said. 'We're both in trouble if you don't stay strong. This is worth a try, even if I have to cut down on the amount of Sendings I do. You're more hurt than you pretend to be.'

'I don't feel it when you're around,' he answered, smiling up at her. And it was true: he was willing to bear all the aches and pains in the world for the sight of her.

'That's not good enough. I can see you're in a bad way, whatever you feel.' She bent close to him, entreating, her hair hanging down in a softly glowing curtain. 'Our connection is strong. Usually a Grafter can't touch a Sending, but you did. Let me help you, Tymon. I can take it.'

He hesitated. He did not wish to deprive her of anything, especially when she told him that she was already weak, running out of strength to perform the Sendings. But his pulse quickened as he thought of their one brief touch. What harm would it do? Even the shadow of intimacy was better than none at all. She seemed confident she could keep back enough vitality while helping him: he decided to trust her judgment. Besides, he could not refuse her anything when she begged him like this, so close, so glowing.

'How do we do it?' he asked cautiously.

'It works by proximity,' she said. 'Touch me, like before.'

He held up his hand, palm-outwards, and she laid her own against his. The slight, tingling sensation as their fingers met and twined was exhilarating.

'My little night-wife,' he said softly.

'I will be,' she promised. 'We've never had enough time together. It isn't fair. If we get out of this, Tymon, it'll just be you and me. No more epic quests. Just ordinary human life, and love. We deserve it.' She closed her eyes. 'Now. You have to want it. I'm ready. Reach through the connection, and pull the energy into you.'

When he, too, closed his eyes, he was able to sense the tug and stretch of a faint Grafter's connection between them, even as he did with Jedda. On this occasion, it did not appear to him as a shining cord, but filled every part of his body with a dim, tingling wash of sensation. As he concentrated, pulling more of the energy through the link as he had been told to do, the tingle became a rush of pleasure, overwhelmingly intense. It was nothing like the flow of the Sap he had felt in the Tree of Being; this sensation was harder, coarser, fascinating. It reminded him fleetingly of the Doctor's chair.

His eyes flew open in surprise. 'What's this?' He searched Samiha's face, troubled. He resisted the urge to drink more and greedily of that heady brew, wary of the effect it would have on her. Was she playing the martyr again for him?

'Don't stop,' she whispered. She bent down and kissed him, a stab of light on his lips. 'This is my love. Don't refuse it.'

He could not resist for long, in any case. The link to her, once opened, almost engulfed him in its embrace. It was like the physical desire between a man and a woman, but also the unconditional love of a parent. It was all the different kinds of comfort and approval he had yearned for in his life, and had never been given. The mother he had not known, the wife who had been ripped away from him too soon — all these he found again, cradled in one complete sensation. Compared to the relentless punishment of the past few weeks, it was bliss. After a moment of confusion, he allowed the flow from Samiha to fill him to the brim. There was no harm, he thought. He would do the same for her in a heartbeat.

'This was how it was, in the beginning,' said the vision, though he no longer heard her, his eyelids drifting shut in ecstasy. The bending figure caressed his forehead with her pale fingers, musing aloud. 'Pure love. We gave you everything, and yet you walked away from us. You chose to live alone, in hardship and in pain. How strange.'

The *Syon*'s spirits, Zero thought to himself, trudging behind Tymon two days later, were exacting creatures, requiring great personal sacrifice in exchange for their wisdom. They took as much as they gave, that was clear enough. Zero did not believe for one minute that Samiha, the Nurian queen, was still alive, for Tymon's spirit guide behaved exactly like a hungry ghost.

Tymon had not been himself since they set out again, on what Zero guessed was the morning of the day before. After picking at his crumbs of breakfast, the *Syon* had hardly spoken a word as they walked, refusing lunch when they stopped to rest several hours later. By that time, the passage had indeed turned vertical, becoming a plunging well of darkness almost fifty feet across. But as Tymon had predicted — as the Kion apparently had told him — it was passable. A perfect, ten-foot wide ramp spiralled down into the hole, a corkscrew ledge cut into the sides of the well. Zero would have assumed the construction was manmade, had it not been so smooth, lacking any evidence of tool work. The edges were cut into the wood-grain with impossible precision, the gradient absolutely even. No hammer or chisel he knew of could have achieved that feat of engineering; he assumed, therefore, that they were walking down a spirit road.

The supernatural existed with complete ease alongside the physical for Zero. Why should spirits not have their own roads, houses and cities in the secret core of the Tree, as humans did? It seemed natural to him that a spirit guide would take them down a spirit road. But the toll required for passage through these sacred sites was heavy on the living. Tymon had descended into the well like a sleepwalker, in a waking dream. It was clear to Zero that his friend had bartered up a corner of his sanity in order to complete their journey, receiving in exchange a febrile power of endurance. They had stopped their day's march only when Zero was staggering with weariness, and they had used up their quota of twelve torches. Tymon, for his part, seemed ready to walk on completely blind, and consented only grudgingly to a halt. That night, or what they guessed was night in the dark eternity of the Tree, Zero had convinced his friend to eat some of the Freeholders' food, and the *Syon* had behaved more like his usual self for a little while. They had camped on the ramp in absolute gloom, saving their light for the journey ahead.

But the spirit would not leave Tymon alone. Zero could see that it gave him no rest; even at night, it demanded its ransom. The Marak boy had gathered from many and garbled sources that certain ghosts were hungry for only one thing, and that was to live again. Their current guide was no exception. The shade evidently wished to eat, sleep and love as humans did, and the more it sought those satisfactions, the less Tymon was accorded their benefits. As far as Zero was aware, his friend did not sleep a wink the first night on the ramp, ridden by the ghost to distraction. Whenever the Marak lad awoke it was to hear Tymon twisting about from side to side, mumbling to himself or crying aloud in pain or pleasure, it was difficult to tell. Once, the young Argosian jumped to his feet and paced up and down the road for several yards in complete darkness, returning only to begin the restless circuit again. When Zero arose after an insufficient night's sleep, and lit his torch on what he guessed was the following morning, he found Tymon already awake and crouched before him, wild-haired and grinning, his eyes ringed with shadow.

'What are the children of Love?' he said in a hoarse whisper to Zero, before scrambling to his feet with a dry, croaking laugh. 'Never mind,' he said. 'Let's get on.'

He waited neither for the torch nor his breakfast, but began reeling away down the ramp. Just as Zero was about to stumble after him, however, he caught sight of something small and reflective on the ramp, a shard gleaming in the torchlight. He bent down and picked up the hardwood pendant Tymon had always worn about his neck, its bright inlay shining like starlight. The cord had been untied, rather than broken, the pendant simply dropped on the ramp. Zero wondered at his companion's abandonment of something he had formerly considered so precious. He stuffed the pendant into his tunic pocket, ready to give back later, and hurried after the disappearing figure of his friend.

He watched Tymon with increasing concern during the course of that day, noting in dismay that the *Syon* would take neither rest nor food, only walking on with relentless determination. The spirit-energy given by the hungry ghost may have been boundless, but a body was a body, with its own requirements and rules, to be ignored at one's peril. Zero hoped their journey would not continue much longer, for Tymon's sake. His own moral compass may have been idiosyncratic, lacking a coherent interior logic, but he was sure of one thing. Good and evil were purely human concerns. Ghosts had no use for such ideas, and this one seemed bent on riding Tymon until he broke.

13

The forms of Oren, Ara and Mata were grey and bowed in the morning mist, seated in the little clearing among the twig-thickets near Farhang, where they had once performed a Reading with Tymon. Only their eyes glinted over folds of the long wraps used by the northerners, covering them from head to foot. Noni was missing, away on her trip across the Gap, but the young Focals unconsciously left a space for her in the circle, an opening on Mata's right side. Their breath whitened the chill air as they spoke in low voices, in Nurian.

'What did you see this time?' asked Oren. 'The attack again?'

'The attack,' the twins confirmed, in unison.

'Was this vision like the others?' pressed Oren. 'Did the ships arrive under a black cloud?'

'The cloud that darkens, but gives no rain,' said Ara, as Mata nodded. 'But it was worse this time. The whole canopy was shrouded. There was only one spot of light, over Marak.'

'The power of the Envoy,' muttered Oren. 'Though I don't know why it wouldn't touch Marak, too. Well, the fleet won't be long in arriving, I suppose.'

'Mid-morning, three days from now,' said Mata without hesitation.

'And what about you?' Ara asked Oren.

'The usual. Fire, destruction and the end of things,' replied the other Grafter, as if such news were negligible. 'It's what I don't See that disturbs me. I can't feel Tymon any more. He's clouded. This time I was wandering through a burning city in search of him. I thought he might be buried under a pile of ash, and dug into it with my bare hands, but couldn't find him.'

'The visions aren't so different then,' said Ara with a grimace.

'Well,' continued Oren after a moment, standing up and stamping his feet on the frosty floor of the clearing, 'I suppose we'd better go tell the judges about the fleet.'

'Not that it'll do any good,' sighed Mata, as he and his brother arose in their turn.

'Or save us,' added Ara mournfully.

'Nonsense,' said Oren, with an attempt at cheerfulness. 'We can always prepare. A fleet is a fleet, and the judges can deal with that. As to the rest, being upset about it isn't going to help.' But his expression was grim as he followed the other two through the misty stands of twigs, towards the village dining hall.

The communal hall was already bustling with Freeholders from both Farhang and Sheb, gathered in the main room to take their breakfast. The young Grafters approached Gardan, Aythan and three other judges seated in a loose group on the floor. The Freehold leaders were accompanied by a newcomer: a lean, weathered Nurian who, judging from his generally dusty and travel-worn state, had only just arrived in Farhang, though the hour was early. Everyone stopped talking as the Grafters approached, and turned expectantly, if a little warily, towards them.

'Respected *syors*,' said Oren, bowing deeply and speaking in Argosian out of deference to the northerners, 'we come to you this morning with troubling news.'

'Welcome, Oren,' answered Gardan. 'Sit down, please, all of you. I'd like to introduce you to Halas Melat, from Marak.'

She indicated the newcomer, who inclined his head in polite greeting, gazing with a curious intensity at the Grafters. Oren gave the stranger an answering nod before turning back to the judges. Although Ara and Mata had seated themselves at Gardan's request, he remained standing in urgent supplication.

'I regret, this report is of great importance,' he began. 'It cannot wait —'

'You wish to tell us that an Argosian fleet will attack within the next couple of days,' interrupted Aythan, in his rumbling baritone.

'We've just heard the news,' continued Gardan, as Oren stared in surprise, then slowly sank down on the floor next to his friends, 'from Halas, who walked day and night from Marak city to bring us the Argosian edict.'

She retrieved an impressive-looking green velvet bag from the folds of her cloak and handed it to Oren. It was a seminary post-bag of the finest variety, reserved for Council missives. The young Grafter unknotted the drawstring with trembling fingers and drew out the document within, paying no heed to the ornate lettering but focusing instead on the ancient Seal of the Prophets affixed to the bottom. The Argosians had not dared use that mark for centuries.

'Ah,' he said unhappily. 'I see that Fallow has declared a crusade.'

'The letter is dated almost four weeks ago,' said Gardan, plucking back the paper with its florid signature and folding it away in the soft green bag again. 'It was supposed to be sent out to the northern Freeholds more than a week ago but, oddly enough, no trader could be found travelling in these parts this time

of year. Halas was the only one able to bring it —
which means the Argosians are right on his heels.'

The grey-garbed man nodded again in corroboration
of this. 'I came as quick as I could,' he remarked, in the
harsh accent of a Marak dweller. 'Twenty ships docked
before I left, about half the fleet if I guess right. The
others were due in the next few days. It took me a week
to get here, though I rode on a farmer's barge and
shortened the trip. They'll be right behind.'

'Arriving in three days,' put in Mata glumly. 'In the
morning.'

Gardan glanced up at this. 'That's helpful to know,'
she said with relief, as several of the judges whispered
excitedly to each other in response to the revelation.
'We feared it might be sooner. Thank you, friends. This
means we have more time for the evacuation of our
families. As you know, the United Freeholds have been
preparing for just such an attack. We're as ready as we'll
ever be.'

'Begging your pardon, *syors*, but preparation does
little good,' blurted Oren. 'This is only first attack.
There will be many more: even if we survive this one,
we are doomed. All Freeholds are doomed.'

His comment provoked another flurry of whispers.
Some of the judges openly rolled their eyes, while
Gardan stifled a sigh.

'Oren,' she said, 'we understand your desire to warn
us. We appreciate any information you can give us, like
the time of attack. That's a great help.' She took hold
of his arm with a strained smile and a swift glance at
the people scattered about the meal hall, and pulled
him closer before continuing. 'But these Grafters'
prophecies of doom and gloom — it just kills morale,
old friend,' she hissed in his ear. 'We'd much rather you
didn't announce such things in public.'

'All the same, *syora*, it is true,' replied Oren, lowering his voice in response. 'We will not win final war with Argosians, not in End Times.'

'What do you suggest?' she murmured to him in the Sheb dialect, as the other judges continued to talk among themselves, ignoring the Grafters now. 'That we surrender? It's fight or die, Oren. The Saint has been quite clear about that. He accuses us of conspiring with Lantrians against the Holy Seat, though everyone knows that was Caro's game, may the Sap leave him dry. Fallow has officially declared the Freeholds heretic nations to be cleansed by fire and the sword. We have no rights; we have no recourse. Everything we ever negotiated or signed means nothing. There are no civilised options open to us any more. Do you understand?'

The Speaker's voice had become a harsh whisper, belying her usual calm, her gaze full of bright intensity. Oren opened his mouth to answer, then thought better of it. He knew she hated what she was saying, but was driven to such measures out of desperation.

'Yes,' said Gardan. 'Kill or be killed. If you have an objection to that, you're welcome to return to Marak. I'm sure we're all doomed. This is probably the end. Just don't, for the love of the Sap, start dispiriting these poor people with advance notice of the fact. I suggest you and your friends evacuate with the non-combatants tomorrow, and do the best you can to protect them. That would be useful to us.'

Oren bowed his head in silent acquiescence, alerted at that moment to the sound of distant throbbing in the sky. An air-chariot was approaching the Freehold. Was Noni back already? He scrambled to his feet with a whispered word to Ara and Mata, bid a polite farewell to the judges, and turned to leave the room. As he hastened away, the man from Marak looked up and caught his eye, flashing him a rueful half-smile, as if to apologise for being the bearer of bad news.

Noni stared out of the round windows of the *Dev* as the new machine descended over the northern Freehold, spiralling down towards the bare, up-thrust crest of the docking limb. Even from this height, she could see her brother waiting below on the crest of the branch in the watery afternoon light, his long Farhang cloak wrapped about his ears. Oren had not brought Ara or Mata with him to welcome her home, which meant that he was anxious, and wished to speak with her alone. Noni could guess at some of the subjects preoccupying him. She hunched her shoulders as she sat by the window, dreading the inevitable conversation about Tymon.

Beside her, the eight Saffid workers crammed into the passenger section of the air-chariot whooped and cheered at the sight of the Freehold buildings half-hidden in the twig-thickets. It seemed unbelievable that they had been marching through the South Canopy only two days before. After bidding farewell to Tymon and Zero, she and the mineworkers who were well enough to walk had journeyed north along the many interconnecting ledges in the trunk-face, making for the bulging outcrop of the Spur of Sails. Those who were ill or weary had accompanied them in the *Dev*. The weather had remained fine, and it had been a pleasant enough trip, scrambling through the trailing vines and beds of moss that colonised the Tree at this point. They had walked with the cloudy expanse of the Gap to their right, exposed against the face of the Tree the whole time; luckily, the only visitors approaching from above happened to be friends. The three other Freehold pilots had spotted them long before they reached their destination of the Spur, picking them up after only one day of travel.

They had made the Gap-crossing in good time and good weather, travelling together in the air-chariots. Noni had found herself regretting the luxurious, leafy regions they left behind as they set out for Farhang, but her Saffid companions seemed eager enough to be done with the South Canopy, and the memories it contained. They had cheered when they first sighted the arid branches of their home, and cheered again the next day, with undiminished enthusiasm, when they arrived in the northern Freehold. She wondered privately what advantages they thought they could look forward to. Although they were no longer slaves, they would still live under the threat of permanent war, their so-called curse affecting them in spite of their fervent beliefs. It was a depressing thought, and she pushed it aside, fixing her gaze on her brother standing on the branch below. Perhaps Oren would have some advice for the Saffid.

The air-chariots made the descent one at a time, alighting on different sections of the horizontal limb. All the machines were of a new design developed by the Farhang engineers; they were more stable and less likely to be buffeted by wind, but required a slightly longer docking strip as a result. Oren stayed well out of the way as the *Dev* rolled to a halt on its creaking wooden wheels. As soon as the machine had stopped, he hurried eagerly forward, reaching the hatch even as it opened.

'Where is he?' he burst out to Noni as she emerged. 'Where is Tymon?'

She did not immediately respond, but searched her brother's strained face for some sign of greeting. It was not there. The workers stepping out of the machine behind her bowed respectfully to Oren, but he only half-bowed back, distracted.

'Where is Tymon?' he repeated impatiently, as his

sister stretched her cramped joints after the long flight. 'I haven't been able to See him for days!'

'He went back into the mine,' she finally replied with deep reluctance.

Oren blanched. 'Why?'

'He insisted,' she shrugged uncomfortably. 'He said he Saw the Kion.'

'He Saw nothing of the kind!' cried Oren. 'I don't know what was in the mine, but it wasn't the Kion!'

Noni's spirits sank. Her brother was almost beside himself: she had rarely seen him so upset. They were communicating in the Sheb dialect, their native tongue, which Oren spoke more easily than either Argosian or the patois current in the northern Freeholds. The pilots from Farhang did not understand what they said, but the Saffid workers did. They politely ignored Oren and Noni, standing in a tight knot to one side of the air-chariot, having perhaps learned from experience with the Oracle that the affairs of Grafters were best left to Grafters. Oren did not take the time to welcome them to their new home, as he would normally have done, but tugged Noni up the path that followed the crest of the limb.

'I tried to warn him,' she told her brother, when they were out of earshot of the others. 'He wouldn't believe me.'

'A warning is not enough!' Oren admonished her sharply. 'You should have stopped him.'

'How was I to do that?' she asked. She felt overwhelmingly tired, and wished only to find her tent and lie down, though she knew she would have to give her report to Gardan first. 'He's a grown man, Oren. He makes his own decisions.'

'You could have told him it was a trick of the Masters.'

'Are you sure it is? He's had visions of her before that could have been real — the one at Hayman's Point, for example.'

'There's something very wrong happening.' Oren knit his brows unhappily. 'First Pallas, then *Ama*, now this! Why else wouldn't I See Tymon, Noni? Think about it. Maybe it isn't a trick, but the fact that he's gone down into those tunnels is playing directly into our enemies' hands. He's not with us, and without him we haven't a chance. You could have lied, Noni!' he concluded in despair. 'Anything to get him back here.'

'I seem to remember having this conversation with you before he set out for Argos,' she retorted, somewhat tight-lipped. 'Then, you told me it was important he made his own decisions.'

'This isn't the same!' said Oren, seething with frustration at her side. 'Apart from the mess this leaves us in, he's heading into a trap, I can feel it! We won't be able to help him. We won't even know if he's dead or alive.'

She stopped on the path, exasperated in her turn. 'What would you have me do? When I wish to act, you persuade me to wait. Now that I wait, you prefer me to act. Tell me, brother, how may I please you?'

He looked away from her then, stung. 'The Oracle's gone,' he muttered. 'Our Fifth, the one remaining link to her, has been taken from us too. If you appreciated the danger, you'd realise this has nothing to do with pleasing me. Our enemies are attacking on two fronts, just like *Ama* warned. This time, it won't just be dirigibles and armies, though we'll have that to look forward to as well. The Masters are holding our very souls to ransom, Noni.'

He turned to go, but after a few steps faced her again, his mouth twitching with emotion. 'I'm not sure what we're going to tell Galliano,' he said. 'He's been waiting for Tymon's arrival ever since you left: he's going to be devastated.'

And with that, he strode away up the path to the village, leaving her to follow behind, slow and heavy of heart.

He did not join her in the meeting hall for her report to the judges, or hear her being commended for the rescue of the mineworkers. The Freehold leaders also brought her up to date with news of the Saint's crusade, which Oren had not mentioned when he met her on the docking branch. The omission did not surprise her. The loss of the Oracle and Tymon's disastrous abandonment of them would be a far more serious concern to her brother than the arrival of enemy ships. For their part, the judges reacted with some disappointment to the news of Tymon's departure, but no real surprise. They had grown used to the young Argosian's headstrong ways, Noni realised sadly, and had already dismissed him from their minds as someone who could not be relied on.

As Gardan and the others did not ask her to stay on during subsequent discussions about the housing and employment of the Saffid, and indeed appeared as eager to be rid of her as Oren was, she returned, dispirited, to the tent she shared with her brother in the refugees' quarter. Many of the temporary dwellings in the camp, including their own, had by now been converted to semi-permanent constructions, built on high platforms. The twenty Saffid from the mine were just the latest addition to the throng; following the rumours of marauding Argosian soldiers to the west and Lantrian pirates to the south, more refugees from the surrounding area were arriving day by day. But there would be little respite for them on the Freehold. All about her in the camp, Noni could see signs of travel preparations as the young families, the old and the infirm readied themselves for yet another upheaval, yet another evacuation. They would leave the following day, marching deep into the tangled twig-thickets east of the Freehold to wait out the attack.

Oren was not in the tent when she arrived. Noni washed herself sparingly with water from the rain-cistern and lay down on her sleeping mat to rest. After a few minutes, she heard her brother entering through the door-flap. Although she had her face turned to the canvas wall, she could hear, simply from the way he walked, that he was no longer angry.

'Sister,' he whispered, kneeling down beside her on the mat. 'I apologise for my words. You are not Tymon's keeper.'

She rolled over and took his hand, squeezing it. 'You're right to be worried,' she said. 'Without our Fifth, what hope have we of bringing the fledgling Grafters to safety? What hope have we of combating the Envoy?'

'None.' Her brother seemed utterly crestfallen, she thought, more sad than she had ever seen him, including in the Marak jail. 'Actually, there was little hope even with Tymon,' he sighed. 'The Reading visions have been pretty plain about that since you left and Grafter tradition backs them up. The Saint has begun his Last Crusade. There will be attack after attack, and the Freeholds will be wiped out. We can't withstand the Envoy — not alone, not without the Oracle.'

Noni gazed at him in dismay. 'You've told the judges this?'

'We told them this morning. They were grateful for information about the attack, but didn't seem in a hurry to believe the rest. Honestly, Non, sometimes I wish Caro hadn't left us. At least when he was around, the judges opposed to his faction actually listened to us. Now no one does.'

'That's just nostalgia,' she said dryly. 'Only Laska ever listened to us. I'm glad Caro's gone: it lances the sore. What are the judges going to do?'

'They've already sent scouts with messages to Majad and Tuman — I expect the United Fleet will be assembled in two days. They're keeping the rest a secret, to maintain morale, they say. Really, they've just invested too much in our defence to believe it's hopeless.'

'We can't go on like this,' exclaimed Noni, letting go of his hand and sitting up on the mat. 'We have to do something. *Ama* is relying on us to protect these people. We're failing them.'

'That's what I came here to talk to you about,' he said slowly. 'It may be time to start thinking of training another Fifth. I know,' he continued, as his sister winced with distaste. 'It's a terrible wrench. We're twined with Tymon, and we'll have to cut him loose. This shouldn't have to happen, but it sometimes does. Ishi from the north holdings might be a good replacement, and he's young enough to leave with us if we evacuate. We should consult with Ara and Mata, anyway.'

'What about the Oracle? She always praised Tymon, however much trouble he was. He was our last link to her. What if by cutting loose from him, we lose her for good, as well?'

Oren's face fell, as if that particular question distressed him most. 'Then we'll follow her directives and keep the spirit of her work alive, as we do for the Kion,' he replied with some difficulty. 'To try to help her in the Veil, or go on some foolish search for her body, would only take us away from those who need us most. Our mandate is to defend the defenceless. We won't let ourselves be distracted from doing that. It would be just what our enemies wish for.'

As he spoke, the door-flap opened and Ara and Mata entered the tent. The twins smiled in relief when they set eyes on Noni, quickly bending down to embrace her.

'It's good,' began Ara.

'To have the family together again,' finished Mata as they settled themselves on the floor in their usual circle.

There was a pause. Although nobody mentioned Tymon's name, it echoed in all the Grafters' minds like a chime. The four young people did not always need to speak aloud when they were together, even outside the trance. They were deeply attuned to one another's moods, acting as a close-knit, surrogate family. That was indeed an important aspect of the Focal group, for Noni and Oren had lost both parents to illness years ago, while the twins never mentioned theirs, keeping an almost total blank drawn over their origins. The two boys had simply appeared one day in Farhang, out of thin air, attaching themselves to a refugee convoy bound for the village. Such stories were common in the Eastern Domains, and no one pressed them for more information. The Focals, in any case, could never lie to each other; the shared experience of a Reading would not permit it. Ara and Mata did not ask about their absent Fifth, but shared instinctively in Oren and Noni's concern, their eyes growing round and solemn in the silence. The same questions preoccupied all of them.

Tymon had always perceived this close connection with his fellow Grafters as an invasion of privacy, and shut himself off from it. Without him, the young Focals felt stunted; with him, they were forever battling to be heard. And now he had disappeared completely, leaving them adrift. There was a decision to be made.

'A new Fifth,' murmured Mata, after a moment of deliberation.

'I don't want to,' said Ara emphatically.

The Focals' intimacy did not preclude disagreements. On this occasion, Ara was adamantly opposed to the general sentiments of the group.

'None of us wants to,' replied Noni. 'It's a last resort.'

'It's a terrible idea.' Ara set his mouth. Noni and Mata felt his disapproval like a prickling heat and shifted uncomfortably where they sat. Only Oren remained unwavering, cool.

'We needn't decide this ourselves,' he suggested. 'We could ask the Sap.'

'The Sap,' agreed Mata and Noni in unison.

'The Sap won't touch this question,' said Ara. 'It won't take the responsibility away from us, and make everything neat. It's our business, we can't wiggle out of it. We have to decide on our own. *As it should be.*'

'Are you sure of that?' asked Noni. 'Don't we run the risk of doing what we want, instead of what we must?'

Ara did not have to answer: his eyes burned with an unshakable conviction. After a moment the other Grafters nodded.

'Well then, we decide it,' conceded Oren. 'What does everyone think?'

'We're weak without a Fifth,' said Mata.

'Limited in our scope,' added Noni.

'If we cut off the Witness,' argued Ara, 'we'll be blinding ourselves further.'

'So,' said Oren. 'It's a choice between blindness and weakness.'

Outside the tent, evening had fallen and the smell of cooking drifted over the camp. The four young people continued to sit in the gathering twilight, eyes closed or downcast as they considered their situation. They would reach a unanimous decision eventually — they always did. In the meantime, they mulled over this snarl in the fabric of their cohesion, prodding restlessly at it in their minds. A long, silent while passed.

'Weakness,' murmured Oren eventually, 'is strength.' He looked up at his fellows with dawning realisation. 'I apologise, my friends,' he said. 'I've been too upset to think clearly. Ara's right, of course. The cure for a rotting limb may be amputation, but the cure for a broken one is to bind it closer.'

Noni's and Mata's expressions mirrored this complete turnaround. It was not that the other two Focals lacked personal will, or were easily influenced and swayed. They had simply followed the same silent line of reasoning as Oren, and reached a similar conclusion. The atmosphere of the gathering became more relaxed.

'So, we'll limp along,' laughed Noni regretfully, 'and wait for our broken wing to mend, come Storm or Maelstrom.'

'Maybe we'll never be whole —' said Ara

'But at least we won't be blind,' finished Mata.

'We should begin training Ishi during the evacuation, all the same, and maybe young Tudah from the farm-hold, too,' said Oren. 'We can still teach, even if we aren't strong —'

'Excuse me,' called a voice from the entrance to the tent, cutting him short. 'May I come in?'

The Focals glanced up in surprise, as yet another visitor stepped through the door-flap, and Halas stood blinking in the gloom of the tent.

'I was told I could find Oren the Grafter here. Is that correct?' he asked.

Noni, who had not met the messenger from Marak that morning, stared in astonishment at the newcomer still dressed in his dusty travel clothes, carrying a worn and patched backpack. The others smiled and waved him in. During the meeting with the judges, he had spoken in his heavily accented Argosian. Now, he used the Grafters' own lilting, decorous brand of Nurian, and the change was striking to those who had heard him before.

'I wished to speak with you in the hall, but you left too quickly,' he told Oren with a weary grin. 'Afterwards, Gardan had me visiting every blessed judge who didn't make it to the meeting. It took all day, but I can finally make my delivery. I was supposed to give this to you, and only you.'

'Delivery?' echoed Oren, rising politely as the messenger retrieved a neat bundle of paper from his pack. Ara and Mata stirred restlessly where they sat, craning their necks to see what he held.

'There's a peculiar story connected with these papers,' continued Halas, passing the sheaf to Oren. 'By the way, I'm an old acquaintance of Judge Laska's, an undercover agent in the Domains, if you like. You don't know me, but I know you. I've been on a mission out east for the past three months — curse those bastards in Cherk for killing the best captain that ever was.'

He sat down cross-legged on the floor with a grunt of disgust, even as Oren knelt beside him, already lost in perusal of the papers. The young Grafter did not answer his visitor; the others, too, appeared almost to have forgotten Halas, gathering in a semicircle about Oren to see what he was reading. Noni hastily rose and lit a basket lamp, before peering curiously over her brother's shoulder.

'I only found out about it when I returned to Marak,' the agent resumed, when no one responded to his introductions. His expression was ironic, but kind, as he surveyed the young people engrossed in the papers. 'Even the colonial cities haven't escaped the Saint's wrath, you know. He's put Marak under military rule. The Governor answers to Admiral Greenly. The whole city's in an uproar about it —'

'Do you realise what this is?' exclaimed Oren, interrupting the messenger as if he had not listened to a word of his speech.

'Where did you find these papers?' asked Noni, immediately afterwards.

'I'm getting to that,' protested Halas mildly. 'Anyway, part of my mission in Marak was to keep an eye on Caro's *kafa*-heads, as well as the other groups out and about. The Freehold judges like to know what sort of shenanigans they're going to be blamed for next. The newest lot we've seen agitating for reform, religious this time, are the so-called "Kion's Disciples".'

'Tanata,' said Oren. 'But she never wrote this. Not these verses.'

'I didn't say so.'

'Well, who did?' prompted Mata, as their guest hesitated.

'I paid a visit to the Disciples,' resumed Halas, apparently determined to tell his story in his own way, and in his own time, 'because I had reports they were consorting with Argosian missionaries. I knew Tanata was full of tales of brotherly love and so on, but this just struck me as impossible. So I went to talk to them, and found the stories were half-true. They'd been in contact with travelling Argosian performers — Jays. They're an Impure caste, and never cross the Gap, in normal circumstances. Colonials hate them, as you probably know.'

He paused to let the implications of his tale sink in, scrutinising each of the Grafters in turn. 'These Jays came all the way from Argos city,' he continued, seeing with some satisfaction the quick succession of emotions — hope, excitement, disbelief — crossing their faces. 'They brought with them something they considered very important: the last testament of the Kion of Nur, smuggled out before her death.'

The bold declaration seemed to strike the Focals dumb. They crouched on the floor of the tent in a tight knot about Oren, gaping first at the bundle of paper in his hands, then at the calmly smiling messenger. The Oracle had told them of the testament when they spoke in Chal, but they had all thought it beyond their reach, in the Central Canopy. To be given this unexpected insight into the Kion's final hours filled them with unspeakable emotions; it brought tears to their eyes. But it also left them in a state of shock.

'Impossible!' said Noni, in a choked voice.

'It isn't even in Samiha's handwriting!' muttered Oren.

'No, it's a copy,' said Halas. 'The original was lost.'

'How do we know it's authentic?' asked Ara.

'How can we be sure the copy was faithful?' said Mata, almost at the same time.

'We can't be, entirely,' replied the Freehold agent. 'But there are certain indicators that lead me to suppose the Jays were telling the truth. They knew a friend of yours, a young man named Tymon. He's the one who obtained the testament, according to Tanata. She's convinced their story is genuine, by the way, and I had a hard time persuading her to let me bring the papers here. She only agreed to it after she'd had her own people take down a copy for themselves. She says it's holy writ. They all do, even the Jays.' He chuckled as the Grafters drank in his words; he had their entire attention now. 'But it was what happened afterwards that actually convinced me. I wasn't going to take Tanata's word for it. Who knows what games the Saint will play? I went down to the docks myself that day, making enquiries. It was the day the last ships of the admiral's fleet arrived, ready for the start of the crusade. I found the Jay dirigibles. But before I reached them, just as I was walking down the quays, in fact, I saw everyone on board those vessels arrested. I saw the Jays marched out of the air-harbour to the city jail, and I don't think they got a hero's welcome there. The Argosian soldiers turned their barges upside down. They were looking for something. I believe you have what they want.'

'Our only hope,' muttered Oren, relief dawning on his face.

'A gap over Marak!' breathed Ara and Mata together.

'The Witness' gift,' said Noni. 'Ah, Tymon.'

She rubbed her hand over her eyes, weeping freely. About her, her fellow Focals sat with their heads bowed. She knew they felt the same turmoil in their hearts — a mixture of gratitude towards Tymon for stubbornly insisting on the trip to Argos city, of shame that they had ever considered replacing him, and of acute distress that he might not see the fruits of his labours.

Halas declined their belated offers of *yosha* and hospitality, apparently content to have made his delivery. Soon afterwards he left, returning to the tent that had been assigned to him to wash and prepare for the evening meal. The Focals themselves decided to skip supper in the dining hall, remaining together to do the only thing that seemed important to them at that moment. They read and discussed the Kion's testament far into the night, by the light of the basket lantern. When Ara and Mata finally stumbled back to their own tent to snatch an hour of sleep, the moon was setting behind the western twig-thickets and the first traces of dawn were in the sky. The coming day, the day of the evacuation from the Freehold, would not permit any study at all.

The young Grafters met again later that morning, carrying their scanty belongings and exchanging nods of greeting as they joined the noisy, slightly chaotic assemblage on the path that ran through the centre of the camp. Gardan and two other judges passed up and down the line of evacuees, speaking with the heads of households and exchanging notes with the expedition leader — a tall, formidable-looking Farhang woman, wrapped in grey cloth up to her eyes, like a human pillar. Children shrieked with excitement and ran to and fro, unaware of the gravity of their situation. Those from Sheb were generally quieter than their companions from Farhang; they had seen two previous evacuations, and were becoming practised nomads, patient with upheaval. A few of the refugees had only just arrived the day before, to hear that they would be leaving again. Noni glimpsed the Saffid workers sitting on their haunches in a group near the back of the line. She smiled and waved to them. A few slowly raised their hands in response.

The Focals did not say much to each other as they stood in the queue. They were still brimful of Samiha's words, unable to speak any of their own. The testament lay safe in Oren's backpack, practically the only thing he had bothered to take with him apart from the rations doled out to every evacuee. The four Focals no longer doubted the authenticity of the papers, for they had recognised the Kion's inimitable voice in the lines, precious and familiar, giving them hope. They yearned to share their discovery with others, but knew the time was not right.

A short while later, the line began moving sluggishly forward as the refugees filed down the path that led out of the camp, one by one. But Noni walked with a light and buoyant step, the Kion's words reverberating through her whole being. She felt the verses rising up in her throat, pushing against her palate, clamouring to be heard. *I rely on you, Tymon, to tell my story as it was, without embellishment.* The testament was written in the traditional style of a mystic love-poem, supposedly intimate but actually addressed to all. Even so, the epistolary style did give Noni some hope for Tymon's survival. Perhaps he would read and tell that story for himself, one day. The testament, she knew, was primarily a public declaration — holy writ to some, but also a frank and open challenge to the Argosian priests and busy war-mongers everywhere. No wonder the Saint had given orders to suppress it! It was meant to be shared widely, its intimacy taken symbolically, something no literal-minded priest would ever understand. Preoccupied by these thoughts, Noni did not immediately hear the thin voice crying out behind her. She only stopped in her tracks when Oren grabbed her arm.

'Look!' he said, as she glanced over her shoulder to see the familiar form of Galliano stumbling at the rear of the queue.

They had been told that the scientist would remain in the camp with a few of the judges, leaving just before the attack, in an air-chariot. Noni had been secretly relieved not to meet him the day before in the dining hall, dreading the old man's reaction to Tymon's absence. But Galliano had caught up with them, now. He was almost falling over on the path in his haste to catch up with them, waving his cane in the air. The people at the end of the line cried out in warning as he bumped into them, caught his elbow as he half-collided with a nearby twig-stump and staggered on.

'Noni? Oren?' he called to the air about him, in Argosian. 'Are you there?'

'We are, *syor*,' Oren replied in the foreign tongue. He pushed past those in the queue behind him, and hurried back to the blind scientist with Noni close on his heels. 'What can we do for you? We thought you stay in Farhang!'

'I'm staying,' gasped Galliano, wheezing for breath. 'And so should you. I'll explain why in a moment. Come close, so I can feel I'm speaking to your faces. It's difficult, talking to a void.'

He reached out his gnarled, trembling hands to grasp their shoulders as he spoke. 'I understand,' he continued, as they glanced at one another anxiously, 'I understand that you left my boy behind in the South Canopy. I won't ask what possessed you to do it, because I know him. He insisted on staying. He always does exactly as he pleases.'

'We're so sorry, *syor*,' said Noni regretfully. 'We know Tymon was like a son to you.'

'Believe me, I'm used to it,' snorted Galliano. 'That scamp will think of everything farthest away from him before he thinks of home. That's how his mind works — he draws a wide arc before returning to the beginning. No, no. Something else troubles me. I also suspect — correct me if I'm wrong — that you're unable to See him in your Grafting visions. Is that right?'

'It's true,' said Oren. 'But you do not believe in those, I think, *syor*?'

'I don't pronounce any judgment on the Grafting. It's not my area of expertise. But I do know one thing. What you two believe will affect how you react to my boy's disappearance. It's as if he's dead, am I right?' There was a note of distress in the old man's voice; his fingers gripped their shoulders with unconscious anxiety.

'Alas, *syor*,' answered Noni, 'when another Grafter, especially one as deeply connected to us as Tymon was, is no longer visible in the world of the trance, it can mean only two things. Either he's dead, or he has been engulfed in our enemies' power. If that's the case, then he might as well be dead. He's lost to us for now —'

'Nonsense!' interrupted Galliano. 'No one's ever lost! Not really. You don't give up on people who matter, after only two days! You try to reach them, and try again. When that's over, you try once more. You won't wash your hands of Tymon while I'm around!'

'That's not what we're doing,' said Noni, her pale face flushing in embarrassment. 'We're not washing our hands of him. Please don't think that.'

The long line of refugees continued to walk by them, swelling and dividing into two rivulets on the path before closing ranks to trickle out of the camp. Some glanced back curiously to watch the altercation taking place behind them. Last in line, the Saffid group trudged by, whispering to each other as the old scientist harangued the young Grafters, his beard fairly bristling with outrage. Although Galliano kept a tight grip on Oren's shoulder with one hand, he let go of Noni with the other in order to gesticulate impatiently in the air.

'Then do something about it!' he harrumphed. 'Why don't you go after him? Why don't you even think to talk it through with me? I might be able to help, you know.'

Oren and Noni glanced at each other again, full of pity for the old man. Noni began to wonder whether the scientist had not begun to go senile. His love for Tymon was blinding him still further. 'Did it ever occur to you,' he was spluttering now, 'not to rely on all your mystic wisdom for once, but ask for a practical man's advice?'

'What do you suggest, *syor*?' asked Oren. 'Do you wish to go after him, into tunnels, into mines? We wish also, but this is impossible task. How do we know where he goes if we cannot Read him?'

'Not the mine,' said Galliano. 'I know where he's gone, and I know another way of getting there. I have plans in my tent I could show you — ah, I wish you'd come and seen me before! If he's determined to go into the Tree, as I hear from your Saffid workers, he'll reach the rhizome layer, one way or another. The centre of the Tree is hollow, riddled with gaps and old sap-conduits. They all lead to the same place.'

This time, the look the Grafters exchanged was one of astonishment. 'How do you know this, *syor*?' Oren enquired.

'I'm a professor in applied Treeology,' answered the scientist, with a degree of weariness. 'What do you think we studied at the seminary? The priests aren't only about killing heretics and preaching to the wayward, you know. They have plenty of perfectly good scientific and historical knowledge in their library, which they sit on like a flock of brooding buzzards. Oh yes, the Council knew about *Lacuna*.'

Galliano was perfectly fine, thought Noni suddenly. It was they who had been blind, yet again: there was something important here, something to what the old man was saying. She felt it instinctively; sensed Oren's shiver of shock as he stood by her, on hearing the legendary name given to the World Below.

'A century ago, they sent Explorers under the Storm, to verify the stories,' Galliano continued, his voice dropping low, though the last of the refugees had passed them by and disappeared through a tunnel of twigs at the borders of the camp. 'Contrary to what was reported, those people didn't travel through the clouds in a ship — not on their most successful journeys, anyway. They used a natural shaft near Argos city to descend. What they found was so troubling that it was kept a secret by the Council, the tunnel sealed and all further travel below. the Storm banned. They throw a poor pilgrim into the remains of the shaft each year, as you know. A cynical exercise to keep a cynical secret. Of course, secrets work only when people have forgotten what was common knowledge to begin with. I believe Nurian Grafters remember the civilisations that once flourished at the base of the Tree …'

Noni could feel her brother's unease radiating out of him. 'Those cities were filled with bad people, *syor*,' he told Galliano. 'Perhaps it is best Argosians forget them.'

'That's what the Council decided,' replied the scientist. 'They decided to bury the truth. I personally think they were wrong. Be that as it may, if Tymon has gone into a mine in search of Samiha, there's every chance he'll end up in the sap-conduits, because that's where the Lantrians dig for their blessed corewood. Luckily, we don't need to follow him there. The Tree has lost integrity at its base because of its age, and many of the shafts merge together to form big hollow spaces at the foot of the trunk. Tymon will end up in one of those chambers, mark my words. He's going to walk out of the Tree and find himself in the World Below.'

'And so you wish to meet him there,' burst out Noni, her heartbeat quickening. 'Now I understand. Yes, *syor*! It's worth a try.'

But Oren did not echo her joy. He stood silent and troubled beside her. She wondered why he was so reticent: this was a chance to help Tymon. Wasn't it?

'We could cross the clouds, and do a sweep of the whole area underneath the mine,' said Galliano eagerly. 'The judges have already agreed to a voyage below the Storm, on principle —'

'Wait,' interrupted Oren, holding up his hands. 'Wait, both of you. We forget what is most important, in seeking what is important. We must think of all, not one. Right now we must help Freeholders. First survive attack, then go on rescue mission, *syor*.'

Although all was peaceful and sunlit around them, the twig-thickets emptied of the refugees' noise and clamour, Noni noticed that her brother's face had lost its colour. His hand was trembling on her shoulder as he promised Galliano that the trip to the World Below would take precedence over all else, after the Argosian attack. She realised with dismay that something had frightened him deeply. But he said nothing more about it, taking the old scientist into his arms and embracing him in a fond and wordless farewell. Galliano refused to let them conduct him back to his tent, remaining poised like a bent twig on the borders of the empty camp as they left, his arm raised in farewell.

Oren's unease did not diminish after they had set off down the path in the wake of the other refugees. Noni watched him covertly as they walked, wondering when he would confess to what preoccupied him. Whatever her brother had to say, she guessed it would not be pleasant.

'You realise what this means,' he muttered to her at last, in their own language, after they had lost sight of Galliano among the twigs.

'I thought it might be good news,' she answered, wistful. 'Some hope for our friend.'

'It's terrible news,' said Oren flatly. 'It means Tymon has definitely Seen a shadow-form sent by the Masters. Who else would know the paths into the Old Places? Who else would be interested in luring him there? They've been working on him ever since he began having those accursed visions. They chased away the Oracle to get to him. Now, they're leading him to *Lacuna*. Think, Noni. What do they do to Grafters? He'll be lost to us by the time we reach him — Eaten.'

The word was like a physical blow to Noni, knocking all joy out of her. Even the triumph of retrieving the Kion's testament drained away. To be truly Eaten was no glorious martyr's fate, as the priests in Argos liked to claim. The victim lost his mind, driven mad by the parasitic attacks of the rogue Born. The worst of it, thought Noni grimly, was her own lack of surprise at the conclusion. Now that Oren had articulated the idea, she realised she had half-suspected it herself. She had dreaded that Tymon was being lured into the tunnels by a creature more deadly than the Envoy himself, and tried to forget that the possibility existed.

'There was a moment, talking to him, when I think I guessed it …' Her admission trailed off miserably before she started again. 'He described how he felt with this — Samiha. It seemed odd. I didn't let myself think. I hoped for the best.'

'You couldn't have known for sure,' Oren told her.

But Noni felt she might have known, should have known, had known, if she had only listened to her own instincts. She was devastated by her wilful blindness, berating herself bitterly for it.

'So, what do we do?' she asked in a small voice, as they caught up with the straggling line of evacuees.

'What we said we'd do,' said Oren. 'Take care of the others, then go after him. But we won't find him when we get there. We'll find a raving shell.'

Noni walked in wordless misery after that, not even managing to greet their companions when they rejoined the line. Ara and Mata immediately picked up on their fellow Grafters' mood, growing subdued when Oren and Noni arrived; they reacted to Oren's whispered report of the conversation with Galliano, and his fears for Tymon, with deep distress. The journey went on in dismal silence. They covered a little over five miles that day with the slow-moving train, winding up and down branches and through the twig-thickets east of the Freehold to reach their camp site for the night. The judges had decided to use a clump of thick, serried twigs as a hideout, a cave-like enclosure formed where the tops of several branches met and intermingled. If the Argosians wished to find them there, they would have to come on foot and in single file, picking their way between the close-growing shafts.

The refugees set up camp in a sloping clearing, hardly more than a wider path or furrow between the twigs. No one spoke much, everyone feeling either tired or downhearted. Noni carried out the mechanical tasks of unpacking canvas and hammocks in an anxious daze. But even in her preoccupied state, it occurred to her to wonder, after a while, why the Farhang Freeholders were bothering to establish two separate sleeping areas in the clearing. There was the main one in the highest and widest part of the furrow, where it ought to be, but also another at the far end, where the growth underfoot was rough and uncomfortable. It doubled the work of building shelters and created a very inferior second camp. At last, she took her courage in hand and questioned Adhama Sing, the pillar of grey strength who had led the evacuation, as to the reason for the choice.

'Separate sleep for cursed ones,' replied Adhama in her clipped, guttural Nurian. She indicated the Saffid sitting in a quiet knot on the far side of the clearing with a flip of her fingers. 'Don't want 'em infecting others. Feel sorry for 'em and all, but won't have 'em round babies.'

'But they're not infectious,' protested Noni, taken aback. 'Everyone knows that. It's not really the Slow Death — it affects them, and no one else.'

'Decided while walking,' declared the woman, fixing her with eyes as flat and grey as the folds of her cloak. 'Whiteskins are sick. Told 'em already. Everyone's choice: fine with you.'

'No, it's not fine with me,' said Noni, growing hot in the face. 'I never made that choice. I don't think it's right to make the Saffid feel unwelcome, for no reason. They've come a long way looking for a better life.'

'Everyone's choice,' repeated Adhama, slowly and clearly, as if to a child. 'Fine with you.'

It would have to be fine with her whether she liked it or not, Noni realised, staring in consternation as Adhama gave her a curt nod, and moved away to oversee the cooking area. This decision was doubtless what most of the northerners, perhaps even the people of Sheb wanted. They had accepted her and Oren without question, but drew the line at the Saffid. Maybe that was also what was meant by the 'fine with you': Adhama was telling Noni, in a veiled threat, that she must toe the line, or face being labelled a pariah, too.

It was all too much for the Grafter girl, after a day of self-recrimination over Tymon. She stamped off to the corner of the main camp where the Focals were hanging their hammocks between twigs, and picked up her own pack, red-faced and trembling. The others gazed after her in surprise as she turned and marched without a word to the narrow and uncomfortable corner where the Saffid had gathered. Placing her belongings by theirs, she sat pointedly down beside them.

14

'Open the keg, you scum!' roared a voice on the deck above Bolas, thickened by Treesap wine.

Bolas recognised it immediately. He also recognised his corporal's stamping tread on the deck-boards. A tremendous thump sent a plume of wood-dust down to settle on his head as he crouched miserably on the floor of the hold, sharpening hardwood spears in the dirigible's barracks. His fellow soldiers were all above deck, enjoying their night off in Marak before embarking on the journey north the next day, and the real start of the crusade. He had been singled out by his corporal to remain below, given a heap of spears to polish while his fellows celebrated under the stars. The weather continued to oblige them, remaining as cold and dry as on their journey through the Upper Fringes, and later across the Gap. It seemed the Tree had blessed the Saint's war, keeping its winter storms at bay while the fleet gathered in Marak. The soldiers were warming themselves with wine, egged on by their superior officer.

The corporal did not think much of Bolas. The young architect did not, according to his bellowing superior, sing patriotic ballads with sufficient fervour, which is why he had been left out of the party. Everyone else was anticipating the upcoming battle with sickening enthusiasm. All the other youths like himself, who had been confined to the ship on the journey from Argos city, were now permitted to drink their fill to make up for not receiving passes to the town. They were due to set sail for their first Freehold target tomorrow morning. But for now, the Argosian soldiers were singing their hearts out, thumping their boots off, as well as drinking a great deal, with all the consequences that entailed. The first cask of Treesap wine must have been drained already, if the corporal was braying for a second to be opened.

As far as Bolas was concerned, there was little reason to celebrate the prospect of wiping out the 'Nurry problem'. Since Admiral Greenly could not subdue every last louse with his newfangled blast-cannons, that singular pleasure had been reserved for the young soldiers. They would erupt from the dirigible in three days' time, at a signal from the corporal, and crush everything that moved in the woodwork. They were under strict orders to give no quarter when they attacked the Freehold. This time, there would be no prisoners taken or exchanged by the Argosian infantry, no opportunity for the damn Nurries and their traitor allies to pull any tricks. The surrounding canopy would be wiped clean of survivors — man, woman or child — and Farhang pummelled to ash.

Bolas anticipated the coming battle with the numb patience of a creature snatched up by a bird of prey, unable to avoid his fate. He sighed as another loud thump on deck shed dust all over him, and spat half-heartedly on the point of the lance he was polishing. The name of the Freehold target was not lost on him. He remembered the honest face of the Nurian scout named Pallas, and the tale Tymon had told of his adopted home. He thought of the people who had helped his old friend, and how they were no better or worse than his own people. All those lives, doomed in advance by the sharpened spearheads in his lap, the pile of gleaming crossbow bolts by his side. He was in half a mind to blunt the blades, except he knew that would merely increase the suffering of those struck down. The rough whetting tool made of pulped fibre rubbed his palms raw as he worked in rhythm to the thump of feet and the roar of the merrymakers overhead.

'Come on, open it up!' bellowed the corporal, to the sound of general laughter.

The barracks where Bolas was confined for the night were a long, low-ceilinged room at the aft of the dirigible, equipped with hammocks and little else. The windows, he had already ascertained, were too small to fit through, even if he had had the heart to dream of escape. The only glimpse of Marak city afforded by the portholes was the far right-hand corner of the ruined Governor's palace, brooding over the town. He inspected the shining blade in his lap, considering that falcons, despite their cruel and sharp talons, were as helpless as the creatures they preyed on. He was as bound to his fate as the innocent people he would be required to kill. Except that the greater disaster was theirs.

There was naturally no one to confide his woes to on the crusader ship. Overhead, his comrades-in-arms had begun to sing again: the Four Canopies would bloom, they chanted, watered by the blood of martyrs. The Lawgiver's rule would bring eternal peace, but first his faithful servants must wipe their enemies from the face of the Tree. The Nurians, bastard spawn of wayward tribes and demons from the Storm, had had their chance at repentance, and would now be obliterated. Praise be the Tree, sang the soldiers in the barracks ship, for any man who died in this holy struggle would go straight to Paradise, to be waited on by the willing maids of Heaven. The fact that the soldiers were more like boys than men themselves, and that most had never touched a maid of any sort, heavenly or not, seemed only to fuel their eagerness. They had been drilled by their roaring corporal to anticipate death, primed for the inevitable day when they would be disgorged from the ship with the name of the Saint on their lips.

Bolas listened to the carousing of his drunken comrades, a hundred desperate resolutions forming in his mind. He would desert at the first opportunity, he thought, setting the gnarled fibre to the spear's edge and wincing as it seared his skin yet again. He would raise his bow, he decided, but not fire. He would fire high. He would fire low. When he finally wondered, with a sore heart as well as bleeding hands, whether he should kill himself rather than harm Tymon's friends, he was honest enough to discount that option quickly. He did not want to die by any means. He wanted to live, and hold Nell in his arms once more.

'Why can't you open the damn thing?' belched the corporal from up above. 'It's only a cask of Treesap, not a bloody virgin! Come on!'

Bolas shuddered as he finished sharpening the blade. He must be a terrible person, he told himself, to have ended up in this situation. He must be paying the price for going to the Green Rites, for allowing an innocent man to be put to death without lifting a finger to help. For it was the events of that terrible day, less than a year ago, which haunted him now, on the eve of war. And to think he had been so eager to participate! The solemn rite he had been led to expect had turned out to be a travesty. He knew, now, that the Rites were for appearance only, for the crowd on the quays. Once they were inside, the Divine Mouth had proved to be a disappointingly shallow cavern, the black crack at its heart deep enough for murder, but not Sacrifice. There had been no willing surrender at the last — only hesitation, a dawning doubt on the part of the poor, befuddled pilgrim. The Nurian had been as confused as those burping fools on the deck tonight, prepared for glory and martyrdom on the morrow.

The priests had not waited for the pilgrim to change his mind. Bolas had seen the brutal deed with his own eyes. At a word from the Dean, a guard had stepped up and stabbed the Nurian in the back as he teetered at the edge of the hole, pushing the man into the shaft without further ceremony. Standing nearby with the other stunned Green Year students, Bolas had turned aside from the abrupt execution, doubled over with nausea. When he vomited on the floor of the Tree-cave, a probable blasphemy, no one had bothered to make him clean it up. For most of those present at the Rites, the horror they had witnessed simply brought them closer together, reminding them of a shared responsibility. But for Bolas, it had been a wake-up call. Never again, he had sworn to himself, kneeling on the soiled bark. Never again would he allow the priests to dupe him.

And yet here he was, obliged to serve the murderers once more. No amount of swearing on his part could save him now. None of his oaths would stand between him and the coming crusade.

'For heaven's sake, you damned fools, get out of the way and give me that crowbar!' roared the corporal. 'I'll show you how to deal with this!'

What happened next was hard for Bolas to remember. He sensed, rather than saw, a blinding flash as he was thrown backwards by a tremendous force, and dashed against the side of the hold. The flash was followed by red-tinged darkness and searing pain, mixed with the hot, scorched smell of cooked flesh.

He sat where he had been thrown with the memory of bright light dancing in his eyes, unable to move his legs, pinned by some heavy object to the floor. It was a long while before the pain caused him to pass out, and forgiving blackness enveloped him.

The wine cask, he learned later, had been tampered with by Nurian rebels, filled with blast-poison as part of a ploy to undermine the Saint's success. It had exploded, killing most of the ship's company and leaving a hole twenty feet wide in the hull. Bolas escaped with his life, but sustained injuries to both his legs, crushed by a beam from the collapsing ceiling. But in his fevered recollections, it was the head of the corporal that fell on top of him, pinning him down. It lay in his lap for a considerable length of time, staring up at him with bloodshot eyes, still roaring and braying out orders to kill those Nurries, damn them, kill, kill, kill.

The Envoy sat in silence in his garret room at the seminary, feeling the College humming with energy beneath him, purring with accumulated power. He was at the hub of the world and the centre of the web: all the Saint's busy plots and plans, the sticky strands of domination, poured forth from here to capture their unwary prey. That day, Fallow had received encouraging reports from spies in Lantria maintaining that the southern offensive was a success, their enemies in retreat. There were, moreover, rumours of the destruction of a Tree-mine key to the war effort, apparently in a natural disaster. Lace was unsurprised, having long foreseen the structural weakness of the South Canopy. The Tree, it seemed, smiled on the Saint's endeavours, to the extent of self-destruction. Tomorrow, the offensive against the Nurian Freeholds would finally begin. The *orah*-clock predicted success after success, a string of military triumphs.

Lace, however, sat brooding on his narrow bed, as if all these evidences of manifest destiny were not enough for him. He did not doubt the outcome of the Saint's crusade, heralding a spate of victories that would bring the Four Canopies under the Lawgiver's sway. But something else troubled him, pricking at the back of his mind even as he prepared himself to play his own part in that grand offensive. His Masters had been silent for days. They had not yanked on his leash since he sent the acolytes on their mission, refraining from calling him to the Veil for further reports, though he had information that might influence their plans in the World Below. Wick and Gowron, as he had observed to his annoyance in his last session with the *orah*-clock, had picked up an additional passenger, one they should by rights have left behind.

It was not that the girl, Jedda, could prevent the Oracle's death. The SAP-measure was clear about that. Her presence would only exacerbate the existing rivalry between the Envoy's two acolytes, a rivalry inevitably resulting in the death of the weaker one. This was all *as it should be*, if he might indulge in the phrase. But Jedda meant something else to Lace, something he was loath to admit even to himself. She reminded him starkly of his own failure. She had resisted him to the last, ridding herself of the addictive *orah* and escaping the curses he sent after her. Her strength of mind was galling. He doubted she could stymie his plans alone and unaided, but would have liked to report her presence all the same. And yet his Masters had given him strict instructions, at the end of their last interview, not to return until he was called. They had informed him that they would be engaged in delicate work over the next few days, work that required all their powers of concentration. They did not wish to be disturbed. He had been told that they had no time left for his whining; they had kicked him away like a begging cur.

He snorted softly to himself in derision, lying down on the mattress. So be it. His Masters could take care of themselves. He would win the Saint's little war for him, dust up the Freeholds and keep an eye on his errant acolytes, when and where he could. He had already taken leave of his seminary colleagues, ostensibly to depart at dawn on one of his private retreats; it would take a fair amount of time, a week perhaps, to ensure the smooth operation of the Saint's will beyond the coercive sphere of the *orah*-clock. And then he would be free to make the World Key his.

On this occasion, Eblas did not quit his false body to enter the Veil. He allowed the construct of Father Lace to lose cohesion, sighing apart on the bed so that he could channel the few molecules of real matter it contained to other uses. The sands of him melted and dispersed into separate clumps, a seething heap that spawned new forms like heavy smoke, spilling and tumbling off the mattress onto the floor. The smaller constructs were vaguely bird- or bat-shaped, but wispy and tenuous, lacking the physical presence of the curses produced by Wick. They rose up in a ghostly, flapping swarm and flew out of the open window of the room, darkening the moonlight outside by their passage. If any of the Fathers had glanced out of the College windows at that moment, they would have assumed a flock of bats had been disturbed from their roosts behind the seminary bell tower, flying eastwards into the canopy.

The swarm wheeled over Argos city then streamed away, rising in a grey cloud up the face of the trunk. They were speedy and tireless, fearing neither cold nor hunger. In this shape, he knew, the Envoy would be able to reach the Eastern Canopy within days.

15

The silence at the heart of the Tree was not complete, nor was it devoid of life. What seemed, at first glance, to be acres of dry bark and fathoms of dead wood, proved on closer inspection to be teeming with tiny communities: bugs and beetles, patient spiders and stalwart woodlice that scattered in panic at the approach of a torch. These busy denizens were of course the first signs of apocalypse — the secret, ticking clockwork of decay. The covert agents of destruction acted without any regard for the wars or ambitions of humanity, bringing to an inevitable close the millennia-long lifespan of the Tree. Woodworms had been chewing holes beneath the priests' feet for centuries, and termites had colonised the dry sap-conduits, leaving heaps of red dust on the floors of the tunnels through which Tymon and Zero passed. Where the hollow shafts were more accessible to the outer strata of the Tree, moths had bored their way through the bark, laid their eggs in the walls and left generations of pupae to chew tiny channels into the wood grain. The sides of the dry sap-well with its evenly cut ramp were riddled with these reminders of mortality. Zero ran his left hand lightly over the wandering script of wormholes as he walked after Tymon, his fingers deciphering the language of endings.

The busy work of deconstruction only grew more pronounced as they reached the end of the ramp, and entered the large hollow spaces at the base of the Tree. Before Zero's last torch was consumed they were already travelling through a series of caverns opening one into another, a rotting honeycomb of wood. The walls in this labyrinth were moist and clammy, blooming with lichen and fungus, the air filled with the whispering echo of running water. When the final shred of torch-rope fizzled out in his hand, Zero blinked away the memory of flame to find that he could still see.

Some of the fields of fungus produced a phosphorescent light as strong as the lodes of corewood in the upper passages, and he was able to pick his way over the spongy growth in pursuit of his companion. The ramp had disappeared, or was buried under the mounds of mildew; it had been colonised by crops of mushrooms that quivered on stalks like the twig-forests of the upper canopies. But if Zero ever doubted his path, he had only to glance up at Tymon. The young Argosian walked through the fungus forest and across the fields of bubbling decay as if they did not exist. He never once hesitated, though he stumbled with fatigue. His expression was set and distant, and he walked with his gaze trained on his invisible guide.

Zero ached with concern as he watched his friend march on. Tymon seemed to slip farther from him with every hour they journeyed into the depths of the Tree: the *Syon's* eyes were glazed over and heavy lidded, his skin glistening with sweat in the cool tunnels. He had spoken little to Zero after his comment about love, unable or unwilling to reply to his companion's questions. But his lips moved in whispered answer to a voice Zero could not hear, and he would occasionally blurt out a word or phrase, laughing aloud. He walked fast for all his dazed state, unmindful of any danger in the dimly lit caverns. If he lost his footing on the slippery fungus and fell, scraping the skin of his palms on the wet bark, he simply rose again and carried on, as if he felt no pain. Zero was hard put to keep up with him.

Still the Marak lad struggled on, clinging to a faint hope. Tymon's madness was not complete; there were moments of lucidity, brief episodes during which he would behave normally for a few minutes, before lapsing into non-communication again. Even in his current state, he must not have entirely forgotten Zero, for after each long march he halted and waited for his companion to catch up. When Zero trudged wearily over to where he sat on his haunches, staring blankly ahead, Tymon registered his presence as though waking from a dream. He would jump up and ask Zero whether he was tired; he was very kind on these occasions, before the distant daze set in again. Once or twice he even humbly asked Zero's forgiveness, berating himself for leaving his friend behind. But after a brief exchange, he usually sank into his thoughts once more and became oblivious, mumbling to himself in the green-tinged darkness.

And so it carried on, hour after hour, day after day, until Zero despaired of ever seeing the light again, either at the end of the tunnel or in Tymon's eyes. They had spent one full day descending the ramp in the sap-well, according to the Marak lad's calculations, and two more traversing the lower caverns. On the fifth morning after leaving Noni and the mineworkers, they glimpsed a bright gleam in the darkness ahead, paler than any corewood or fungal phosphorescence. The glowing lichen had petered out by this time, and they were obliged to grope their way blindly towards the sliver of light, emerging at last onto a ledge about halfway up the wall of another massive cavern. This final hollow — a great, gutted hall of rot, hundreds of feet wide and high — culminated in an open archway, filled with filtered afternoon sunlight. The glow from the outside was as bright as noon to the travellers, though the mouth of the hollow was still about a quarter of a mile distant.

Zero could not help wondering, as he stared at that radiance, if the Argosian priests had been right about Hell being at the foot of the Tree. He had grown intensely suspicious of Tymon's invisible guide during their journey, convinced that the hungry ghost was leading them both to their death, which he now suspected would be a watery one. For fifteen yards below the ledge a black river flowed, the sum of countless rainwater channels running down and through the Tree to wash out again into the sunlit world. The mysterious ramp they had followed into the sap-well had reappeared, cut into the bark wall on their right. The path here was scored with fissures and blocked by debris, but Zero could see it led in a gentle slope all the way down to that infernal river. And as he scrambled after Tymon over lumps of fallen bark and yards of trailing moss, he became increasingly convinced that the spirit road was taking them where no mortal man could survive. But there was no way he could let his friend know they were on the wrong path.

The denizens of the rotted Tree-hall turned out to be suitable guardians for a passage to Hell. Before long, the travellers' progress disturbed a huge flock of bats nesting in the cavern ceiling. Even Tymon had to halt and press himself against the wall, as myriad black shapes rose in an outraged cloud to swoop by their ears; Zero flung his arms over his head in superstitious dread, though the bats deftly circumnavigated him, never once brushing his skin with their wings. Like the river, which was wider than any Zero had seen gushing through the canopies, the flock was gigantic. The whirring cloud seemed to take forever to pass. At last, the bats wheeled in a vast arc and streamed out of the hollow, shrieking faintly into Hell.

'Better them than the Envoy's curses, any day,' remarked a quiet voice beside Zero, as the flock disappeared.

Zero lowered his arms in surprise to see Tymon smiling tiredly at him. The *Syon* was exhausted, haggard-looking and streaked with dirt in the unforgiving daylight, but clearly himself again.

'You're better, *Syon!*' exclaimed the Marak boy in relief.

'I wasn't sick.' Tymon shrugged his pack off onto the ramp before opening up the bag. 'But I'm incredibly hungry, for some reason. Let's stop and rest, if you don't mind.'

Zero was delighted with the prospect and began to rummage inside his own pack for rations. Oh, if only this could last, he thought, glancing surreptitiously at his gaunt-faced friend. No food had passed Tymon's lips for two days. Although their rations were low, perhaps only enough to last them another week, Zero was happy to see his friend consume two full packets from the stores. The *Syon's* appetite had come to symbolise their shared survival.

'Is the spirit gone?' he enquired cautiously, as he sat down on the tumbledown ramp beside Tymon. He restricted himself to a bare minimum of food, grateful to see his companion still chewing.

'Just for a while,' mumbled Tymon through a dried-fruit roll. 'The connection lasts longer down here than it did in the mine, but I suppose she's as tired as we are. She'll be back, never fear.'

'It's the coming back I fear,' said Zero, grasping at this opportunity for communication. 'When she's with you, *Syon*, you don't act right.'

Tymon peered at him in amused surprise. 'What do you mean?' he said. 'Of course it's a bit odd, me talking to thin air and all. That's to be expected.'

'It's more than that,' insisted Zero. 'You don't eat — you don't sleep. She uses up your evil. It's very worrying.'

Tymon stared at him a moment, then burst out laughing as he wiped the crumbs from his knees. 'Why would I waste time sleeping all day, while we have a job to do?' he said.

'But you can't go on like this,' protested Zero. 'It'll kill you. She'll kill you.'

A shadow passed across Tymon's face. 'I'm surprised at you, Zero,' he admonished. 'Does it really kill you to go a few hours without a rest stop?'

'A few hours?' asked the Nurian, aghast. 'Is that how long you think we've been travelling?'

'A day and a night. Why? How long do you think it's been?'

'Five days, *Syon*. We've been walking for five days.'

This response seemed to confound Tymon. He frowned, passing a hand across his eyes. 'But we're almost there,' he muttered, more to himself than to Zero. 'We're close to the body now — she told me. It's just outside. We can't give up now.'

'I thought she didn't know where the body was,' said Zero unhappily. 'What's outside, anyway?' he added, desperate to hold on to this brief instant of lucidity. 'Where are we going? Is it Hell?'

But Tymon did not hear him, or did not want to hear him. To Zero's dismay, he was already rising to his feet on the ramp, heaving up his backpack. 'I can See her,' he called over his shoulder, his eyes bright with excitement. 'She's waiting for us at the mouth of the cavern, where the ramp ends. I told you she'd be back soon.'

'No!' cried Zero. 'Don't follow, *Syon!*'

It was too late. Tymon was running down the ramp, almost tripping over himself in his eagerness, as he waded through the mouldy bark and mossy debris. Zero picked up his own bag and trailed reluctantly after him down to the riverbank. By the time he caught up with his friend by the shallows, the *Syon* was lost to him once more, his lips moving silently and his face full of exultation as he greeted whoever, or whatever, it was he saw. He followed his guide without a second glance at Zero, striding into the vast empty spaces of Hell.

'Long ago,' said Samiha, 'long ago, my love, we were one. There was no division between the Born and their creations, no line between Gods and men.'

Tymon was aware that he must be hearing her in his mind, as he had the Oracle, although his recollection of what his teacher had told him when they were together had grown vague. Indeed, all his recent memories had grown peculiarly distant, as if the experiences might or might not have been his own. The events after Samiha's execution — the battle with Wick and the journey on the South Road, his trials and triumphs in Chal, even the flogging at Hayman's Point — had taken on the quality of a dream. He still saw the old scars on his body when he looked for them, a mute testament to the reality of pain, but they were disconnected from him, unimportant. Pain no longer existed in Samiha's presence. He did not remember the brightness of the Sap filling him when he fought off the Envoy's curses, or the sensation of the Oracle's power when she spoke through him in the trance.

Irresistibly exhilarating, the connection to Samiha had erased all else. Her presence left no room for doubt, personal recall, even a sense of responsibility. He shook off the thought of Zero dragging at his heels in order to concentrate wholly on his love. She was all he had and all he needed, he told himself, following her as loyally as the Tree-hounds had followed Lord Dayan. Even so, he was not entirely blind to the changes that had taken place since he first glimpsed Samiha in the mine.

In the darkness of the tunnels, her figure had shone like a gentle, guiding light. Then, she had seemed unsure of where they were going, needing him as much as he needed her. Now all that had changed. Though still dear and familiar, her form had become tinged with a strange electric blue that was a little disconcerting, and she walked with single-minded purpose along the bark banks of the river flowing out of the hollow. This Samiha was all-knowing in a way that astounded him. She could read his thoughts and answer any question he cared to ask about the Born.

'In ancient times,' she was telling him, her blue form drifting lightly over the bark just a few steps ahead, 'we Born did not seek to manipulate humans from the realm of the Sap. We stayed here with you, our children, in this universe, sharing in your everyday lives and loves.'

They were walking through a bark gully, flanked on either side by sheer cliffs and surmounted by a strip of lowering, cloudy sky. They could see no more of their surroundings, apart from a rising hillock of grey bark ahead. It occurred to Tymon, dimly, that they had emerged beneath the Storm, but the astonishing fact of reaching the World Below was also swallowed up by Samiha's all-engrossing presence. He registered that the Tree was not sheer at its base, but scored with gorges miles deep, a labyrinth of gnarled cliffs and bark buttresses. Its exposed roots rose dramatically in rift valleys near the trunk-wall, before dwindling into undulating hills and hummocks. Samiha led him on without hesitation through these winding gullies of bark. All the time, as she spoke and they walked, his heart leapt towards her, even as his body struggled to keep up with her light pace. He tried to banish the warning whisper of contrition in his mind, telling him that Zero was lagging further and further behind in this alien country.

'We constructed a garden of delights for you,' Samiha was saying. 'A perfect society. War, disease and oppression were unknown. People died, of course, but after many centuries, and in peace. It was a paradise, the one true heaven, and it existed right here at the base of the Tree.'

They had quit the banks of the cavern-river now, climbing out of the gully onto the slope of the bark hillock above. It was steep and, even before they had reached the halfway point, Tymon was breathing with difficulty. The air of the World Below felt heavier than in the canopies above, muggy and laden with moisture.

'Were you there?' he called to Samiha hoarsely, as she floated ahead. 'I mean, here? You sound as if you knew it well …'

'I was,' Samiha answered, glancing back at him, 'but in another form. The Born always return to this universe. It's our workshop: long ago you called us Gods, because we built you. We built everything — the Tree and its flora and fauna, including humans. We made you to be our friends and companions.'

Tymon felt a sudden stab of guilt at her words, as he stopped a moment to catch his breath. His own friend must be far in the rear by now. He turned and searched for Zero in the gully behind him, and after a few minutes of anxiety saw the Marak lad's matted red head appearing around a corner by the riverbank. If only he would hurry up, Tymon thought impatiently. He ought to wait for the boy, he realised, but could not risk losing sight of Samiha. Her voice was growing fainter now, whipped away by the persistent wind. Turning his face uphill again, Tymon willed himself to press on. If Zero could not keep up, it was his problem.

'The Born ruled in the old days, certainly,' Samiha continued, as he struggled up the slope after her. 'But we did so in the open, with justice and mercy. None of this fiddling around with prophecies, while supposedly endorsing free will. Humanity obeyed us out of love and we gave it unending bliss. The civilisation of the Old Ones was the brightest and best this world has ever known. And it was all here, in front of you.'

Her last comment was accompanied by a dramatic gesture, as he rejoined her at the top of the hillock, breathless. Her arm swept in a wide arc, taking in the immensity before them.

'Here?' Tymon gasped at the scene before him. 'Where ...?'

The view from the summit snatched the question from his lips, for the vast spaces opening up before his eyes were another world indeed. The trunk spread its skirts for miles around, surmounted by the rolling grey ceiling of the Storm. Beyond the last outflung roots lay a shimmering plain of water, stretching to the horizon.

The World Below was drowned in a gleaming deluge. The waters seemed to go on forever, a flat mirror beneath the cloud-cover, reflecting the Storm's shadow. It reminded Tymon of the Veil, except that instead of being plunged in darkness the watery plain glinted in the hazy light of an overcast afternoon. The upside-down Storm covered all the points where the Tree was not, lapping right up against the foot of the hillock where they stood. Tymon's heart beat wildly in his chest at the unexpected vastness of the world. The Tree was great, but the un-Tree was far greater. There was silence about them, the smell of loam and water on the wind; he suddenly felt very small.

'How could such a civilisation disappear completely?' he asked Samiha.

'There was a war,' she sighed. 'A great conflict that levelled everything — all the cities, all the beauty. It's something I regret, especially now that I have almost died myself, and had a chance to think things through. But the old world didn't completely disappear. Not if you know where to look.'

She pointed to his right, drawing his attention to an area near the base of one of the outflung roots. He saw that the watery plain beside it was not continuous after all, but broken in the distance by curious mounds and protuberances. He assumed this archipelago of grey atolls was more of the Tree's exposed root system.

'There lies one of the old cities, or what's left of it,' Samiha continued. 'I shall not speak its name, for it grieves me to remember what once was. Even so, that is where we are bound.' And with these words, growing faint as she turned from him, she proceeded down the side of the bark escarpment towards the waters. Tymon stared after her departing form with its nimbus of blue.

'Wait!' he cried. 'How do we get over the water?'

'We'll walk,' she said, as if this were self-evident. He was suddenly conscious that she had no shadow, walking down the bare bark in the hazy sunshine.

It gave him quite a turn, though he told himself there was no reason a Sending should look like a normal object in daylight. How long had it been since they left the hollow Tree-hall? he wondered, sensing a chill in the air. He searched the sky in an attempt to guess the time. As far as he could judge from the vague white point of the sun in the Storm clouds, the trunk-wall behind him ran from east to west, falling slightly away to the north in the barest indication of a curve. It was perhaps late morning in the canopies above, though he felt now as if he had been walking for far longer than a few hours. He recalled what Zero had told him when they stopped to eat. Had their journey really lasted five days?

With that memory came belated concern for his friend. But just as he turned to search behind him for Zero, he heard a gasp of astonishment. His faithful companion had caught up with him already, and was crouched on top of the slope, a few feet away. The hulking red-haired lad clung to the bark as if he were afraid he might fall, his simple face blanched with terror as he stared out over the shining waters. And although Tymon had been gazing for the past few minutes at the expanse, he saw it again through Zero's eyes, as it would seem to someone who had barely witnessed the Gap, let alone stranger worlds like the Veil. He could just imagine what the poor fellow must be feeling. How could such an immense body of water exist? How could the universe be so endlessly flat and huge? It went against all experience for a Tree-dweller.

'Don't be afraid,' he told Zero kindly, feeling ashamed that he had abandoned his friend at such a time. For some reason — the shock of seeing the World Below, perhaps — he had half-convinced himself, in the past few minutes, that he was travelling alone with Samiha. He shrugged off the sensation, telling himself that he must be tired, and offered Zero his hand, helping him rise.

'Just follow me,' he urged, as the lad clung desperately to him. 'I'll show you where to go. You won't fall if you stay close to me.'

'Why don't you stop worrying about him?' Samiha called from some distance down the slope. 'He can take care of himself.'

She had turned to wait, her expression marked by annoyance. The disapproval in her voice caused a shiver to pass down Tymon's spine.

'He's shocked by all this flat space,' he tried to explain, shaking Zero off as gently as he could, and letting go of the other lad's hand. 'He's never seen anything like this, not even the Veil.'

He began to hurry down the slope after Samiha, in spite of Zero's faint cry behind him. The vision of his love frowned as he drew near.

'I wish you wouldn't call it the Veil,' she said with some severity. 'That's misleading, as if one could just step in and out at whim. Call it what it is: the Prison.'

'Of course. The Prison,' said Tymon, abashed, as they continued on. He glanced back only once, surreptitiously so as not to make Samiha angry, to be sure that Zero was following.

After one last steep section of the escarpment, where Tymon almost lost his balance as he slithered down the bark, the hillock levelled off, bordered by a wide strip of loam before the waters. Up close, the vast lake at the foot of the Tree was a muddy grey, losing its reflective sheen. The waters seemed mournful-looking, rippled by the now stiffening wind. Before they reached the water's edge, however, Tymon stopped and squatted down, his interest caught by a tuft of green sprouting out of the loam. He tore up a handful of grass, scrutinising the blades.

'Just ordinary grass,' he said in astonishment.

'What did you expect?' asked Samiha. 'What else would grow here?'

'I wasn't aware anything at all grew here,' replied Tymon mildly.

But he did not follow her when she walked out over the waters, her blue-bright figure hovering just above the surface of the lake. 'Why don't you come?' she called to him, surprised, as he continued to squat by the lakeshore.

'I'm not a Sending,' he reminded her. 'Nor a Saint unburdened by the weight of sin, much as I hate to admit it. I'll sink, Samiha. It looks too wide to swim.'

'Oh, don't worry about that,' she said. 'It's not deep, up to your knees at most. The ground rises under the city. We'll be on dry earth soon.'

'*Earth*,' he repeated, trying out the unfamiliar word. It lay thick on his tongue. 'Is that the same as loam?' he asked. 'That's what it looks like, from here.'

He peered doubtfully at the sediment that had gathered in the shallows of the pool, sprouting more plants of the kind he had pulled up, tough hardy bog-grass he had seen growing in the loamy troughs and hollows of the Central Canopy. All at once, his mind was overtaken by another image, a fleeting memory of the rolling expanse of grass and loam beyond the Tree of Being, as endless as the Veil, but smelling of home.

'The world beyond the world!' he exclaimed, jumping to his feet. 'You know, Samiha, that's what this place reminds me of, not the V— I mean, Prison. I don't know why I didn't think of it before. When I stepped outside the Tree of Being —'

'Are you coming, or not?' she interrupted peevishly. 'Or are you going to talk Sap-talk until the sun goes down, and my body expires?'

Her tone was so jarring, the reaction so unexpected, that he stood blinking at her in confusion. He remembered, then, in a disconnected rush of remorse, that he had not contacted the Grafters in the trance for five whole days, if Zero could be believed, and that they would be deeply worried about him. And what had possessed him to leave his young Nurian friend behind again? He turned to see the red-headed boy inching his way down the difficult section of the slope. Despite his fear, Zero was doing his best to follow him.

'My love,' cried Samiha from behind him. There was a note of panic in her voice, a new urgency that made Tymon spin guiltily round. 'Hurry,' she entreated. 'I grow weak. I don't know what they're doing to me.'

He saw that her trance-form had faded, now no more than a wavering blue candle over the surface of the lake. 'No!' he exclaimed, splashing into the water after her, the wetness penetrating his clothes and boots in a cold rush. 'Wait, Samiha! I'm coming!'

The sight of Tymon stepping into the Storm below the Storm filled Zero with instinctive panic. When he had peered over the top of the high escarpment after toiling up the bark for what felt like a good half-hour, and seen that vastness of rolling grey on the other side, a cry had escaped his lips, half-croak, half-exclamation, all shock. He had been unable to restrain it. But when Tymon went on to actually step into the dreadful immensity, wading through the clouds, Zero's shout of warning died in his throat. He stared from where he sat on the slope, frozen and dry-lipped, as his friend walked to his death.

He expected to see Tymon disappear within seconds. That was what normally happened when people fell into the Storm, or were flung into it as a punishment, or were thrown as corpses, over the edge. You saw them for a few seconds and that was it: they hurtled down and disappeared forever. And so he expected Tymon to disappear too, swallowed by this last, gaping void that would surely plunge him into the farthest reaches of Hell. Or perhaps it was worse. Perhaps this Hell was bottomless. For what if each time you stepped into the Storm, you hurtled down and fell into another world, where there was another Storm which sent you headlong into yet another world, in which you fell into another Storm, then world and Storm over and over again — forever? Zero stared in horror at the distant figure splashing through the shallows, knowing that the surface beneath the *Syon's* feet could not hold. Any minute now, his friend would tumble forward — any second, and he would disappear into the emptiness.

And yet, somehow, he did not. Tymon kept moving, step after step into the clouds. First his ankles vanished. Then his calves went under. Then the Storm rose right up to his knees. And as he walked into it, Zero saw with amazement that dark, swirling eddies were spreading in his friend's wake. Tymon's passage was stirring up black sediment from below. That was when the Marak boy finally understood that the second Storm did not consist of cloud at all, but water. There was a bottom to this Hell, and it was made of loam and water.

And there was also something more than cloud above him. When Zero saw the first flash, he thought it was lightning. It seemed to burst out of the heavens, a stab of blue. But there was no accompanying thunder and the light, arcing over Tymon's head, lasted only an instant. Strange, thought Zero, looking up in expectation of rain; in spite of all this water down below, storms under the Storm seem drier than the ones above. And then he saw it again. Another crackle of light shot over Tymon's head, closer this time, circling over him in a flash only to vanish seconds later. Zero thought again, anxiously, of the fire-demons the Argosian missionaries had warned him about. It was as though the spirits of this underworld were using the *Syon* for target practice, or the hungry ghost had decided to play bowls with him. Another such throw and he would be knocked over. Then, Zero was sure, he would disappear beneath the waves.

He waited no longer. Though he trembled with trepidation at what he might find below, he slid down on his rump over the last outcrop of bark and slithered to the foot of the escarpment. By the time he reached the bottom of the slope, his trousers were torn and his fingers and knees grazed. But he was there, standing on the loam shore at the edge of the water, with Tymon far ahead of him now, wading out into the endless lake.

'Be strong!' He heard the words as though they were addressed to him. But it was Tymon's voice, Tymon who was unaware of the spirits flashing above his head, Tymon who was speaking to the hungry ghost that lured him into the depths.

Zero paused to take a deep breath before stepping gingerly into the muddy shallows.

Samiha held her hands out to Tymon. 'I've been short with you because I'm afraid,' she whispered anxiously as he drew close. 'Time is running out.'

He brushed her flickering fingers with his own, and shivered as the touch of her sent the familiar shock of pleasure through him. She seemed to glow a little brighter.

'Why don't you rest yourself?' Although he forced himself to say the words, he only wished for her to stay with him. 'Stop the Sending, and come back when you feel better. I'll use the opportunity to contact the Focals. They'll be wondering where I am.'

'Hush,' she said, pressing a burry finger against his lips. 'There's no time for that. They'll See you in their Readings, anyway. This is our last chance. If we don't find my body today, I'll be gone.'

Tymon waded further into the lake after the blue haze of her form, pressing on without too much difficulty. The water was cold but not deep, and it was not long before the lake bed rose, just as Samiha had said it would. By the time they skirted the outflung root to reach the area she had pointed out to him from above, the lake was no more than a squelching few inches about his boots. The atolls he had glimpsed were all about him now, towering columns and lumps of grey matter jutting up from the water, larger than he had thought they would be. He realised, with a jolt of shock, that the islands were in fact the remains of a city, crumbling remnants of buildings. The hard stuff the columns were made of was like no material he had ever seen. He laid the palm of his hand against one of the blocks, a roughly rectangular slab about the size of a small dirigible; it was as cold as *orah*, pocked and eroded by a thousand tiny marks.

The bases of the columns were colonised by lichen, but Tymon saw no other plants growing among the jungle of grey pillars. The place was bleak and silent, devoid of birdsong. The last animals he had seen in the World Below were the bats in the Tree-cave, and the last ordinary human sound had been Zero's cry, asking him to wait. He winced at the thought of the lad trudging faithfully behind him, and resisted the urge to turn around. Samiha was watching him.

'What could destroy buildings this big?' he asked her.

'The Born used weapons of unimaginable strength,' she said, beckoning him on between the columns. 'Blast-poison is only a shadow of that power.'

'It seems like such a waste,' he muttered. When she did not answer but walked ahead, he left the pockmarked block and splashed in her wake. 'Where are we going in exactly?' he called to her. 'Do you know where your body is?'

She nodded. 'Everything's clear to me now. It's kept in a certain building at the heart of the city. That's the only one of the Ancients' constructions that would have survived: it was built after the end of the war, and built to last.'

'Why? What was it?' he asked.

Again she did not reply, walking swiftly over the last puddles of water. He bit his lip and followed, aware that she probably thought he was wasting precious time with questions. They soon left the lake behind and were walking on dry loam, winding between the silent ruins. Tymon felt the prick of rain on his face, and glanced anxiously at the Storm clouds. As he did so, he caught a brief flash, a prickling brightness like lightning leaping between the tops of two of the towers. He squinted at the space between the columns in perplexity. Again, there was a fork of blue light, unmistakable this time.

'Tymon.' Samiha waited ahead of him again, her flickering form bright against the grey ruins.

'There's something up there,' he answered. 'I see a light ...'

At that moment someone grabbed his arm, stopping him in his tracks. Zero was beside him.

'No further, *Syon*!' gasped the red-haired lad, clinging to the tattered sleeve of Tymon's jacket. Zero's eyes were wild, the pupils dilated; he was panting with the exertion of trying to catch up with Tymon. 'Go no further!'

Zero was breathing so noisily and babbling so quickly that Tymon could hardly follow what he was saying, though he saw that his friend was clearly exhausted, terrified out of his wits. He squinted at Zero, feeling the spongy loam ooze under his feet, and tried to shake off the lethargy that plagued him lately with regards to the Marak lad. He wished he could say something to reassure him.

'Hold up,' he replied, to Zero's babble. 'Start again. Why no further?'

'It's a hungry ghost, *Syon*,' said the Nurian boy in a loud whisper, his eyes rolling with terror. 'It calls down lightning! It's trying to kill you!'

Samiha had halted on a set of crumbling steps, and was looking back at them both. 'This fellow has done all he can for us,' she said coldly to Tymon. 'His ignorance is becoming a real hindrance.'

'There's no reason to be afraid,' protested Tymon. 'The Kion won't hurt me.'

He was speaking to Zero, but he suddenly realised he was reassuring himself, too. The mention of lightning made him uncomfortable. He did not dare look up at Samiha, afraid she would insist he leave his hapless companion behind.

'You're going to have to make a choice,' she said, giving voice to the very sentiment he feared. 'Either you help me, or you stay with him. You can't do both.'

When Tymon whirled around to face her, intending to plead for her patience with Zero, he found that she had not waited for an answer. She was already walking up the steps, disappearing over the top. The sight of her leaving caused his throat to tighten in panic. He tried to stumble after her, but was hindered by Zero.

'You don't understand,' Tymon cried in annoyance, attempting to free his arm of Zero's tight grasp. 'She isn't a ghost, and she can't control lightning. She's just using a Grafter's Sending. I keep telling you that.'

But Zero clung doggedly to him, apparently intending to stop him from following Samiha by sheer force. He wrapped both of his hulking arms about Tymon and held on with all his considerable strength, digging his heels into the mud. This misguided attempt to separate Tymon from, as he saw it, his love, was infuriating to the young man.

'Let me go, you fool!' he shouted. 'If you stop me, she'll die!'

Summoning up all the strength that remained to him, he fought against Zero more violently than he would have done in any other circumstance. But each time he wrested himself away from the Marak lad, Zero simply blundered towards him again, determined not to let go. Tymon was beside himself, desperate to catch up with Samiha.

'Leave me alone, you idiot!' he yelled at last. And raising his fist, he punched Zero in the mouth, drawing blood.

The hurt in his friend's eyes was hard for Tymon to bear, an emotional blow far worse than a split lip. He backed away, unable to look at the reproach in Zero's open, trusting face.

'I'm sorry,' he said as the other lad stood stock-still, staring after him. 'You don't understand. I have to do this. I can't waste any more time.'

With that he hurried away, stumbling up the cracked steps after Samiha. He did not know how he found her again, in the lifeless maze of the old city; it was as though he sensed her passage on the crumbling pavements, drawn after her like a fly to honey. Or perhaps he saw the trace of her blue shadow under the broken arches. Her smile when he caught up with her, in any case, was gratifying, though it did not banish the galling memory of what he had just done to Zero.

'You had to defend yourself,' she told him, as they walked on together. 'He shouldn't have attacked you. You can apologise later — you can make it alright again.'

If there is a later, thought Tymon, fighting off a rush of shame. 'Let's get this over with,' he said with a shudder. 'I want to take you away from here.'

'You're a very kind person,' she remarked, gazing at him with grave compassion. 'Your Marak friend will see that in the end. They all will — all those who never listened, or believed in you when you said you'd find me.'

They were just the words he yearned to hear at that moment. His shame over Zero and the underlying nagging worry about not contacting the Focals ebbed away as he listened to that smooth voice of reassurance. It was true, he thought with a pang of self-pity. No one had supported him in his quest to find Samiha. No one ever listened to him. Now even Zero had turned against him, he told himself gloomily, staring up at the massive walls on either side. The towers had grown taller as they marched towards the centre of the city, the hulking remains of what must once have been monumental constructions. Tymon remembered the light he had seen.

'Do you think this place is guarded? Where they keep your body, I mean?' he asked Samiha, sounding a belated note of caution. 'I saw something odd before —' he had a hard time using her word for it — 'before Zero attacked me. A light leaping between the tops of the towers like lightning.'

'I don't know what that could be,' she said, smiling at him again. 'I see only darkness when I wake. But I suggest we approach carefully. There may be guards, yes.'

'Maybe we should find something to use as a weapon —' he began again, only to be cut short by a whirring, humming, bristling explosion of movement in the air in front of his face.

At first, he thought it was a species of bird or giant bat, for he glimpsed reddish hairs that might have been fur on its body. It did not appear to have a head, however, and hovered in the air without the aid of wings, darting like a mayfly about three feet from him and emitting an insect-like, buzzing noise. Its body was the size of a Tree-dog's, a lumpy central sphere attached to a long, stiff appendage like a tail. The creature, Tymon realised in astonishment, was belching white smoke in the manner of Galliano's steam-engines. It smelled of burning hair and another bitter odour he could not identify.

'These are the guards!' shouted Samiha, as he gaped at the whirring, smoking beast. 'Throw something at it, quickly! Don't let it touch or stun you!'

The thing had arms, Tymon saw. They had been folded in tight, and now rose slowly above the lumpy body: two gleaming stick-like protuberances. He retrieved from the loam the heaviest piece of tower-rubble that he could find, aimed for the central portion of the beast, and threw with all his might.

To his surprise, the projectile knocked the body off the tail. The creature was now in two parts. The central lump crashed onto the ground and rolled over at the base of a ruin, before extending two more limbs from its body and attempting to drag itself away. But one of the long, thin legs was badly bent by Tymon's throw and the creature wobbled precariously as it moved, bumping over the rubble like a wounded spider. The tail portion spun away and collided with a wall on his right, tumbling down to lie on the loam, trembling and belching smoke. It looked insentient and appeared to be made of some hard, unyielding material. In fact, it looked very much like a grey broom-handle with smoke for bristles. It shuddered where it lay, but did not seem disposed to rise. It was, Tymon grasped, not alive at all, but a flying machine that the other half rode.

'Demons riding on brooms,' he mumbled aloud, in consternation.

16

The turbulence of the Storm seemed to last an eternity. Jedda gripped the edges of the bench in the air-chariot, while Wick grovelled, groaning on the floor. Gowron stood tense and immobile, his legs well apart and his shoulders hunched as he guided the *Lyla* through the clouds. The wind shrieked past the open windows, buffeting Jedda's short hair, and rain battered the sides of the vessel in brief gusts, spattering her face. Bags tumbled back and forth across the pitching floor, spilling their contents. A water gourd rolled into Jedda's feet. She pressed herself close to the window, wondering what in the world had just happened to her. There had been a voice in her mind. Was this another trick of the Envoy's, or simply fatigue, the effect of the accumulated stress of the last few weeks?

It did not feel like a trick. The brief chant left her heart as light as a feather. She could not remember if the voice had spoken in Nurian or Argosian; she had repeated it in her native tongue, but the verse might have been sung in a different language, for all she knew. All she had registered was its familiarity. She must have been dreaming, she told herself: she must have been half-stunned by the rattling cacophony of the air-chariot and imagining things. She shook her head, glad of the water whipping her cheeks through the window, for at least she could be sure she was not still asleep. She concentrated on keeping her gaze trained on the front of the craft and her stomach steady. The squall battered the sides of the *Lyla* with intermittent fury, but Galliano's miraculous little creation held true, the propellers thudding faithfully through the clouds, where a larger dirigible's ether sacks would have been torn to shreds.

The crossing was over abruptly. They passed through the lower strata of cloud and hurtled without warning into open air again, bursting into muted grey daylight. Under the Storm! Jedda caught her breath. The air-chariot no longer leapt and shook; she was able to relax to some degree on the bench, staring out of the window in amazement at the immensity of the World Below.

It was larger than she had thought, and surprisingly wet. Instead of the piles of blasted loam she had expected — the scale of her fantasies had been far short of the mark, she realised — a vast body of water stretched out to the horizon, flat and shiny as a hardwood mirror. Its gleaming blue-grey surface reflected the underbelly of the Storm, as well as a few branches of the South Canopy snaking down through the clouds. One such limb in the distance caught her attention, for it had broken off and leaned at an angle against the trunk, a vast and lonely ruin on the western horizon. It must have been gigantic, one of the supporting struts of the South Canopy, for it looked at least five miles long. She noted in surprise that the leaf-forests at its tip were still green, joining their own reflection in the water. This disaster had occurred recently.

None of the Envoy's schooling had prepared her for how very huge, and how very drowned, the World Below would be. Hell was made, bafflingly, of water. The wispy shadow of the air-chariot moved over the reflective surface like a dancing fly; Jedda understood how a glimpse of that mirror from high above might have sparked the legend of *Lacuna*, the second canopy beneath the Storm. A moment later, the craft banked steeply to the right, and she lost sight of the broken branch in the distance. Before her, the southern marches of the Tree trunk stretched out in a long, wriggling line, bathed in hazy sunlight. When she craned through the window towards the *Lyla*'s tail, she could just make out the sweeping curve where the trunk bent north into the Gap, then east once more. The Tree was indeed all one beneath the clouds, the Four Canopies merging together in a single, colossal base. She guessed that parts of the lake at the foot of the trunk were not deep, for she saw the reflective surface was broken by blackened mounds, humps scattered across the water in oddly regular configurations — squares, circles and spirals, the half-drowned traces of deliberate design.

There was other evidence of an ancient order in the World Below. Even at this height, Jedda could see the unusual marks on the trunk, the straight line slashing across the face of the Tree from west to east, patently artificial. No ordinary growth pattern would create such a sharp, exact gradient. Her suspicions were confirmed as Gowron steered them in a northbound arc towards the trunk-wall. The line proved on closer inspection to be a giant causeway more than fifty feet across, constructed with skill and precision and rising to regions beneath the Gap. Just before reaching the clouds, however, it came to an abrupt end. It had been gouged out, obliterated by an unimaginable force that had left a crater a mile wide in the bark. Even blast-poison would not wreak so great a devastation on the Tree, Jedda thought with a shiver. The Old Ones, she remembered, had been great architects and engineers, but equally skilled in the arts of destruction. She recalled the Envoy's lessons, delivered in the College library, while he had still been well-disposed towards her.

The Born were the masters of this universe, possessed of the secrets of creation. Long ago, they shaped the world, the plants and animals, out of three primary elements: air, water and loam. The sacred element of fire they kept for themselves. They made human beings, your ancestors, to be their servants and companions, sharing their ancient knowledge with them, and causing them to resemble their makers to a degree. That was their greatest mistake. It caused the people to become proud and rebel, and sparked the war that tore apart the Born.

'Well, that's one lie,' murmured the voice in Jedda's head.

The Nurian girl sat up, ramrod-straight on the bench, her nerves tingling. A brief glance about her confirmed that no one else in the air-chariot had spoken. Wick was still crouched on the floor in a far corner, clutching his stomach with his face pressed between his knees. Gowron was bent over his controls, oblivious to them both.

'What did you say?' Jedda whispered.

But the voice was silent, replaced by the thudding cacophony of the propellers. She prayed that she had only imagined it again, and leaned back against the shuddering wall of the air-chariot, her heart beating uncomfortably fast. Gowron was bringing the air-chariot down in slow spirals over one of the hummocks of bark at the foot of the ramp, overlooking the grey waters. Just where the great causeway began, Jedda caught a glimpse of the ruined remains of an arch, gutted even as the road had been by an unthinkable blow.

The great war destroyed the old world and scattered its inhabitants. The Envoy's lectures echoed again in her memory, haunting her. Had he lied to her about everything, then? *Only the Tree survived, where humans took shelter.* She had wondered, on hearing the story, why the Born had made the World Tree in the first place; it seemed a curious inversion of causality to create first the means of deliverance from apocalypse, then the apocalypse itself.

'A very good point,' observed the alien voice between her ears, causing Jedda to stiffen with alarm. 'It only makes sense if you realise that the war lasted for centuries. It was, of course, the weapons like those Eblas used that caused the old cities to be poisoned, and brought the Storm into being.'

'Who are you?' muttered Jedda, clutching the bench as if she might anchor the part of her mind that seemed to be detaching itself and growing its own personality. Even through her shock, she understood that the tone of the disembodied commentator was familiar, recalling someone she had known before.

'Hello, Jedda.' The Oracle's voice was more strained than she remembered it, and deeply weary, though it contained a trace of her old dry humour. 'I'm very glad to find you listening. I was afraid I'd be shut out.'

'You?' gasped the girl, turning her face away hastily as Wick moaned with queasy annoyance from his corner. 'How can you be talking to me?' she murmured into the wall of the air-chariot. 'How can you even want to talk to me, after all I've done?'

'I can always reach my students, when they're ready,' said the Oracle. 'And when the attacks against me subside.'

All of a sudden, the image of Lai standing in the grass by the abandoned mine rose up in Jedda's mind like an accusation. She hung her head in wordless shame.

'Be assured, you didn't cause the death of Lai,' said the Oracle, with a gentleness that took Jedda's breath away. 'That was only a Seeming. She died, but later, and through no fault of yours.'

Jedda could not answer immediately. The knowledge that she had not been an accessory to murder was a deep relief, but it also shook her to the core, releasing a floodgate. Emotions held back for months welled up, and she found herself weeping, pressing her cheek to the smooth planks of the air-chariot's wall. The Oracle waited patiently for her to be ready to speak, but Jedda felt a mounting urgency in her silence, like a beating pulse.

'I'm sorry for everything, *Ama*,' she whispered to her teacher, at last.

'I know. Jedda, we haven't much time.'

The girl blinked her tears away, with another glance at the still-incapacitated Wick. The urgency lay in the Oracle's voice, now, not just in her silences.

'Tymon's in grave danger.' The words whistled like the wind in Jedda's ear.

'Tymon?' she exclaimed, then hastily cupped her hand over her mouth, grateful that the cacophony of the propellers drowned out her voice. 'What's happened?'

'Can't you feel him?'

Jedda had not immediately remarked the familiar tug in her belly, confronted with so many other overwhelming changes since they passed through the Storm. But the minute the Oracle mentioned his name, she realised the connection with her twining partner was present once again.

'He's in the World Below?' she breathed. 'Where, *Ama*? And why?'

'About five miles west of you, right now. But he's moving.' The Oracle's voice was muffled, as if she spoke behind a thick barrier, and punctuated from time to time by a noise like the rushing wind. 'He thinks he's saving Samiha. Recovering her body.'

'So the Kion's alive?' The news caused Jedda's heart to leap, a brief stab of joy. She quelled it: the Oracle did not seem enthusiastic.

'In a sense. She's being kept —'

The Oracle's voice faded away frustratingly and Jedda did not catch the next few words. She thought she heard the Oracle mention the Envoy. Or was it his Masters? If they were involved, Samiha had little chance of survival. Even Lace had spoken of those shadowy entities with fear.

'Are you alright, *Ama?*' she said with concern, when the Oracle was audible again. Her teacher was evidently harried, her voice increasingly distant. She appeared to be buffeted by forces as strong as that which caused the air-chariot to drop alarmingly into air-pockets during their descent.

'Attacked … Veil,' came the faint answer. There was another gust of air that swept her words away. 'Not long now,' she concluded.

'What about the acolytes?' Jedda glanced anxiously at the miserably groaning Wick, then back to Gowron hunched over the controls. Did the Oracle know what the Envoy's servants were doing in the World Below? Jedda guessed it could not be good. Should she ask about their intentions, find out what they were up to?

'Tymon first.' The voice of the Oracle was broken and drowned in the distant roar. 'Find him, Jedda. Find him, before it's too late —'

And with that, suddenly she was gone, leaving an emptiness in Jedda's mind like an echo of bereavement. She shivered. Her teacher had sounded as if she were in pain, as though she were suffering. She had mentioned attacks. If anyone were capable of assaulting the Oracle, Jedda suspected it could only be the Envoy's Masters.

Preoccupied by the Oracle's trouble and Tymon's mysterious plight, Jedda barely noticed the air-chariot bouncing to a halt on a bark hummock about a quarter of a mile from the start of the causeway and the ruined archway. The cessation of the propellers and the ringing silence that followed recalled her to the present moment. They had arrived. They were actually in the World Below. As she stumbled out of the *Lyla*'s hatch after the two acolytes, her legs trembling on the hard bark, Jedda was amazed by the sheer solidity of *Lacuna*. The juddering racket of the air-chariot seemed suddenly unreal: vast silence greeted her as she stepped out onto the crest of the hummock. The flat, glistening waters stretched southwards from the foot of the slope, as far as the eye could see.

Jedda gazed out over the lake in awe. The air was mild, spring-like, but not a single bird sang in the immensity. Behind her, to the north, the flanks of the Tree rose up in long folds, the trunk-wall broken by deep rifts and valleys filled with rising mist. The ruined arch at the base of the old road was a mute 'o' of dismay. Her fellow travellers reacted in different ways to the enormity of the World Below, though they must have been groomed by Lace as to what they would find on their mission. Gowron strode to the edge of the slope, and surveyed the glittering expanse of water below with a proprietary air, as if he were a plantation-owner taking stock of his fields. Wick staggered a few paces from the air-chariot and sat down again, hiding his face in his arms; he was evidently still feeling air-sick, and more concerned with the solidity of the bark under him than the sight before his eyes. Jedda pretended to stretch her legs and surreptitiously inspected her surroundings, wondering how she might escape.

All within at least a mile radius was bare and open, humps of exposed bark and stretches of empty water.

If Tymon were as much as five miles away, then she must give the acolytes the slip soon, in order to have a chance of reaching him that day. But she could see no place to hide, no opportunity to break free of her enemies. She no longer feared the Envoy's curses, for she guessed the birds would not be able to follow her all the way here before they lost cohesion. Besides, the Oracle would not have suggested she try to escape, if it meant she would be pecked to death. The voice in her mind had always wished her well — Jedda knew that now. But although she no longer doubted the Oracle, she had no idea how she could break free of her captors, without being instantly caught and killed.

'We head west,' announced Gowron, interrupting her thoughts. He was speaking to Wick. 'The location we need to find is three miles from here, but we must go on foot to be sure we don't miss it.'

'What about her?' Wick peered groggily in Jedda's direction.

Gowron's eye slid disdainfully towards the Nurian girl. 'The whore's not welcome on this journey,' he snapped. 'It's private seminary business. I'd suggest you tie her up and leave her in the air-chariot. But she's your problem now. Deal with her, will you?'

Wick had managed to readjust his face in an infernal smile by the time he rose shakily and walked over to Jedda. 'Sorry, m'dear,' he murmured in her ear. 'The grumpy old bastard is right, for once. You'll have to stay behind and I'll have to restrain you — can't have you flying away in our transport, can we? My promise to you still stands for afterwards, of course.'

'Wait,' she whispered to him, as he attempted to lead her away. 'There's something you should know. It's about Tymon.'

She did not know whether she was making the right decision to tell Wick about her twining partner, but spoke on impulse. She knew she would waste valuable time if she were left behind in the machine, bound and trapped. 'I feel him,' she murmured to Wick as he pushed her towards the air-chariot. 'He must be down here somewhere.'

Wick's step faltered and he gazed into her eyes, searching for the lie. 'I'm not making this up, I swear,' said Jedda, keeping her voice low. 'He's in the World Below. I think I can help you find him.'

But Gowron had heard her. 'Oh, for heaven's sake,' he barked from the edge of the escarpment. 'Don't tell me you believe her. You feel Tymon, do you, Nurry whore? Well, feel my fist, too.'

He strode towards Jedda, his face darker than the Storm, raising his hand as if he were about to strike her. But Wick placed himself between them.

'What if she's right?' he countered. 'Can we really take the risk that the Grafter is here, probably trying to stop us? We need her, Gowron.'

The older acolyte glowered over Jedda. If he could have squashed her where she stood, like a crawling, irritating insect, he would have done so, she knew.

'By the bells!' he burst out. 'I'm sick of this. Bring her, fine: but tie her wrists and keep an eye on her. And you.' He spat on the bark at Jedda's feet. 'You'd better not be lying. Because your kind protector here might be obliged to leave you in my tender care, if you are.'

He stalked away from them on the slope, leaving Wick to salvage a length of rope from the air-chariot on his own, grumbling under his breath.

A short while later, Jedda was trudging along behind Gowron and in front of Wick, over the bark hills and dales by the shores of the gleaming lake. Her hands were tied behind her back, and her back was loaded with the day's provisions. The Envoy's acolytes had brought the minimum with them on this trek, evidently intending to return to the air-chariot to camp that night, but the load felt heavy enough. Gowron strode some distance ahead of his companions, scowling furiously; he was taking swigs of *kush* from his gourd again. Wick had wrapped the long lead attached to Jedda's bonds around his own right arm, and gave her irritating little jerks from time to time, as though she were a beast of burden. She had no hope of running away without dragging him and his confounded smile along with her, and comforted herself with the fact that they were at least moving in the right direction. She could not have travelled faster by herself, and still remained hidden from her enemies.

They were walking towards the broken branch again, she noticed, picking out the fallen arch of the great Tree-limb in the distant haze. It was massive, the ruin of it taking up half the western horizon. She wondered what unthinkable calamity had made it fall, for it seemed impossible that the Saint's little war in Lantria had anything to do with the disaster. Even lightning did not usually dislodge the largest limbs of the Tree — only the Ancients' weapons might once have been capable of that. The thought made her slow her pace to walk beside Wick, determined to use this opportunity to learn more about his mission. She had to know why the Envoy was suddenly so interested in the World Below; it struck her, with a chill, that Lace might be after some remnant of those weapons that had blighted the world of the Old Ones.

'Why do you think Tymon's here?' she asked Wick. She knew he would be susceptible to flattery, if he believed he possessed more information than she did. 'What does he want to stop you from doing?'

'That's for me to know and you to wonder,' quipped Wick complacently.

As he spoke, they reached the bottom of the bark hummock and the edge of one of the crescent-shaped beaches immediately bordering the lake. Wick had recovered from his nausea, but seemed to be having trouble breathing in the World Below. His attempt at a smug chuckle after his last comment dissolved into a hacking cough, and he paused, spluttering and wheezing, before stepping onto the black silt of the beach.

The loam here was grittier than any found in the upper canopies, Jedda saw, consisting of tiny black granules. She crouched down on her haunches as she waited for Wick to recover, feeling the comforting crackle of Samiha's papers under her clothes, and ran her fingers through the gravelly substance. It was gleaming wet; it moved under her fingertips as she caressed it. Were these the seeds of the World Below? she wondered. What might they grow? Ahead of them, Gowron crunched on along the shoreline, stolidly oblivious to the mysteries of this strange new world.

'It's all this damp air,' Wick wheezed, struggling to catch his breath. He pressed the ball of his foot doubtfully into the silt. It pooled with water when he lifted it. 'So much moisture. Can't do the lungs any good.' He peered with evident dislike at the softly lapping lake to their left. 'Damned unnatural place,' he muttered.

He still hesitated, though Gowron's figure had dwindled in the distance. Jedda scooped up a handful of the granules to her nose and sniffed, curious. The silt was less redolent of decay than Tree-loam, cleaner than its namesake in the canopies, and somehow stripped down to essentials. It continued under the lake, so it was fair to assume this world was made of loam after all, beneath all that water. Jedda almost laughed aloud, remembering her own confusion in trying to imagine such a thing, based on what the Envoy had told her: she had thought of the World Tree sitting on a lump of loam barely larger than itself, like a plant in a pot.

'I didn't expect so much water, from the tales Lace told us,' she admitted to Wick. 'I expected blasted ruins, evidence of the Born war ... It's funny that all these years the priests have been talking about fire below the Storm, it's really the exact opposite.'

Despite the tension with Gowron, Jedda had recovered much of her youthful vigour and optimism over the last few days, and the spark was back in her eye as she spoke. Though the scratches inflicted by the Envoy's birds still wove a web of discomfort over her neck and the pack of provisions rubbed against her back, she felt alive again, filled with a tentative hope. The openness of the waters gave her a sense of freedom, and she found the clean loam of the shoreline pleasing. She let it fall between her fingers with a noisy clatter.

'Stories fit for children,' sniffed Wick, stepping onto the beach at last with an air of bravado. 'Tales to frighten simple-minded folk into behaving themselves, or discourage them from going where they'll inevitably come to grief. We're the initiated. We know better.'

'Do we?' she said, rising to follow him. 'Maybe it was fiery, once. Maybe those stories about Hell were based on something that happened a long time ago, a memory from the war. Then the rain came and covered everything.'

Wick shrugged, evidently uninterested in ancient history. 'Fire or water, it's all the same to me,' he snuffled. 'I hate this place. The sooner we get done and get out, the better. I feel like I'm choking.'

'Lace said you used to be able to journey for miles, straight ahead,' mused Jedda as they walked on. 'The world was like a giant ball, and you could go all the way around it, until you arrived back where you started.'

There was indeed a dark mass on the southern horizon, as if the surface beneath the waters rose up again in hills and mounds of loam. Jedda could not help envying those ancient travellers, able to walk in any direction, without fear of the world coming to an end beneath their feet.

'Miles of pointlessness,' said Wick. 'How could it be straight ahead if you went in a circle? And why would anyone want to live on a ball? You'd fall off on the underside, wouldn't you?'

'It doesn't work like that, apparently —' began Jedda.

She broke off, distracted by a bright flash like lightning, arcing briefly westwards ahead of them. 'What was that?' she exclaimed.

'What?' gasped Wick. He had been overtaken by another fit of coughing just as the lightning had appeared, and had doubled over, missing the flash.

Jedda stared over the black crescent of the shore, flanked by bark escarpments. To her right rose the frowning wall of the trunk, its rift valleys now overflowing with mist. She shivered in the mild breeze. Perhaps there was fire in this unlikely Hell, after all. The lightning was either a natural phenomenon striking dangerously close to where they were standing or, far more worryingly, evidence of weaponry. Were there others here, lurking denizens of a dead world, unimaginable descendants of the Ancients? Had they been the ones to bring down the massive limb of the Tree? Worse still, could the flash be the work of the Masters? Or was it just a faint reminder of the endless storms beneath the Storm, a premonition of rain and the cause of all this water in the World Below?

'Nothing,' she said cautiously. 'I thought I saw something. I made a mistake.'

She did not know whether the lightning had something to do with Wick's mission, and now feared he would leave her behind if she appeared too well-informed. She did not want him to tie her to some stump of bark, ruining her chances of reaching Tymon.

'We'd better catch up with old grumpy, then.' Wick heaved a sigh as he peered at the tiny figure of Gowron, already winding up a bark slope at the far end of the beach. 'He's working himself into one of his tempers again. I don't want to give him any more reason to take it out on us.'

Wick made light of Gowron's moods in the presence of Jedda, his show of nonchalance sustained by the suave Seeming of the mask. But he knew, as he trudged over the gritty loam, feeling the tug and pull of the invisible scars on his face, that the older acolyte was mortally angry. He sensed Gowron's rage boiling ahead of him in the monstrous spaces of the World Below, bubbling and seething beside the endless placidity of these objectionable waters. It was the heat of his associate's fury, rather than any demon-fire, that inhabited this Hell, Wick thought dismally. He was sure Gowron's anger would translate into violence in the end, culminating in a final murderous showdown. It was inevitable. The older man would not allow himself to be bested at the game of *orah* again, and would attempt to do away with Wick as soon as they had attained their objective. Only one of them could claim the credit of finding the World Key, after all; only one could step into the Veil and obtain his rightful reward from the Masters. Wick anticipated the final confrontation between them, his heart sinking further with every slippery step on the lake-side loam.

One comfort remained to him: the business with Tymon might grant him a slight reprieve. While there was still a possibility their mission would be stymied by the Grafter, Gowron would let his seminary ally live.

Wick almost preferred the possibility of battling Tymon to the certainty of dealing with Gowron's hulking menace, though he guessed that the Envoy's curses, left far behind in the upper canopies, would be of little use to him now. He followed the other acolyte along the shore, breathless with trepidation.

Indeed, he could hardly breathe at all these days, every gulp of air a struggle. Since they had set out that morning, he had felt the Explorer mask constricting over his face, the air-passages over the nose and mouth becoming unbearably tight. He realised he had kept the artefact on too long, ignoring the Envoy's advice to remove it for at least as long as he wore it. But he could not bear the thought of appearing as he truly was before Jedda, in all his naked ugliness. He still clung to the notion that he might seduce her, only daring to remove the disguise when she was sound asleep. Each time he did so, the exercise grew more difficult, the mask more tight. The night before, after the disastrous argument with Gowron, he had waited until very late to pry it off. The edges of the mask had stuck stubbornly to his cheeks before coming off with a soft, sucking pop. Now, as he walked after Gowron up the bark slope, he allowed Jedda to trudge a few paces ahead, intending to lift the mask and gulp a mouthful of air while she had her back to him.

Turning his face aside, he surreptitiously tried to pry the rim of the mask loose. But it was completely stuck. The *orah* had bound to his skin since that morning, becoming one with it; try as he might, he could not budge it an inch without feeling the seamed scars on his face begin to stretch and tear dangerously. He let go of the mask in dismay, as Jedda came to the end of her rope and faced him again.

'Are you alright?' she called down to him.

He was anything but alright. He felt trapped, his pulse racing with sudden panic. He had omitted to ask

Lace what the long-term effects of wearing the mask beyond the allotted time would be. Now he knew. He was not only forced to associate on a daily basis with a man who intended to murder him, but might be obliged to wear this horrid, constricting thing for the rest of his life. It was intolerable.

'I'm fine,' he lied, hurrying up to where Jedda stood. She stared at him curiously, as if she doubted his word, and he avoided her gaze.

There was nothing for it but to carry on, for they had fallen far behind Gowron and the older acolyte showed no signs of stopping to rest. Wick marched in front of Jedda in order to avoid further questions and scrutiny. Once, he asked her whether she felt as if they were getting closer to Tymon, but when she told him that the twining connection remained the same, he lapsed into silence again. They wound steadily up and down the humps of bark and exposed roots by the lake, for what might have been the better part of an hour. At last, they crested a final hillock to see Gowron squatting on a patch of shoreline on the far side, under the sheer north escarpment that enclosed the beach. He was gazing intently at something on the ground, at the foot of the bark wall.

Wick allowed Jedda to accompany him to the bottom of the slope, but once on the shores of the lake, he cut off a section of his rope lead with a pocketknife and used it to bind her ankles together, relieving her of the backpack. He did not speak as he immobilised her, and she did not protest the treatment, intrigued by what Gowron had found on the north side of the beach. All she could see from where she sat, bound hand and foot at the base of the slope, was a circular hatch set into a flat slab of grey material, buried at a forty-five degree angle in the loam. Wick abandoned her by the lakeshore and walked up to his fellow acolyte.

'It's locked,' grunted Gowron, as the younger man knelt down beside him. 'Just like our master said.'

The trapdoor was buried under years of accumulated sediment. Gowron had already dug away layers of silt around it, loosening the bark and grass with his bare hands and creating a sizeable mound of discarded debris beside the hatch. If he had not been given the exact coordinates of the location leading to the Oracle's body, he would have passed by the place without realising it, Wick thought. Instead of relief, he felt dread that they had reached their destination. He eyed Gowron warily, for the end of the journey could mean only one thing: his associate would wish to keep whatever they found inside the door to himself. But Gowron's attention was absorbed for the moment, and he did not seem to be spoiling for a fight. Wick reached out to brush the top of the hatch with his fingers; the convex lid radiated cold. Lace had warned them about the properties of the door. It would be secured by a code-lock and made of a material impervious to blast-poison. Very few constructions dating from the time of the Old Ones were intact, but this was one of them, and it had survived centuries. The surface of the hatch was hard and coarse to Wick's touch.

The name the Envoy had given to the Ancients' building material had sounded equally harsh, a pair of clanging syllables Wick could not quite recall: *core cret. Con crud.* The coldness of it reminded him of *orah*, but where the Grafter's material was bright and precious-looking, the dull material of the door seemed to have a stolidly utilitarian nature. It was mottled by patient years under the silt, streaked with water and loam. The only mark it bore was a curious pattern of dots at the centre — nodules about the size of peas arranged in five spiral arms like the petals of a flower, or one of the stylised stars on the seminary's maps of

Heaven. The dots, Wick noticed with growing excitement, gleamed with a familiar yellow glint under the streaks of grime.

'Maybe the *orah* unlocks it,' he whispered to Gowron, aware of Jedda watching them from her post further down the beach. He should have blindfolded her, he thought. 'Maybe that flowery thing will respond to our own pieces.'

His fingers had already gone up to the pendant at his neck when Gowron shook his head curtly. 'I already tried with mine,' he said. 'Nothing happened.'

Wick felt a sudden stab of annoyance. *Of course you already tried*, he wanted to shout at his rival. The unremitting tension of the past few days, and now the problem with the mask, conspired to rob him of patience; frustration welled up inside him in a hot rush.

'Naturally, you couldn't wait a few more moments for me to arrive,' he snapped. 'Naturally, you wanted to get in first.'

'What do you mean?' asked Gowron, swivelling his gaze around to rest on Wick.

'You know exactly what I mean,' said the younger acolyte. 'Now we've reached our destination, you don't think you need me any more, do you? Well, I've got news for you. I'm not going to be shunted aside while you claim your prize.'

'I think,' drawled Gowron, eyeing him steadily, 'you need to calm down. The stress of the mission is clouding your judgment. We haven't got the Key yet. We can hate each other cordially, all we like: we still need to work together to deal with whatever's on the other side of this door.'

Wick subsided with an angry shrug. Gowron's face, he thought, bore a striking resemblance in both colour and texture to the material of the door. His fellow acolyte was like a heavy lump of *con crud*.

'Well, how do we get in, then?' he said. 'If the code isn't *orah*, what is it?'

'It must be mathematical,' replied Gowron, turning his deadly scrutiny to the spiral design again. 'The dots need to be touched in a certain order. They go in, see. Lace gave me some different *abjat* phrases to try in case the code was based on prophecy. He didn't tell you about them, eh?'

The words were like a blow to Wick. Their master had not given him any formulas, clearly favouring Gowron with this information as with other secrets, such as the mysterious leather pouch the other acolyte still carried, hidden in his jacket pocket. From Gowron's satisfied leer, half-visible as he bent over the door, it was fair to assume that he knew it, too. Wick crouched silent by the door, struck dumb with dismay, as his rival set about pressing the nodules inwards. The knobs of *orah* shifted sluggishly under pressure, slow and stiff with age.

The sight of Gowron's slab-like finger, its yellow nail jabbing away at the *orah*, reminded Wick disagreeably of the Envoy's thumb jabbing into his collar bone. He thought with revulsion of the so-called 'work' he did for his master, feeding Lace with the energy required to maintain his shadowy presence in the world. That was all he was to the Envoy, he ruminated grimly: a convenience, a food-source. He would always be second best to Gowron.

He stood up, trembling, his breath rasping under the mask. 'I need some air,' he mumbled to Gowron's uncaring back. 'I'll return in a moment.'

Jedda had been watching from a distance as the two acolytes knelt by the door, spitting their bile at each other in mounting disagreement. Throughout the altercation, she had been furtively rubbing the rope bound about her wrists against the rough slope of bark behind her, hoping to fray the knot. She had been obliged to halt her attempts when Wick stood up and strode down the beach towards her. He did not appear to notice what she was doing, however, his expression frozen with hatred; he only retrieved a large hunk of water-smoothed bark from the loam, weighing it in his hand as if gauging it as a weapon. Then he discarded it.

'What's going on?' she asked him.

He did not answer, pacing to and fro on the beach in silence. From time to time he picked up and tested the weight of a fragment of wood, or one of the larger lumps of hard loam. There was an odd light in his eyes, she noticed, the unhinged gleam of madness. It sent a shiver down her spine. She wondered how she was ever going to escape him: the longer she waited, trapped there as the minutes of the cloudy afternoon slipped by, the further Tymon strayed out of her reach. She had lied to Wick regarding her twining partner's position, for the pull of the link had grown fainter over the past hour, indicating that Tymon was moving away. The knowledge of it made her seethe with impatience.

'Why don't you tell me what's bothering you?' she tried again, in an attempt to engage Wick. 'I might be able to help.'

He stopped to survey her, then, as if he had just seen her for the first time. 'I doubt it, sweetheart,' he rasped. His smile was ghastly now.

'Try me. I might be able to open that door for you.'

'No, no.' He shook a slightly manic finger at her. 'Don't you start trying to wheedle information out of me. Can't have that. Oh, which reminds me. There's something I should have done a while ago.'

He squatted down beside her and, with a flick of his

small belt-knife, ripped out a section from the hem of her borrowed cloak.

'Oh, not that,' she pleaded, as he lifted the strip of cloth over her eyes. 'What if your friend over there decides to bother me again, and I don't see him coming? It's bad enough that I'm tied and can't keep him off. Actually, I was going to beg you to cut at least the leg ropes. Where would I go down here? I'd starve to death if I left you. Please, Wick.'

The young acolyte hesitated. The mad light faded from his eyes, and a more ordinary cruelty, an enjoyment of her dependence, replaced it. He gazed at her with hard satisfaction, as if she were a prizewinning herd-beast he was just beginning to break in. 'What guarantee do I have you're going to behave yourself?' he murmured.

It did not please Jedda to deceive even her enemy, but she told herself this was the only way to help Tymon. She picked up on the note of conceit in Wick's voice, and played on it. 'I was mean to you at the seminary,' she said, dropping her voice and peering at Gowron on the other side of the beach; he still had his back to them. 'I was too proud, and didn't know a good thing when I saw it. I regret what I said to you, that first day, when you came up to my room.'

'Ah?' Wick's eyebrows lifted, two perfect arcs on that smooth, unblemished face. 'So, what are you going to do about it?'

'This,' she said.

As she spoke, Gowron struck the grey slab with the flat of his hand, clearly frustrated with his failure to open the door. Jedda took advantage of his preoccupation to lean closer to Wick. *It's Varana all over again*, she thought gloomily, as she planted a kiss on his lips.

She did not feel the slightest attraction to the young acolyte. In fact, his gangling frame and smooth, cherubic face repelled her. But she had not expected to find an actual, physical barrier between them. It was as if Wick's lips were encased in an invisible shell. She pulled back from him in perplexity. He did not notice her reaction, however, his smile self-satisfied again.

'Oho,' he breathed. 'It's like that, is it? Well, you might just have yourself a deal.' He unsheathed his knife to saw through the cord on her ankles, kneeling by her side on the gravelly loam. 'The rest comes off later,' he grinned. 'When I've seen how well you behave.'

False face. Was it the Oracle's voice? Jedda was not sure where the words echoing in her mind had come from, as Wick helped her to her feet and drew her towards him again, still smugly smiling. There was no further sign of her teacher after those two brief syllables. But when Wick pulled her close, glancing surreptitiously over his shoulder at Gowron, she finally saw it: saw why she had been troubled by his expression for days now, by the jarring reality beneath that smooth smile. For a fleeting instant, she glimpsed his true features, hidden beneath a powerful Seeming of normality. His real face was wounded beyond recognition, a map of bubbling blisters and cratered burns.

'*Ama?*' she gasped in shock, reaching out for reassurance from her absent teacher. Then she bit her lip at having spoken the Oracle's name aloud.

'What?' asked Wick. 'What did you say?'

'Nothing,' she replied, shaken by a rush of unanticipated pity for Wick. *What happened to him?* she cried to her teacher silently. But the Oracle was gone, or else had never returned. Jedda was alone with her maimed and twisted companion.

He must have received the horrific injuries after she had left Argos city, she thought, for she could have sworn he did not have them on the fateful morning before the Kion's execution. The Seeming that disguised him was strong, the illusion breached only a moment before the false smile was back again. Now that Jedda knew the truth, however, Wick's expression seemed as rigid as a wax cast. Everything about him was hollow, a lie. Only his eyes blinked at her with any semblance of humanity. Her stomach churned as he bent towards her with that perfect, smiling mouth, but it was the smooth falsehood of the Seeming, rather than what lay beneath, that sickened her. The brush of those unreal lips almost caused her to cry aloud in horror. She stood as rigid as a statue.

'What,' Wick whispered in her ear, as he ran his hands over her shoulders and breasts, 'what in heaven's name do you wear, stuffed up inside your undershirt like that? It feels like paper.'

Jedda felt her heart skip a beat as Wick plucked one of the pages of the testament out of her bodice. Her hands were still tied, and she could not snatch it back.

'*If you can do that — if you can unbind yourself from wanting and winning — then we will meet again at the heart of the world, where all divisions cease,*' Wick read with a sarcastic flourish. 'What's all this nonsense?' he snorted.

Jedda stared at him, speechless with terror. If he realised what she carried, if he so much as guessed that the verses were addressed to Tymon, he would destroy them and kill her immediately. She waited in anguish. In that same instant, she would have given anything — her chances at safety or comfort, body and soul — to keep Samiha's words intact. But Wick appeared to have already lost interest in the testament. Incredibly, he let the loose leaf slip from his fingers, and swaggered up to Jedda again.

'Reading romances, are you?' he murmured, with an attempt at suavity. 'I could show you another way to keep warm.'

She could not help it. She jerked away from him as he drew close, unable to bear the cold brush of that death-mask. He took hold of her shoulders and held her in place, frowning a little as he bent towards her. But she could not abide his proximity and turned her face away.

He was silent, then. When she looked up at him, she found that his smug smile had disappeared. There was no need for words. The look they exchanged was the final admission. She saw him as he was, and he knew that she did. For an instant, there was a spark of something like hurt in the acolyte's eyes. He would think she spurned him out of squeamish disgust for his injuries, she realised. Her heart was wrung once more with pity for this cruel, broken boy, who hid from everything and everyone, including himself. A moment later, Wick's vulnerability was gone: cynicism closed over his face like a shutter, and his eyes became veiled.

'So, can't bring yourself to touch a cripple, eh?' he whispered. 'That's a shame. It might have saved you some trouble. Maybe you'll feel differently tonight, when there's two of us to hold you down.'

Jedda's eyes jerked instinctively towards Gowron. The older acolyte had given up whatever battle he was having with the door and had thrown himself down in exasperation on the piled loam, his head in his hands. '*Green grace*,' he could be heard swearing. 'None of 'em. Not a single, green, blooming mother of 'em.'

'It's not you, Wick —' Jedda began.

'Save it,' interrupted her captor with a dry laugh, as he retrieved the discarded length of rope, and made her sit down on the wet silt, securing her ankles. 'You know, you really had me taken in for a while there. Oh, I didn't believe it was love or anything, I don't ask for that much.' The mad gleam was back in his eye, his grin the cackling grimace of a skull. 'But I thought:

"She's a reasonable lass, she sees what I can do for her. We can be civilised about this." That'll teach me.'

His voice had become harsh and wheezing, each phrase accompanied by a savage pull of the rope. He tied her legs far more securely this time, kicking off her boots and pulling the knots tight around her ankles. When he had finished, he picked up the strip of torn cloth from where it lay on the beach. But he did not bind it about her eyes, weighing it in his hand as he watched her.

'I was going to protect you with this,' he said in a low, vindictive murmur. 'The less you knew about our mission here in the World Below, the more likely Gowron would have been to let you live. But now, I don't really care what he does with you. As you seem to be calling on your *Ama* to help you, you might as well know. She won't. She never will again.'

He bent close to her, smiling cruelly. 'We're going to finish the job you couldn't do in Cherk Harbour,' he continued. 'We're going to kill your stinking Nurian Oracle, once and for all. We've found her real body. It's buried beyond that door. And we're going to get in eventually, believe me.'

'No, Wick,' she exclaimed. 'You mustn't. You have no idea what you're doing.'

But he had already turned his back on her, and was walking away, crunching up the beach towards Gowron.

'No,' she said again, despairing, and bowed her forehead to her knees.

She had no doubt whatsoever that the Oracle was aware of the danger. Her teacher had refrained from mentioning the threat to herself, and begged her to help Tymon instead. And now, Jedda thought in anguish, she was unable to help either of them. It was agonising, her weakness; it was a trial to her as it had

389

never been before. She yearned for one last possibility of escape, regretting again her decision to throw away the *orah*, and more bitterly still her inability to put up with Wick's mask of lies. The dampness of the silt seeped through her stockings as she cried tears of frustration into her knees. Nearby, on the beach, the page discarded by Wick tumbled back and forth on the wet black lakeshore, worried by the breeze.

After a few minutes, however, Jedda raised her head, a slow hope dawning in her heart. The quality of the fluttering connection in her belly had changed. Tymon was no longer moving away from her, but drawing steadily closer.

17

Tymon bent down to inspect the crumpled form of the creature that had attacked him in the ruins of the city. He had followed and incapacitated the thing, at Samiha's direction, with a few more lumps of the heavy stuff she called *rock*. When the creature lay helpless, softly whirring and clicking at him through invisible mandibles, he had crushed it with a final massive *rock* slab he could barely lift, beneath which it had fallen silent at last.

On heaving up the slab, he found the so-called demon flattened, its stick-limbs folded up for all the world like a dead spider. It was covered in clumps of reddish fur, festooned with fragments of cloth and other objects unrecognisable to him at first. Now, on closer inspection, he realised the dangling materials were all foreign matter affixed to a squatly spherical core. The inner body and legs were made of the same unyielding substance as the broom-handle, a dull grey colour. When he reached out cautiously to poke the sphere with his index finger, he found it warm and hard to the touch.

'They're called Collectors,' said Samiha, hovering at his elbow. 'Machines the Ancients made to guard and clean their cities. They have a rudimentary intelligence, but they aren't alive.' She peered in distaste at the amalgam of materials stuck to the creature's body. 'The program must be corrupted. Look at all these trophies,' she muttered to herself.

Trophies. As she said it, Tymon realised with a prickling rush of revulsion what was actually stuck to the Collector's body. Tufts of human hair hung from its back, bleached red by time. Fragments of bone and other organic remains he shrank from identifying were carefully stuck to its greyish belly with gobs of adhesive. He glimpsed a tiny straw effigy dangling between its legs, of the kind thrown into the Void by mourners during a funeral service; the ragged ends of cloth, he realised as he jerked his hand away from the Collector in disgust, were fragments of white shroud.

'By the bells!' he gasped, scrambling to his feet. 'It's been collecting parts of corpses! Things that fell from the Tree — it's scavenged them!'

'Yes,' said Samiha, gazing thoughtfully at the broken machine. 'That would be logical, very like a Collector. It was originally built to guard and maintain ... bodies. It has degenerated. Well. We should go now.' She roused herself, brisk again. 'Come, Tymon, before more of these things find us.'

Tymon did not need to be told twice. 'What would it have done to me, if I hadn't stopped it?' he asked, shuddering, as he followed her glowing silhouette over the rubble.

'It would have collected you,' she said simply. 'As it does the other remains it finds. That's what it thinks it must do.'

'How can a machine think?' he objected.

'How can you think?' she countered from several paces ahead, without turning around. 'In a sense, you're like a more nuanced version of that machine. The Born made your ancestors, and your ancestors made the Collectors. It's possible, I assure you.'

It might have been possible, but the idea disturbed Tymon more than he cared to admit as he hurried after Samiha. When she had first murmured her story to him of the idyllic life shared by the Born and their creations, he had thought of the sacred ties of family. The relationship between the Born and humanity had seemed to him like that of parent and child. Now, as Samiha threw out the comparison with the machine, he was taken aback. Could the analogy be appropriate? Was he just a mechanical, half-living thing to her, an organic machine endowed with *rudimentary intelligence* — rather like the Envoy's constructs? Jedda's accusations in Argos city drifted back to him, half-remembered. *They cultivate us.*

He pushed away the thought as merely a product of his own fears and anxieties. Samiha loved and respected him; he was simply on edge, he thought, troubled by his strange surroundings. But his unease remained, threading through his shame at how he had treated Zero. He could no longer bring himself to call his friend's intervention an attack, and the taste of his own dismay lingered, a bitterness in his mouth. The eager daze that had taken hold of him in the Tree-tunnels had begun to wear off: he no longer followed Samiha without a thought for the consequences. As he trudged after her through the ruins, eyeing the shadows between the gutted towers for any sign of the Collectors, he found himself questioning certain aspects of his mission for the first time.

There were important issues about the World Below that he realised he had not considered. Was this the same region the Explorers had visited on their journeys, where the Dean had recovered his *orah*-clock and the Doctor had found his abominable chair? He had so far seen no evidence of any expedition, old or new, in the ruins or near the base of the Tree. Of course, Argos city was hundreds of miles away, and any traces the Explorers might have left behind would likely be closer to that point of origin. The idea reminded Tymon of the sheer distances involved in transferring Samiha from the place of her execution to this location, a journey of at least three weeks in an ordinary dirigible. It was odd, he thought to himself as he walked, that in all the time he had spent in the wide-open spaces of the World Below, he had seen no indication of the Envoy's servants — unless it was the unexplained flashes of light. Who had brought Samiha's body all the way from Argos? Who kept her prisoner now? Might she herself have worked out that puzzle, as she appeared to have worked out so much else since he first found her in the Tree-mine?

But before he could open his mouth to speak to her about it, he glimpsed a sight ahead that banished all other considerations. In front of them, on the summit of a gentle slope, a building had come into view. Though ancient and weathered by the elements, this construction was not a gutted remnant, like the others in the ruined city. It was free-standing and rectangular, its peaked roof intact and made of what appeared to be overlapping tiles. The whole building was more than two hundred feet long and at least three storeys high, built of a whitish-grey substance like *rock*. Fluted columns ran along its four sides, enclosing a portico that reminded Tymon very much of the temple Hall in Argos city. In fact, his first reaction was that it must be a place of worship. There was even a decorative frieze on the triangular pediment that depicted human figures, so eroded over time as to be almost invisible. A long flight of stairs led up to a porch on the front façade, and beyond that to a pair of gigantic double doors, fashioned from what appeared to be a yellowish polished hardwood.

The area immediately around the hall had been cleared of debris, swept clean of the rubble that littered the rest of the city. There must be more Collectors about, Tymon thought, with a twinge of anxiety; he hesitated a long moment before following Samiha out of the shadow of the ruins. When no sound or movement broke the pervasive silence, he hurried across the open space towards the hall, pursuing her blue form up the front steps. His breath seemed loud and harsh in the echoing space of the portico. As he stepped up to the doors, he realised they could not be made of ordinary hardwood, their polished surface glinting coldly in the light of noon. Even the handles were oversized, two tawny discs the size of Tymon's chest. There was neither lock nor keyhole.

'Orah?' he muttered doubtfully to Samiha. He touched his fingers to the burnished material of the doors: it was cool.

'They're made of *metal*,' Samiha answered, using another word he was unfamiliar with. 'The Ancients extracted this stuff from rocks, and used it for building. *Orah* doesn't come from this world at all. Go on, try the door, I don't think it's locked.'

Tymon reached up with both hands to take hold of one of the discs, feeling like a tiny child faced with its gigantic proportions, but hesitated at the last minute. 'Why not?' he whispered to Samiha. 'Why would they leave your body in an unlocked building? Wouldn't it be a trap?'

'I don't know.' She seemed anxious and unsure again, glancing over her shoulder at the silent ruins. Her voice was pleading. 'We haven't any choice. We have to go in and find out.'

It seemed to him that she was right. Anything was worth the risk, if they could recover her body. Resigned to the danger, he leaned his weight against the handle.

He had expected the door to be stuck with age, or at least heavy, requiring all his strength to budge, but to his surprise it swung open with hardly a push, perfectly balanced on silent hinges. Beyond it yawned a cavernous space. But just as he was about to step over the threshold, he heard a sound that brought him up short — a dim, thrumming echo, somewhere behind and high overhead. He turned and frowned at the rolling grey of the Storm; the sound reminded him incongruously of an air-chariot's propellers.

'Don't wait!' hissed Samiha urgently, at his side. 'Quick, before the Collectors find us again!'

The wind changed and the thrumming faded. After one last wary glance at the sky, Tymon slipped through the doors into the gloom. He did not see the blue flash that arced above the portico just at that moment, a buzzing tongue of energy that leapt straight up from the roof of the hall.

Inside, cold air washed over him in a tingling wave. The main chamber of the hall was as frigid as an ice-box, a shadowy central nave with columns marching down each side. There were no windows in the walls but, as Tymon's eyes adjusted, he saw a small amount of daylight filtering down through hidden openings in the roof. There was also a greenish glow, clearly artificial, welling out of a small, enclosed chamber at the far end of the hall. Just as he noticed this, the main door swung shut behind him with a soft click, causing him to jump.

'Come on.' Samiha's whisper was eager, her blue silhouette already gliding down the central nave. 'My body's in the back room, I can feel it.'

Tymon followed her as quietly and cautiously as he could, unable to quell the anxiety that had taken hold of him at the sound of the closing door. This was all too easy. He did not believe for a minute that the Envoy's servants would have left their prisoner unguarded, not even locking up the building where her body was kept. And had he heard an air-chariot, after all? He peered at the flickering green light ahead, then over his shoulder, into the dim recesses between the columns, expecting at any moment to see a figure outlined there.

Even so, he could not help noticing the austere beauty of the hall as he continued down the nave. The main chamber was empty of furniture or other items, offering no clue as to what the function of the building might once have been. But there were intricate friezes on the walls, better preserved than their counterparts outside. Scenes melted in and out of the darkness above Tymon's head as he walked, fine relief-work adorning the columns. One of the first he passed on his right depicted the stars and constellations, some of which he vaguely remembered from his studies at the seminary. But here, the heavenly bodies were not shown dangling like fruit in the upper branches of the World Tree, as was traditionally the case on seminary maps. The stars seemed to move purely in relation to each other, conducting a stately procession across the column, and there were a great many of them. Stranger still, tiny figures floated incongruously between the constellations, as if a group of people had flown up to dance among the stars.

The subsequent friezes had more recognisable settings, showing the loam slopes and waters of the World Below, though again, no Tree. A column about a third of the way down the hall on Tymon's left depicted a bustling city with tall buildings, and what must have been airships of a variety that used neither ether sacks nor propellers. But as the scenes went on, the character of the friezes changed dramatically. Instead of simple records of human activity, they all appeared to deal with a single, defining historical event. Halfway along the nave, Tymon came across an image of people gathered about what must have been a judge or other representative of justice, for the feminine figure was shown blindfolded and holding a pair of scales, a symbol still used to denote impartiality in Argos. The people held up petitions to the presiding figure, their expressions angry or woeful, clamouring for retribution.

The Ancients could not have been too different from their descendants today, Tymon thought, struck by how unhappy the faces on the later friezes looked. This was no idyllic history of the Born and their creations. He shivered as the columns marched relentlessly on, and he passed scene after scene of conflict and misery, growing more violent as he approached the rear of the building. All-out war was depicted on the final columns and, to Tymon's distress, heaps of dead bodies. The city was now a gutted ruin surmounted by a rain of fire, clearly a reference to the Born war. The air was growing steadily colder towards the back of the hall, too; he noticed that his breath was smoking and that his footsteps left dark patches on the coating of frost on the floor. He took some comfort from the fact that there were no visible marks in front of him, indicating that no one had passed there recently. He almost tripped, slithering to a stop on the icy flags, when he looked up at the last column on his right, and saw the woman in the tree.

The frieze depicted a female head and torso emerging seamlessly from a stylised tangle of trunk and branches. Leafy fronds sprouted from her hair and limbs. The design reminded Tymon, with a shock of recognition, of Samiha, as she had been when he found her mysteriously intertwined with the Tree of Being. He had almost forgotten that experience, obsessed with the newer, glimmering vision from the mine. The woman on the column was pointing upwards, indicating something to the people gathered about her.

'What's taking you so long?'

The peevish note was back in the Kion's voice. As Tymon glanced towards the current version of his love, standing in the greenish light that spilled out of the small chamber at the back of the main hall, he felt a sense of aching loss. Samiha had changed so much since the execution, he thought. She had lost her depth of humanity and compassion, the capacity he had noticed in her long ago of queenliness, of seeing to the needs of others before herself. She was a mere shadow of her former self, as impatient as a child, her arms folded over her chest as she waited for him by the half-open door.

'Do hurry up,' she said.

But as he approached she smiled again, winsome as ever. 'Come, my love,' she said. 'We're almost there. It'll all be better soon, the way it was before.'

He nodded wordlessly, following her into the smaller chamber lit with its green glow. This room was equipped with a series of nine rectangular blocks set against the back wall of the hall, each one surmounted by a decorative, arched frieze at the head. They would have reminded Tymon incongruously of nine empty beds, had they not been hugely oversized and made of what he assumed was more of the hard, burnished *metal*. The cold was intense in this part of the building and all the surfaces were covered in a thick layer of white frost. A quick glance about the room showed Tymon that it was empty of intruders, the white blanket on the floor unbroken. It crunched under his feet as he followed Samiha towards the source of the green glow, an alcove on the right-hand side of the room. The silence was now filled with a barely perceptible, continuous hum.

Tymon almost cried aloud when he saw the clear-walled tank at the rear of the alcove, about the height of a man and filled with a viscous-looking liquid. Within it, floating upright and festooned with tubes like tangled vines, was Samiha's body. He ran up to the tank, pressing his palms against the coldly transparent sides; they were made of another unfamiliar material, like hardened Treesap but more sheer. He stared through that window, devouring Samiha with his eyes, torn between relief at finding her and pity for her state. The mass of tubes snaked about her naked body, plugging her nostrils and her mouth, wrapped about her belly and inserted into the skin of her arms; he could not guess the utility of them, unless they were somehow keeping her alive in the liquid. For he saw her chest rise and fall, a faint indication of breath beneath all the paraphernalia.

This was no sweet vision of the past. Samiha's physical reality was the battered one he had witnessed in Argos city, her hair hacked short and her face drawn with pain, even while unconscious. But there was no mistaking the identity of the woman in the tank. This was the Samiha who had stood in the prisoner's dock during the trial, who had spoken to him briefly in the bell tower, then fallen into blank emptiness from the air-harbour quays. And she was here, really here, separated from him only by a sheet of what looked like clear ice.

'How do we wake you up?' he breathed to the apparition, though his eyes were still fixed on the floating body in the tank. 'Do we turn off this machine?'

For that was what he assumed the tangle of pipes and humming boxes behind the tank must be. They produced the steady mechanical humming; the green glow that filled the alcove emanated from two lamp-like protuberances on the topmost box. The whole contraption reminded him uneasily of the Collectors. Galliano would have found it fascinating, he thought —

and then wondered, with a pang, why he had not remembered his old friend before. He was living the scientist's dream, after all, walking in the World Below.

'No,' answered the Sending, from behind him. 'You have to do it from here.'

Tymon turned to see the vision of his love, half-reclining on the nearest long block by the door of the alcove. Except that she did not recline, but hovered, her shimmering form only mimicking contact with the hard surface, whitened by frost. She beckoned to him.

'Come,' she said with a teasing smile. 'Lie with me.'

When he gazed at her in confusion, wondering if she could really be offering him her strange, incorporeal love right now, in these circumstances, she laughed. 'I can help you launch the Grafter's trance,' she explained. 'You have to go in and bring me back: I can't wake up on my own.'

There was something jarring about her laugh, a slight edge of mockery to her smile. He took her outstretched fingers, allowing her tingling touch to draw him closer to the block, but gazed searchingly into her eyes, desperate to find a glimmer of the person she had been before. The reality of Samiha's body, so clearly marked by her trials and suffering, only underscored the change that had come over her as a Sending. It was not just the externals: such things would mean little in the world of the Sap, he knew. It was her behaviour. The Samiha of before had been high-minded in all her dealings. She had loved him, but never manipulated him with the promise of pleasure. In fact, she had been independent of him to a degree that was almost vexing. The vision, by contrast, alternated between neediness and domination, seductive and scolding by turns. She was intent on achieving her personal goals, and intolerant of anyone, like Zero, who stood in her way. She had become, Tymon thought in dismay, a profoundly ordinary person.

He winced as he lay down on the icy block, shivering when the frost seeped through the back of his tunic, melting with his body's heat. 'I can launch the trance myself,' he sighed. 'I don't need your help.'

'This way is quicker,' she told him. 'And we need to hurry.'

Though he half-raised his head, protesting when she climbed astride him, she did not pay him the slightest heed. 'Relax,' she said.

Before he could object, she ran her prickling blue fingers down his chest. The effect of her touch was overpoweringly strong, sending a jolt of intense sensation through him. He almost fainted from the shock, his vision reeling. It was not right, he thought, shaking his head groggily in an attempt to recover his senses. What she was doing to him was not right: she should not be ignoring his wishes so completely.

'Samiha,' he began again, as soon as he could, 'I don't want this —'

'Will you ever be quiet?' she interrupted, peremptory.

And suddenly she slapped him, with the flat of her hand, even as he had struck Zero. The force of her half-real blow on his cheek was a trembling, biting rush, both pleasant and painful. He stared at her, deeply shaken, but she only laughed as if it were all a joke.

'I've had enough,' he muttered, trying to rise from the hard couch.

But he could not. The strength had fled from his limbs, and he lay sprawled and helpless on the block. The act of touching it seemed to have drained his vitality, and he was reminded again, alarmingly, of the Doctor's chair. A terrible suspicion gripped him; he raised his sluggish hand to rub away the frost on the right side of the slab, craning to see the surface beneath. Why was Samiha behaving so strangely?

Beneath his fingers, under the coating of white on

the block, he caught the unmistakable, yellowish glint of *orah*.

Even as he peered at it in dismay, the slab warmed beneath him, and the energy drained out of him in waves. A spray of cold fell on his face. With a supreme effort, he glanced up at the wall behind his head, to see separate discs of *orah* spinning in what he had thought was a decorative arch. The block was another of the Old Ones' machines, its mechanism now whirring to life, shedding its coat of frost. And all the while, Samiha threw back her head and laughed, and laughed again, as if this were the best game in the world. When she looked down again, there was a wild blue light in her eyes, as blue as the flash he had seen above the city.

'What are you doing?' he mumbled thickly, staring up at her in anguish. Understanding had dawned. His love had not changed after all. This was simply not Samiha: it never had been.

'What am I doing?' echoed the false vision, her expression frankly scornful. 'I'm taking you for all you're worth, little man. I'm emptying you. You're all mine now.'

'Why?' he gasped, though he could piece together what had happened to him, berating himself for his own stupidity. He remembered the Oracle's warning: *they can enter this world through our dreams.* The Masters, he thought. He had allowed himself to be tricked by the Masters.

'Why, it asks?' The Samiha-that-was-not-Samiha burst out laughing again, a harsh, grating sound. Her eyes flashed a venomous blue. 'Because I can. Because that's all you're good for, worm of the Tree.'

Her voice changed on the last phrase, growing raucous and rasping, breaking into several different voices that spoke as one. As Tymon looked on in horror, unable to move, the vision passed through a hideous metamorphosis, the blue haze of the Sending stretching and bulging out. The likeness to Samiha fell away, and a nightmarish creature emerged, squatting over him on the couch — part man, part woman, part ghastly bird. Three monstrous beaked heads sprouted from its shoulders, long-necked as vultures, staring at him sidelong with their mouths agape. The great wings that unfurled from its back were as dark as Storm clouds.

'Why, why, why,' jeered the heads, together. 'Did you expect us to cherish you, worm? Did you expect us to stroke you, and whisper sweet nothings to you? Heaven knows, it was bad enough doing that on the way down here.' One of the bird heads took on a vague resemblance to Samiha again. 'Hold me, my love,' it mocked in a high falsetto. 'Oh please, yes, more. Pah, disgusting.'

Then the wavering face of Samiha disappeared and the bird-thing drew itself up, its wings beating, the vulture heads emitting a multiple laugh. 'The Masters of this universe, love a maggot like yourself?' they sneered to Tymon. 'Hardly.'

All at once, the harpy-creature pounced down on him again, plunging its ghostly blue hands into his chest. Tymon howled in pain; the Masters' disembodied touch was no longer remotely pleasurable. He felt as if his heart were being gouged out.

'You make us sick,' rasped his tormentors. 'Love me, love me. Like a puking infant. You're all the same. Can't figure out what their Heavenly Highnesses see in you squealing worms. All you're good for is eating. Well, if they won't eat you, we will. Hear that, Matrya? Samaya, do you hear?'

The Masters suddenly let go of Tymon, arching back to shake a fist at the heavens, the three heads emitting a defiant shriek. Tymon let out a shuddering breath, weeping from pain. There was one word his enemies had pronounced that he clung to, one thought that kept their horror from driving him mad.

'Samaya?' he whispered. 'Do you mean Samiha?'

The Masters bent over him again, gloating. 'She won't help you now,' they said.

And with one more pounce, one more tearing, excruciating plunge of their talons, they ripped the very pith out of him, tore up the plant from its casing and cast his consciousness spinning away into a howling vortex.

He imagined, then, that he would die. But the whirlwind that tore him apart and sucked him under was as brief as it was brutal. It did not deliver him to oblivion. After an interval the howling noise and fury drained away, and silence descended on him like a shroud. He found he was still lying on his back, still on a hard cold surface, with his eyes squeezed shut.

The first thing he noticed as he opened them was that the pain caused by the Masters was gone, and that his fingers, like the rest of his body, shone with the starry glow of the trance-form.

The second was that he was no longer in the great hall of the ruined city in the World Below, but confined in a cramped space, just large enough to contain him. When he raised his glowing hand to touch the cold grey ceiling above, claustrophobically close to his face, he recognised the deadly, dense material of the Veil.

Panic rose inside him in a choking wave. They had not killed him, no. Why go through all the trouble of bringing him to the World Below, just to kill him? What the Masters had done was to eject his soul from his body, and incarcerate it in the Veil. This was a burial of the spirit. He pounded both fists against the unmoving ice; there was no change in the grey surface.

He shouted, screamed for help until he was hoarse, but no answer broke the silence of the Veil.

The young man who left the building with the columns was not the same one who had entered it, Zero knew that much. He had already forgiven Tymon for hitting him, knowing his friend had been under the spell of the hungry ghost. After their argument, he had waited for his companion to hurry off through the ruins, then followed, tracking him from afar. He had watched in awe as Tymon battled a flying creature he could only assume was a lesser demon, knocking it to the ground. Then he had followed his friend here, to this Ghost House, the one intact construction in all the spirit-city.

Zero quailed when he saw Tymon enter the shining double doors. He was not able to summon up the courage to pursue him there, for the building looked exactly like the shrines his people still carved in the Eastern Canopy, complete with surrounding columns and peaked roof. These so-called Ghost Houses, little hollow box-altars built by peasant folk in Nur, were remnants of a religion far older than that of the Grafters or the Argosian priests. They were built to honour the ancestors. The sight of a life-size version filled Zero with superstitious terror. He sat down at the base of a crumbling wall, ashamed of his fear but unable to enter that seat of blue, crackling spirit-power. For tongues of lightning struck the top of the Ghost House at regular intervals, as if called down from the Storm above. The House ate lightning.

He did not have to berate himself for his cowardice too long. After only a few minutes, Tymon obliged him by walking out of the building again. Zero's joy was short-lived, however, for he realised his friend had paid a terrible price for entering the Ghost House. The young man walking down the steps had eyes that shone as blue and bright as the lightning that leapt above the roof. Zero had only to glance at the host's dead, emotionless expression to know that the hungry ghost had possessed Tymon's body, filling it with its own uncanny essence.

The Marak boy crouched in the shadow of the wall, his heart beating wildly. But to his relief, the thing inhabiting Tymon's form did not appear to see him. Or perhaps it saw, and simply did not care that he was there. The blue spark faded from its eyes and it strode away through the gutted buildings. It chose a slightly different trajectory through the city than the one they had taken while coming in, heading almost due east. Zero rose cautiously and followed, feeling that he should at least keep what had been Tymon's body in sight. He had little hope his friend had survived the possession, but did not know what else to do. Nothing could have induced him to enter the Ghost House. So he shadowed the spirit-Tymon, dodging through the ruins to a point where the shallow, lapping waters invaded the city. There he hesitated, miserably unwilling to step into the cloudy reflection again, though he knew now the loamy base would hold beneath his feet.

He waited until the figure of the spirit-Tymon was a faraway dot. He was just working up the courage to step into the waters, when he heard a buzzing, whirring sound behind him, reminiscent of the flying demon. Before he could turn around and investigate the noise, however, something hit his neck with a sharp, lancing pain. His hand went up to feel the gently fanning end of a dart; a moment later, blackness surrounded him, and he crumpled unconscious in the shallows of the lake.

18

The canopy of stars had already given fair warning of it the previous night, as had the stiff breeze at dawn, but the sky was swept clean of any cloud on the morning chosen for the attack on the Freehold. It was a depressingly clear blue, and provided a perfect contrast to the Argosian dirigibles, with their reddish bark hulls and green sails. Admiral Greenly cursed under his breath as he stood on the deck of the flagship *Green Lady*, and squinted across the twig horizon, shielding his eyes against the bright sunlight.

'They'll see us coming from miles away,' he muttered.

'They won't be able to do much about it, sir,' barked his companion by the deck-rail.

The stiffness of Sergeant Pumble's posture was only exceeded by that of his coat collar. To the surprise of his baffled associates, his linen seemed to have suffered little diminution of starch since their last encounter with the laundry services of Argos city. But the gruelling voyage to Farhang had taken a toll on his appearance, all the same, which was why he now had to keep his double chin rigidly down in the breeze, clamped over his shirtfront, even as he fixed his eye on the far horizon. It was an awkward position, giving him an air of severity that was not normally appropriate when addressing a superior officer. But he felt he had to keep his collar from flapping. A man could not fulfil his duties properly if his collars were limp, in the sergeant's opinion.

Pumble was suffering a promotion to the colonial forces due to his deft handling of an awkward case in Argos city, several weeks before. In his more lucid moments, when the collar was off and he had allowed himself the latitude of a cup or two of Treesap wine, the sergeant heartily wished he had not been quite so deft in the discharge of his duties. He wished he had not alerted anyone to the possible Lantrian connections of the seminary lad, Tymon, who had caused so much trouble to the authorities. Had Pumble not been raised to the rank of Greenly's liaison due to that episode, he might still be wearing clean collars today.

The admiral shifted away from his companion at the rail. There was an unpleasant odour of frogapple blossom hovering about his secretary, who was inclined to anoint himself liberally with perfume. Greenly sometimes suspected that Pumble communicated with the Saint on the basis of long-distance odours. But however stiff the sergeant's collars and malodorous his choice of ointments, he was blessed by a far-seeing eye, as well as a gratifyingly literal mind. He was now using both to excellent effect, thought the admiral.

'Those fools in Farhang have joined up with rebels from Majad and Tuman,' continued Pumble, gazing at the distant twig-forests. 'They've formed a United Front against us. Not that it'll help them.'

Admiral Greenly, who suffered from dry eyes and a condition known by the medical establishment at the seminary as 'spider vision', could not see a thing on the horizon but the usual wafting of cobwebs across his sight — an irritating effect that caused his eyes to sting and water in the bright sun. After a few moments of straining uncomfortably, he finally glimpsed, in the uncertain distance, the masts and ether sacs of a pitiful cluster of dirigibles bobbing up and down in front of the village. The admiral smiled to himself in relief. If this was all the Nurian rebels had to show for their unification, then the crusade would soon be over. Perhaps one of his adjunct's United Shirt Fronts might have served the lice better, he thought scornfully.

'But if we can see them, Pumble, can't they see us?' he asked aloud.

'Not for much longer, sir,' said his poker-faced secretary. 'It seems we have the advantage, sir, under current meteorological conditions.'

And he pointed towards the western horizon. When the admiral turned obediently to gaze in the opposite direction, he saw to his astonishment that a black cloud had appeared out of the clear blue sky. He was certain it had not been there a few moments ago. He blinked at it several times but, unlike the usual trailing wisps that complicated his vision, this cloud was dense and did not slide to one side in order to reform and drift before his eyes again. It was scudding towards them at a considerable rate, growing larger by the minute.

'Good grief, man, get them to lower the sacks and lash the sails immediately!' gasped the admiral. 'It's a freak storm!'

The Argosian ships were not at first visible to the refugees in the hideout nestled beneath the bleak twigs, some miles east of Farhang. Noni could not even see the western horizon from the edge of the Saffid camp. It was only as she was making her way back to Oren's tent that she glimpsed the ominous green smudge of the armada drifting over the distant branches, bearing down on the Freehold.

She had spent an uncomfortable and indignant

night away from her fellow Grafters, and awoken early to news of the fleet's arrival, when a Farhang runner had reported the lookout's sighting soon after dawn. But Noni had remained with the Saffid until Ishi and Tudah, the fledgling Grafters, came to fetch her. Together, they trudged wearily back up the slope to the upper camp. The sad irony was not lost on Noni that Gardan had sent the message about the approaching armada to Adhama Sing, the grey-robed steward-in-chief, and not to Oren.

'There was no message for the Grafters at all,' Ishi told her breathlessly as they walked.

The older of the two fledglings, a gangly youth from the north holdings, had broken a front tooth some time in his rough and tumble past and had a ramshackle grin; he was very keen to get into the 'action', as he called it, and was in a continuous fidget. When Noni had first seen his young female companion, she had not thought such a milksop could ever prove to be Grafter material. Tudah was a rosy-cheeked girl from the outlying western farms, as different from Ishi as a lamb to a wolf. But she had proven to be remarkably lucid.

'They're on high alert at the Freehold,' she said. 'All the men and ships have come from Majad and Tuman to join them. But it's not enough, Noni.' Even though her voice was low, Noni could see the glow of ardour lighting her warm brown eyes. 'Can't we help?' she urged. 'Can't we stop the attack?'

'Surely we can!' exploded Ishi. 'That's what Grafters are for!'

Noni sighed as they walked together up towards Oren's tent. It would take patience to disabuse these young ones of their illusions. It would take time before they learned that a Grafter's power lay in the knowledge of its limitations. Oh, Tymon! she thought sadly. How much we miss you! But she knew that Oren had summoned her for the same reason. Something had to be done to protect the Freehold.

The others were already sitting in their circle when she lifted the tent flap. Ara and Mata rose to their feet and embraced Noni, asking anxiously how she was, for they had been grieved by their parting the previous evening — not because she had taken a stand in going to the Saffid camp, but because she had been forcibly separated from her companions as a result. They hovered protectively over her. Oren, however, did not waste time on greetings. His glance told her all.

'Have you seen it?' he murmured eagerly.

There was no shred of reproach in his tone. He was in no way rebuking her for her absence. But he was clearly preoccupied by an important matter that went above and beyond the Freeholders' sleeping arrangements.

'The fleet?' began Noni. 'Yes, I saw it just as we were coming up —'

'No,' her brother interrupted. 'I meant the cloud.'

Her eyes widened. The fledglings had mentioned no cloud. Neither had the message from the Freehold that morning. What she had heard whispered among the Saffid was that a fleet of at least fifty Argosian warships was hovering over Farhang, the Saint's army, poised to obliterate the Freehold. But there had been no talk of a cloud.

'It's no ordinary one, Noni,' murmured Oren. 'It's accompanying the ships like a blanket, shrouding them from view. I'm afraid the Envoy is with us.'

Even as an intake of collective breath rippled round the Grafters at his words, they heard a shuffle of steps outside the tent. The entrance flap was lifted and a tall, grey swathed figure blocked the morning light. They could see Adhama's broad feet in the doorway, like some old statue's, in heavy bark sandals; they could see the thick folds of her woollen cloak caked with grime. Noni felt her throat tighten as the implacable steward bent her veiled head to peer inside the tent.

'What's this?' snapped Adhama. 'Why is she here?'

There was no doubt whom she was referring to, though she evidently did not consider Noni worth addressing to her face. Ara and Mata closed ranks on each side of their fellow Grafter, standing by her defensively, but Oren remained seated and still.

'This is my sister,' he said quietly, to Adhama.

'There's a war out there, you know,' rasped the overseer.

'I know,' answered Oren. 'And we have urgent work to do.'

'Can't have this sort of hanky-panky going on, in wartime,' continued Adhama imperturbably. 'Rules are rules. She's a bad example for the younger ones. Come on, you. Out.'

Her eyes flicked over Noni at last, dismissive. The fledglings stared open-mouthed as Adhama yanked the tent flap open and held it up. She was evidently waiting for Noni to bow her head and go out after her, like a five-year-old child or an obedient margoose.

'She's staying here,' said Oren, with rigid calm.

'If it wasn't fine for her before, it won't be now,' sneered the grey-robed overseer. 'She's going back to 'em, in the other camp. Her choice.'

'It's not going to be fine for anyone much longer,' replied Oren coldly, 'if you don't let us do our work. Now. We cannot delay.'

Noni did not know what power her brother used then, but Adhama shrank back. Perhaps it was because of the fixed intensity in Oren's eyes, which Noni knew was worse than any curse. Or perhaps it was because of the strange rustling that passed through the twig-forests at that moment, followed by a perceptible darkening of the air. There was no time to lose. Oren called out urgently to his companions as the tent filled with whispering shadows and a whirl of invisible wings.

'Quick!' he exclaimed. 'My friends! Form the circle!'

The others hastily gathered in the Grafter's ring, while Noni stepped forward and pulled the flap of the tent out of Adhama's grasp.

'I'll leave as soon as I can,' she said. 'But now I must work.'

And as the chant of her fellow Grafters rose up in the tent, swelling out, drawing her into the circle of acceptance, she closed the entrance flap and knotted it firmly shut in the face of the outraged overseer.

Farhang was built for defence. The houses were constructed deep within the twig-forests at the summit of the canopy, surrounded by a labyrinth of dense growth and inaccessible by air, all paths inward equipped with booby traps and mobile blocks. When one protective circle was broken, another always remained; the Freehold leadership itself was divided into separate cells, self-sufficient in case of emergency. The dining hall had been set up as the main battle headquarters, but it was not the only one. And yet, thought Gardan, as she stood just outside the hall, squinting up at the vast black cloud rolling over the twig-forests, one could not be prepared for everything. One could not foresee all consequences. The freak storm cloud had completely engulfed the Argosian fleet, rendering the enemy ships invisible. The usually level-headed judge felt a shiver go down her spine, as she gazed up at the roiling vapours advancing over the Freehold. She did not like the oily density of the cloud. She did not like the way it moved so quickly, and without the benefit of the wind.

A moment later, she noticed that the men and women who were meant to be defending the perimeter of the hall were standing idly in the clearing outside the building, staring up at the unnatural cloud, even as she did. She realised that they were all wasting precious time.

'Battle stations,' she called, with some irritation.

The Freeholders responded to her command, shaking off the numb daze that had taken hold of them, and returning to their posts at the palisade of cut and sharpened twigs around the hall. Gardan took a deep breath and strode up the ramp into the building, taking up her position at a western window. The cloud gradually cut off the sun, plunging the environs of the village in shadow.

'That's odd,' remarked Galliano, from where he sat on the floor of the hall. 'The temperature's rising. That's not seasonal.'

'Weather's gone all muggy,' Gardan answered briefly. 'There's a freak storm coming up. It's hiding the enemy ships.'

'A freak storm?' The old scientist had turned his empty eye-sockets on her, frowning. 'Now? In the month of Sunlight Return? I doubt it.'

But Gardan was not listening, her gaze fixed on the darkening sky. She realised she was being assailed with emotions she had not experienced since the last Argosian attack on Sheb, when she had watched her colleague, Kosta, inexplicably lose his mind in the midst of negotiations with the enemy. She was overcome by the same clammy sense of horror she had felt that day, the desire to run and hide, entirely contrary to her character and training. She looked about her and saw the expressions of the other soldiers in the hall reflecting similar sentiments, their faces drained of all colour. She took a deep breath, forcing herself to remain calm.

'Battle stations,' she repeated to the Freeholders in the hall, more to rally and comfort them than to remind them of their duty. And then, with a stab of compunction, she remembered Oren's warning to her the day before.

We will not win a final war. Not now, in the End Times.

Perhaps she should have listened a little better to the Grafters, thought Gardan.

On board the *Green Lady* and the other ships of the Argosian fleet, sails had been rolled up, ether sacks double-lashed and anchors dropped to the twig-forests below. The entire flotilla was poised for a battering in the tempest. Pumble held surreptitiously onto his collar as he stood on deck, for the cloud that had been scudding towards them from the west was now directly overhead. It was dense and almost tangibly dark, a seething mass of shadows. But it was also remarkably un-moist, for a storm cloud, and very well-behaved, thought Pumble. No wind. No rain. His collar had not budged. As the cloud continued to hang over them without releasing the slightest speck of humidity, an idea occurred to the sergeant.

'An excellent opportunity, sir,' he said to the admiral, 'to attack under cover.'

But Admiral Greenly was not convinced. 'Yes,' he said doubtfully. 'Perhaps. We should wait for the first downpour before doing anything, however. I'm afraid the rain might put out the flames and waste ammunition, otherwise.'

He blinked and rubbed his eyes. There was something about this cloud that disturbed him. It seethed, clotting in the air overhead; he fancied he saw shapes in it, like bat wings or savage birds. Damned spider vision, he thought. Flies in the eyes.

The sergeant could not understand why the admiral

was dragging his heels. Their course of action was obvious. 'We should act fast, sir,' he urged, 'before it dissipates.'

Admiral Greenly took out a handkerchief and mopped his brow. It was supernaturally hot, this storm cloud. It breathed like a furnace in his face. No chance of it quenching the cannon flames, he thought dismally: quite the contrary. There wasn't a breath of wind in the air. And where was the rain, anyway?

Pumble, who had shuddered involuntarily at the sight of the rumpled handkerchief emerging from his superior's breast pocket, decided to take the shillee by the horns. A chap without pride in his personal linen could not be a proper leader of men, in his opinion. He pushed out his chest, pulled back his shoulders and clamped his chin rigidly down on his collar. As far as he was concerned, storm clouds that appeared out of nowhere just before an attack were custom-made for the Saint's crusade, especially when they were shorn of wind and rain. To use them for any other purpose would be outright negligence. Even if it only resulted in yet another confounded promotion, he had no choice but to insist on the proper action in the present circumstances.

'Shall we order the ships to advance, and fire the first volley, sir?' he said stiffly.

And barely waited for the admiral's weary nod to do so himself.

It came down on Farhang like burning rain: a barrage of blast-poison out of the black cloud, a hail of deadly, devastating flame. Volley after volley ripped through the twig-forests, shaking the bark beneath the villagers' feet, sending clouds of dust and blinding splinters into their eyes. The soldiers from Sheb, who had experience of the new Argosian weaponry, crouched down and took cover beneath loose building planks and sections of bark as best they could, grateful for the twig-thickets that sheltered much of the village. But they knew that even those barriers would not hold for long. They had little hope of prevailing against the enemy while the Argosians remained on their ships, pelting them with explosive shot. They could only hunker down, waiting for the bombardment to stop, and the Saint's foot soldiers to move in.

They had not banked, even so, on the full effect of the cloud.

It was of course demoralising not to know where the explosive volleys were coming from. While the Freeholders judged the general position of the fleet to be somewhere in the heart of the freak storm, they could not see each ship. But what they did not expect, what truly took them by surprise, was how the storm cloud itself behaved. The vapours were tangible in a way ordinary fog should never be; with every new series of bombardments, the black miasma descended lower over the village, sliding its oily tendrils through the buildings and by-ways. It was like a clotting of feathers, a seething of cobwebs, a stinging of bat wings in the air. The Freeholders choked and coughed on it.

And there were other effects, too: an assault on the mind. Even as the soldiers' limbs were being dismembered by the conventional barrage of blast-poison, they felt slithery horrors coiling around their arms and ankles, tangling them in knots. They found themselves clawing the air in front of their faces, scrambling away from their posts in panic and tripping into the fires that had started to blaze all over the village, their hearts filled with ashy fear. The cloud drained all will to fight out of them; they were terrorised, fleeing before it when they should have stood their ground.

The outer defences were soon broken. The Nurians retreated into the core of the village, fighting hand to hand with the Argosian foot soldiers who had begun their advance through the twig-thickets in the wake of the bombardment. By the time the inner cadre of defenders had fallen back to the barricade around the dining hall, the Freeholders had lost five entire fighting units, either to the disheartening effect of the cloud or to the explosions. Gardan was obliged to take her place at the thinly manned palisade herself. She crouched behind the barrier of sharpened twigs next to Halas, fingering a hardwood spear and listening to the steadily approaching din of combat. Nearby, her fellow soldiers at the palisade gripped their weapons with whitened knuckles, whispering nervously to each other. The miasma of the cloud drifted through the twigs along with the smell of burning. So far, the vapours had not produced a single drop of rain.

Gardan's face was smeared with soot, her clothes and cropped hair covered in dust and bark chips. Her eyes stared wearily out of a background of grime, for her earlier terror had been replaced by a quiet despair, confronted with what seemed like overwhelming odds. Beside her, Halas squinted into the smoky gloom between the twig-shafts in grim silence, waiting for a glimpse of the enemy.

'We should try to get the scientist out, at least,' murmured Gardan, glancing over her shoulder at the dining hall. 'Things don't look good and, besides, he's starting to annoy the troops. We're cut off from the squadrons, anyway: he doesn't need to stay.'

Halas shrugged unenthusiastically, following her gaze to the building where Galliano's bent figure could be seen leaning out of a window, apparently oblivious to any danger. 'Won't it be more risky,' he said, 'to leave now, under enemy fire?'

'It's more of a responsibility to keep him in Farhang at such a time,' Gardan replied. 'Look at him! He's starting up his nonsense again.'

She gestured in mute exasperation towards Galliano, who had begun to call once more out of the window, shouting to the soldiers cowering by the palisade. The scientist had refused to take cover when the cloud of poisonous fear descended over the village: it did not seem to affect him as it did so many other people, and as a result he would not believe in its influence.

'It's pure illusion!' he was roaring, as the cries of approaching combat grew louder, mingled with the occasional distant explosion. 'Bats in the fog — nothing but imagination!'

'Just because he can't see what's going on,' hissed Gardan to Halas, 'he thinks it's all in our minds. I'm afraid his is turning,' she concluded, shaking her head. 'I should have insisted he leave earlier, with the others.'

Galliano had claimed, to begin with, that he was trying to rouse the soldiers' courage, but the tenor of his shouts had changed in the last few minutes. He was scolding them now. 'Don't buy into that humbug,' he was yelling. 'Don't fall for those tricks. The Argosians just want to frighten you: they're nothing but stupid little boys. Listen — they're singing playground songs!'

And it was practically true, thought Gardan. In addition to the roar of blast-poison and the terrifying rush of flying spears in the air, she could hear a strident anthem rising in the distance, all bravado and childish rage. The enemy soldiers were drawing nearer, singing raucous battle songs.

In the steps of the Saint we come!
To the sound of his marching drum!
Dip your hands in gore,

Give your life to war,
Clean the Tree, in his name, of scum!

'I want you to go with him,' said Gardan, turning to Halas once more. 'It's pointless to lose everyone, we're not going to survive here —'

She was not given the opportunity to finish her sentence. At that instant, a dark figure rose up from behind the palisade, vaulting with a shout over the barrier of twigs. Gardan barely had time to realise, with a stab of terror, that one of the enemy soldiers had crept up to the palisade, before she was thrown down on the bark with the weight of the foreigner on top of her, her spear knocked from her grasp. She struggled against her assailant, expecting at any moment to feel the bite of his blade.

But instead of encountering her death, she found herself gazing into the face of a young Argosian boy. He was a lad of barely seventeen or eighteen, black-haired and wearing a wisp of a beard, his hazel eyes wide as he slumped on top of her. He made no further move after his first leap, his expression frozen in surprise. Gardan wondered fleetingly why he did not kill her. Then, as he continued to lie inert, she rolled him over with some difficulty to see Halas' spear rooted between his shoulder blades. She watched in horror as a dark stain spread through the young Argosian's clothing, soaking symmetrically on either side of his back like a pair of wings. Halas also stood staring down in consternation at the dead boy.

'They're just children!' he muttered in disgust. 'They've sent us a bunch of children!'

Gardan struggled to her feet, shocked out of the sense of hopelessness that had overcome her. There was a reason for this reprieve, she thought, a cause to cling to that went beyond survival. She took hold of Halas' arm, her voice soft and urgent in his ear.

'Leave now,' she told him, as the manic chant of the Saint's boy army drew ever closer. 'Find Oren and his sister, I beg of you. They're our only hope, I see that now. I should have sent this message earlier, but it may not be too late if you bring it yourself. You're a brave man, our bravest. Protect the Grafters with your life. They're the ones who can lift this cloud from our hearts. Do it,' she whispered, as lurid flames lit up the darkness and Galliano finally stopped shouting out of the window, doubled up with coughing, 'do it in the name of our old friend Laska.'

In the twig-thickets beyond the palisade, flames, smoke, and the black fog of despair consumed Farhang. The Argosians were torching the Freehold, house by house, heart by heart, song by song.

The beating of dark wings was suffocating in the Grafters' tent. The Focals' chant fought, but could not banish it. Gripping her brother's hand, Noni felt the fog brush her cheek and clammy tendrils smear the surface of her lips. She had difficulty in resisting the impulse to pull her fingers away from Oren's in order to wipe the slime off her forehead. The cloud descending over the Freehold was made of some viscous substance, seeping into every nook and cranny. Psychic constructs, she thought with a shudder. Half-real pieces of matter spread out in a choking miasma. The camp of the refugees might have been hidden from the admiral's fleet, but it was at the mercy of the Envoy. The heavy air closed in around the young Grafters, oozing between them, clogging their nostrils and hair. Lace was everywhere. They resisted his pernicious influence by entering the trance.

Their strength depended on unity, thought Noni. It did not matter how weak they might be individually, so long as their union was strong. A brief glance round the circle before shutting her eyes confirmed it. Oren was holding her right hand, and had Ishi's left in his firm grasp; Ishi was holding Ara's right hand and Ara was holding Mata's left; Mata had laced Tudah's right fingers in his own and Tudah's grip tightened on Noni's left. The circle was complete. Their voices grew firmer and more confident as they felt the Sap surge through them. It passed like a fiery thread from hand to hand, glowing warmer, growing wider as they confronted Lace in the trance. If they could draw his attention to themselves, they might help release the Freeholders from his grip.

Worlds made one, thought Noni, remembering the Oracle's lessons from long ago. If they were one, their influence could reach out into the world. One, unified.

'Use the Letter of Union,' said Oren, echoing her thoughts.

Noni knew what he meant them to do, to banish the slithering fog. She held tightly to her companions' hands and opened her eyes again, concentrating not on leaving her body but on the space at the centre of their circle. She visualised the Letter of Union there, an unbroken ring of light, and felt the others doing the same as they wove the trance, adding their strength to her own. A glowing point appeared in the air and expanded into a sphere of light, a pool of energy throbbing with the Sap. The pieces of Lace, the bats' wings and puddles of frogspawn, the dead birds' feathers and lumps of wet shadow, were repelled from it. Everything depended on their holding firm, Noni told herself. Everything depended on their widening that little globe of light, outwards from this tent across the camp, bringing Adhama and the Saffid into the circle and reaching further, wider, until they reached Farhang and beyond. They must stretch their unity out to where Nurians and Argosians were fighting their futile battle, extend their globe of light and wellbeing to push the Envoy's cloud away —

Mother help us, she thought suddenly, *for we are weak.*

And as she contemplated how far this tiny circle of unity would have to stretch to fight the fog, considered the vast impossibility of their light reaching out and including every dark crevice of the canopy, Noni felt the slap of something feathered and sticky across her mouth. She almost cried aloud in revulsion, breaking her focus to shake her head and be rid of the filthy thing. But the next minute, the disgusting fragment flew back into her face from the other side, covering her mouth and nostrils completely. She felt she was choking. It took the greatest will in the world not to tear her hand from Tudah's trembling fingers, or pull free from Oren and wipe the horrid clot off her skin.

In weakness find strength. Oren was chanting the Grafter's litany beside her, calling desperately on the Leaf Letters. *In emptiness, power.*

She realised from the tenor of his voice that he was being similarly attacked. They all must be. She had to stay firm! She had to keep the circle true. Noni gathered up her courage and joined her brother in the chant, singing despite the slimy fragments of the Envoy that seethed through the air, slipping between her lips and thickening her tongue.

Worlds that were severed, we now bind together.

But the pool of light between them was becoming clouded. The emptiness that had allowed the Sap to flow from hand to hand was being blocked, even as they struggled to maintain the trance. They were only as strong as the weakest links in their chain, thought Noni in dismay, and one of the fledgling Grafters — she sensed it was Ishi — had already broken away. She could see him across the circle from her, batting his arms about his head, furiously swinging his fists in the air. Into the breach he had created surged a dark puddle of filth, a viscous arm dividing the Grafters' circle in half. It muddied the Sap globe and darkened the light, causing Tudah to squirm with discomfort and assailing Mata and Ara in a similar fashion. They held firm another long moment, and Noni hoped they would prevail: in spite of the breach, she imagined the Sap would still flow, the light still pulse between them. Then Tudah finally tore her hand from Mata's grasp, Ara coughed and groaned and Ishi scrambled out of the circle. The trance began to disintegrate.

Oren had not stopped chanting the Grafter's song all this while, but Noni could see he was straining to concentrate. Tudah retreated to the back of the tent, weeping bitterly, while Ishi still lunged about in a fruitless fight against the Envoy's vile particles. Noni saw Oren reach out and grasp Ara's hand in an attempt to maintain the circle. So she did the same. Still chanting despite the choking air, she held out her free hand to Mata to keep the trance intact. If they could just maintain the flow of the Sap, even if they were only four — ah, Tymon! mourned Noni's heart, silently, as her lips kept moving. If only you had returned to us.

But Ara and Mata could not sustain it. They broke apart, retching in the fog. Mata doubled up and starting vomiting. Trembling with nausea herself, Noni fancied she heard a jeering echo in the clotted air. Lace was laughing at them. She felt the wet slap across her face again and an insidious finger of slime being traced across her neck. It was all too much for her; she shuddered in horror and pulled away from Oren, covering her face with her hands.

At that moment, a dreadful cry rent the air. It sounded like a creature in terrible pain.

* * *

The cry catapulted Oren from the shredded remains of the trance and he opened his eyes, shaking. He did not know whether the scream had come from Noni's lips, or from one of the others. Was it was poor Ishi asking for help as he writhed on the ground, or Mata gagging on the other side of the tent? Was it Ara, or perhaps little Tudah, hunched in the far corner weeping her heart out? He felt a terrible sense of responsibility for the fate of whoever had called out between the suffocating echoes of their enemy's laughter. He felt he was to blame for that cry.

Oren ground his hands together after Noni let him go, balling his fists in his lap. He knew that the glowing globe was extinguished, and that the waves of Sap had spiralled away, useless; the trance was a failure. He ached all over, and there was a dead weight lodged in the middle of his chest that made it difficult to breathe. It was a wrench to have been torn apart from his fellow Grafters in the middle of their chant. He felt bruised and broken, crushed and beaten by the Envoy's cloud of despair, as if the shreds of cobweb and clogging feathers had been whips and hooked thongs rather than a fog, finally settling like hardwood in his lungs. But that cry had been the most painful of all. Such a call it was! Such agony! It tugged at his heart, filling him with remorse. He should not have permitted the fledglings to take part in the trance, he reproached himself. They had not been ready for such a test.

But though he sensed the pain that rose from the ruins of their little circle, he could not banish the persistent feeling that the cry itself had come from far away. Whose voice was reaching out to him from the distance? Who was suffering so? And with the thought of Ishi and Tudah, Oren suddenly remembered Jedda, combating the Envoy's curses. And Tymon, lost and invisible to them.

Protect the fledglings, the Oracle had told him.

Those two had been inexperienced Grafters, too, placed under his care. And although Oren had been angry with the one for betraying them and the other for abandoning them, he suddenly realised he had expected far more of Jedda and Tymon than he had of himself. He had hardly thought of them at all in his concern to defend the Freehold. What if they were the ones crying out to him, across the reaches of the Tree? If he could not keep faith with those earlier fledglings, how could he protect the new ones?

It was then, as he listened to Noni trying to comfort Tudah in one corner and Ara whispering to Mata in another and Ishi grumbling in the middle of it all about not having had his chance to knock the skittles out of that beastly Envoy, that Oren knew. He understood at last who had given the heartrending cry, and leapt to his feet.

'*Ama!*' he coughed, staggering to the corner of the tent where he kept his backpack. 'I've been such a fool!'

Noni surfaced from her own torpor, startled. Her brother was fumbling with the ties on the bag, his face deathly pale. 'What do you mean, Oren?' she said anxiously.

'We've been tricked!' he wheezed as he bent over his pack. He seemed to be having difficulty opening it and breathing, too. 'The attack was a feint, Noni!'

'For goodness sake!' his sister remonstrated as he doubled up in a fit of coughing. She jumped to her feet and thumped him on the back. 'What are you talking about?'

'The cry,' he gasped. 'Didn't you hear it?'

'I thought it was you,' answered Noni.

Oren gave another hacking cough, finally clearing the dead weight from his lungs. 'It was her,' he said. 'The Oracle. The Envoy's been trying to blind us with his fog and his blast-poison. He's been keeping us busy, gathering his filthy cloud in our little buckets.' He was shaking with emotion as he pulled the bag open with Noni's help. 'When all this time, we should have been trying to contact Jedda. Through her we might have found Tymon, and through him the Oracle. Our duty was to protect the fledglings — all of them, even the ones that had strayed.'

'That's not fair,' Noni protested. 'We tried and tried to contact Tymon —'

'Not enough. Not the right way,' said Oren hoarsely. 'But it may not be too late. That cry — it came from the future. We have to prevent it from happening!'

'But what can we do?' asked his sister. 'We tried to launch the trance, we sang the songs —'

'The old chants are not enough.' Oren shook his head. 'We need new songs, songs for the future. It's the Year of Fire, remember? The beginning and the end.'

He straightened up with a soft exclamation of triumph, having finally retrieved what he had been looking for in his backpack. Samiha's testament had been hidden at the very bottom. Noni felt herself breathe more freely as Oren drew the bundle out. The sight of the papers seemed to banish the fog a little, and the air felt cleaner in the tent. She fixed her eyes on the testament, recalling the words that gave her hope. The verses were already growing green in her heart, spreading through every part of her, ready to leap through her lips.

'Ara! Come, Mata, Ishi, Tudah!' cried Oren, beckoning the Grafters towards him again. The twins gathered around him instinctively, while the younger ones looked up, summoned by the urgency in his voice.

'We need to launch the Reading again,' he continued, as Ishi scrambled off the floor and Tudah blinked and blew her nose in a rag. 'But not to go into battle this time, not to play more paltry games. Not even to create the globe of Union. No, Ishi —' he added, holding up a hand in warning as the fledgling opened his mouth to protest. 'That's not the way, not this time. We're going to enter the world of the Sap, where Lace cannot follow us. We're going to sing her words — Samiha's words. Only they have the power to reach our friends. Come, now. For Tymon's life, and for Jedda's! For the sake of the Oracle!'

Lace stretched himself luxuriously through the air, like a shimmering swarm of buzzing black flies over the crumbling sweetmeat that was the Freehold. Though he would rather have plunged a knife into the Oracle's heart himself, it was some comfort to mop up the upstart Nurians instead. He was enjoying the feast of fear and mayhem he had cast over them, choking the last dregs of courage out of them with his cloud. The village was ablaze, the Freehold dead piled by their useless barricades. As the Saint had ordered, the Argosian soldiers took no living prisoners. They were now scouring the village for survivors, singing as they went. Soon they would move on to the refugee camp five miles away where, if the Envoy guessed aright, they might sniff out the Grafters. Lace was looking forward to a little further amusement after routing the Focals' trance so successfully.

They had been too weak to combat him, and had withdrawn with barely a fight. For the moment, he let them be. He had another adversary in his sights, for he had glimpsed old Galliano stumbling out of the burning dining hall at the height of the fighting, crawling blindly through the embers with the last group of evacuees. They had been headed for the refugee hideout, five miles away. The Envoy had no intention of allowing the infuriating scientist to escape with his life again. It was time to put an end to Galliano's little inventions.

For the scientist's air-chariots were proving troublesome, the one hiccup in an otherwise flawless battle plan. The armies of the Saint might have succeeded in burning Farhang to ashes, but the job of crushing the Freehold was far from finished. Hand-to-hand fighting was persistent in the thick undergrowth around the village, where the Argosian soldiers were having greater difficulties, harried by the Nurian flying squadrons. The Freeholders had built hidden platforms in the twig-thickets from which their abominable machines took off and returned at high speed; the Saint's army had become the target of a horde of wasps that swooped down over the twig-forests to pick them off, one by one. Had their visibility not been reduced by the Envoy's cloud, the Freeholders on the ground would have seen that Galliano's machines were providing an indomitable counter-offensive to the admiral's attack. These infernal little air-chariots were harrying their enemies relentlessly, impeding their progress as they tried to finish the job on foot. But for the Envoy, the armies of the Saint might have been at a distinct disadvantage.

First, thought Lace, settling his tendrils over the Freehold, he would deal with the irritating, stinging wasps, then he would crush the crawling louse that invented them. He turned his attention to the buzz of air-chariots that tried to compete with his cloud, sending his blanket of black flies and crawling spiders towards them. He gathered himself into a vast and clotted web over the Freehold, while the squadron swung round for another attack. Their leader had evidently seen the line of the Saint's soldiers below, making their way towards the refugee camps; he must have imagined that three of the air-chariots would be sufficient to stop the Argosians in their tracks as they marched single file through the twig-forests. He was wrong, thought the Envoy sardonically.

The minute the air-chariots swooped down, the Envoy thickened his cloud around them like frog-pea soup. Finding visibility drastically reduced, the first pilot swerved violently to avoid crashing into the twigs, and tumbled headlong into a vine plantation. The second turned a somersault in the heavy mist and nose-dived into a branch, breaking all his propellers. And the third, overcome with dismay, beat a hasty retreat to higher air.

Once more, the wasps rose from their launching pads; once more, they swept in a wide arc over the twig-forest. And again the Envoy smiled in anticipation and spread out his hazy tentacles to receive them. His wisps and trails of mist were as sticky as cobwebs and clung to the sides of the Nurian machines like an enormous butterfly net from which they could not escape. Their air-chariots were buffeted about without the benefit of any wind. They were nudged in directions they had no intention of going, their craft careening out of control. When the sole survivor of the second squadron limped back to safety in his stuttering machine, he raved to his fellows about bats' wings and birds' eyes in the unnatural fog.

There was a lull, then, and no further attacks occurred. For the Envoy's cloud blotted out confidence as well as visibility. It filled the Nurians with bewilderment and despair. The United Freeholds could not come up with a new plan of action, although the Argosian soldiers were hacking their way step by step closer to the refugee camp, singing their ribald songs of victory.

Come out, scum! Taste my bum! Eat my spear, let's have some fun!

Eager fools! thought the Envoy complacently, as the strident chorus reached up to his cloud. He was doing what he could to conceal the whereabouts of the Saint's army, but if they were not careful, the Nurians would hear the soldiers' idiotic rhymes and hunt them down. They would attack that infernal noise, if they were not so duped by fear themselves. Lace sniggered, a cackle of mean-spirited merriment. The battle was almost over: he could practically smell the coming Nurian defeat, a heady mixture of smoke, dust and burning bodies.

But just as he had his moment of gloating anticipation, in the midst of his laughter he heard another far-off song through the din of war. It was a very different melody from the soldiers' anthem.

Ye are the wind that carries forth the flame …

Lace concentrated all his fragments, gathered all his droning flies together to listen. The sound was coming from the refugee camp, a music more felt than heard. The Grafters! They were chanting again in an attempt to launch another trance. He listened with growing fury as the music from the Focals' inner world echoed through the thrum of propellers in the outer one. For it seemed the confounded Freehold wasps had also chosen that very moment to begin a counter-offensive. The squadrons were rising again, all of them at once, in a concerted effort, a distracting hum to his right.

Ye are the call raised at the break of day.

Lace felt himself shrivelling at the edges, his bat-cloud shrinking. He thought he had snuffed out the little Grafter wimps, but no! They were at it again. Just like the air-chariots swooping out of their hiding places. What were they up to now? There were four squadrons of three machines each: they split ranks and closed in on the admiral's fleet from the south, north and east.

Before you, armies lay their arms to rest …

Lace flung his tendrils out in disgust, and gave chase. But he was no longer bothering with the air squadrons of the United Freeholds. He was lunging back towards the Grafters' tent. For their song filled the air with a bright shimmer he dreaded. A fiery river of Sap was flowing strong between them again. They were slipping away from him, swirling beyond him to a place and state he could not reach. It was an insult far more vexing than the stinging air-chariots on the fringes of his cloud.

The promise kept and all signs manifest.

The Grafters had entered the world of the Sap. They were communing directly with the Tree of Being, a condition from which Lace was forever excluded. He seethed with rage on the perimeter of their circle, whirling his tendrils of fog about their tent, unable this time to distract them. He fumed frogspawn and salivated bat wings and spat bird feathers into the air, not caring for the moment that the Freehold squadrons were carrying out their first successful attack on the fleet. Greenly could deal with the wasps himself, for once, the Envoy decided. He had had enough of babysitting the Argosian army. He sulked, wrapping his miasma about the Focals' tent.

Let the fools sing and pray all they liked, he thought savagely. Let them stay trapped in their bubble of a Sap-world, like flies caught in amber. Much good might it do them! The minute they stopped their caterwauling, the minute they broke their confounded unity, he would throw a tendril of fog around their necks and strangle each one of them. Once the Saint's army managed to reach the camp, their prayers would be of no use to them, anyway. He had their bodies at his mercy. All that was left to be done was for the Argosian soldiers to search through the twig-thickets, and find and crush every last remaining louse.

19

Jedda's initial joy at sensing Tymon's approach was quickly replaced by confusion. The twinge in her belly had acquired a queasy edge of duality she did not understand, an inherent contradiction. Tymon drew closer, and yet he did not; he was obviously moving towards her, but remained distant. There was a paradox or, more precisely, a *wrongness* to the twining link that caused her to feel faintly ill. She bowed her head to her knees again, concentrating instead on loosening the bonds about her wrists, for she wanted to be able to jump up and help Tymon when he arrived. If he really was on his way towards them, he would need her help to resist the two acolytes.

It might have been an hour or more that she sat on the wet granules of the beach, while Wick and Gowron crouched on the higher ground by the Oracle's door, arguing with each other about which prophecies to translate into the *abjat* numerals. The acolytes mercifully ignored her, preferring to vent their bile on each other. And all the while the odd, queasy sensation in Jedda's stomach grew stronger. At last, after steadily and grimly twisting her wrists beneath the ropes until the skin of her arms was raw, she noticed the bonds slowly beginning to loosen, and simultaneously felt something soft brush against her right hand. Craning her neck to peer behind her shoulder, she saw the loose page from Samiha's testament that Wick had abandoned fluttering on the loam, tantalisingly within reach.

She glanced at the two companions under the escarpment. They had their backs to her, bent over the door, and paid her no heed. She inched her body over the gritty loam and with infinite care caught the sheet between her thumb and forefinger. But even as she drew it into her palms, crumpled it between her fingers and tried as best she could to shove it back up her sleeve, the verses on the page sang in her memory, like the lapping of the waters of the lake.

Far from you, I wander lost, tattered, searching through the dust …

'I don't care if it isn't part of the canon.' Wick's voice rose up, strident, breaking through Jedda's thoughts. 'It's old. Try it anyway.'

The acolytes seemed to be having such difficulty with the hatchway, and such a difference of opinion about how to open it, that Jedda began to hope they would never break the code. Perhaps the Oracle would be saved through the influence of other, more subtle powers than those of the Envoy. But although Jedda had called out silently to her teacher many times as she sat on the beach, there was still no breath of response. Matrya's presence no longer inhabited her mind. She had also tried to reach out through the twining connection to Tymon, to touch his consciousness, as she had done in Argos city. But the character of the link between them had definitely changed. He was no longer open to her. He did not answer when she called but simply approached, or rather both approached and did not. The effect made her feel decidedly dizzy. She found herself feeling sorry for the air-sick Wick, for the tug and pull in her belly was nauseating.

The two acolytes had just begun a fresh round of arguments, their voices rising vociferously from the top of the beach, when Jedda's nausea abruptly increased. She gasped for air, feeling violently ill; the skewed twining link had intensified and was like a clanging bell in her gut. She glanced across the lake, her eyes dragged towards the source of the call. Far off to the southwest, hardly more than a sliver of darker grey on the grey waters, a figure had appeared on the horizon. She recognised it long before the features were visible on the face.

In desperate hope that I may find a hint, a remnant left behind of you … she thought, frowning at the faraway figure. Tymon appeared to be walking on the water.

A moment later, she understood that he was wading through it. The lake must have been very shallow, barely up to his knees. She wondered in consternation why he approached so openly, and without bothering to hide from his enemies. Even as she watched him, astonished, she realised Wick and Gowron were no longer arguing. The two acolytes stood as still as statues on either side of the door, staring out over the water as she did, hypnotised by the approaching figure. They neither spoke nor moved, apparently in no hurry to attack their enemy. All three of them watched Tymon in absolute silence. The plash of waters grew louder and louder against the beach.

Jedda gazed at her twining partner in mounting dismay. With every step he took towards her, the humming dissonance of the link that bound them became more distracting, more unbearable, until she could almost hear as well as feel the skewed connection in her gut. She did not know what to call the twisting *wrongness*. Nothing she had experienced before, no violation of body or mind had ever felt so terrible. She both anticipated and dreaded the moment when

Tymon's eyes would turn on her — and why did he take so long to turn towards her? He did not even recognise her! His gaze, she saw with alarm, was trained on the Oracle's door, never once deviating as he strode purposefully through the water. She stared, amazed, as he splashed out of the shallows and passed her without a shred of acknowledgment, making for the top of the beach where the acolytes stood transfixed by the hatchway.

'Tymon?' she croaked as he passed, voiceless in her surprise.

She could barely force the word out, overcome by waves of nausea. Tymon did not pause or answer, though his eyes darted towards her briefly, then, a flicker of blue. Had his eyes been blue before? she wondered groggily. She watched with sick dread as he reached the door and extended his hand in greeting to Wick and Gowron. The two acolytes appeared bewildered by his arrival, but did not behave towards him with hostility. Instead, to her amazement, they responded to his greeting with dazed respect. Jedda was about to call out to Tymon again, to ask him, aghast, what he thought he was doing, when he spoke. And at the sound of his voice, the protest died on her lips.

'Well met, my friends.' The tone was flat and harsh, lacking all emotion, entirely unlike the Tymon Jedda had once known. 'We see you've found the location Eblas gave you. Excellent work.'

Gowron had shaken Tymon's hand when it was first extended, but now drew back. At the mention of 'Eblas' — a name Jedda did not recognise — the older acolyte immediately sank down on one knee before their visitor. A realisation seemed to have dawned on him that was not altogether reassuring. He pulled the gaping and astonished Wick down onto the loam beside him, whispering in his ear before turning to Tymon.

'We bow to you, great Masters,' he said huskily. 'We are honoured by your presence.'

Masters. With another sick wrench of the belly, Jedda began to understand. This was no Seeming: the real, physical presence of Tymon harped unmistakably in her gut. But neither was it properly her former friend and fellow student, for the mind inhabiting the body was not Tymon's. Her twining partner had been ripped out of himself, banished to make room for the Envoy's Masters. They had somehow taken his body over, for she could not imagine that he had been a willing party to an Exchange. That was why he had felt both near and far to her, close and yet at the same time coldly remote. Jedda watched in horror as the false Tymon acknowledged his servants with a nod, and raised them to their feet. Wick and Gowron stood respectfully aside to allow the Masters' host to approach the hatch. Jedda's chest felt unbearably constricted as she watched, helpless. The Masters were going to open the door. They were going to kill the Oracle.

'Your information was incomplete.' The false Tymon's voice was as flat and hard as the lumps of grit at Jedda's feet. 'The combination is not drawn from human prophecy at all, but from a word in the true First Tongue.' The invisible beings that had inhabited the body of her twining partner began to press what she guessed was a mathematical combination into the door lock. 'Eblas, it seems, has forgotten the language of the Born!' The host gave a harsh laugh that seemed to escape from a cacophony of different throats.

All three men had their backs to Jedda, absorbed in the door again. With a final, desperate burst of energy, she struggled to free herself from her bonds. She had already made the mistake of misjudging the Oracle, had been tricked and used by Lace and his Masters as they sought by any means to overcome their enemy. She could not allow it to happen again. Twisting her wrists and kicking her legs, she strained against the ropes until her skin bled.

At the foot of the escarpment, the acolytes hovered on either side of the false Tymon like two wings on a hunched and evil-minded bird, their green cloaks billowing in the stiffening breeze of afternoon. The Masters' combination took a long time to enter in the door, though the host's fingers moved quickly, punching in the required pattern. This was no ordinary *abjat*. Jedda found herself wondering, as she felt the ropes grow slippery with blood beneath her fingers, how long a single word in the Born language could be.

'What's the word that opens the door?' Wick's question repeated her thoughts, rising plaintively from the top of the beach.

He had not been able to resist drifting closer to the Masters' host, and now stood perilously near, peering over the shoulder of the false Tymon as he worked. Although Gowron glowered at him from a few paces away, clearly wary of the Masters' power, Wick seemed fascinated by this puppet-Tymon, entirely controlled by an outside will. His eyes devoured its features hungrily, following its every move. Jedda caught the flash of blue in the host's gaze as the Masters swivelled round to face the younger acolyte.

'Only we can pronounce it,' answered the harsh voice. 'Only we know the generative language of the universe, which you humans see in fragments, as Leaf Letters. To speak a single word of that language would consume your entire lifetime. Luckily, this particular word can be translated into one of your numbers, albeit inexactly.'

Oh let it not be too late, Jedda prayed. With her eyes fixed on the host's back, she gave her bleeding wrists another wrenching twist, biting her lip to avoid crying out as her right hand broke free at last. With her wrists liberated, it was easier to deal with the ankles. After a final heave, she kicked the loops off her legs and stood up, trembling. At that very moment, the hatch in the slab swung open, with a soft sound like an indrawn breath. Beyond it yawned a long, low-roofed tunnel, disappearing into the blackness beneath the roots of the Tree.

'You can't do this!' cried Jedda hoarsely.

She quelled her rebellious stomach, and began to lurch up the beach in her stockinged feet, her muscles deadened and her legs tingling from the tight bonds. She did not know what exactly she was trying to achieve. Not only did she have no *orah* with which to focus her Grafter powers, but her physical strength in her current state was barely enough to tackle Wick, let alone Gowron. She was certainly not equal to opposing the Masters in their stolen body, which seemed to be full of a crackling blue energy she had not encountered before. She simply knew that she could not let them enter that tunnel without a fight.

'*Ama* is our guide and teacher,' she shouted as she stumbled up the beach, her voice shaking. *The Sap give me strength*, she thought. 'You have no right to take her away from us!'

She did not even reach the door. In a flash, Gowron had stepped behind her and grasped her by the arms, pinning her elbows behind her back and thrusting her down on her knees before the false Tymon. But she found that she did not care what happened to her now, staring up into the host's deadly blue eyes. She could plainly see the multiple horror that inhabited Tymon's body, its seething desire for power. Paradoxically, the sight steadied her, calming the contradictory pull of the twining connection. She was filled with indignation at what the Masters had done to Tymon; she would have words with them, she thought, even if they killed her for it.

'What's this?' demanded the host of the two acolytes. 'If you want to bring a pet animal on a serious mission, at least keep it under control.'

'It won't happen again,' muttered Gowron from behind Jedda, gripping her arms so tightly that she gasped. Wick winced in embarrassment and turned his face away, as if he were ashamed of associating with her now.

'I don't care what you do to me,' said Jedda, through gritted teeth. Her fear faded, and she never took her eyes off the Masters, defiant in her single-mindedness. 'You won't succeed, not for long. You know it better than I do: there are powers in this world greater than yours, powers that imprison you. They won't let you go on like this, bending the rules, using a human body without consent.'

This answer, delivered without any premeditation on Jedda's part, seemed to infuriate the Masters. The features on the false Tymon's face lost their rigidity, a flash of fury jarring the implacable expression. The Masters' voice cracked like lightning through Tymon's pale lips.

'There was consent,' they rasped, bending close enough to Jedda to spit in her face. 'The young Grafter invited us right in.'

'Then he didn't know what he was doing,' she replied without hesitation. 'You know Tymon doesn't belong to you. He loves another. *They'll meet again, in the heart of the world, where all divisions cease —*'

'Silence!' snapped the Masters. The host recoiled from Jedda as she quoted Samiha's testament, its eyes burning as blue as the lightning. 'You have no right to speak those words, Tree-bitch!'

'I'd listen, if I were you,' murmured Gowron, a breath of warning in Jedda's ear, unheeded.

'The words are for everyone.' Jedda smiled up at the Masters. The defiant mood had taken hold of her again, and she felt like laughing in the face of death. 'They were written to be shared. *Ye are the wind that carries forth the flame* —'

'We shall cut out your tongue, slut!' snapped the host in fury. It swivelled its coldly burning gaze onto the acolytes who cowered beside Jedda. 'What have you brought here with you, fools?' it hissed. 'How does the bitch know these words?'

'I know them because I read them,' replied Jedda imperturbably, though the question was not addressed to her. 'The Kion lives on in her testament, and there's nothing you can do to stop it. *There is no triumph without loss, no power without weakness* —'

'We said silence!' roared the Masters, rounding on Jedda once more with eyes that were now a dangerous, pulsing blue. A raucous cacophony of voices emerged from the host's throat, grinding out the words. 'Eat dust and be still!' they all shrieked.

Jedda would not be cowed; she opened her mouth to speak again. But even as she did so, the Masters reached out and smote her forehead with one palm, quick as a striking snake. Their touch sent a bolt of burning energy through Jedda and she stiffened in pain, before sagging limp in Gowron's grasp. The blow chased the breath from her lungs and caused her tongue to cleave to the roof of her mouth. Both acolytes stared at her in consternation as she collapsed. Gowron let her slip down onto the silt on the shores of the lake, where she lay shaking, her back arched by convulsions.

'There.' The Masters drew themselves up again within the host body, the multiple rasp of their voices subsiding. 'Now she'll be quiet. What has this hell cat been reading?'

'I think it's the papers she was carrying,' whispered Wick, cringing in fear. 'These ones, in her clothes. We saw them, but we didn't think they were important.'

He bent down and withdrew some of the sheets stuffed into Jedda's sleeve. But when he held them out, the Masters pulled away from the scrolls with a raucous cry.

'Fools! Idiots!' Multiple voices burst through the false Tymon's lips again like cracks of thunder. 'Those are the Kion's verses. Be rid of them. Tear them up, throw them in the lake — do what you will, but destroy them now, this instant, if you want our good pleasure. Don't let that harridan's words survive!'

Jedda lay on the wet silt, paralysed and unable to protest as Wick and Gowron obeyed. One by one, they pulled the pages of the testament from under her clothes. They searched every corner of her body, ripping off the old undergarments, tearing out the rolled sheets of bark-paper, strawpaper, smooth pulp and rough parchment she had kept next to her skin since fleeing the Jays. She lay speechless and half-naked on the gritty loam, watching them tear and crumple, stamp and smash the precious sheets to shreds beneath their boots. Wick, even more than Gowron, carried out his task with complete dedication. Fleetingly, Jedda wondered if perhaps he were inspired by the prospect of earning the Masters' 'good pleasure', so eager was he to brutally destroy what was most sacred to her. And she pitied him once more, for she knew he was incapable of comprehending a word of what Samiha had written.

When the acolytes had reduced the testament to tatters, they collected up the mangled papers and strode down to the edge of the water, dumping them into the lake. A breath of relief issued through the Masters' stiff lips.

'Now,' they sighed, as the last sheets sank from view, the ink blurring the translucence of the waters, 'let's get on with our business.'

The host turned and began walking towards the open hatch of the tunnel. Wick hurried back from the shoreline, hastening up the beach after him without a second glance at Jedda. He had eyes now only for the body housing the so-called Masters of the universe.

'What about her?' Gowron called, pausing uncertainly by the Nurian girl. 'What happens to her?'

The Masters barely slowed their pace. 'She'll die,' they said.

With that, the false Tymon slipped effortlessly into the low-roofed tunnel. Wick caught up with him, peering briefly over his shoulder at the pair on the beach before plunging after the Masters. But Gowron hesitated, looking down at Jedda after the others had gone. She could not escape him: she could do nothing but watch him, her strength ebbing further with every instant. The blow she had received from the Masters had sent her soul reeling from her body. But there was still enough life left in her for her to quail as Gowron knelt down by her. Her body was arced at a skewed angle on the gritty loam, paralysed; she was at his mercy now.

But all he did was reach out with rough, square-tipped fingers to brush her cheek, in an oddly tender gesture.

'You should have listened to me,' he whispered to her. 'You should have stayed with me, all those months ago, and never gone to Argos city.'

And then he rose and was gone, striding after the other two. Jedda lay alone on the beach as the wind sighed through the grass and the life spilled out of her, grain by trickling grain.

Tymon beat against the ceiling of his prison, his voice spent from shouting into the icy darkness of the Veil. He felt as if he had been pounding on that immovable surface, crying out in rage and despair for years. How long he might exist like this, as a glimmering shade divorced from his body, he did not know; the thought that it might be a lasting state, unrelieved even by death, caused a wave of panic to rise up inside him, and he pounded again on the ice, screaming until he was hoarse.

In his misery, he fell back on his first schooling by the priests, on the notion that his misfortune was a punishment. It was his own fault he had come here, he thought with savage self-recrimination. He had let himself be taken in by a lie, betrayed his true love and lain with his enemy. He deserved to be trapped in his own personal hell of cold isolation. Now that he thought back over his encounter with the false Samiha, he could not believe how easily he had allowed himself to be duped. The paucity of the Seeming, its reliance on externals rather than any real appreciation of how Samiha would behave, hit him with renewed force. And he had actually seen through the travesty: he had doubted the vision on more than one occasion. He had known something was wrong when the false Samiha denigrated Zero, ignored the dead mineworkers and finally treated Tymon himself with such disrespect. If he had only listened to that instinct! But he had chosen to ignore the warning signals. He had followed her around like a benighted Tree-puppy, letting her pat him on the head and feed him treats.

The thought made him groan with shame and fury in his icy tomb. He had been wandering like a fool after the Masters' delusion for five whole days, with hardly any consideration for what might have become of the Focals and his other friends. And what in the name of the Tree had been happening to the Oracle during all this time? He began to wonder, belatedly, if the attack on her was linked to the one on him. Why had the Masters wanted his body?

'Green grace!' he whispered to himself in sudden realisation. 'They'll use it to kill her!'

How or when it would happen, he did not know. But it was clear to him now that the Masters, locked away in the Veil and planning their revenge against their jailor, must have somehow located the Oracle's hiding place in the physical world. They had been trying to do away with her, attacking her hosts through the Envoy's agency for years, and now they had a chance to deal with her themselves. He wanted to scream aloud at his stupidity in handing them precisely what they wanted, without the slightest resistance.

In that bleak moment, as he contemplated the full folly of what he had done, Tymon heard a faint sound. Or was it music, the echo of a song? It seemed to come from very far away.

'You can still choose.' The Oracle's voice was a faint breath in his ear, no more than a sigh.

'Ama!' he cried aloud, setting his palms on the ceiling of his prison and straining against it. But the voice, or perhaps the memory of it, like the music, faded away. He guessed he had only imagined it in his despair, and wept then, for there seemed to be no choices left to him at all.

'Oh, my love,' he whispered to the ice, forgetting his own troubles as he remembered Samiha's body, floating in the tank. 'What have they done to you?'

To have come so close to her, to have stood beside her, then allowed himself to be snatched away through his own stupidity, was excruciating; he yearned to return to that chamber and truly help her this time, even if it meant plucking her out of the tank and allowing her to die at last. And yet here he was, trapped and unable to do anything for her, or for his teacher. He could not bear it. It was not right, not *as it should be*.

He had just begun pounding on the unresponsive ice with his half-real hands once more, when he was arrested by another faint breath of melody. Again? He paused to listen. Was it possible? Had he actually heard music coming from outside the Veil?

The World Below was not entirely abandoned, thought Jedda dreamily as the darkness crept over her, eating away first at the edges of her vision, then moving inwards, towards the core. Some sensation persisted in her body, ebbing along with the light. When the sense of wet silt at her back faded and the creeping gloom reached the centre of her vision, she knew she would be gone. But the journey to oblivion was slow and by now quite painless. Her sense of hearing sharpened for a while as movement and vision were curtailed, and the world around her that had seemed so empty and silent before became full of busy new sounds. The soft lap of the waters grew loud in her left ear, a repetitive cycle amplified from time to time as a larger wave hit the shore. Other presences made themselves known in the absence of human cacophony: the faint buzz of flying insects, an occasional pop and ripple in the water and the surreptitious burrowing sound of some tiny creature in the granules of the beach. The wind sighed through the grasses at the edge of the lake.

Jedda was aware that she was dying, the intricate mechanisms of her body fatally disrupted. It did not matter to her now. She let go of her anxieties one by one, bidding farewell to her existence without rancour.

It had been a journey of light and dark, pain and joy, nearness and separation, a dance of opposites that did not always contradict. She understood, now, how to pronounce the Letter of Knowledge, having grown it in her own heart even as the Masters had said, for a lifetime. They were wrong about humans, she thought, as the circle of light in her vision shrank to a bright tunnel and the sensation of wetness on her back dissipated. The members of her species, so small and weak in every other way, spoke the First Tongue all the time: they pronounced it in thought and deed, spinning out the fabric of the universe with their lives. So much for the Masters, who had once possessed such power but could not even begin to Read humanity. They were blind to the story unfolding all around them.

Weakness is strength.

Existence was full of the Grafter's song, thought Jedda. The whole world was shouting it out, for any who would listen. She heard the ground beneath her tell its story as her other faculties dimmed, sensed the shards of the old cities floating like so much jetsam on its surface, unimportant. This loam, this *earth* as she somehow knew it was called, was no dead thing, nor was it merely the ruined receptacle of an ancient civilisation. It had been blasted by fire, scarred and poisoned, but it endured. It had lain dormant for centuries, until the clouds lifted and the poison drained away. It was miraculous and sacred. As the last bright point of light in her vision winked out, Jedda thought she heard a deep, swelling music, the song of the Sap, rising from every atom and particle of earth, *the Earth*, her home.

It was music, Tymon realised, the faint strains of voices chanting. It came from outside the Veil but also from within himself, carried by an invisible connection that persisted at his heart. And all at once, he remembered the twining. No wonder he had thought he was hearing the Oracle! He was still tenuously linked to his fellow Grafters in the world of the Sap. The link appeared to be functioning in the Veil, at least in part. He was sure now that Oren and the other young Focals were calling to him.

'I'm here!' he cried out joyfully.

But there was a strange echo in reply. *Here, here, here*, mocked his own voice, reverberating back on him. Tymon shook his head in frustration till the echo faded. As silence surged back into the tomb, he could still hear the Focals singing, distant as the stars. He could not distinguish the words, but the music was so familiar.

'I'm with you,' he responded eagerly, straining to be in tune with them.

With you with you with you, came the mocking echo.

It was a hard blow when he finally grasped that the Veil must be permeable in one direction, but not the other. The Focals could not hear him. They did not even know if he were alive. They were only reaching out to him in an act of faith, without hope of an answer. The realisation sent him reeling back into the depths of despair, and he lay speechless in his cramped and icy tomb. The Focals' voices continued faintly for a while, then faded away. Tymon closed his eyes, forlorn.

Jedda opened her eyes and found herself standing on the beach, blinking down at her own body on the silt. She was in the trance-form, she understood calmly, for the last time. She was leaving the Tree of Being. The music of the Sap welled up about her, within her. The whole world was growing bright with that subtle fire: soon the light would spill over, sweeping her away. Whether she would survive that final disintegration she did not know, but she was content, either way.

As if in response to her contentment, another music welled up through the song of the Sap, a haunting melody that beckoned to her. Voices, it seemed, were summoning her into a well of light. She strained to hear them. Who was calling?

'Who are you?' she whispered, stretching up her fingers to the bright sky. She knew she might step into the light, if she liked: she might go home.

Jedda. Her name? Another stray sound snagged at the enveloping light, interfering with the heavenly music that would dissolve her once and for all. Jedda hesitated on the brink of departure. 'What?' she murmured in exasperation.

Jedda. The voices of Oren and Noni were crying out to her. She recognised the faint echo. They were trying to reach her through an invisible wall, a thick bank of mist that hid their forms and muffled their words. There was someone they were reminding her of, someone who needed her and was ebbing fast. 'Who?' she asked.

But it was the Oracle who answered. 'You have a choice,' she said, a brief breath in Jedda's ear. And then she was gone once more.

Jedda glanced about her. The light and music were in abeyance. She was on the empty beach again, standing over her own unconscious body, though she was sure she had been about to go somewhere else, somewhere she would much rather be. She might yet go, she understood. No one would blame her if she chose the light. Or she could stay here, and help a friend in need. *Tymon*.

'For heaven's sake,' she muttered aloud. 'That's not a choice.'

* * *

What are you doing, kneeling in the dust, Juno, oh Juno?

Had he imagined the words? Tymon blinked awake again, through his torpor. He strained to catch the sound that came from above and beyond his prison. Not the Focals this time, but another, very different voice, closer and oddly jaunty in the gloom.

I kneel here only because I must: I seek my Lyla, wherever she roams.

Tymon remembered. It was a popular folk song from the days of his childhood, one of the many based on the fable of Juno and Lyla, a tale as ancient as the Tree. How had the story gone again? The lover had searched the world for his absent beloved, sifting through the dust in his desire to find her. The people had mocked him, calling his devotion mad. Tymon wondered if he were going mad himself, hearing the words of the old tale now, at such a time and in such a place. This version was wonderfully inappropriate to the darkness of the Veil, filled with salty humour.

Why do you look for her in such a place, Juno, oh Juno?

It was all so odd. Tymon shook his head again on the cold ice. He recognised the singer, sensing a connection with her in the world of the trance, as if she were a long-lost friend. Could it be? he wondered. Could it really be?

'Jedda?' he whispered, hardly daring to believe.

I only wish for a glimpse of her face: I seek my Lyla, whatever the trace.

'Jedda!' called Tymon. He raised his cramped hands once again, pounding against the ice with the dregs of his strength. 'Jedda! I'm here!'

You won't find her here, you poor lost soul.
Your love is sublime, this isn't her home.

Someone was bending over him. He could see the faint light of another trance-form now, gleaming

452

through the translucent roof of the cavity, just an arm's length away.

'*Ama* didn't say you'd be under the Veil, as well as in it.' Jedda's voice sounded amused, though her tone grew serious again as she pressed her palm on the ice above him, a bright smudge. 'Goodness, it's hard stuff,' she said.

'The Oracle? She's alive?' Tymon felt a rush of joy. 'I feared ... Jedda, I've been so foolish —'

'Then that makes two of us. The Oracle's in grave danger, Tymon. The Envoy's acolytes have found her body. We might still be able to help, but we have to get you out of here ...' There was a moment of silence as her voice trailed off. Tymon waited, breathless, his eyes fixed on the faint light of her through the ice, a lifeline in the gloom. 'Have you tried the Grafter words?' she suggested. 'These are mental worlds, so they might respond to your concentration.'

'No, I haven't!' What an imbecile he was, he thought, coming to his senses. He kept forgetting that the Veil, despite its tactile qualities, was as subtle a plane as the shining world of the Sap. The branches of the Tree of Being had grown and changed in response to the Grafters' watchwords: might the Veil not do the same?

He tried. She tried. Both of them repeated every single phrase the Oracle had ever taught Tymon, recited the watchwords, chanted the Grafter's song, even muttered the names of the individual Leaf Letters over and over again. But it was no use. When Tymon pronounced the word of Union, he thought the ice shuddered a little, the barest tremble. But after repeating the Letter countless times, nothing further happened. The stubborn surface of the Veil did not open for him. Nor did the walls break for Jedda, when she spoke the same phrases from outside his prison.

'Well,' she said, after Tymon had cursed the ice roundly, 'I guess that's that.'

There was a moment of silence as this fact sank in. 'What have I done?' whispered Tymon, miserably trapped in his prison. 'I just handed the Masters a way to kill *Ama* …'

'They were going after her anyway, with or without your body,' Jedda assured him. 'They might have been able to help the acolytes without you. Maybe tried a sort of temporary Exchange …'

He knew she was only trying to comfort him. 'How did you get involved in all this?' he asked, in an effort to distract himself. 'I heard you'd broken with the Envoy. How do you know about the Masters?'

'I wanted to find you,' she answered simply, 'and say I was sorry. It's a long story. I had Samiha's testament and wanted to bring it to you. I thought, if I could give it to you, it would make up for everything. Another one of my bad choices, I suppose. The Masters found it anyway, and destroyed it.'

'Ah.' He barely had the heart to think about the ramifications of all she was telling him. He closed his eyes again, seeing for a fleeting moment the bleachers, the Jays' circus, the package slipped behind the seats before the guards came. 'Tell me what you remember of it,' he whispered. 'Let me hear her words.'

If he were going to expire here, he thought, trapped in darkness, then let it be with the memory of Samiha's voice in his ears.

His companion obliged him, singing. It was not the Kion's voice, of course: it was Jedda's. But the sound of Samiha's words in his fellow student's husky tones was pleasing in a way Tymon had not expected. And it was also surprisingly powerful.

There is no triumph without loss, no power without weakness. The verse had barely passed Jedda's lips when the ice shook again, a sudden jolt. Tymon's eyes flew open as the formerly impassive substance of the Veil trembled beneath him.

'Go on!' he cried to Jedda when she stopped in confusion. 'Sing more,' he begged her. 'It works.'

So she began again. *Do not fear darkness or defeat. Do not fear loss …*

The Veil shrieked and groaned, the ice shuddering to life around Tymon like a waking beast.

The voice in the Veil gave Eblas pause. He felt it like a distant clanging alarm, niggling him even as he wrapped his tendrils about the Focals' tent. This was no whining of the Grafters in their Sap-world. Someone had entered his own realm while his back was turned: there was an interloper in the kennels. How could it be? The defences were all firmly in place for the battle, debarring the Nurian Grafters from entering the Masters' domain. No one should have been able to step into the Veil.

No one, except for one of his own acolytes.

It took less than a fleeting moment for the incredible truth to be conceived and admitted. The Envoy gathered himself up; he became dog-like again in his bristling outrage, his vaporous limbs knotting together in the cloud. The howl that escaped from his invisible mouth was a thunderclap, his rage a flash of blue lightning as he raised one smoky talon to tear a hole between the worlds. He was already shrinking, becoming again the dense and four-footed Beast as he leapt into the Veil, leaving nebulous wisps of himself behind. And as Eblas streaked like a ragged black comet back into those realms of ice, the final remnants of the cloud that had so terrorised the Freehold wavered, dissipated and lost cohesion. Fragments of bat wing and bird feather, cobweb and fly spit rolled off the twig-forests of Farhang and disappeared, and sunbeams broke through the smoke over the Freehold. Lace left a startlingly blue sky in his wake.

The songs of victory died on the Argosian soldiers' lips as they gazed up at the bright heavens in consternation, wondering where the storm that had accompanied them and given them such an advantage could have gone. The harried Freeholders, too, halted and passed their hands over their eyes in astonishment, feeling the fog of panic lift. The village buildings still blazed, smoke rose into the blue sky, and the Argosian fleet was regrouping overhead, recovering from the air-chariots' attack. The battle was not yet over. But the day had grown ordinary again, its fears and dangers distinctly human.

Gardan rallied the units that had already been chased to the borders of the village, and led them in a coordinated offensive against the enemy foot soldiers, before they were able to close in on the refugee camp. The young Argosians responded in kind, crying out their battle songs with renewed fervour as they prepared to fight the Freeholders close and hard among the twig-thickets. They knew the Saint was always watching over them, after all. It was clear, as Admiral Greenly muttered to Pumble, when the strange cloud had vanished as if it had never been, that a freak storm, no matter how spectacular its effects, could not help you win a proper war.

Although the ice shook spasmodically as Jedda sang, the surface above Tymon did not finally begin to crack open until he, too, took up the chant. It was not hard to repeat the words from Samiha's testament: he found he half-remembered them, though he had barely glanced at the papers.

Do not fear darkness or defeat.
Do not fear loss, and you and I shall meet

in the heart of the world, where all divisions cease …

It took no more than a single verse to break through the ice of the Veil. The tomb cracked abruptly open with a heave, vomiting Tymon out as if the ice itself could not wait to be rid of him. Jedda helped him stand up on the hard floor of the prison world, his trance-form shedding glittering particles of frost.

'Something's coming,' she said, glancing uneasily at the faint unknown canopy of stars.

Tymon could feel it, too: their song had drawn unwanted attention. An invisible malevolence had turned its gaze on them, and was sending its agents to hunt them down at high speed. They would be found, and soon.

'Quick,' exclaimed Jedda. She broke into a sprint on the dark plain. 'My door. Maybe it's still open.'

'Door?' Tymon cried as he ran after her. 'You know how to make a world-door?'

'Lace taught us,' Jedda shouted over her shoulder. 'Only useful thing he ever did. There, see? The light. But hurry: I can only open it in one direction.'

Tymon could see it now, barely more than a sliver in the gloom. 'It's shrunk,' gasped Jedda as they came to a panting halt by the bright gap. She reached up her hand and gingerly tested out the ragged edges of the hole, bleeding light.

'Go through, quick,' Tymon told her, peering in trepidation at the sky. The stars were being blotted out one by one, filled with huge, winged shapes.

'Not me, you. It'll take a while to squeeze through: you go first. You have more of a chance of surviving on the other side.'

'What?' Tymon stared at her. Her expression was calm, perhaps a little sad. He was struck by how much older and graver she looked than the last time he had seen her, even in the trance-form. 'Why?' he objected.

'Just go!' she said, gazing anxiously up at the wheeling blots of darkness.

Aware that there was no time to waste on argument, he bowed to her wishes and slipped his arm and shoulder through the opening, wincing as the unpleasant sawing edges of the Veil clamped down around him. He turned his head to one side, looking back at Jedda as he inched his way through the opening. Above her, the winged clouds had spread over the stars of the prison dimension, rapidly approaching. And something else was running over the plain of ice: a blot appeared on the horizon, a thundering black bolt of malevolence. The Beast, thought Tymon grimly.

It took several moments of breathless, struggling labour before he burst through the door and staggered onto one of the loamy beaches of the World Below. His trance-form felt tingling and sore, but otherwise unharmed. The door to the Veil was a shrinking black line in front of him.

'Quick!' he cried, extending his hand to Jedda through the opening.

She shook her head, her face pale in the gloom of the Veil. 'Get out of there!' she whispered through the gap. 'The door's going to close on you!'

'It will, if you don't come quickly,' he said, stubborn.

She hesitated, glancing upwards again. Tymon could hear the raucous shrieks of some horrific creature on the other side of the door, neither bird nor beast but a foul travesty of the Veil. Beyond it echoed the howling, baying cacophony of Eblas. Jedda came to an abrupt decision: she grasped Tymon's hand, and set her own shoulder to the narrow opening, squeezing through.

'Push,' he urged her, as she grimaced with pain, caught between the edges of the door.

'I can't.'

'You can. Push. It's still big enough.'

'I'm being torn apart!'

'You're strong.' He smiled encouragingly at her, clasping her arm from the other side of the gap. The touch of her trance-form was a light burr beneath his fingers.

'It hurts,' she muttered, as with their combined strength they pulled, yanked, and finally wrenched her through the opening.

Jedda stumbled onto the beach with a strangled cry. Behind her, the edges of the door sucked shut, but not before something heavy blundered against the gap, flapping and shrieking in rage. In the last instant that the door was open, a blue eye stared out at them, full of unblinking hatred. Then the gap closed, and the air above the beach was clean again, suffused with the waning light of afternoon.

'Are you alright?' Tymon asked Jedda.

Her flickering trance-form was fading in the daylight, he saw, growing faint and transparent. She gazed at him wordlessly, but did not seem to be in pain any longer. He assumed she was being called back to her physical form, for he felt the faraway tug of his own body, muffled and stymied by the Masters' influence. It drew him to a location some distance from where he was standing.

'Goodbye, my friend.' Jedda's voice was barely a whisper, as her form wavered and winked out.

It was only then that Tymon noticed Jedda's body, lying sprawled on the silt to his right. But she was not asleep: she was not in the Grafter's trance at all. She lay at his feet, pale and rigid. Dead, he realised with a sickening lurch.

'Jedda!' he gasped, falling to his knees beside her. He understood, too late, what she meant when she had said he would be the one to survive. 'Don't go!' he cried, bereft.

There was no answer but the lapping of the lake waters and the soft, plaintive murmur of his own body, calling to him in the trance.

Tymon stood up. Fury surged through him, quenching the flood of grief. Slow and potent, he felt the righteous heat of the Sap well up inside him, even as it had faced with the Envoy's curses. This time, the flame of reckoning was deeper, stronger, burning not only in response to his own need, but on behalf of all those hurt by the Masters. The Sap-waves started at his feet, by Jedda's body, then travelled up to his chest and arms, running down in rivulets to his fingertips. He raised his right hand to see the old scars throbbing again, a fiery red. Turning away from the corpse of the Nurian girl, grim-faced and burning bright as a torch, he strode towards the tunnel entrance at the foot of the Tree.

20

Tymon sped down the tunnel, following the call of his stolen body. The journey did not take more than a few moments, though he was dimly aware that he had traversed a significant distance, moving far faster in the trance-form than he would physically. Even as he rushed through the dark, he felt a wrenching urgency, over and above the pull of his body. Someone ahead of him was in pain; someone dear to him was dying. He hurtled through the tunnel and burst into a circle of torchlight, a bright spot in a large gloomy hollow beneath the roots of the Tree.

It was a natural cavern in the *earth*, its domed ceiling lost in shadow. Tymon had noticed in passing that the tunnel was fashioned at least in part from the Ancients' tough grey building material, but this chamber was different, all made of loam and choked with Tree-roots. Beside him, at the tunnel entrance, someone had planted a torch in the floor. A second circle of torchlight danced in the darkness ahead. The burning Sap-fire within him dropped to a quiescent glow as he took in his surroundings. The mute mental echo of pain was all around him, so that he could not at first pinpoint the source. The chamber was filled with winding columns and tangled spires of roots. Large and small, they twisted through the hollow hall in a bewildering net, but all seemed to radiate from a central point. It was there,

Tymon realised, that the pain originated. When his gaze came to rest on the figure at the heart of the root system, he almost sank to his knees again in astonishment.

Before him was a giant, a woman, more than twice the height of an ordinary person. She stood, or rather hung, about ten feet from the floor, her body cradled and transpersed in a hundred places by the roots of the World Tree. Tymon was reminded once more of Samiha's Tree-form, for the giant's grey, bark-like flesh was almost identical in colour and texture to the woody roots, merging seamlessly with them. He had already witnessed the Masters' nightmare harpy, the Envoy's Beast-shape, and Wick's aping version of it in the Veil. But he had never seen a Being like this, completely inhuman and yet somehow belonging wholeheartedly to his universe, a part of the natural order and not some sorcerer's travesty. The giant amazed but did not horrify him.

He did not know whether the creature before him had grown the great tendrils that burgeoned from her body, or was trapped by them; he did not know either whether she was holding up the Tree, or being crushed under its weight. But if he read her expression aright, she was in terrible pain, her shoulders bowed with suffering. She held something in her hands, cradling it protectively against her belly. She was old, very old, Tymon thought, in awe. She raised her head at his approach and he could tell that she Saw him in the trance. Her smooth face with its high brow and pronounced cheekbones was unlined, her large eyes a deep and liquid blue. She was one of the Born, he grasped, though how he was so sure of it he did not know. This was what they must originally have looked like, when they lived among humans; the giant was the last of her kind. And then, with a final thrill of surprise, he identified that steady blue gaze.

'This is my seed-form.' The Oracle's lips did not move when she spoke to him. Her voice was a weary gasp in his mind, taut with pain. 'My first body in this world.'

At the comprehension of her agony, Tymon glanced downwards, towards the second sphere of torchlight at the Oracle's feet. There, wriggling like termites through the nest of roots, three traitorous creatures moved, bent on destruction. The human acolytes and their Masters had chewed through the protective net enclosing Matrya, leaving a trail of gouged-out tendrils and severed connections. The Oracle could not get away from them, merged as she was with the root system. They were killing her, ripping out her entrails, hurting her, and hurting the Tree.

'No!' exclaimed Tymon. The Sap brimmed up in him again, a hot surge of outrage as he leapt through the tunnel of broken roots.

Neither Wick nor Gowron Saw into his trance, unaware of him as he arrived beneath Matrya's towering form. The two acolytes and the Masters' host had climbed high into the root-tangle, to stand about level with her waist. Wick held up a torch, while Gowron was busily hacking with a knife at the innermost net of tendrils encasing the Oracle. Tymon identified the slick gleam of *orah* in the cruel-looking blade. The deadly tool cut through the Tree-roots with hardly a pause, every hacking strike setting Tymon's teeth on edge. He writhed in empathy, as if he were being cut himself.

But the Masters had a specific goal in mind over and above hurting Matrya. Tymon caught sight of the bright gleam of *orah* between the Oracle's fingers; the object cupped in her palms was entirely made of the stuff, a roughly egg-shaped mass. The Masters in Tymon's stolen body balanced on one of the roots to Gowron's right, their attention focused greedily on the egg, waiting for the last strands protecting the treasure to be ripped away.

It was unspeakably strange for Tymon to see his own body moved by another, relentless will. He could not enter his physical home, though it called to him. And others must have heard that call, too. Unlike the acolytes, the Masters were able to sense his approach. Tymon shivered as the host's head swivelled abruptly round, its cold gaze piercing him in the trance. The Masters' eyes flashed an uncanny blue and they bent down to whisper in Gowron's ear; the older acolyte then murmured something to Wick, and both priests peered uneasily over their shoulders.

'So, you got away,' the Masters called out to Tymon, smiling insolently at him from their perch. 'No matter. You can't stop us now, Grafter. You know your order doesn't hold with violence.'

'You have something that isn't yours,' said Tymon calmly, ignoring the jibe. 'That's my body. And I'm going to take it back.'

He raised his right hand and stepped forward, the flaming energy of the Sap surging in his palm. The consciousness of the Oracle's suffering gave him a bleak confidence: he would defend her to the death, if it came down to it, he thought. There might have been the briefest spasm of doubt in the Masters' expression, quickly replaced by blank hatred.

'Oho, so you do want to fight!' they snapped. 'Have it your way, worm.'

The host slithered down through the roots and landed on the floor of the cavern in front of Tymon, simultaneously raising its right hand to conjure up a blue, crackling ball of energy.

'Eat this,' hissed the Masters, throwing the blue bolt straight at Tymon.

The young man did not stop to think, but reached quickly up to catch the bolt with his scarred right hand, before it hit his face. The energy prickled in his palm for an instant, then dissipated.

'You'll have to do better than that,' he said, advancing on the Masters.

They glared at him in surprise and dawning apprehension, then shrieked with fury, casting bolt after crackling bolt at him. Tymon continued to catch each one, advancing step by step on the host; when he missed one of the balls and it struck his shoulder, a wave of searing cold passed through him. But a moment later the Sap-fire returned, burning hot and bright in his red right hand, banishing the Masters' crackling power. The pain he had once endured now gave him strength, even as the Oracle had promised.

'Laska and Pallas,' he muttered as he strode towards his enemy, summoning up the memory of those in whose name he fought. 'Dawn and Nightside.'

This time the Masters produced a twisting lump of blue energy as large as Tymon's head, casting it at him with both hands.

'Samiha!' gasped Tymon, grimacing with shock as he caught the lump. The massive bolt shook him to the core before dissipating.

The host was backing away now, howling up to the acolytes to hurry, hurry and finish the job. It leapt into the tangled roots again; Tymon jumped after it.

'Solis and Zero,' he shouted to the fleeing Masters. 'The Saffid and the Freeholders. You and your Envoy are responsible. You will pay.'

'Human fool,' cried the Masters, almost spitting down on him in fear and rage. 'You can't possibly hold us responsible for every ounce of suffering in existence. Do you think we orchestrate your pathetic world? Far from it. You control your destiny: you make your own mistakes.'

The host dodged past Tymon, leaping nimbly from root to root to reach Gowron, just as the older acolyte broke through the final tendrils encasing the Oracle.

'That, after all, is what Matrya in all her infinite wisdom wanted,' continued the Masters savagely, rounding on the giant trapped amid the severed roots. 'Free will for humanity. And look what it's produced.'

As he spoke, Gowron took hold of one of the last and largest roots emerging over the Oracle's heart, and severed it at the base. The Oracle cried aloud, a terrible, gut-wrenching sound. It shook Tymon to his very core; he could not have felt worse if he had seen poor Masha, the closest person he had to a mother, writhing in agony under Gowron's knife. All the roots in the chamber shuddered as the Masters gleefully snatched the *orah*-egg from Matrya's trembling hands, climbing up ever further into the net of tendrils.

'Leave her alone,' yelled Tymon in outrage.

He remembered belatedly, as he was scrambling after his stolen body, that he did not have to traipse from one point to another as he normally would. Instead, he willed himself forward as he had in the passage — shot upwards through the trembling roots to alight in an instant beside the Masters, even as they raised the egg, gloating over it.

'For Jedda,' said Tymon. And with the Nurian girl's name on his lips, he summoned up all his courage, and grasped the host's neck firmly with his right hand.

He did not touch his physical body, of course. But his insubstantial fingers closed over a film of crackling energy within it, a sticky blue miasma that clogged up the casing. He struggled to detach the blue lightning from his body, pulling the Masters out of their host, hand over hand. They resisted, their sticky energy spitting out sparks, changing shape like viscous Tree-gum beneath his grasp. The blue miasma transformed into a nest of snakes, hissing in his face, but Tymon held on. Then the snakes wilted like an old bouquet, and the Masters' energy bloomed into the shape of a slavering beast's head, snapping at Tymon with its fanged jaws. Still he did not let go, wrestling his opponents loose with all his might. His body slumped against the shuddering Tree-roots as it lost its guiding impetus, the *orah*-egg slipping from its grasp to tumble to the cavern floor. The Masters fought to stay in the host, snapping and snarling and shifting into a bewildering array of forms.

'My love, you're hurting me.' The miasma settled into the likeness of Samiha, gazing pitifully at Tymon as he held her by the throat. 'Let go, you're killing me!'

Tymon looked her steadily in the eye, holding on until the likeness transformed with a savage howl into the three-headed harpy again. The bird heads shrieked and stabbed at him with their hooked beaks.

'Maggot!' screamed the Masters. 'Creeping worm! If we were not bound by our sentence, we would peck out your mind's eye! We would rip your soul to shreds!'

Tymon did not answer, holding the jabbing beaks away from his face as the roots of the Tree continued to heave and shake in response to the Oracle's pain. He had to regain control of his body to help her; there was no other way. He held on grimly while the Masters' blue light grew gradually weaker and more transparent. At last, with a final yank, he ripped them clean out of their host.

'You're too late to help her,' snarled the Masters vindictively, even as he shook them loose.

They loomed like a blue cloud over Tymon, beaks agape, and reached their snapping fingers towards him, seeking to rake him in the trance with their cruel talons. But at that moment, a vortex opened up directly behind them, a whirlwind glimpse of the Veil.

The shrieking harpy dissolved and was whipped away into the maelstrom, the three straining heads sucked away with a last drawn-out howl.

'Late, late, late …' wailed the Masters. The vortex swallowed them, diminished to a point, and was gone.

Emptied of their will, the pull of Tymon's body became inescapable. It drew his spirit home, and a moment later he blinked awake from the trance, only to find himself half-slipping off the shuddering roots of the Tree. He barely caught hold of a tendril in time, swinging a good twenty feet over the floor of the chamber. The whole cavern was shaking, the *rock* groaning in sympathy with the Oracle. Tymon scrambled frantically down the trembling ladder of roots towards his teacher.

But even as he approached her, even as he slid down the intervening roots with a defiant yell, Gowron cleared the final tendrils away from the Oracle's chest. The acolyte raised the *orah*-knife high in both hands and, with a yell of triumph, plunged it deep into Matrya's heart.

The convulsion that passed through the Tree was tremendous. All Tymon could do was cling to the quaking roots to stop from falling, as the Oracle's body shuddered in its death throes. Wick was already far below them, he noticed dimly, scrambling over the cavern floor towards the abandoned *orah*-egg. Gowron lost no time in wrenching the knife out of Matrya's chest and leaping after his fellow acolyte. Tymon caught a stray yellow gleam as Wick picked up the Oracle's treasure and bundled it in his cloak, then turned and fled from the chamber without waiting for Gowron. The older man howled in fury and sped down the tunnel in hot pursuit. The cavern was plunged in shifting shadows in their wake, with only the half-spent torch by the tunnel-mouth remaining.

'*Ama!*' cried Tymon in distress, as he arrived by the Oracle's side. The giant's beautiful old face was tilted upwards in pain, her eyes darkened now almost to black. Her breast ran with blue-black blood where the savage knife had bitten deep.

'I'm sorry, I'm so sorry,' he murmured to her, weeping freely now. Unable to think of what else to do, he climbed the roots, so that he could caress her great face with his small hand.

'There's nothing to be sorry about.' He heard her voice in his mind, but her lips were unmoving as she gazed at him out of those dark pools. 'You've done well. You have to leave now, it's all going to collapse on this side. You must retrieve the World Key, and you must bury me.'

'What's the World Key?' asked Tymon anxiously. 'Is that what the acolytes took from you? The egg?'

She was right, he thought: the cavern would not survive the shaking roots. Already, sections of loose *earth* were dislodging from the chamber walls, and he could feel the rumble of disquiet spreading far beyond them, through the Tree.

'You know where it is.' Her voice in his mind was hardly a breath, and it seemed she was raving in her final moments. 'You know where to find the Key,' she whispered. 'Bury me on the mountain, where the sky meets earth. Bury me where the sun shines and clear water rises.'

With that, she closed her eyes and spoke no more. He knew he could not free her from the enclosing net of tendrils before the chamber caved in, or drag her body out to bury it anywhere, let alone on a *mountain*. He did not even know what the word meant. He only felt he had failed her as he dropped awkwardly to the floor, his arm raised to protect himself against the lumps of loam raining down from the roof. He grabbed the guttering torch by the tunnel-mouth and stumbled into the passage, blinded by tears. His last glimpse of the Oracle was of her marvellously tall form cradled amid the roots, great eyes closed and peaceful, while the walls of the cavern slowly collapsed and the Tree trembled to its core.

The torch soon guttered out. Tymon stumbled down the tunnel from the Oracle's chamber in total darkness, with one arm pressed against the wall to keep himself upright. A fine, choking dust had begun to fall from the roof of the passage, coating his hair and clothes. It did not look as if even the Ancients' tough grey building material would survive the bereavement of the Tree. Tymon wept for his teacher as he staggered down the juddering passageway, hardly caring whether the whole construction fell on his head, for the cruelty of ending that ancient and benevolent life had struck him afresh. He knew instinctively he would not see Matrya's like again in his world. Whatever the Born were now, they had ceased walking among humans in those gentle, giant bodies.

The journey out of the chamber was far longer than it had seemed on the way in. Befuddled by the Masters' sorcery, he had forgotten how many aches and bruises his body had endured in the past few weeks. Now his muscles were reminding him of it, his tendons shrieking with pain, clamouring that they were alive, he was alive, even as he mourned the death of the Oracle. He gritted his teeth and carried on, steadying himself on the left-hand wall as the *earth* beneath shook and trembled. To his surprise the tunnel walls held for the moment, despite the tremors. After what felt like an eternity, but was probably little more than half a mile, he glimpsed the grey smudge of the exit hatch ahead. A few minutes later, he was out and on the beach again, blinking in the dimmed light of the World Below.

The first thing he noticed was that Jedda's body had vanished. There was a depression in the silt where it had lain, but the corpse itself was nowhere to be seen. He did not know if it had rolled away into the lake, or come to grief by some other means; he had no time to solve the puzzle, for a glance at his surroundings showed him that it was not only the roots but the entire Tree, and everything close to it, that was affected by the Oracle's passing. The beach was shuddering beneath his feet, the waters of the lake rising in waves that crashed on the trembling shore. He peered up in alarm at the towering buttresses and deep clefts of the trunk behind him, to see bark slabs breaking off the shivering slopes, whole sections of the Tree slithering down in clouds of dust that turned the late afternoon light a murky brown. High overhead, the Storm itself was seething. Frothing leaves alternated with grey cloud as the great branches of the South Canopy pitched and swayed, sending down a rain of dust and small particles of bark that caused the waters of the lake to boil. The whole world was filled with a deafening, ruinous roar.

The Oracle had said it was going to collapse on this side, Tymon remembered numbly. She had meant the whole South Canopy of the Tree. And he was right under it.

He staggered on in panic, splashing into the unquiet lake, his mouth and nostrils caked with the falling dust. Coughing and choking, he waded as fast as he could through the rising waves and away from the collapsing trunk, in the direction of the ruined city. If this were his final hour, he thought, and he was about to join the Oracle in death, he would like to see Samiha's body one last time. He would like to live just long enough to return to the building where she was held. But he was still some distance from the ruins, two miles perhaps, when a large section of branch and leaves plummeted through the clouds about a mile to his right, falling with a thunderous crash into the waters.

The shallow lake became suddenly riotous, and a single massive wave slammed into Tymon, sending him sprawling. When he picked himself up again, dripping and terrified, something else hard and about the size of a child's fist hit his head with a stinging thump. It was followed by several similar missiles. The rain of bark was becoming a lethal hail; the South Canopy was disintegrating about his ears. He broke into a run with his arms curled over his head and one thought in mind. He must fend off death for just a little while, delaying the end until he reached Samiha.

The race to the ruins was an obstacle course. Once Tymon entered the environs of the ancient city, he was able to take some cover from the rain of bark beneath its overhanging towers. He knew that even the ancient hall would not stand up beneath the weight of a whole limb of the Tree, were one to fall on top of it. He slipped, dripping wet and half-blinded by dust, from the shelter of one ruined wall to the next, leaving the boiling lake behind him. Between the periodic showers of bark and twig particles, he glimpsed the demise of two more huge supporting branches, one far to the west and the other worryingly close to the east, the vast forms detaching themselves from the clouds and falling into the lake with a slow, grinding roar. The ground heaved and trembled when they hit, but the real danger came from above.

He was exhausted by the time he reached the region of the city where he knew the hall should be. For a few anguished moments, he feared it had been crushed already, for a massive section of bark the size of the building itself had flattened one of the ancient towers in front of it, blocking his view. The *earth* beneath the ruins was already thick with splintered twig-shafts, shards of bark and torn leaves, and Tymon waded through a pile of debris almost as deep as the lake itself, passing under the tipped-up slab of bark to reach what he hoped would be the hall stairs. They were still there, he saw with relief, the building intact by a hair's breadth. He hastened up to the double doors, and slipped into the gloomy hall as the South Canopy continued to rain down in ruin on the World Below. The fall of bark pounded against the roof of the building, echoing through the central nave like an endless drum roll.

He did not immediately notice the movement in the rear chamber, hurrying between the rows of columns. The green light still welled out of the door to the room where Samiha's body was kept, and the rain of shattered bark overhead drowned out all other sounds. But just as he stepped over the threshold, a shadow flitted across his vision. Then he caught sight of the ominous flash of a flying stick, and heard a Collector's telltale hum. An instant later, a pale and grim-faced figure staggered into his line of sight, wielding one of the dormant flying machines like a weapon.

'Jedda?' cried Tymon, in utter astonishment.

Jedda swung the grey broom-handle up above her head and brought it down hard, with a grunt of effort, on top of something close to Tymon's right-hand side. One of the Ancients' addled machines had been sliding towards him, he realised as he stumbled back. The Collector gave a despairing sputter and dropped out of the air, tumbling to the floor of the chamber. It tried to grow legs and scuttle away, but Jedda lurched towards it, smashing it with her weapon until it was still. Then, there was only the thunderous clatter of falling bark above them, and a choked sound as Jedda began to sob.

Tymon caught her in his arms as she collapsed. She was shaking all over, the tears spilling. 'Jedda, Jedda!' he murmured in wonder. 'How did you get here? I thought you were dead on that beach. I wouldn't have left you if I'd known you were alive!'

'I was dead,' Jedda panted, gazing at him through eyes that were ringed with blue shadow. She looked little better than dead now, he thought: her complexion was almost the same ghastly shade as the frost on the walls. 'Suffice to say, I was sent back. I have to tell you what happened — another time. What about you? And *Ama?*' she finished, without much hope.

He shook his head sadly. 'I was too late. By the time I fought off the Masters and took back my body, Gowron had got to her. I failed absolutely, Jedda.'

He saw his own grief reflected in Jedda's face, and wondered if he should tell her about the Key, and the Oracle's true form. But the memory of the ancient Being in the roots of the Tree was still too raw. He could not speak.

Jedda gave a final shudder and pulled herself together. 'This is the end, then,' she said. 'When someone of that power goes ... well. You can hear it, outside.'

'The South Canopy is falling down.' Even as Tymon uttered the words, another crash echoed overhead.

'*A third of what lies above* ...' Jedda murmured the old prophecy, considering the crushed machine at her feet. 'And here's *what lies below*, or some of it. I must have been brought here by some of these bizarre creatures. There's no way else it could have happened. I think they saved me, in spite of themselves, though I doubt they had that objective in mind. I woke up on one of those hard beds, with them trying to attach their cursed tubes to me, like they've done to that poor fellow over there.'

She pointed to a frost-encoated *orah*-couch on the far left of the chamber, on the opposite side to Samiha's alcove. To his joy, Tymon glimpsed a familiar, red-headed figure stretched out on the table. 'Zero!' he exclaimed, hastening to his friend's side, filled with anxious recognition and relief combined. 'But what have they done to him?'

The Marak boy was still alive, but deeply asleep, his body festooned with transparent tubes and other, nameless Collector paraphernalia. His breath was the faintest curl of white on the cold air. Jedda joined Tymon, peering curiously down at Zero.

'The creatures must have ambushed him,' she said. 'I think they put people to sleep with poisoned darts. There's another around here somewhere, and it's been trying to stick me for about an hour. It's hiding, waiting for me to let down my guard.'

'Asleep, but not in the Veil,' muttered Tymon, inspecting Zero's pale features. It was clear that his friend was not held in a trance: the *orah* disc behind his table was undisturbed, still wearing its coat of frost. Instead, the Collector tubes snaked off in a long winding mass towards a bank of machinery on the far wall, similar to one other Tymon had seen in the building.

'Just like Samiha,' he said, glancing up with alarm, in the direction of the alcove. He had been overcome by a sudden fear that the Collectors had moved the Kion's tank, or somehow tampered with it.

'Samiha?' echoed Jedda, pursuing him as he set off abruptly across the chamber. 'Is she here, too? What is this place, Tymon? You act like you've seen it before.'

'This is where it all happened,' he answered, reluctant to go into detail. 'This is where the Masters stole my body, and threw me into the Veil.'

'But how would they do that?' Jedda was hard-pressed to keep up with him as he hurried towards the alcove, panting in her exhaustion. 'With the tubes?'

'The couches are made of *orah*,' he explained briefly. 'The mechanism forces people into a trance. But our flying friends haven't done that to Samiha, or to Zero. Or perhaps they don't know how ...'

'Careful,' Jedda said, as they stepped over the threshold, into the shadows of the alcove. 'Remember, there's another one of those things, somewhere.' She handed Tymon the grey stick. 'You'd better take this.'

To his great relief, the tank was still there, along with its slumbering occupant, the green light pulsing in the machinery behind. Jedda hastened with him to the side of the tank, gazing up in awe at the floating form of the Kion.

'I should have known!' she breathed. 'She said she'd come back, for a while.'

'Come back?' asked Tymon in confusion. 'She spoke to you?'

'In my head. After I died.' Jedda's eyes slid away from his, as if the admission embarrassed her. 'She told me a few things I ought to know, before I was granted my life again ... about the choices I've made, and how they've affected people ... Not quite in the way I thought, actually, but still. Consequences ...'

Her voice trailed off awkwardly. Tymon could not help feeling a pang of envy; Samiha had not spoken to him at all, in any state, not even about his own very questionable choices.

'Well,' resumed Jedda, taking a deep breath. 'How shall we get her out of there? Do you think she'd wake up if we unplugged her?'

'It's worth a try,' said Tymon, inspecting the back of the tank, where another tangle of large tubes connected Samiha to the green-lit machine. 'For her and for Zero. I'm beginning to understand now, Jedda. The Collectors — those flying things — they keep people alive, or half-alive. That's all they know how to do. They're just complicated machines, built to tend unconscious bodies.'

'So that the Masters can use them?' Jedda shuddered.

'I don't think so.' Tymon made a full circuit and emerged from the other side of the tank, his face pensive as he pieced the possibilities together. 'The Masters can't take over just any sleeping body. They needed to use the *orah*-couches. And the Collectors haven't sent Zero or Samiha to the Veil. They've just drugged them and stuck them full of tubes.'

'That's bad enough,' muttered Jedda, rubbing her arms in the chill of the hall and glancing nervously up as the rain of bark on the roof grew louder, a drumming roar.

But Tymon had been carried away by his ideas. 'You know, I think this was a prison in the old days,' he said to Jedda. 'The criminals' minds were locked in the Veil while their bodies were kept alive by the Collectors. Think of it, it's the perfect sentence.' He turned excitedly to the Nurian girl, standing shivering beside him. 'Maybe the Masters were even the ones imprisoned here, all those centuries ago. The bodies on the couches must have disintegrated, leaving nothing for the Collectors to tend or guard. The machines didn't stop wanting to do their jobs, though, in a broken sort of way. They scavenged for bodies under the Tree, collecting corpses as far as Argos city. The Masters would have known they would collect Samiha, too. They couldn't force her spirit into the Veil, and this was the next best thing. They wanted her helpless, unconscious, but not dead!'

He stopped talking then, because Jedda's expression was aghast, as if he had spoken a blasphemy. A split second later, he realised she was looking over his shoulder. He spun around to see the familiar humped silhouette of the missing Collector rising up in a shadowy corner of the alcove, its thin arm poised to hurl a dart.

'Look out!' he cried, leaping forward and pulling Jedda bodily down to the floor.

It was not a moment too soon. The whir of the dart clipped Tymon's right ear even as he tumbled on top of Jedda. The Nurian girl was cursing roundly but not at him, as they scrambled up to face their floating nemesis together. The remaining Collector did not survive another encounter with both of them. Tymon gave it a resounding whack with his stick, sending it reeling into the nearest wall with a crash. Jedda grasped one of its hanging legs, and dragged it back as it sought to slip away from them, out of the door. After that, Tymon bashed the contraption to the floor, and continued to deal it blows until it gave a final coughing whir and lay silent. In the pause that followed, the bark rain thundered loudly on the roof.

'Let's do it,' said Tymon, hurrying towards the tubes that linked Samiha to the green-lit machine. 'Let's wake her up. All we need to do is disconnect her —'

He never finished his phrase, for at that instant something huge fell on the hall roof with a deafening crash, and the green lights in the alcove went out.

The World Tree shook and groaned as the spark of life at its heart ebbed away. The tremors in the Oracle's cavern extended for miles, the vibrations shuddering up the network of roots and causing the flanks of the Tree to quake. The South Canopy, already weakened by old age, decay, constant mining of its corewood and finally the Saint's blast-cannons, could not take the strain; one by one, the massive branches that had held up the Lantrian leaf-table for so many centuries succumbed to the stress. The great southern sisters to the mining limb of Chal began to show small fractures, then wider cracks. Gaping fissures opened at their bases, and one by one they tipped, toppled and finally crashed down on the watery plain. The Tree was too vast for the southern disaster to cause significant damage outside a radius of about a hundred miles, but the vibrations of the dying canopy were felt everywhere, echoing dimly through the human world above.

The tremors could be detected as far away as Farhang. In the refugee camp five miles from the Freehold, the young Grafters emerged from their trance to find the bark shivering beneath them. Halas, Gardan and the other evacuees, who had safely reached the camp and were watching and cheering from the twig-thickets as the air-chariots doubled back for yet another assault on the Argosian fleet, fell silent, then and glanced at one another, frowning. Gardan reached up in anxiety to feel a trembling twig-shaft beside her; Galliano, pacing impatiently outside the Focals' tent, stopped short, then lay down flat on his stomach before the astonished eyes of Adhama Sing, his ear pressed to the bark. And on the admiral's ship, as the drums of the fleet began to sound the signal for a tactical retreat, Pumble clutched the deck-rail and most particularly his collar, as a sudden and powerful gale from the south threatened to rip away that final shard of dignity.

In Argos city, slightly closer to the epicentre of the disaster, buildings shook and a few of the new sappanes in the windows of the College burst from their hardwood frames. The Saint, celebrating the recent Lantrian victories with his colleagues in the state banqueting hall, found himself showered with shards of dried Tree-gum even as he raised his goblet in a toast to himself. Nothing further happened in the College, but an uneasy silence fell over the company and the Fathers paused, listening to the echoes of the disaster. From outside the seminary, in the direction of the trunk, came a dim crashing and splintering sound. It was followed by a babble of shocked voices, then wails of dismay. Without a word, Fallow rose from the table and marched out of the hall, pursued by a gaggle of whispering priests. They emerged onto the College quadrangle to join a crowd of seminary students and workers, all staring up at the sheer wall of bark over the city.

It was easy to see the source of their consternation. From the spot where a dark and sacred cleft had once marked the trunk, there now rose a plume of dust and nothing else. The entire Tree-rift had been erased: it had caved in, filled with fallen shards of bark and betrayed by a swift stroke from within. The Divine Mouth had closed.

21

'Jedda?' called Tymon, to the dust-filled hall.

He peered shakily over one of the huge grey blocks that had fallen from the roof of the Ancients' building, crouching close to Samiha's tank. The block had missed them both by inches as the roof caved in: the hall, it appeared, had finally been caught beneath one of the falling branches of the South Canopy. The central nave was obliterated, replaced by the massive flank of a Tree-limb. Hazy light and thick clouds of dust penetrated the gaping hole in the roof. Outside, the shards of bark continued to fall, a pattering grey rain. Tymon coughed through the dust as he stood up, gazing about him. He could hardly see in the thick air.

'Jedda —' he began again.

He was arrested by a tapping noise behind him, and whirled around to find that the figure in the tank was moving. Samiha's eyes were open and fixed on him, her hand fluttering urgently against the transparent side of the container. She was drowning, he thought in panic. Whatever the Collectors' machines had done to keep her alive, they were no longer working, smashed to smithereens by the falling blocks.

'Samiha!' he exclaimed, desperately searching the container for a door as she struggled to free herself of the cumbersome tubes.

It was useless. He could see no obvious access to the tank. Faced with Samiha's increasingly frantic struggles, he climbed on top of one of the nearest fallen blocks and heaved against the container with all his might. Slowly, excruciatingly, it tipped, teetered and finally fell over with a crash on the floor, the transparent material bursting open and spraying its contents in all directions.

And then he was beside Samiha, holding her dripping form entangled in tubes tight against him. He watched anxiously until she coughed and spat up the liquid that clogged her lungs, took a ragged breath, and opened her eyes once more.

'Hello, my love,' she said, a choked whisper.

'Hello,' he murmured. He could only gaze at her like a fool, drinking her in with his eyes, incapable of saying more or believing as yet in his good fortune.

'Is this the World Below?' asked Samiha, peering up at the ruined roof and the continuous rain of dust. The larger pieces of bark had ceased falling, but distant crashes still echoed over the ancient city, proof that the danger was not over.

It did not seem odd to him that she had guessed it. For all he knew, she had indeed walked here long ago, in another form, even as the Masters claimed. They had liberally mixed the truth in with their lies.

'We're in one of the old cities,' he told her. 'The Masters let the Collectors take your body. They didn't want you to die.' He had really found her this time, he thought numbly; against all hope, he had his Samiha back.

Her answering chuckle was more of a gasp. 'No, they wouldn't, would they,' she said. 'Help me sit up, Tymon, so I may catch my breath. And help me remove all this nonsense stuck to me.'

He raised her up with great care, as if she were breakable, and gently assisted her to disengage the tubes that adhered like transparent leeches to her arms and stomach. She winced as he unhooked their clinging teeth from her. When he had cleared them all away and kicked them into a corner, he took off his own coat — the old House slave's coat from Chal, torn and dusty from his journeys — and wrapped her thin body in it, securing it about the waist with one of the discarded tubes.

'Thank you,' she said softly. 'Someone's coming now.'

Tymon glanced up to see Jedda emerging through the clouds of dust, picking her way slowly over the debris in the hall, skirting the fallen limb. The Nurian girl appeared bruised and tumbled, but otherwise unharmed. To Tymon's great relief, she supported a dazed-looking but wakeful Zero by the arm, aiding him to cross the wreckage. When she arrived before Samiha, she did not speak, but helped Zero to sit down on the floor. Then she knelt in front of her sovereign, bowing her head before Samiha, as if to receive judgment.

'Rise, Jedda.' The Kion's voice was strong and joyous as she gave her hand to Jedda, lifting her up. 'Fear nothing, for you have pleased me.'

Jedda went red to her ears, stood up and backed away behind Zero. Tymon gazed at Samiha in astonishment. There was a ringing confidence in her tone that he had never heard before. Her body was the same — fragile and marked by her ordeals — but the voice was that of a Being whose inhuman power and authority he felt emanating like heat from her. He could hardly look in her direction. Fleetingly, he missed the old Samiha he had known: the imperfect, very human Samiha who had loved, lived and argued with him on the Freehold. But even as she turned towards him again he knew, drawn to gaze into those fathomless eyes once more, that the girl from Sheb was still there, a spark of laughter at the centre of the power.

'Yes,' she said, just as if she had heard his thoughts. 'It's different. You'll find me happier now, and stranger. You're Seeing me almost clearly, Tymon.'

He was overcome then with the recollection of just how foolish he had been, mistaking the Masters' paltry shade for his true love, and sank to his knees in front of her just as Jedda had, too ashamed to speak. But Samiha would not allow him to grovel, raising him up with a touch of her hand on his cheek.

'We have far to go before evening,' she told him. 'The Tree mourns Matrya: it is not safe here. We must leave this place.'

'The World Key!' cried Tymon, remembering. 'The Oracle told me to find it before she died ...' Then his shoulders sagged in disappointment. 'But the acolytes took it. Who knows where it is, now.'

'The acolytes took a husk, a sham,' said Samiha, shaking her head. 'They have nothing.'

'Nothing?' he echoed in wonderment. 'Then ... where's the Key?'

'Don't you know?' she asked, fixing him with those compelling eyes.

And then, suddenly, he did know. She was what he sought, of course. She always had been. From his first muddled dreams regarding her arrival in Argos city, to the title of the Nurian queen — all had proclaimed it. She had been the one who opened her mysteries to him, door upon door. He felt as if he had been discovering who she really was, unlocking new facets of her ever since they first met. Every time he thought he finally knew her, she had revealed another persona: pilgrim and priestess, sovereign and martyr, human and Born. Now he sensed he was coming close to the very heart of her. She was the Judge. She was the Key. But what did it all mean?

'Spirits,' murmured Zero, from the background. The

Nurian lad was looking sidelong at Samiha, but smiling, as if they shared a secret. 'Not cold this time. Hot.'

Samiha only laughed, inclining her head to Zero in acknowledgment before addressing Tymon again. 'We should go while the light lasts,' she said, as he continued to gaze speechlessly at her. 'Much has become clear to me since you freed me from that tank. We must get to higher ground.' She held her hand out to him. 'I'll need your assistance to make it,' she said, apologetic.

'That much I can do,' he answered, rising and helping her up.

A thousand questions crowded his mind: how much had Samiha, and even the Oracle known in advance about the Masters' attack? If they had foreseen enough to plant a false World Key for the acolytes, why put up with their enemies' mischief at all? Why allow Matrya to die and everyone else to suffer needlessly at the hands of the Masters and their Envoy? Although Tymon had come to appreciate his teacher's tactics and Samiha's convictions by now, and was sure they both had good reason to do what they did, he would have liked to have a better explanation. He privately determined to seek one, when the time was right.

That time was not now, however. They needed to leave the unstable hall and the dangerous environs of the city behind as soon as possible. Though the fall of bark had lessened to a steady trickle of dust as Tymon helped Samiha hobble out of the gutted hall, the far-off booming crash of falling limbs could still be heard. Behind them walked Jedda, assisting a wheezing Zero. They found the front stairs and central nave of the building smashed to atoms, but were spared the task of seeking another way to descend from the hall, for the ruin of the South Canopy had engulfed the city in a layer of debris so thick that the bark was piled up almost to the level of the columns. Many of the ancient towers had been crushed or buried under a heap of broken branches, twigs and leaves of the Tree, and Tymon's main difficulty lay in finding a safe path over the rubble. For a long time he and his friends wandered like ants across the vast plain of the World Below, too anxious and breathless to do more than negotiate the path ahead. Samiha in particular was hard put to clamber through the devastation in her weakened state, though she seemed to know the way out of the city. She guided Tymon unfalteringly forward, leading them roughly south.

He half-carried her in his arms as they walked, his head bent close to hear her whispered instructions. She told him to make for a line of dark slopes that stood up like a beacon above the dust and chaos on the south horizon. *Mountains*, she called them, using another of the old words that had fallen into disuse after humanity abandoned the World Below. Tymon could not help remembering the Oracle's impossible request and puzzling over it. He also watched Samiha with the concerned attention of a mother hawk, lifting her over one broken fragment of branch after another. She was too thin, he told himself worriedly. She looked brittle, her skin like paper stretched tight over the bones. He dreaded she would trip on the jumbled wreckage and break apart. He could see the journey wearing her out rapidly, consuming her small reserves of strength.

And yet, in a reversal he could not fathom, he knew also that she was strong, far stronger than she had ever been before. Within her frail body burned an indomitable will; her eyes were bright with a knowledge he could not bear to contemplate. As much as the Oracle's true form had seemed strange to Tymon, Samiha was ten times stranger. His questions returned to consume him — what did it mean, exactly, that she was the World Key? Why had the Masters wished to retrieve such a thing, and what would happen now that their servants had made off with the wrong artefact? What secret was so important that the Oracle had given her life to protect it? By the time the four travellers had left the debris-clogged plain and begun to climb the first rising slopes of grass and *rock* beyond, the unanswered questions were building up and seething against Tymon's lips.

By then, the sun was making its final descent to the west, stretching an occasional ruddy finger through the Storm clouds to touch the *mountains*. Tymon felt abruptly and ravenously hungry. There seemed no hope of satisfying such banal needs, for now: he saw nothing edible growing in the World Below, nothing but feathery grass on the slopes, and not a bird in sight. The thought made him remember the last meal he had snatched with Zero that morning, at the foot of the Tree. He could hardly believe it had happened on the same day as this, and glanced over his shoulder towards the towering trunk, just to reassure himself that it was still there. It was the first time he had seen the Tree from such a distance. It rose about ten miles behind them, in his estimation, a bank of shadow stretching from east to west. The vista of destruction lying at its foot, though expected, took his breath away.

The remains of the South Canopy lay scattered for miles beneath a veil of dust. The southern marches of the trunk had suffered a terrible transformation, and a new topography of heaped bark and jagged rifts spread about the great roots of the Tree. The valleys through which Tymon had walked in a dream that morning were congested with the leaning carcasses of broken limbs and shattered bark; the steep slopes and rising cliffs of roots over which he had toiled, deep in the grip of his illusions, were filled now with new chasms of collapsed branch and bough. The whole plain was littered with fragments of the Tree, the shallow lake choked and obliterated with debris. And above it all, the Storm itself was ragged-edged and incomplete, the clouds swirling about the glittering funnel of red dust rising over the plain.

High overhead, Tymon glimpsed fitful swathes of azure sky. It seemed the turbulence of the collapse had created two distinct weather systems that spun silently about each other, the sky above encountering the sky below, disturbing the implacable complacency of the Storm for the first time in millennia. He wondered briefly what had become of Wick and Gowron in the cataclysm, but shrank from contemplating the fate of the inhabitants of the South Canopy, the people who had once lived among the fallen branches. It seemed unlikely that anyone could survive such a catastrophe. Slaves and slave-owners of Lantria, young and old alike, were gone. No trace of humanity remained in the grey and broken shards strewn over the World Below. It seemed unjust that both the innocent and the guilty had been destroyed together.

'It's a tragedy,' Samiha remarked at his elbow.

He had not realised that he had stopped walking, and glanced up to see the Kion standing patiently beside him. Jedda and Zero were knee-deep in grass, further up the slope. 'It's not fair,' he muttered, indicating the spectacle of the ruined canopy with a helpless gesture. 'They didn't all deserve to die.'

'No, they didn't.' She fixed him with those eyes again, waiting for him to express his questions.

'Why, Samiha?' he asked, searching her face. 'You're a Born. You know. Why lose the innocent along with the guilty? Why do people in one place die because of the actions of others, far away? The guilty ones never pay.'

'It's unjust,' she said quietly. 'It can't go on.'

She was only repeating his points. He gazed at her in

dim frustration, unwilling to be brusque with her, but wishing she would say more.

'You want me to explain it,' she sighed, after a moment. 'You want me to make it all alright. I'll do my best, Tymon. But first you have to get me where I need to go, which is the top of this slope.'

She must have sensed his dissatisfaction, however, for as they walked on she resumed speaking, her voice subdued with fatigue.

'What happened to you in Hayman's Point,' she said. 'That was unjust.'

'So you know about that?' He glanced quizzically at her. 'Do you know everything, then? Do the Born See it all in advance?'

She shook her head ruefully. 'I've been trapped in a coma, remember, though admittedly much has become clear since I awoke. Matrya Saw that the Masters would eventually find the Seed prophecies and her body, but she kept that knowledge to herself. She was ready to give up her life to save mine, if necessary, and chose to do so when the time came. But prophecies are only the bare root of the matter! How it all happens, the colour and flowering of the whole — that's what's important, and can never be predicted. Even in that tank, I was aware of a few things. I dreamed of you at Hayman's Point, felt your pain, and tried to reach out to you.'

'Then it was you I Saw, after all, standing there during my flogging,' he whispered, the knowledge warming him in the rapidly cooling evening air. 'Not all of my visions were false.'

'Certainly not! But what I mean is this: you suffered that injustice for my sake, and for the sake of your friends. Looking back now, would you have refused to go to Argos and stand up to the priests, knowing it would result in great pain?'

'No,' he said. 'I'd do it all again, to try to help you.'

'Then you understand why Matrya Saw her own death, and allowed it to happen. Because of what comes after.'

He digested this as they trudged along in the failing light, thinking that he did not understand, no. Why suffer the Masters at all? But the thought of his enemies always reminded him of his own foolishness, and he could not help asking her another one of his burning questions. He allowed Jedda and Zero to draw several paces ahead, before whispering his chagrin to Samiha.

'Would they … the Masters, I mean … have found another way to open that door and get to the Oracle, if they hadn't stolen my body?'

She did not answer immediately, and this time he could not meet her eye.

'Probably,' she said. 'They are very stubborn and very resourceful when they want something. This is not the first time they've sought to overturn the sentence imposed on them, and probably won't be the last.'

Her reply did not make him feel any better. He remained miserably silent.

'Tymon,' she continued after a moment. 'There are other forces at work in the world besides our enemies. Forget the Masters. Ultimately they have no power at all. People would still do whatever it is they do without them.'

She was telling him what the Oracle had told him after Laska's death, that evil had no real existence, and was just a form of blindness or disease in the souls of the living. It was a cold and philosophical comfort, and did not in any way lessen his sense of his own stupidity. He said nothing, staring at Jedda's back as she helped Zero over the humped grasses. His fellow student had made her own mistakes, and still come out shining, the object of Samiha's praise. What had he done?

'Not now, later,' murmured Samiha. Her voice was

hardly audible in her fatigue, and she seemed to be speaking to herself, stumbling and almost falling over the tussocks.

He steadied her, biting his lip with remorse at having troubled her with his questions, after all. 'We should rest,' he said. 'The light's almost gone and you're in no state to walk further. We're safe from the falling branches, we should stop —'

'No!' she gasped. 'We must go on. We must reach the top.'

'Just a short rest.' He peered into her face, coaxing. 'And then we go on, I promise. Look, Zero needs a break too.'

He pointed ahead, where Jedda was lowering the evidently exhausted Nurian boy down into the grass. Samiha swayed on her feet, then nodded reluctantly.

'Just a short while,' she sighed, sinking to the ground.

Tymon left her sitting in the grass and joined Jedda, drawing her aside to speak privately. 'Are we making a mistake?' he asked, glancing back at Samiha's slight, straight form on the slope. 'Are we fools to let her drive herself to death? Is there any other way to help her, besides walking on and on like this?'

'I don't think we have many options left.' Jedda's expression was resigned. 'The acolytes had an air-chariot, but it was parked too close to the trunk. My guess is that either it's been crushed, or Gowron and Wick have taken it already. The Kion would have led us there if it were usable. She obviously has another plan, and wants to carry it out, whatever the cost.'

'What about Zero? Can he pay the cost?' objected Tymon.

'He's tired, but he says he wants to go on. He says the Kion is a strong, hot spirit, whatever that means. He wants to follow her.'

'And you? What do you think?'

'I think,' she said, looking at him out of sad eyes, 'that we should respect Samiha's wishes at this point, whatever they are. We owe her that much.'

'Very well.' He bowed his head. 'So be it.'

A few moments later, Samiha struggled to her feet and he hastened to help her. She clung to his shoulder and he almost took her whole weight as they continued up the steep slope, though she could hardly be called a burden. She was like a little child, a feather-light, intense presence at his side.

Jedda walked more slowly, supporting Zero, and the two fell behind in the deepening twilight. After a while the moon appeared, a disk the size of an Argosian half-*talek* over the eastern horizon, stained orange by the dust in the atmosphere. As its light grew stronger, Tymon realised that the Storm had cleared to an unprecedented degree. He could see the stars shining through a massive circular gap in the clouds.

He had been walking in a reverie for a weary hour, concentrating on holding Samiha upright and placing one foot in front of the other, when he saw the slope had almost levelled out. He had been waiting for the *mountain* to fall away again on the other side, as a branch of the Tree would, but the loamy topography of the World Below seemed endless. The moon was paler, shining directly through the gap in the Storm to pick out a peculiar crop of looming grey *rocks* strewn over the grassy slope, each one as tall as a man. Tymon fancied in his tiredness that they resembled an army of barrel-chested giants squatting on the *mountaintop*, silent sentinels hunched in the grass. Their bowed shapes were disquieting, and he did not like to pass between them, crossing their bars of black shadow; he did so only on sufferance, when Samiha threw him a pleading glance. They had left Jedda and Zero completely behind by now. As they crossed the field, a faint noise echoed ahead of them, the first extraneous sound in a long while, apart from their own footsteps and Samiha's gasping breaths. Light but unmistakable, the tinkling of water reverberated between the humped silhouettes of the sentinels.

'This is it.' Samiha's husky whisper seemed loud in the darkness. 'This is the place.'

She pointed towards a ring of five *rocks* standing at the foot of a low cliff, leaning into each other as if sharing a secret. Fifteen feet or so above, the flattened summit of the slope was a bare tabletop of the same cracked grey *rock*, gleaming in the moonlight. A spring gushed from the base of the cliff, the waters collecting in a pool between the five whispering sentinels, before gurgling off in a little stream to Tymon's left.

'The place for what, Samiha?' he asked as she tugged him into the ring. In one respect, she had not changed at all: she was as driven and determined as ever, in spite of her body's frailty.

'The place to rest,' she answered.

He was glad to hear her say it, though why she could not have stopped an hour ago at the foot of the slope was beyond him. He helped her find a comfortable spot to lie down under one of the *rocks*, a nest of grassy tussocks beside the pool, wishing he had more to put over her in the way of a blanket. She wore only his tattered coat wrapped tightly about her to fend off the night air, her calves and bony wrists poking out from under the garment; he longed to gather her up and hold her close, lending her his own warmth, but did not know how to approach her, overcome with awkwardness. She was still his wife in one sense, and yet she was infinitely more.

'Shall I bring some more grass to put on top of you?' he asked. 'I don't think I can manage a fire without

tinder, I'm afraid, I've never been good at doing that …
Maybe Jedda will be able to help when she gets here.'

'Don't worry, Tymon, I feel just fine,' she said,
smiling up at him. 'But I would like a bit of water.
Would you mind bringing me a drink from the spring?'

He nodded and moved to where the water trickled
down the cliff. The *rock* was like Tree-bark in many
ways, he thought as he washed his hands and face
under the spring. It was riven by furrows and striated
like the Tree, though colder to the touch. He glimpsed
moss growing in the crevices. When his hands were
clean, he cupped them together and filled them with
the clear water, for he had no other container. He
heard another slight sound from behind him then, and
thought it was Samiha moving in her bed of grass. He
turned carefully around to bear her the water without
spilling it.

'I'm sorry there's no cup …' he began.

The words died on his lips, for kneeling on the grass
beside Samiha, holding her up and pressing the
gleaming blade of the *orah*-knife against her throat, was
a smugly smiling Wick.

Tymon stood frozen with shock, staring at his enemy.
There was something wrong with the acolyte's face in
the moonlight, he thought idiotically. For to think of
anything else at that moment was unbearable. He
grasped slowly that Wick was wearing a mask, so closely
fitted to the contours of his face as to reproduce his
exact features in a milky white veneer. Tymon did not
remember seeing him wear it in the Oracle's chamber.
It created a rigid, though naturalistic, expression on the
acolyte's face, a permanent leer of gloating satisfaction.
Samiha stared up at Tymon from where she sat trapped
in the crook of Wick's knife-arm, almost as white-faced
as her captor. The water dripped through Tymon's
fingers and drained away.

'You tricked me.' Wick's voice seethed with anger through a gap in the improbably smiling mouth. 'You knew about the World Key: you knew this one was empty.'

With his free hand, he withdrew the two halves of the Oracle's egg from the pocket of his cloak, and threw them with a clatter onto the ground by the pool. They lay dully shining in the moonlight, a hollow shell of *orah*.

'You know where the real one is,' Wick continued, his eyes a mad flash behind the mask-holes as he gripped Samiha. His breath was wheezing and difficult, his voice slightly hysterical. His chest heaved as he spoke. 'You're going to tell me. Now. Otherwise she gets it.'

He had no idea, thought Tymon, almost with pity. Wick would never guess in a thousand years that the Kion was the World Key. Even Tymon was unsure of what that really meant: the mystery of Samiha was still complete. He knew, however, that her life depended on him telling Wick some half-truth that would satisfy him.

'We have it,' he assured the acolyte. 'We'll give it to you. Just let her be.'

He took a step forward, but Wick scrambled to his feet, holding Samiha against him, his voice a gasp behind the rigid smile. 'Not another step!' he said. 'Give it — now! Then she goes free.'

'I have to go over there.' Tymon had seen Jedda circling in the shadows to the rear of Wick, and Zero's silhouette with its large ears poking out from behind a tall tussock; he only had to buy a little more time for his friends. He indicated the far side of the pool to Wick. 'There. Far away from you. I put it down.'

'Go on, then. Hurry.' Wick watched him with glittering eyes as he began to skirt the pool, still pressing the knife to Samiha's throat. The Kion herself said no word: she gazed at Tymon steadily, silently, willing him on.

'Where's Gowron?' asked Tymon, in order to distract the acolyte and keep him from noticing Jedda.

'He won't be joining us.'

The way Wick said it, the distinct note of gratification in his voice, caused a shiver to pass down Tymon's spine. He had no doubt, then, that the younger acolyte had killed his associate. The mask seemed to proclaim it: there, stamped permanently over Wick's features for all to see, was the cold self-satisfaction of an accomplished murderer. Taking care not to look in Jedda's direction, Tymon reached the opposite side of the pool and bent over the grass, making a show of rummaging behind a tussock.

'It's just over here,' he said.

At that instant, Zero rose up from the grass to grab Wick's ankles. Jedda leapt simultaneously on the acolyte from behind, grasping his knife-hand and jerking him away from Samiha. Tymon turned and splashed back hurriedly through the pool. In the short scuffle that followed, Wick rolled with Jedda on top of him down into the shallows. They struggled briefly while Zero hovered nearby, seeking an opening in which to pin down Wick; Jedda, engaged in fending off the arm with the *orah*-knife, was unable to bear down on her enemy with all her strength. But by that time, Tymon had raised his hand high to summon up the righteous power of the Sap.

To his shock and dismay, nothing happened. No cleansing flame leapt up in response to his need: no searing heat enveloped him as it had done when faced with the Masters and the Envoy's curses. As Tymon frowned over his empty and scarred right palm, Wick raised his weapon and slashed it across Jedda's cheek, causing her to utter a cry and pull back.

Zero was on top of Wick an instant later, as he struggled to rise. Tymon was beside him almost as quickly, determined to use the power of his back and muscles, even if the Sap had deserted him. Wick had a lunatic's tenacious strength, fending them both off with grim vigour. But after a panting struggle, Tymon was able to twist his adversary's right wrist behind his back and wrench the knife out of his hand. It dropped with a clatter into the pool. Gasping with pain and pressing one palm to her bleeding cheek, Jedda stepped forward, ripping the mask off Wick's face as he knelt by the pool.

The acolyte's shriek reverberated through the night air, a howl of pain and humiliation that caused the hairs on the back of Tymon's neck to prickle. The mask burst into pieces in Jedda's hand with a resounding crack, the gleaming *orah* in its interior going dark. She dropped it hurriedly to the ground, as if it burned, while Wick sobbed in pain, raising his hands to his face but unable to touch the raw flesh. The topmost layer of skin had been ripped off with the mask, and all that was left was a mass of reopened wounds. Wick's eyes were white and staring, his mouth a grimace of agony. Tymon let go of him, gazing at his former schoolmate in horror and pity.

'Damn you,' croaked the wounded acolyte, half-weeping and half-enraged. 'I hope you all rot in this Hell. I hope you regret the day you were born.'

Then, in one swift motion, dodging away from Tymon, he snatched up the knife glinting in the shallows and leapt towards Samiha. Before Tymon could prevent it, before Jedda or Zero could make a move, he had plunged the *orah*-knife deep between the Kion's ribs. He gave it a final, savage twist and pulled it out.

'Not so proud of yourselves now, are you?' he sneered, as Tymon stumbled forward with a cry, catching Samiha's body when it slumped to the ground.

'Not so damned righteous! Well, you can eat me, my pretties: life's a Tree-bitch.'

Tymon hardly heard him, bent in anguish over Samiha. Wick jumped back neatly and sidestepped Jedda as she lunged towards him, dancing around the opposite side of the pool with by now lunatic glee, waving the knife.

'Eat me!' he cried, breaking into hysterical, croaking laughter. 'Eat me if you can!'

He turned and fled into the darkness, an echo of mad laughter between the *rocks*. Jedda leapt after him with a shout, pursued by the shambling Zero. Tymon knelt with Samiha's crumpled form in his arms, rocking backwards and forwards in his grief.

'No, no, no.'

He did not realise that he was the one saying it: the repetitive murmur seemed to come from somewhere else, outside him. He tore a section from his linen shirt and did his best to staunch the blood flowing from Samiha's side. She was no weight at all now in his lap, her face luminous in the moonlight and dangerously free of pain. She struggled to speak, her expression too exultant to give him cause for joy. He tried to make her rest, but she insisted on uttering the usual fervent words he had come to expect from her.

'Don't be sad, Tymon,' she said. 'We're moving through the Letter of Union, when all things return to what they should be. The old world is dead. The new one will be born. It's my job to bring the prophecies to fruition.'

'Don't you dare,' he told her, despairing. 'I don't care about prophecies! I only care about you. Don't you dare leave me again!'

'You wanted me to be free,' she whispered, collapsing back on his knees as her strength gave out. 'This is the only way.'

He glanced away from her, his throat painfully tight. 'Then the way is too hard,' he said. 'Too hard, Samiha.'

She did not answer. Her eyes drifted shut and her breathing was rapid and shallow. The linen bandage was wet through; he used the thicker folds of the coat to staunch the bleeding, but her life was flowing away, draining through his fingers like the water he had never given her from the spring. When she spoke again, the words were so faint that he almost brushed against her lips when he bent to listen.

'You must bring them down,' she said. 'The people of the Tree. All of them. It's time, the cycle is complete. Will you do that, Tymon?'

'I will,' he promised her. 'I will.'

He was willing to promise her anything, if only she would not leave him for good. Here she was, dying, and all she could talk about was time-cycles and prophecies. The words of a Born, he thought bitterly. She had probably known Wick would ambush them on the *mountain*, and had embraced her end without a qualm. He could not bear it.

'Do you know why the Born come to this world?' she murmured.

The night was still except for the wind sighing through the grass, all sounds of pursuit having faded away. The moon shone down through the wisps of scudding cloud.

'Why?' he asked hoarsely, little caring for the answer in his misery.

'Because you call us. We left, but you call us back. Every cry for justice or freedom, every life ended too soon — it calls out to us. The ones who have been silenced and have no voices of their own …' She paused, struggling to form the words. 'They cry out in the Tree of Being, life after life, Leaf after Leaf. They grow us. You make the prophecies, Tymon. How could

499

we not come, when you petition us, generation after generation? You asked for justice: here I am. You asked for a better world. Here I am.'

But you're going, he cried out in silence. *How can it be better without you?*

She did not say more. After a few moments, her body grew still on his knees, and the breath ceased rising in her chest. She was gone. Immortal she may have been, in other worlds, but in this one she was gone. And Tymon knew that whatever her true nature was, he would never again see her as she had been here, as the girl from Sheb, the girl he loved.

A furious despair took hold of him. No tears came: he could not weep. But after he laid Samiha's body down, he staggered about the rock ring and the pool, kicking the patient ground in his grief, cursing the stars above and the *earth* below. Most of all, he cursed his own inability to summon up the Sap-fire to combat Wick. He beat the uncaring faces of the *rocks* with his fists until his palms grew raw, until his breath came in gasps and the mood passed, replaced by an aching emptiness. Then he returned to kneel over Samiha's thin body, while the wind tugged at the grass and the immovable *rocks* looked on.

So Jedda found him, when she walked slowly back up the slope, accompanied by Zero. A glance at his face told them all, and a glimpse of their dispirited ones showed Tymon they had not caught up with Wick. For a while, they all stood beside Samiha's body with their heads bowed, the others weeping while Tymon remained grimly silent.

Despite their grief and weariness, he would not let them rest for long. It seemed to his friends that with this final incomprehensible loss, a mood of bleak determination had come over Tymon. He announced that since Wick was on the loose, he intended to protect Samiha's body from any further indignities. He insisted, with a stubborn resolve the others dared not oppose, on interring the Kion's corpse as he had heard some ancient tribes used to do with their dead, entombing them in the Tree to protect them from carrion birds. Instead of a carved tomb of wood, they would place Samiha in a grave of loam, fulfilling the Oracle's instructions in some sense at least. They would bury one of them on the *mountain*.

With the aid of sharp *rocks* they found scattered in the field, they set about digging as deep a hole by the pool as they had the strength to make at that late hour. Tymon urged his companions on ceaselessly when they flagged; he could not bear the thought of a lunatic Wick scratching up Samiha's corpse with his nails. After a while, Zero fell asleep, leaning against a tussock where he had only meant to take a short rest. Tymon and Jedda continued to dig until the moon had crossed half the sky and they were both reeling with exhaustion. Finally, when the depth of the hole was satisfactory to Tymon, they lifted Samiha's body into it, still dressed in the houseboy's coat. They laid the two halves of the false World Key and the shards of Wick's mask at her side, for they could think of no safer place to put the artefacts, and had no desire to keep them.

Then they filled the grave up with loam and painstakingly dragged two large, flat *rocks* on top of it. After that last task was done, they threw themselves down on the grass and slept, no longer caring if the blood-mad Wick should return to find them.

22

Bolas could only see one of his legs as he lay supine in his hammock. He had been dosed to the gills with Treesap wine in the dim hours after the terrible explosion, and had not been entirely himself when the ship's surgeon cut the other one off at the knees. His other leg. He had even giggled at the sight of the poor crushed thing with a foot dangling incongruously from the end. What was his foot doing lying there in a bloody basket, with various other chopped-off limbs and members belonging to the rest of the crew?

'Hey, that's my foot!' he wanted to shout, with dawning recognition, as the surgeon pulled it out of sight, but his tongue was not his own at that moment. Too much Treesap, he thought vaguely. Had he been at a party?

It was with difficulty that he remembered how he came to lose it. His leg, that was. Bolas gazed with disbelief at the stump below his left thigh, drenched in unguents, wrapped in yards of fine leaf-gauze spun by the deft fingers of Argosian maids and housewives. Lovely girls sewing on the stoops of their homes. Pretty girls, like Nell, he thought, a lump rising in his throat, who would have been scandalised to know to what bloody ends their lace was being spun. Nell would scold him dreadfully when she learned that he had lost a leg in Marak.

'How careless can you be!' she would say. Bolas fought back his tears as he turned away from the distressing absence to gaze through the portholes.

There were six of them spanning the right side of the ship. Six whole portholes, Bolas thought in amazement; this cabin was larger than any he had occupied since leaving Argos. He could not figure out where he was, but he did dimly register that he could now see more of a large building at the summit of this tawdry town that rose in three tiers between the bare twig-thickets. Marak, he remembered. He was in Marak. He had only glimpsed a broken wall of the palace before. Last night, during the party.

'Oh, mother, let me go!' moaned a voice beside him, light as a feather.

Bolas struggled to find a comfortable position that did not involve increasing pain. His hammock was stretched between two thick rafters, and he entertained himself for a few moments with the possibility that one of them was actually his leg. It would be difficult to walk around with a tree below his knees, he thought, but perhaps no worse than drifting along as he had been doing, with his head in the clouds, since being drugged for the operation. The operation. He was in a hospice dirigible, he suddenly realised, tethered in Marak air-harbour and awaiting instructions to proceed back to Argos with the war wounded. But what war, he wondered in bewilderment, staring through the portholes at the ridiculously ugly Governor's palace. As far as he could remember, there had only been a party.

'Why did this have to happen to me?' wailed the fragile voice beside him plaintively. 'Why me, mother? Tell me why?'

'Shut up, you stupid nut-head,' mumbled a deeper voice on Bolas' left. 'At least you're still talking.'

The bright sunlight, the airy cabin, and the comfort of the hammock might have been positively luxurious had he been able to enjoy them in the company of his own right leg rather than the wounded soldiers. As Bolas resurfaced to full consciousness, he began to make out the other hammocks slung down the length of the cabin in rows on each side of him. There were grumbling and groaning bodies rolled up in these cocoons, in various positions and varying states of cleanliness. All these soldiers had been immobilised, just like him, by wounds sustained last night, during the party.

Someone further down the cabin suddenly let out a stream of invective. 'To hell with them all!' he yelled. 'A total waste! Give me one reason for it!'

Bolas was not sure whether his companion's fury was directed at the Nurians or the Saint, but he shared it fully when he remembered how his leg had been crushed under the falling deck beams of his ship, after a cask of Treesap wine exploded at the soldiers' celebrations.

During the course of that afternoon, as Bolas turned and twisted miserably in his hammock, he heard many such curses and cries of condemnation. He also heard rumours about the cause of the accident and its consequences. One was that the wine cask had been rigged up with blast-poison by a bunch of Jays intent on disrupting the crusade, though why Jays should care about such things was a mystery; they had never meddled in the Saint's affairs before. Another was that they were all trapped in this choking hole of a fly-infested colony because the captain was waiting for paperwork transferring the Jays from the Marak jail to their ship, before setting sail for Argos. And a third rumour was circulating that the person who tipped the Argosians off about the Jays was a blond-haired Nurian claiming to be an enemy of the Freeholders. His name was Caro, and he had sent his condolences to the wounded soldiers.

'Curse him!' bellowed a voice at the far end of the cabin. 'You can't trust a white maggot further than a corpse. I bet he set the whole thing up himself, this Caro.'

The Tree knew what was true. But then, one only entertained rumours for lack of more congenial company, thought Bolas bitterly. To find himself trapped like this among the idiots who had been carousing on deck the night before, singing their stupid songs to the Saint, and who were now bellowing and bawling with pain, was an irony he did not appreciate. He had avoided these men from the day he had been press-ganged onto the ship, preferring to polish hardwood spears rather than participate in their Tree-forsaken party. And now, he was imprisoned in their company for the duration of their journey home. Without a leg. It was too much!

'Oh, mother!' groaned the feeble voice from the hammock beside him. 'Take me home!'

Bolas finally glanced towards it, and saw a boy lying in the bloody hammock to his right. The kid was about fifteen, and had no arms. He was evidently suffering horribly. From the flush in his cheeks and the way he tossed his head back and forth, Bolas guessed he might be delirious. He craned his neck to look in the direction of the door, but there was no nurse in sight. The hospice boat was overcrowded, and the few female assistants who had come from Argos, to do the laundry and keep the medical supplies clean, were hard-pressed to keep up with their multiple duties.

The boy was moaning again. 'Mother, mother —' he began.

But their neighbour to the left, the one who had already called the boy a nut-head, interrupted him.

'Ow shut up, yer silly sod!' the man growled in a choked voice. Bolas noticed that his head was entirely wrapped in gauze. 'You'd have a different song to sing if your face was blown away like mine,' he muttered.

Bolas shuddered and looked back out of the portholes. The boy without arms continued whimpering. Bolas no longer noticed him, absorbed in his own misery and trembling with shooting pains that rose from his missing knee. He had to bite his lips to avoid crying out, and had reached the point where he could barely hold back tears of self-pity, when the doors of the cabin opened and the ship's surgeon entered.

Doctor Swallow had no tolerance with maudlin patients. He was a tough old bird, and had seen worse than the wounded he was currently tending. When the soldiers moaned about the loss of their limbs, he invariably reminded them of the number of dead that had been tipped over the side of the ship after the explosion.

'So be thankful you're around to feel anything,' he trumpeted, as he stomped through the ward on his rounds.

Bolas wondered, with rising irritation, why Swallow felt obliged to place each foot down so heavily when he walked around the cabin.

'If you haven't been blown apart by blast-poison, then gangrene or fly fever will probably do it,' Swallow barked at the poor man on Bolas' left, the one without a face.

You would think he was paid to cure his patients of their hopes rather than their wounds, thought Bolas angrily, as the surgeon approached his hammock.

'As long as you're still in pain, you know you're in tip-top shape,' Swallow announced to him, before passing on to the boy without arms.

Bolas noted, grimly, that the surgeon did not have

anything to say to the youth who continued to call for his mother. He knew Swallow was right, and that he had been lucky to escape with his life, but as the Treesap wine wore off and the pain in his absent leg grew worse, Bolas was becoming more and more conscious of those around him, and less and less thankful as a result.

'If blast-poison and gangrene don't do it,' Nell would have reprimanded him, 'then anger will.'

The memory of her sweet voice was all that kept him from screaming aloud in pain and despair. Thank the Tree he still had arms to hold her! If he survived this, he vowed, it would only be to see Nell again. Nothing else mattered.

It was late that night when the armless youth finally stopped raving. His incessant cries had provoked a storm of protest around the ward. He had been told to hold his tongue or the Saint would cut it out; he had been invited to dive in the Gap and get lost; he had been urged to go bury himself in Nurian manure; and finally there was an appeal, by the faceless man on Bolas' other side, that he might just please hurry up and die, so they could all sleep a little. This last request the boy appeared inclined to obey, though he was oblivious to the rest. For delirium had set in. It was only after the harassed nurse had changed his dressings and administered a dose of something to calm the boy, which she confessed to Bolas was a little stronger than wine and not strictly on the record, that silence finally filled the ward.

The youth's calm might have been ominous, but the other patients were grateful for it. There was a chorus of faint cheers all round and the faceless man was soon snoring noisily through the gap in his bandages. Despite the nightcap he too had been given, however,

Bolas found himself fidgeting restlessly in his hammock as the moon rose outside the portholes. It was difficult to lie in the same position for hours, unbearable to be rolled up in this cocoon without being able to move. But when he tried to find a comfortable position on his opposite side, the pain was so piercing that he gave an involuntary groan.

There was a shift in the silence. He heard something, the trace of a sound that had coincided with his own. Had he roused the armless boy? Would the cripple now begin his endless babbling again? Bolas lay rigid, until the waves of his own pain subsided, listening to the laboured breath of his sleeping companions. They were all like some huge animal extended across different bodies, breathing through separate mouths, struggling through individual dreams, but feeling one common pain. For the first time since he had joined their company, he felt a kinship with the wounded soldiers around him, a deepening compassion. They were just grown-up babies, most of them, hardly weaned before they had been thrust into this war. Perhaps the lad had called out in a nightmare; perhaps he was simply missing his mother. Whatever the sound was, Bolas decided he had better check on him.

Inching himself up on his shaking arms and doing his utmost to avoid putting pressure on the bleeding stump of his left leg, he leaned over carefully in his swaying hammock to look down on his companion. The armless youth was lying in a shaft of moonlight with his eyes wide open.

'Did you hear it too?' he breathed.

Bolas' heart was in his mouth. The boy was as pale as a ghost already.

'It's a kind of singing,' said the boy, staring at Bolas. 'Listen!'

And as he spoke, Bolas heard it. A faint chanting

came from somewhere deep in the bowels of the ship. It was neither a noise of protest nor of pain. It was not a crying or a moaning or a wailing or a curse. It was a steady, joyful, daunting song.

I pass the torch to you, my love.
Fly fast and free, for you're my messenger.
Set the world alight or be consumed, my love.
Either be the torch or burn away.

Bolas realised he had been holding his breath. 'The Jays!' he murmured, in sudden understanding. 'Must be the prisoners everyone was talking about. What are they singing?'

The armless boy looked up at him, washed white as a shrouded corpse in the moonlight. 'The words of the Nurian prophet,' he said softly, as the chant went on, gradually swelling around them in the listening dark.

I pass the torch to you, my love.

Bolas shuddered. 'How do you know that?' he asked.

Fly fast and free, for you're my messenger.

'I remember her,' said the boy, half to himself. 'The one the Saint had executed, before he started killing us.'

Bolas stared at him. So young and yet so truthful? He had not imagined soldiers could be honest, but pain did strange things to the human spirit.

My story will change hearts, my love.

How arrogant he had been, thought Bolas, and how judgmental of these lads! He was no less stubborn than the Saint's crusaders. His eyes began to sting.

'Hush!' whispered the sick boy as the chant continued, 'listen!'

Don't be blinded by your own desires.

Whether because of the shame he felt to be weeping again, or the shaking of his arms which could no longer sustain his weight, Bolas was obliged to lower himself back into his hammock as the song of the Jays continued.

For this is the Year of Fire, the beginning and the end.

As the last wave of the chant dissolved into silence, the voice of the armless boy washed clear as moonlight through the ward.

'You will tell my mother I never killed a man, won't you?' he said distinctly.

When Bolas had the courage to heave himself up from the hammock and look down at the youth again, he saw that he was dead.

The Jay prisoners, who had been arrested in Marak some days before the wine cask accident, provided the wounded soldiers with their permit to return home on the morrow. While the remaining Argosian vessels headed off to Farhang under the direction of Admiral Greenly, Aran, the captain of the hospice ship, gave orders for their ether sacs to be filled, too. With every hammock in the sick bay taken and the hold stuffed with Jays, there was no need to wait for further casualties from the war with the Freehold.

But as it turned out, their departure was delayed due to a bureaucratic setback. The hospice ship failed its hygiene inspection at the last minute because of two more dead bodies found on board. One of the Jay prisoners, who had been fatally hurt during their arrest, had expired in the hold the same night as the armless soldier died of his wounds upstairs. And so the hospice ship was denied sanitation clearance until the corpses could be tossed into Marak Harbour.

There was a considerable brouhaha about it. No one cared about the Jay, who could hardly be called a casualty of the Saint's war, but the Argosian boy's body ought to be kept on board, according to his wounded comrades, until he could be given a hero's funeral in the Gap. Being blown up by a cask of Treesap wine was just as good as martyrdom in a crusade, after all, and an

Argosian from the Central Canopy deserved better than to be thrown overboard in Marak.

Bolas was sickened when he heard of it. How idiotic to impose the prejudices of the living on the bodies of the dead! As if oblivion recognised one nation over another, he thought in disgust. As if the canopies had a 'right' or 'wrong' side. He had the impression that the two deaths were linked, somehow, for he guessed the songs he and the Argosian boy had been listening to had been sung for the Jay who died. Bolas felt responsibility for both young men, and wished to be present at their last rites. But Swallow refused to let him witness the brief ceremony. He lay in miserable pain in his hammock below deck as the two fragile biers were slipped ignominiously overboard, the Saint's soldier and the Impure Jay united in death.

His one source of comfort, when they finally did set sail from Marak, was the songs of the prisoners in the hold. The remaining Jays kept singing throughout that day and the days after, their voices hauntingly beautiful. Despite the poignant melodies, however, the wounded soldiers took exception to this fresh assault on their ears. They grumbled, then cursed. Swallow complained on medical grounds, and Aran stomped down to the hold, telling the prisoners to be quiet on pain of punishment. But the Jays continued, singing quietly at night when the drugged soldiers slept, instead of in the daytime. Bolas was grateful to them for not obeying.

Had it not been for their sweet chanting, his bitterness would have deepened, for the deaths did not end in Marak Harbour. The man with his face blown off, and another youth no older than Bolas, who had lost one leg to blast-poison and the other to gangrene, were tipped overboard two days later, during the Gap crossing. Now that, agreed the wounded men in their hammocks, was the way to go: much better than being shoved out in the colonies. But Bolas missed those funerals, too. He was suffering from a slight fever at the time, and was banned from going above deck. Swallow had no patience with men who threw their lives away when he had gone to the trouble of saving them.

So Bolas missed seeing the Gap, even on one leg. He had witnessed the cloudy expanse briefly on the way over to Marak, but had not had time to appreciate its awful beauty because of turbulence during the first crossing. He had been too busy climbing up and down ladders, and lashing down cargo on that occasion, to use his eyes. On the way back, the weather was fair and calm, with no funnel-winds between the layers of conflicting cloud. The dirigible drifted across the fleecy immensity with a clear, blue sky overhead, while the Jays kept singing. Bolas only caught a glimpse of the cloudy Void through the portholes.

They had barely touched down in the Central Canopy, docking for the night at a postal relay on the other side of the Gap, when they were overtaken by unexpected and disturbing news. The gaunt-faced monk who manned the bird-station had received new messages from Marak that very afternoon: the Argosian fleet had suffered an unforeseen defeat in Farhang, he informed Aran colourlessly. Scores had been killed under the relentless air-sniping of the United Freeholds, and the fleet forced to retreat and regroup, according to the clipped hand of a certain Sergeant Pumble. Bolas was devastated rather than relieved by the news, for he knew well enough that the Saint had hundreds more young lives to waste at his disposal. Defeat would only lead to further reprisals. The war would go on, and on: there was no chance of the Nurians ultimately winning it, and every likelihood that generations of Argosians would be warped by it. He was heartsick at the thought.

But even after this dreadful news, the Jays kept singing. And as Bolas pondered over the setback suffered by the Saint's armies, the words of their chant began to echo with a new resonance in his ears. He began to suspect that these circus performers had been arrested precisely because of their songs.

Before you, armies lay their arms to rest
And ravening beasts learn gentleness.

Three days after the Gap crossing, Bolas' fever had abated, and his strength was beginning to return. Despite the phantom pain in his thigh, he had made sufficient progress to be able to practise walking up and down the ward on a crutch. But he had still not been permitted on deck, and was heartily sick of being cooped up inside the cabin. The hospice ship was making good headway, in steady, southwesterly winds; with his voyage almost half-over, the prospects of seeing Nell were starting to make the young architect restless. The thought had crossed his mind — with a twinge of shame, for he had no cause to think her so fickle — that his sweetheart might not love a cripple with only one leg. The idea made him desperate, and he was determined not to meet her lying on a stretcher. He wanted to be as well as possible, as strong as possible, by the time he reached Argos city, and resolved to ask the surgeon for his walking papers that very day, come what may.

It was not to be, however. Late that afternoon, approaching the Cape of Green Hope and within sight of the Lantrian leaf-table, the weather took a change for the worse. Bolas was just gathering up the courage to ask Swallow, the next time he appeared on his rounds, if he might spend an evening on deck, when a violent storm hit the ship, out of the blue. The southern climate had been mild for days; there had even been a hint of spring in the air. But all at once, a furious gale leapt out of a clear sky, and the dirigible began to pitch and toss, its ether sacks straining.

The three blasts of the emergency horn put paid to Bolas' hopes of going outside. He listened with gloomy frustration from his hammock as Aran's voice drifted down from above, shouting frantic orders to batten down the hatches, lash the sails and drop anchor. The able-bodied men on the ship deserted the cabins, occupied with coaxing the ship down into the lower twigs. After a while, the shouts receded, and there was only the wind pummelling the dirigible's hull, shaking it like a dried leaf. The wounded men in the hammocks next to Bolas were silent, stunned into rare submission by the noise.

It went on for what seemed like hours, a howling, whistling gale interspersed by distant booming, as if whole sections of the Tree were crashing into each other. At long last, the fury of the gale ebbed away to a degree, though the ship still shook spasmodically, and far-off booms continued to echo through the hull. Another faint sound could also be heard, rising over the whistling wind.

Ye are the wind that carries forth the flame.

Before you, cities crumble, hearts are changed.

The Jays were still singing. No one had bothered to silence them during the storm, occupied with the business of safety and survival. Even Swallow had been press-ganged into active service, as Aran called it, and was nowhere to be seen. Bolas cast a rapid glance over the other hammocks in the ward, swaying with the ship. Surely no one would notice in the midst of this crisis if he, too, broke a few rules. No one would care what he was doing at a time like this, he thought, tipping his one leg carefully onto the floor. He balanced precariously as he groped for his crutch. It was hanging on a hook nearby, and he almost fell, reaching for it. Even if he could not go up on deck, perhaps he could make his way downstairs and talk with the prisoners in the hold.

'Where are you off to, Bolas?' grunted one of his companions as he hopped across the cabin towards the door.

'This place stinks of chamber pots,' Bolas replied. 'I've had enough of it: I'm going to sniff out the Storm.'

It was hard to stagger along on his crutch with the ship listing wildly, and harder to open the latch with one hand, but he was determined to do it. No one called him back as the door slammed shut.

Gingerly, he negotiated the corridor outside the ward, following the sound of singing. He was not familiar with the layout of this dirigible, but guessed he would have to go down at least one more flight of stairs before reaching the hold. He passed steps leading up on his right to an open hatch in the deck, and flattened himself against the opposite wall as someone thudded by the entrance, calling for more rope. He was not sure if he were more fearful of hurting himself, or of getting caught by Swallow. At last, he reached the other end of the corridor and found it blessedly equipped with a stairwell to the lower levels. Step by step he descended, leaning on the handrail, while the voices of the Jays rose ghostly from below, and the wind rattled outside. Foot followed crutch as he went down, drawing ever closer to the haunting chant. Just as he reached the last step, another strong gust of wind hit the dirigible and he almost fell again, slamming his right hip against the door at the bottom of the stairs.

He leaned against it to catch his breath and stop his heart from racing. Footsteps echoed dimly on the deck above, accompanied by renewed cries from the sailors.

Through them the voices of the Jays chanted in descending harmony.

Ye are the call raised at the break of day,
The trumpet blast to banish darkness and dismay.

Bolas opened the door to find himself in a long and lightless corridor, illuminated only by air-shafts leading to the deck two floors higher. There were closed hatches on either side of the corridor, extending the full length of the hold. He guessed from the odour of frogapples, mixed with lint, that he had entered the storage area of the hospice ship. The corridor pitched and creaked alarmingly as he hobbled towards the reinforced hardwood door at the far end. It had a barred hatch for passing food and water to the prisoners, and it was through this opening that the Jays' voices came.

Only when he finally reached it, panting with the effort, did Bolas realise his folly. Why had he come all the way down here? Whatever was he going to say to the Jays? As it turned out, he did not have to say anything because, at that moment, the dirigible tilted violently. His crutch slipped from his grasp and clattered away; he lost his balance and went crashing to the floor with a yelp of pain.

The singing stopped abruptly, and there was an immediate scuffle on the other side of the door. As Bolas struggled up into a sitting position, nursing his half-leg, he heard a whisper through the barred hatch.

'Who's there?' said a voice. It was a woman's. Bolas cursed himself for his stupidity: she would be able to see him lying there, helpless and legless on the floor.

'Friend?' enquired the voice, again.

Bolas caught a glimpse of a dirty face peering down at him through the opening, eyes white in the gloom. He took a deep breath. 'Yes,' he answered, after a beat.

In the pause that followed, the alarm horn sounded

dimly for the second time. 'It's a bad storm,' Bolas muttered, aware of the futility of the remark as the ship was buffeted by the wind.

'This is no storm,' said the girl quietly. 'It's the end of the world.'

Bolas was taken aback. He had heard about the Jays and their odd beliefs, but had not expected anything quite so apocalyptic, on such short acquaintance. He groped on the floor for his crutch, rising with difficulty. He could barely see the girl's face through the hatch, a smudged grey oval framed with black and pierced by two gleaming eyes. He remembered that he should be offering the Jays his condolences.

'One of you died, I think, before we left Marak Harbour?' he asked uncertainly.

The girl's gaze was luminous between the bars. 'My partner,' she answered. 'He was beaten to death by the Saint's soldiers.' And when Bolas could not speak, chagrined, she added, as if it explained everything, 'They took him for a traitor.'

'I'm sorry,' Bolas finally said. He was depressed to be involved in such a loss, if only by association. 'They're ignorant, that lot, and brutal, and they've been lied to.'

The girl might have shrugged, a slight shift in the darkness behind the door, sidestepping issues of pardon or blame. 'You're also wounded, I see,' she said. 'Are you a soldier, too?'

'Hardly,' he mumbled, embarrassed by the stark difference between the loss of life and the loss of a leg. 'I never even fought. Just an accident with blast-poison.'

'No accident,' the Jay said. 'Caro's men rigged the cask.'

Her assurance surprised Bolas. He tried to recall the gossip circulating in the cabin a week before. 'You mean the Nurian with yellow hair?' he asked.

'Tanata, our host and Nurian sister in Marak, knew Caro,' the girl explained. 'She told Anise about the attack, and he tried to warn the Argosian captain on that ship. But they didn't believe him. They arrested him, instead.'

Bolas winced as another roll of the vessel almost sent him hurtling against the opposite wall. He imagined the Jay trying to reason with the soldiers, trying to tell them something about a cask of Treesap wine, and being bludgeoned into silence. Anise: where had he heard the name before?

'Why did they arrest you?' he asked the girl.

'For distributing what they call "rebel tracts".' There was a further gleam of the Jay girl's teeth as she smiled through the bars.

Her cellmates had evidently decided Bolas was no threat, for their voices rose up again in harmony from behind the door. Although the wind had grown fierce once more, rattling the hull, their chant throbbed like the still heart of the storm.

Before you, armies lay their arms to rest
And ravening beasts learn gentleness.

'What are those words?' Bolas asked the girl behind the bars. That, he realised, was what he had come down here to find out. 'Why are you singing them?'

'The words of the Kion,' she replied. 'We sing them because we believe in her. That's what we were arrested for — bringing Samiha's promise back to Nur.'

At the sound of the Kion's name, the others broke off their chant, calling out from behind the door.

'The promise of peace!' cried one.

'The words of the angel,' said another, followed by a babble of other voices.

'She who rose up from the temple into the sky.'

'She who fell into the Storm and returned.'

Bolas found the intense ardour of the Jays easier

to take in song, rather than speech. 'I know she died,' he interrupted them impatiently. 'But how did her testament come to you?'

'Samiha's song belongs to everyone,' said the girl behind the bars. 'But we have it because the *Syon* entrusted it to us.'

'The *Syon*!' echoed the Jays behind her. 'Her flaming messenger!'

'Whoa, just a minute.' Bolas shut his eyes and pressed himself against the door as the dirigible pitched and swayed. He had heard that word, *Syon*, before as well — heard it in Tymon's tale of his adventures, related in Masha's apartment many weeks ago. And then he remembered the Jays who had given shelter to his friend. Anise and Jocaste.

'You knew Tymon!' he blurted out. 'You're the ones who brought him to Argos city! Is your name Jocaste?' he asked the girl belatedly.

'Yes,' she answered, a faint note of surprise in her voice. 'How did you know? The soldiers never asked.'

'Tymon told me about you. He's my friend, too,' said Bolas, thinking with regret of what Tymon had done in Argos. 'He gave himself up to save me from jail ...'

'*Syon!*' breathed the Jays, in a rustling whisper.

'The *Syon* is a friend to all in need.' Jocaste's tone had the conviction of fervent belief. 'Our peace depends upon him.'

Their suffering had made them fanatics, thought Bolas suddenly. They had come to think of Tymon and Samiha as prophets of change and doom, spinning fantasies out of the lives of ordinary people, to give themselves hope. He wondered what violence Jocaste must have suffered for her to speak in that fervent tone, clinging to the idea of peace.

'Peace will come, you know,' she said softly, as if sensing his thoughts.

'Will it?' Bolas replied, glum.

Despite the Jays' optimism, it did not seem a likely prospect, with the threat of the Saint's crusades and the ship shaking and quaking about their ears. There was something different about this storm, Bolas thought, with a stab of uneasiness. It was not like the winter tempests he had seen on the way over to Marak. The turbulence came from below, buffeting the ship like a leaf, and he was hearing strange sounds, a groaning and cracking of wood in the distance, ominous to his ears. After each long, tearing crack came an echoing boom of finality. It sounded, almost unthinkably, like the ruin of entire branches.

'How can you be so sure of that?' he asked Jocaste.

'Because Samiha said so,' the girl answered, her logic unabashedly circular. And the voices of the Jays filled the air. 'Our green lady,' they whispered. 'Our prophetess.'

'But she told us the world would end, first,' continued Jocaste. 'Before peace comes the test. Before light comes the fire. This is just the beginning.'

This is the Fire, this the test, sang the Jays. *The promise kept and all signs manifest.*

Another heart-wrenching crack echoed through the hull. 'Good grief!' gasped Bolas, staggering back from the door. 'If that really is the canopy breaking apart, then we could be swept into the Maelstrom!'

'No, friend,' said Jocaste fervently. 'We will be swept into a new world.'

Bolas frowned. More fanaticism? How could the world be new, if it were ending? But before he could reply there was a cry from above, a panicked shout from the lookout. Something was happening outside. He had to go on deck, thought Bolas. At the risk of Swallow's rage, he had to climb upstairs and see what was going on.

* * *

The sun had set, blood-red in the west, by the time Bolas finally staggered up to the deck. No one reprimanded him for being there, for all the ship's crew and not a few of the wounded were already glued to the deck-rail, peering through the twigs where the dirigible was moored. The gale had lasted two hours and devastated the south fringes of the Central Canopy, stripping foliage from the twigs. No rain had fallen, but every surface of the dirigible was coated with broken bark dust, littered with leaf-shards. Some of the ether sacks had snapped off their tethers, and the safety balloons were torn from their struts and swept away. It was clear that the hospice ship had been lucky to survive at all. But as the moon rose, equally red over a disturbingly low eastern horizon, and flocks of screaming margeese flew high above the ship in droves, the sailors realised that something far more terrible than a storm had occurred. Nothing the Jays had said could have prepared Bolas for the sight that met his eyes as he approached the deck-rail.

To the south, through the wind-bared twigs, he glimpsed a huge cloud of red dust, hanging like a glittering mushroom over the South Canopy. But instead of the misty reaches of the Lantrian leaf-table spreading below him in the evening light, instead of the rolling plateau of green where the Lantrian mines and the Spur of Sails and the Grand Duchy of Lant should have been, there was — nothing.

There was no South Canopy to be seen under the lurid moon. In its place was a New Gap, a southern Void as fathomless as the eastern one was wide. But this Gap was transparent: there was a clear hole in the cloud that had replaced the canopy, quite empty but for wisps of gathering mist. The ship was overlooking a well of nothingness. And through that gaping hole, in the gathering twilight of that unquiet evening, Bolas glimpsed something else, something dark and solid-seeming under the blood-tinged rags and whirling tatters of the Storm.

'*Lacuna*,' he whispered, remembering the old tale in amazement.

The cold of the Veil was absolute, the stars above the plain of ice no more than faraway pinpricks in the dark. A breeze rose up, whipping ice-particles into a vortex in the sky, then died down again, leaving cold, glittering silence in its wake.

A moment later, abrupt as a thunderclap, the icy surface of the Veil cracked open, revealing a black and jagged fissure. As the sides of the hole groaned apart, tall figures were thrown up like flotsam onto the floor of the prison world, rigid and frozen themselves. They were spewed out to lean drunkenly against each other, broken statues vomited up on the plain of ice. Then the fissure snapped shut and the Masters stood speechless, stunned into temporary submission, their faces angled up towards the stars. At that instant, they fleetingly resembled creatures of Matrya's ilk, their wide eyes and deep foreheads marked with the traces of lost wisdom.

The resemblance did not last for long. The Masters soon shook free from the torpor of the ice, the glittering particles streaming from their shoulders as they stirred and settled themselves into their familiar humps of shadow again. Their shapes wavered, their features losing definition. They discarded all hint of ancient majesty, and opted instead for vague, ill-fitting crowns and cloaks, a mere echo of kingliness.

'Well, at least we're rid of Matrya,' said one, spitting out the name with the last of the ice-dust on his lips. 'It took a whole canopy to kill her, but we did it.'

Hollow laughter greeted this comment, an attempt at triumphant bravado from the other Masters, but it soon died out, leaving uncertain silence.

'Shame we lost the boy's body, though,' opined a second.

'Cursed human vermin,' said a third, drawing his tattered robes about him haughtily. 'We don't need their filthy bodies, anyway.'

'But what about the Key?' asked another. 'It wasn't where we thought it would be: the acolytes were mistaken in their choice, it seems. We all were.'

There was an uncomfortable pause as the Masters brooded over this fact, hunched in their shadowy remnants. 'She tricked us,' complained the first. 'Matrya. She let us think the Key was a prize, an object to be won.'

'She led us astray,' said the others. 'She lied to us.'

'So, what now?' persisted the one who had asked the question about the Key. 'Matrya may be gone, but we have a new enemy. What should we do?'

His comments provoked a ripple of nervous reaction. The Masters glanced up at the sky, as if they felt themselves watched over by some nebulous foe. 'Wait and see, wait and see,' they whispered. 'We'll gather our strength, to fight again another day.'

'There is, of course, something else we could do,' put in the questioner.

He seemed less sure than his companions, his expression torn between pride and dim hope as he frowned up at the stars. 'We could sue for mercy,' he said doubtfully. 'We could make an appeal to the New Authority, now that the Old One has gone. We were told we could appeal.'

His comment was met by stony silence in the group. The other Masters seemed almost frozen in place, looming figures in the gloom. No one spoke a word.

'Or perhaps not,' mumbled the questioner, after a moment, faced with this mute resistance. 'Perhaps that won't do.'

He said no more. There was silence in the circle of the Masters, beneath the starry dome of the night sky; silence in the black and frozen wasteland of the Veil.

23

The noise was coming from above. Tymon struggled back to consciousness, feeling the thud of it in his veins, sensing a haze of red through his closed eyelids. He wondered dimly whether more Collectors had found him, and whether he would wake up in the execution chamber again. But that was impossible, he reasoned sleepily. The chamber had been destroyed and, besides, he was feeling warm all over; the hall of the living dead had been ice cold. Or perhaps the glow he felt pulsing on his eyelids was some fearful weapon Wick or the Masters were wielding over him. But no, he remembered with a pang of aching sorrow. Wick had wielded his weapon already, to devastating effect.

The innocence of sleep fled, and the image of Samiha lying dead in his lap flooded back to Tymon. He was no longer angry, no longer blaming himself or others. But his will to live seemed to have fled along with his fury. Now that Samiha really was gone, he felt that nothing he could do would ever matter. And with that thought settling in his chest like one of the sharp *rocks* of the World Below, he rolled over with a groan, and hid his face in his arms.

But the steady thrumming continued, insistent, mocking his despair. The noise grew louder, and the air grew warmer. That was when he finally opened his eyes and glanced about him. The first things he saw were the heads of his sleeping companions, lying on the green grass nearby. Zero's hair was the colour of fire and Jedda's matted curls gleamed like *orah*. Tymon blinked at the angelic creatures beside him in amazement: had they died after all, and was this the heaven the priests of Argos always talked about, where the faces of the blessed shone and their hair was spun of sunbeams and flame? And yet these angels looked decidedly grubby. Their faces were streaked with dust and tears, and Jedda's cheek bore a long red gash from Wick's knife stroke.

The light, Tymon realised, came from the sun itself. Long shafts of sunlight shone down through the fitful gaps in the Storm, bathing his friends' forms in a halo of warmth, and casting a pink and yellow glow over the grassy slope. He blinked up through the ring of *rock* sentinels, at the bright rays spilling through the clouds in the east. And then he saw the specks moving against the light, soaring high over the plain at the foot of the Tree, still plunged in shadow. A line of them, dotted across the low clouds.

His heart misgave: were these the Envoy's infernal curses once again? Had Lace found them, even here? But it was the specks that made the thrumming sound, he realised, and after a moment he recognised the distinctive silhouettes of the new air-chariots. There was a whole squadron of them. The Freeholders had come!

He scrambled up, staring at the five thrumming machines for a moment in disbelief. Then he leapt out of the ring of *rocks* with a cry, waving frantically to catch the attention of the air-chariots. But it seemed the pilots had already seen him. The machines were descending in slow spirals towards a patch of level ground about three hundred feet below, a grassy hillock on the lower slopes of the *mountain*.

'Zero! Jedda!' shouted Tymon over his shoulder to his sleeping companions. 'Look who's come for us!'

As the others sat up, rubbing their eyes and gazing at the arriving squadron in wonder, he began to run down the slope, tripping on the *rocks* and skidding on the *earth* to reach the place where the air-chariots had alighted. Soldiers in the long Farhang cloaks were the first to descend from the machines, equipped with crossbows and striding purposefully out to secure the perimeter of the hillock. They nodded to Tymon as he skidded to the bottom of the slope, but did not approach him. It was only when Oren and Noni stepped out of one of the air-chariots and ran to meet him, beaming with joy, did he realise there had been no need to try to signal their attention. His fellow Grafters had Seen him from afar.

An instant later, he was in their arms. It had been so long since he had tried to contact the Focals, that the first words out of his mouth as they drew apart were a chagrined apology.

'I never kept in touch,' he said. 'I'm so sorry, my friends.'

'It's we who are sorry,' answered Noni. 'We couldn't get through to you — we gave you up for dead. If it wasn't for the old scientist insisting on your behalf, we'd have gone on thinking there was nothing to find, just because we couldn't See it.'

'Even so, fog only lifts from our Sight last night,' said Oren, his merrily truncated Argosian now a balm to Tymon's ears. 'We do not know why: it is miracle. Before that, blindness was cloud.'

'That's partly my fault,' Tymon confessed, shamefaced. 'Since leaving you at the mine, Noni, I've made some horrible mistakes —'

'It wasn't his fault!' interrupted Jedda as she slithered down to the foot of the slope to join them. High above,

Zero could be seen negotiating a slower descent of the *mountain*. 'The Envoy and his Masters are to blame for everything,' Jedda continued, appealing to Oren and Noni. 'Tymon's been through Hell. Don't let him tell you otherwise.'

'And you brought me back from it,' answered Tymon, widening their circle to include her, though the two Freeholders stiffened slightly at Jedda's approach. They had not spoken to her since she defected, Tymon remembered.

'Jedda saved my life, you know,' he told them gently. 'She rescued me from the Veil. It's a long story.'

'It seems we all have tales to tell each other,' said Noni, inclining her head in a restrained but kindly greeting to the red-faced Jedda.

'Well, I'm glad of that,' called out a familiar, jovial voice. 'I love stories, and anyone who manages to prevent this young scamp from throwing his life away deserves my hearty thanks!'

Tymon turned around, with a thrill of surprise, to see a frail figure being helped out of the Grafters' air-chariot by Gardan. When Noni had mentioned Galliano, he had not thought the scientist would have accompanied the Freeholders himself.

'Apu!' he cried in amazement. 'You're here!'

'Did you really expect me to miss out on a trip to the World Below?' scolded Galliano, his sightless eyes fixed unerringly on Tymon. 'I almost thought I'd have to do it without you, though.'

'Well, I'm here now,' said Tymon, as he squeezed his old friend in a tight embrace. 'You've fulfilled the old dream after all, Apu. And you've brought company, it seems!'

Judges from both Farhang and Sheb, as well as others who appeared from the subtle differences in their clothes and dialect to come from further afield, were stepping out of the rest of the air-chariots. They paid Tymon and Jedda little heed, absorbed in the spectacle of the widespread destruction of the South Canopy, laid out below them in the morning light. About twenty Freeholders had travelled to the World Below, and they were clearly not all there to rescue the fugitives.

'Oh yes.' Galliano nodded vigorously to Tymon. 'It's everyone's dream now. Everyone wants to see *Lacuna*.' He bent down with a rheumy grunt to scoop up a handful of *earth* from the hillock, sniffing it and rubbing the granules between his fingers. 'And it's all made of this stuff, they tell me, for miles and miles!' he muttered in awe. 'Well, well. That would account for the extra mass in the equation ...'

'The United Freeholds are considering establishing a base in the World Below,' put in Gardan, stepping up to shake Tymon's hand with a smile, though her expression grew more reserved as she set eyes on Jedda. 'We've survived one of the Saint's crusades, but it won't be long before there's another. We have to think of alternatives. We left Farhang yesterday evening, right after the battle —'

'Battle?' interrupted Tymon, aghast. He turned to the Grafters. 'Is this true? You've been attacked again?'

'More long stories,' said Oren. 'We tell them later. Let *syora* go on.'

'We'd just put down for the night, south of Marak,' continued the Speaker, as Tymon subsided in embarrassment, 'when Oren said they knew where you were. I have to say, Tymon, your friends obviously love you: between Oren, Noni and Galliano, I was given no rest until we'd agreed to travel through the night to find you. It's a good thing there was a moon out.'

She broke off, gazing pensively at the plain of shards below the slope. 'Of course, by then, we knew something far more dramatic than a Tree-quake had occurred in the South, and wanted to see it for ourselves,' she said. 'And what a sight it is.'

'The whole Lantrian leaf-table!' exclaimed Galliano, lifting his face to sniff the wind. 'Though the phenomenon was not entirely unpredictable. Those branches have been weakened for years.'

'It's because the Oracle died,' sighed Tymon. Oren and Noni's faces fell at the news. 'And also — someone else,' he added softly.

He could not bring himself to say Samiha's name, and glanced away, his chest tight. It was Jedda who came to his rescue.

'The Kion wasn't killed in Argos,' she said to the astonished Freeholders. 'Tymon freed her from a prison here in the World Below. But one of the Envoy's servants followed us, and killed her last night.'

'Last night,' said Noni meaningfully to Oren. 'When the blindness lifted.'

Gardan seemed less impressed with Jedda's announcement, however. 'Another interesting tale, I'm sure,' she noted gravely. 'I'm sure we'll want to hear all you have to say for yourselves in a little while — especially you, Jedhartha Aditi.'

She fixed the young girl with her steady blue eyes, and Jedda wilted under her gaze. But Gardan did not push the matter further. 'For now, you have travelled far and sustained great loss,' she continued, turning back to Tymon. 'I suggest we all eat something and replenish our strength. There are provisions in the air-chariots.'

Zero finally reached the bottom of the slope and limped to Tymon's side, grinning. 'Such a fine lot of evil friends you have!' he said approvingly, glancing about him at the Nurian judges strolling around the hillock, or gathered in small groups to inspect the *earth* and *rocks*. 'We'll survive anything now, *Syon*.'

* * *

Although they would have seen any interloper approaching on the open slope from a mile off, no one was able to rest easy with the thought of Wick roaming free. Gardan promised Tymon and his friends, as they all sat down to eat their breakfast on the grassy hillock, that the judges would send out an air-chariot as soon as possible to scour the slopes of the *mountain*, to see if they could pinpoint the whereabouts of their enemy. The assurance was good enough for Tymon, who at that point wished never to speak of Wick again, though he knew very well he would have to relate the story of the acolyte's attack sometime.

For now, after a day of fasting, the simple Nurian travelling rations were a heavenly respite. No seminary banquet had ever tasted better to Tymon than this feast of dried figs, cheese and flatbread. Better yet, he was finally able to dispel his anxieties regarding the battle with the Argosians. During the meal Gardan told him the tale of how the Freeholders had prevailed against the Saint's first crusade, despite the Envoy's near-fatal interference. Sorcerers' powers, it seemed, had been given a little more credence by ordinary Nurians since the encounter with the unnatural cloud. Although the battle was narrowly considered a victory for Farhang, the Freeholders were under no illusion as to their future prospects.

'Fallow will fight this war for another hundred years, with or without his Envoy,' sighed Gardan, when she had finished her account. 'He'll see it as a way of proving his legitimacy as the Saint. And the Argosians have ten such fleets to throw at us. They don't need spooky clouds to wear us down! There's nothing to stop them from doing an about-turn on the question of air-chariots, just as they did with the blast-cannons; and the day they do that, the Freeholds are finished.'

'So you see, I convinced them,' Galliano crowed triumphantly from the sidelines. 'I finally got it through their sensible heads. The Freeholders will never be able to defend themselves, long-term, against Argosian attacks. And a good thing, too.'

Tymon shook his head in puzzlement. 'What's so good about that?' he asked.

'Our future lies not in defending miserable little corners of the Tree, but in settling a whole new world,' said the old man. He ran his fingers through the light loam of the hillock beside him, a smile stretched across his blind face. 'This is perfect soil, by the way. It only needs a bit of sunlight to be useful to us.'

'*Soil?*' Tymon stared at him. It was another one of those words.

'Better yet, grass.' Galliano pulled up a hair of feathery green. 'Anything will grow here now, my friends. Anything!'

To their astonishment, he began a lecture on the fertile properties of *soil*, and how it contained a thousand invisible and ancient grains, known to the Old Ones and long disused in the Tree, some of which were edible and some of which were not. They could establish a colony in the World Below, announced Galliano: they need not fight over the dying Tree and its pitiful rainfall. They could simply start again here, start anew. With that, Tymon remembered Samiha's last injunction: *bring them down, all of them*, and wondered belatedly if she had meant that humanity should settle in the World Below. In that case, he thought ruefully, the old scientist was already far ahead of him in carrying out her wishes.

Tymon's reprieve from the judges' scrutiny did not last for long. Galliano's speech was interrupted when

Aythan joined the group, accompanied by two other sombre-faced judges. They had come, they announced, to hear the testimony of the travellers, if they were sufficiently refreshed; they had come, they said, as their eyes slid coldly towards Jedda, to hear the strangers explain themselves. Aythan, once Jedda's identity had been confirmed, was clearly shocked to see a traitor treated with such hospitality. In fact, he stood up as soon as she was named, pulling his Farhang cloak about him in deep umbrage, and would not even hear her testimony until Gardan vouched personally for her good behaviour.

So it was Jedda, pale and ill at ease before the scowling judges, who gave a first brief account of her break with Lace, testifying to Pallas' death at the hands of the priests and her own departure from Argos, and humbly begging her hosts' forgiveness. A temporary freedom on parole was granted her by Gardan, pending the vote of the judges on her status. When Tymon protested that Jedda deserved a full and immediate pardon for all she had done to help him, and that they had not heard her whole story, Gardan assured him in a kind but brisk manner that the judges would give due weight to his testimony.

'Then you will hear it,' he said hotly. 'The testimony — the whole story. Right now.'

And that was exactly what he did. He told them everything that had happened since he left Noni, making no bones about his own foolishness in following the Masters. He spoke of his journey with Zero through the mine, their arrival in the World Below, and the *orah*-couches in the ancient hall. He told his listeners how he had allowed the Masters to trick him out of his body. Then he told them, insisting on it although she tried to interrupt, of Jedda's battle with the Envoy's curses, a part of her story she had omitted to mention. Two spots of red embarrassment appeared in the Nurian girl's cheeks as he spoke of her bravery, corroborated by Oren and Noni, who shared the details of their vision. She reddened still further as Tymon went on to recount how she had survived capture by the Envoy's acolytes and attempted to save the Kion's testament, only to suffer a mortal attack from the Masters. And he told them all, as Jedda sat hunched and crimson over the remains of the meal, how she had died on the beach and been called to life again — by Samiha's voice.

He choked then with emotion, and there was a moment of silence as the judges and the Focals waited for him to command himself. For in all that had been said, in all that had been shared so far, Tymon had barely been able to speak Samiha's name. Noni gazed at him, her face full of compassion. Oren turned aside and bowed his head. Only Jedda had the courage to reach out, slip a very grimy hand into Tymon's, and squeeze it.

He allowed her to be the one to continue the story of the Kion's awakening in the hall, and all that followed, for he was still unable to put words to that dry lump of grief. Jedda's voice was stronger now as she faced the judges, the confidence back in her tone as she told of their journey up the *mountain* with Samiha, and Wick's final treachery. When she finished recounting their fruitless hunt for the murderer and the Kion's burial, no one said a thing. The other Freeholders, who had gathered one by one at the fringes of the group to listen to the tale, stared at the three travellers with renewed respect. Not even Aythan made any remark; the silence on the hillock was broken only by the wind whispering in the grass.

Tymon cleared his throat and stood up, pulling Jedda to her feet beside him. The young Focals, Gardan and Aythan rose too, feeling the solemnity of the moment.

'I ask the Freeholders to pardon my twining sister, even as the Kion did,' Tymon said to them, lifting Jedda's hand cupped in his own, and directing her towards Gardan and Aythan. 'And I ask my fellow Focals to receive and forgive one of their own, for she is truly a Grafter.' He glanced towards Oren and Noni, who immediately nodded, tears in their eyes.

'I ask you also to receive my brother, Zero,' continued Tymon formally to the gathered judges.

He had to pull the red-haired lad up by the arm and into their circle, for Zero had remained seated by Galliano, preoccupied with his meal. Gardan smiled at him kindly, and Zero's face beamed with joy. With his fellow travellers on either side of him, Tymon looked at each one of the judges, holding their eyes in turn.

'If you must pass judgment on someone after this, do so on me,' he finished quietly.

But his plea had the edge of a challenge, and no one dared speak a word about freedom on parole after that, or voting on Jedda's status. The usually sceptical Freehold judges even refrained from questioning Tymon's story of uncanny creatures from other worlds, though the tale of the Masters went far beyond any accepted notions of what a Grafter could or could not do. Galliano, who had listened to Tymon without making a single objection, nodded and made approving noises at his descriptions of the Old Ones' technology. Perhaps, the young man thought wryly, the Freeholders were feeling more indulgent towards such ideas, because they had recently set foot in another world themselves. *Lacuna*, too, had once been derided as a myth. As to Jedda, she threw a grateful glance at Tymon following his staunch support of her, and held her head higher from then on, meeting the Freeholders' eyes directly and without fear.

While Gardan and the other judges conferred in low voices, and Galliano continued to hold forth on *soil* to anyone who would listen, the young people occupied themselves in activities that were blessedly mundane. They gathered up the remaining food, made a fire with tinder sticks and warmed some water so that Jedda, Tymon and Zero could wash away the stain of their trials. Noni arranged for a bundle of spare supplies to be opened and one of the air-chariots to be used as a changing room, where they were able to strip away their rags, and dress themselves in warmer clothes. The cut on Jedda's cheek proved to be shallow, though long and ugly, and Noni was satisfied it would heal well with proper care and attention.

It was only then, as the five friends talked in the air-chariot, that Tymon and Jedda heard the full tale of the victory in Farhang, beyond air-chariots and military manoeuvres. Oren showed them the precious roll of the Kion's testament which he kept stowed in his pack, passing it with great reverence around the group. At the sight of this full copy written in Anise's flowing script, Jedda burst into another abrupt tempest of tears; all the others were able to understand from her garbled confession was that she was very glad the Jays had survived long enough to bring the Easterners their copy, and that she was very sorry for any indignities they may have suffered as a result.

Then, too, with the Kion's testament in his hands, Tymon related the exact circumstances of Matrya's death to his friends. He had glossed over the details of the Oracle's physiognomy to the judges, unwilling to challenge them further with tales of a blue-eyed giant whose life was enmeshed with that of the Tree. The Focals were as mystified by the Oracle's so-called 'seed-form' as Tymon had been, though Jedda said she had once heard Lace claim the Born had come from another world before creating this one, a world far up in the sky. Perhaps that was why, she suggested humbly, Matrya looked so different.

'There are worlds above and worlds below,' she said. 'Worlds in Trees, and worlds in loam. And also floating up among the stars, apparently.'

'People from the stars?' asked Tymon curiously, remembering the frieze on the first column in the ancient hall. 'But how would they get all the way here?'

Jedda shook her head. 'He never told me. He always acted as if the Born were the only beings that mattered in the universe. Maybe nothing he said was true.'

'Oh, *Syon*.' Zero jumped up from where he had been sitting in the air-chariot's hatchway, half-listening to the Grafters' conversation, and rummaged in the pocket of his dusty slave's uniform lying abandoned on the floor. 'I forgot,' he said. 'I found this when you dropped it in the mine. It shone like a star in the darkness, too.'

He drew out the little pendant Samiha had given to Tymon long ago, marked with the Kion's rune. Tymon accepted it back with mingled joy and sadness, for he had not even realised in the chaos that it was gone. He did not put it on again immediately, however, staring down at the carved pendant on its cord. It seemed to symbolise a part of him that was gone forever. Oren and Noni exchanged a glance at his hesitation.

'I'm no longer the Kion's defender,' Tymon said to them, after a moment. 'Do you know if there will ever be a new king or queen of Nur?'

'No one knows,' replied Noni. 'Samiha did have some distant cousins, but they all gave up ties to the Freeholds when the seminary paid them off. We haven't heard from them in years.'

'Well,' sighed Tymon, 'be that as it may, this should go to the new defender, if there is one.'

He tried to give the pendant back to Oren, but the young Grafter would not accept it. 'Not mine to give,' he said, shaking his head. 'You know right person.'

And then, quite simply, Tymon did. He rose and stepped up to where Jedda was sitting, and slipped the pendant about her neck before she could object.

'You're the perfect person to have this,' he said to her, forestalling her protests. And to her deep embarrassment and surprise, he bent down and kissed her solemnly on the forehead.

Just then, Gardan poked her head through the air-chariot's hatchway. She raised a wry eyebrow when she saw Tymon embracing Jedda, but did not comment on it.

'It's time,' she said to the young people. 'We'd like to pay our respects now — Tymon, we'd appreciate it if you might lead the way up to the Kion's grave.'

The procession bound for Samiha's resting place wound up the grassy slope at a far more leisurely pace than Tymon had descended it that morning, and far more slowly than he would have liked. Apart from the judges, Galliano had joined the company at the last moment, leaning on Gardan's arm. The scientist's shrill tones reached Tymon at the head of the line, claiming that a high place like this was perfect, just perfect, and they should establish the colony right here, where the sunlight was strongest. Galliano stopped every few minutes to wave his arms left and right with blind propriety.

Tymon chafed at the delay. He wanted to run full tilt up to the field of *rocks*, for he was suddenly impatient to be by the graveside again. It was almost as if the spot by the spring called to him. He longed to be watching over it; he half-fancied he could hear a faint voice summoning him to the top of the slope, an intoxicating melody just on the edge of perception. But the judges saw no reason to run, and he was obliged to trudge up the slope at their stately, crawling pace.

Preoccupied by his desire to reach the top, he did not say much to his friends, leaving them to talk quietly among themselves, or sing snatches of Samiha's poetry. Noni and Oren had learned much of the Kion's testament off by heart, as had Jedda, and they exchanged different renditions of the verses as they walked, Jedda sharing the version sung by the Jays while the Focals gave their own chant a distinctly Eastern twist. Their song reminded Tymon of Samiha's call from the temple roof in Marak. To his surprise, the recollection did not sadden him. It echoed the voice — imagined? real? — that throbbed frustratingly just on the edge of his hearing, from the top of the slope.

'Be the wind, be the flame,' hummed Zero, trudging beside him. 'It's pretty, isn't it, Syon? Spirit words have power.'

Tymon nodded, distracted by the peculiar sense of excitement that had taken hold of him. He did not know why, but he could barely breathe for it. As they crested the slope and entered the field of rocks, Oren, Noni and Jedda stopped singing, walking in respectful silence. The judges and Galliano had by this time fallen some distance behind them. Although Tymon peered eagerly about him at the grassy slope, searching for any sign of change, he could see nothing unusual, no reason to be anxious. The serenity of Samiha's grave seemed unbroken as they approached the ring of sentinels, the two flat rocks lying undisturbed on the ground.

But even as he laid eyes on them, Tymon gave a gasp of surprise, and ran the last few feet to the graveside, dropping to his knees on the loam. He heard Jedda's sharp intake of breath behind him. There, where they had buried the body of Samiha — where there had been nothing but loam and grass the night before — a tall green shoot was pushing through the *soil* of the grave, poking out between the flat *rocks*. Its straight stem was robust and elegant, and two delicate green leaves had already unfurled at its crown.

For a long time no one said a word, staring speechless at the young plant. Then Zero clapped his hands. '*Syon*,' he cried. 'It's a new Tree!'

And then Tymon did weep, the sharp lump of grief breaking apart in his heart to release a flood. He bowed his head, his shoulders shaking. Oren and Noni drew back to give him space, and Jedda urged Zero away. The judges now arriving in twos and threes at the ring of *rocks* stopped short, arrested by the sight of the green shoot pushing through the loam. They stared in wonder at the sapling growing with mysterious speed from Samiha's grave.

The bells of Argos seminary were silent in the days following the collapse of the Divine Mouth, though the city teemed with anxious activity. Despite the fact that these were neither designated days of rest nor a holy festival, the markets remained closed. People from all walks of life, fat burghers and seminary students, peasants and moneylenders, hurried like so many ants through the streets, crying that the End was nigh. The weather appeared to agree with them, for since the Tree-quake the Central Canopy had been darkened under an almost perpetual cloud. Signs and omens were noted in the heavens: the moon rose red three nights in a row, and flocks of birds travelled north unseasonably, filling the skies with their mournful cries. Witnesses started up their bloody rituals again, and housewives went out in their nightclothes with their hair pulled down to their shoulders, waving sheets on which they had scrawled messages of doom.

'The Tree is falling!' they wailed. 'Save us, Saint Loa, give us your grace!'

Alone atop the bell tower, on the third overcast morning after the Tree-quake, the Envoy contemplated the scurrying humans below with disgust. He had been too late to catch Tymon and Jedda in the Veil, and had been obliged to return to Argos city the long way round, in physical space, for he could not simply step into the prison dimension in one spot and step out again in another. Such facilities were denied him by his jailors. Three nights and days it had taken him, therefore, flying nonstop in his bat-forms back to his base of operations in Argos, only to find this scene of chaos flowering in his absence. His lips curled in disdain at the sight of the foolish placards of the townsfolk, their silly banners. He paced the space beneath the silent bells, round and round, from side to side, seeing the same panic, the same brainless hysteria everywhere.

His acolytes had succeeded almost too well in their task, he thought grimly. Of course, he knew that the quakes due to the Oracle's death would not undermine the whole Tree, but that was hardly what the good people of Argos were capable of imagining. The celestial omens, of course, were simply an effect of the dust raised by the South Canopy's fall and the homeless birds another sign of that disaster. He knew that the last of the living Born had entwined her body to the Tree-roots many eons ago, and that the area where she was entombed would be the worst affected. Even a scientist as blind as Galliano might have understood that, thought Lace, biting his lip at the annoying reminder of the latter's escape. But from the way these fools were running around, anyone would think the Four Canopies were experiencing their final demise.

Never mind, he told himself as he passed the ladder leading down to the room below the bells, for the third time. This was the moment to gather his resources, to contemplate past victories and measure triumphs to come. He would be able to use these so-called omens to his advantage; he could sway the superstitious, and regain Fallow's allegiance, perhaps, which had been badly shaken by the losses in Farhang. But most importantly, as soon as the World Key was his, he would find favour again with his Masters. Even their minor humiliation at the hands of Tymon, which he felt pressing on him, a bubbling echo from the Veil, caused him no serious anxiety. On the contrary, he was pleased to imagine the bird-kings temporarily humbled by a mere human being, and nursing their outrage.

They needed a reminder every century or so, he sneered to himself, of why they had been imprisoned in the first place; a reminder of just how much they had lost when they refused to be written into the Tree of Being, and born as one of the mortal scum, like Samiha and her ilk. He, Eblas, had chosen to remain pure and strong, sharing his Masters' fate. They would be his to influence again, now, if only through the efforts of this irritating young Grafter — and through Jedda's, the Envoy thought, with a stab of annoyance.

For his former student had been the one to free Tymon, wandering into the Veil with impunity and singing the Kion's hard, bright verses in Eblas' dark kennel. It made him want to throw back his head and howl at the closed Mouth in the trunk-wall opposite. How the humans infuriated him. Despite all their failings, they still somehow managed to escape his influence. How could something so weak be so stubborn?

Not for the first time did Lace feel remorse at having

failed to capture the smoky allegiance of Tymon and Jedda. He had almost had them both, at different moments, almost caught them in the mesh of their own pride and fear. By now, they would have made acolytes worthy of the name, infinitely stronger than Wick, infinitely more intelligent than Gowron. Tymon would not have failed in his missions; Jedda would have lent her master her indomitable strength, without always begging for treats in return. How unlike his own acolytes, who were so ready to assume all rewards in advance, though they had as yet achieved nothing.

In fact, there was just one thing that nagged him about this whole apocalyptic scenario orchestrated by Gowron and Wick. Where in the Hell under the Tree were his acolytes now? Surely they had not been crushed beneath the canopy's fall, for he had warned them of the possibility, told them to exit the Oracle's tomb after her death and seek shelter elsewhere, preferably on higher ground. But if they had reached the air-chariot or escaped by other means, he could not sense it. He had lost touch with them for over twelve hours: he could no longer See them under the Storm. The cloud he had sent to blind the Focals seemed to have descended over his eyes. When would the fools bring him the World Key? Or had they — and the thought gave him pause as he paced beneath the bells — had the idiots actually sought to keep it for themselves? Lace stopped walking and closed his eyes, uttering a soft oath. Of course they had.

It would not help them. He would have it back in a trice, and have their guts too, while he was at it, to dangle from the bells. They did not have the first idea how to work an artefact of the Born. The World Key was an item even the Masters did not possess the secret to, for it could, and did, change form over the centuries. The accounts of it in ancient times would be of no use to him now. Lace would have to study the Key in person. He would get it back from whichever of his imbecile acolytes had it now — for they would be sure to quarrel over it — and inspect it thoroughly and warily, before attempting to use it.

He had taken a step back towards the ladder leading to the room where Samiha had once been kept, determined to seek out and punish his errant servants, when the Envoy had the shock of his life. There on the roof before him, as plain as day, stood the Kion herself. But her form was bleeding light, almost too bright to contemplate.

'Eblas,' she said, in ringing tones. 'Enough.'

Lace felt faint at the sight of her, his construct-body suddenly lacking solidity. He swallowed, eyeing the bright Being on the roof before him.

'My world is weary of your intrigues,' she told him.

Although her words caused the substance of his borrowed flesh to wither, she was beautiful when she spoke. The Envoy quailed. What was this? Why did Samiha's shade radiate such damnable majesty, making him cower before her? And then, he understood. She was free. Her seed-form must have finally expired; it was bound to happen, eventually.

'You have no right to be here,' he barked. 'You're dead.' The memory of uttering those same words to Matrya when she had saved Tymon from the Veil returned, disconcerting him slightly. He pushed the thought away.

'Is that so?' asked Samiha, unmoved.

Her serenity was appalling to him. 'According to your own confounded rules,' he growled, 'if your seed-form dies, you have no right to act in this world directly. You must be content to leave the action to others, just like Matrya did.'

Samiha only smiled. 'You're greatly mistaken in

thinking me dead, or Matrya gone. Both of us,' and she began to laugh, 'are very much here.'

The Envoy shuddered at her laughter. It swept like a sudden gust around him, buffeting him in its breeze, tickling his wraith-like substance apart. He had to rub his arms in order to reassure himself they still existed.

'And you, Eblas.' She did not stop smiling, her gaze too bright and clear to meet. 'Do you know where your World Key is?'

'Certainly!' retorted the Envoy, edging towards the ladder and safety. 'My acolytes have it. They are bringing it to me!'

But Samiha's laughter only increased. She raised her right hand, pointing to the sunlight peeping through the leaf-forests above, a ray of relief after days of grey gloom. The gesture, like a wind, thrust the Envoy backwards and away from the ladder. He was pushed step by step towards the opposite side of the roof alcove, step by inexorable step, until he let out a cry of horror. For there was nothing he could do to stop the wind from pushing him off the tower.

'You have no right!' he shouted to Samiha. 'You can't meddle with humanity directly!'

'Oh, Eblas,' she said, laughing all the more and shaking her head. 'I am not meddling with humanity at all. As far as I can see, I'm meddling with you — and did you not fight for the right to remain "pure of blood", unmixed with the "human taint", as you called it? You refused to live as one of them, shorn of your precious power and influence.' She paused a moment, looking him up and down, as if reconsidering the question. 'No,' she continued, still smiling. 'You are not human. Not even a little bit. Not at all.'

Back, back, and back again the Envoy was thrust. He screamed as he teetered on the edge of the bell tower, pushed by the inexorable force of Samiha's mirth — howled once, in terror and disbelief, then tumbled over the edge.

He fell to his ruin in the quadrangle before the shocked gaze of Fallow and his coterie of priests, just as they were exiting the Library building. Before the Envoy's false body even hit the ground, its component parts were blown to shreds, leaving only a few shards of bone and tufts of hair rolling on the bark at Fallow's feet. And when the priests cast their eyes up to the top of the tower, searching for whoever, or whatever, had caused their Envoy's demise, all they could see were shafts of sunlight breaking through the clouds to strike the alcove beneath the bells.

EPILOGUE

Tymon did not move from the side of the sapling for three days and nights. He watered it carefully from the pool, shifting the flat *rocks* apart on the grave so that the tender plant might have room to grow, and watched over it with jealous care. The others did not ask for his reasons or question his choice, at least to begin with. No one mentioned Wick, either, but they all sensed Tymon's concern to protect the young Tree from the threat that had helped destroy the old one. They knew he wanted to ensure no harm touched the sapling, no mischief came to it. On the first night, Jedda took it in turns with him to guard it, allowing him to snatch a few hours of rest huddled in blankets by the grave.

On the second morning, however, she was drawn away to help Galliano conduct a survey of the surrounding area in one of the air-chariots, and Tymon was left on his own with the young Tree. Thereafter, the Nurian girl spent increasing amounts of time with the scientist, apparently happy to act as Galliano's surrogate eyes. He, for his part, was grateful for her help, and praised her enquiring mind. Zero in the meantime attached himself rather touchingly to Noni, claiming that she also had 'strong spirit-friends'. The young Grafters, used to collecting waifs and strays in their travels, accepted this additional member of their family without a qualm.

The judges and the rest of the Freeholders spent those three days carrying out multiple scouting expeditions in the air-chariots, searching for the best possible location for their base in the World Below. Tymon's companions would sometimes climb up to the grave to visit him, bringing him news of the scouts' latest discoveries, or fresh provisions. On these occasions, they invariably found him kneeling over the sapling, murmuring to the new leaves that sprouted thick and fast from its crown. He would stop talking to the Tree when the others arrived, but they began to suspect there might be another reason for his refusal to leave it, a reason that went over and above any concerns for its safety. Tymon's only personal request was that they bring him the Kion's testament to study. Apart from that, he seemed content to be close to the sapling, and required little else. His friends had the sense that he would have forgotten to eat had they not brought him the food, and placed it on his lap.

On the afternoon of the second day, Jedda set out for Tymon's camp to report an important discovery made by one of the scouting parties. The Tree, she saw as she arrived at the top of the slope, had grown with astonishing speed to about the level of her chest, its trunk as thick as her right arm. She eyed it with awe as she approached the gravesite, its shivering explosion of green leaves bright against the ring of grey rocks. The Grafters could find no reason for its extraordinary growth, except what touched on the mystery of Samiha's being. Tymon was sitting beneath it, apparently deep in thought, a blanket wrapped about his shoulders against the chill breeze. He would not have shown such foresight on his own — Jedda had put the blanket on him herself, on a previous visit. He did not look as if he had moved since then.

The pages of the Kion's testament lay in a neat pile by his side.

'They found Wick,' Jedda told him as she arrived by his side, without preamble.

Tymon glanced up at her, smiling faintly. She felt his preoccupation through the twining link that still existed between them; her news did not shock him in the least. It was as if he had already heard it.

'He was walking far to the west,' she continued, when Tymon did not answer. 'Crossing the plain below the trunk, through a desert of these *rocks*. He didn't look up or notice the air-chariot, and just kept rambling on. They think he's gone mad. Gardan's happy to send soldiers out to deal with him, but wanted to check with you, first. She says he'll die of exposure anyway, given the state he's in.'

Still Tymon remained silent, considering her with his calm smile. She waited patiently, telling herself that his behaviour was perfectly understandable, after all he had gone through, and it would take time for him to return to his normal self. When he spoke to her at last, it was not regarding Wick. His tone was distant but reasonable enough.

'I've finished it,' he said, picking up the sheaf of testament papers and handing it to her. 'I see why you wanted me to read it. Thank you, Jedda. I hope you don't mind returning it now.'

'I'll give it to Oren,' she mumbled, accepting the papers. 'But I need an answer regarding Wick, Tymon.'

'Wick.' He repeated the name, sighing. 'Yes. Of course.' He said no more for a moment, lost in thought. 'It's sad,' he continued, just as she was beginning to fidget with impatience. 'Even when we were at school together, he was the same. Always afraid. Always hiding. He would never show his true face to anyone: he thought we would hate him. And now he has left us, gone as far as he can go.'

Then he fell silent again, so that Jedda was obliged to prompt him. 'Well, do you want us to go after him?' she asked. 'I have to tell Gardan something.'

'Tell her there's no need to send soldiers,' he replied, shaking off his reverie and smiling again. 'Wick won't trouble us. In fact, I think he's going to stay as far away from the new Tree as possible. Don't worry, Jedda. Everything's going to be alright.'

'What about you?' She gazed at him in distress. 'Are you going to be alright, Tymon?'

The worried questions tumbled off her tongue, for she could see he was entirely uninterested in human company. Already, as if he had decided their interview was at a close, his eyes were sliding away from her, concerned only with the Tree.

He did not reply for another heartbeat. When he looked back at Jedda, his expression was perplexed, as if he, too, were asking himself that question.

'I think so,' he said mildly. 'Do you remember how you felt when the Masters almost killed you, and Samiha sent you back? How you knew certain things afterwards, but didn't really want to talk about them? Well, it's like that for me, at the moment. I'm not quite ready to talk about it.'

'I understand,' Jedda whispered, for she knew exactly what he meant.

She still had not spoken to him of all the Kion had told her in that fleeting space between life and death — of the glimpse she had been given of her possible future, her part in creating a new world so that others might be free, even as she had tried so hard to be. It was a vision that concerned Tymon, too, but whether it came to pass depended on what he and the others did in the coming days and weeks. For that was how the Born prophecies worked, Jedda had come to understand: however wonderful the vision, it was only a template, a plan, useless without the will to put it into effect. Like the secret blueprint folded deep within a seed, it gave direction and character to growth. But it did not guarantee results. A seed might never germinate. It was up to ordinary people, with all their faults and blunderings, to bring the prophecies to pass — and when they did, the result would not be perfect, but beautiful, flawed, real. The future, Jedda understood, had been entrusted like a delicate seedling to her care, and it was her responsibility to make it grow.

But would Tymon take up the challenge? Would he lay aside his grief and quit the past for the present, carrying out his task? Jedda could not help wondering, quailing a little for her friend as she left him. Walking down the slope, she glanced over her shoulder to see that he had already turned back to the sapling, stretching out his right hand and placing his palm against the trunk, as if in silent communion. But the Tree, for all its vigorous growth, was only a Tree. It could not talk.

He would come down, she supposed, when he was ready.

She's right, you know. You can't stay here forever.

It was not precisely a voice: more like sunshine slanting on Tymon's mind as he watched Jedda walk away. The words of the Samiha Tree settled in his heart, like leaves on the surface of a clear pool.

'She doesn't know I hear you,' he whispered to the smooth bark of the sapling. 'None of them do. Give me a little longer. One more day.'

After that you must return.

He gave a wry half-smile. 'So, what would you have answered?' he asked the Tree. 'Am I going to be alright?'

I have no doubt of it.

'I won't be what they call normal.'

You speak to trees. There was a quality to the voice in Tymon's mind that might have been laughter, an effect like shivering foliage in the wind. *That's hardly normal.*

'I'd rather be considered mad, and always hear you.'

They will not think you mad. Not those who actually listen to what you have to say.

Tymon did not need the Grafter's Sight to understand that the sapling burgeoning from Samiha's grave was no ordinary plant. Nor was it simply the beginnings of a new World Tree. Whether it would eventually grow into another giant, all-encompassing environment like the world of his birth, he did not know. But even as Matrya's life had been enmeshed with that of the first Tree, the second was mysteriously linked with Samiha. His love was still present, still with him, though in a form most would not recognise. She did not speak to him in words and phrases, as Matrya had done, for she was one step further away, no longer in possession of her 'seed-form'. But she whispered to Tymon in the language of knotted bark and wind on grass, falling water and stirring leaves. He always understood what she meant. And she understood him.

'I'll miss you,' he told the Tree.

You will return here when your work is done. For now, you have a message to deliver.

He glanced again at Jedda's lanky form disappearing down the slope, knee-deep in grass and carrying the bundled testament under her arm.

'You told them everything already, of course,' he remarked to the Tree. 'In your own words. You don't really need me.'

They need you. There is the word, and the one who speaks the word — the story and the storyteller. Two different but complementary things. And you have words of your own to share, a tale only you can tell. The world needs your way of Seeing, and most of all your way of Listening.

Tymon had realised belatedly, after his first pilgrimage to the grave with the Freeholders, that no one else, not even his Grafter friends, heard Samiha's voice. Even Oren and Noni thought the new Tree was just a new Tree, though that was extraordinary enough in itself. The sapling grew with astonishing speed, burgeoning before Tymon's very eyes. If he left the graveside to sleep or refresh himself, he was sure to find the supple trunk taller when he returned; if he glanced away even for an instant, he found fresh green buds when he turned back.

His companions, it seemed, could not bear to contemplate the young Tree's vitality too closely. They gazed at it in awe and fear when they approached, practically running away once their errand was done. To Tymon, their visits were like fleeting dreams, the Freeholders' activity on the slopes below no more than the buzzing of insects. Time had little meaning; it might have been a few minutes that he sat beside the Tree, rather than days. He only knew that hours had passed because his friends told him so. After they left, he returned to his conversation with Samiha as soon as possible, speaking the language of greenness and entirety with her, the language of Union.

For there were no divisions here, in the presence of his Beloved. Tymon's communion with the Tree included all within its circle: the wind in the grass, the *earth* underfoot, the Storm clouds in the sky. It encompassed the busy Nurians who rushed about in their air-chariots, exploring the World Below, and the Argosian sailors in their dirigibles overhead, staring down in shock at the hole where the South Canopy used to be. It reached out to Caro and his rebel forces, holed up in their wilderness hideout in the East, and the Lantrian pirates in Cherk Harbour, already scheming to resurrect their poisonous Company. The circle even included the deranged and murderous Wick, wandering lost on the desert plain, a faraway echo of bloody misery. Going farther still, it encompassed the crouched form of Eblas, cringing before his Masters' wrath in the Veil. All were part of the Letter of Union, whether they knew it or not. All were connected, though they fought each other tooth and nail, struggling for ascendency.

There was no Heaven or Hell, no saved or damned, no us and them in the presence of the Tree. There was only a cycle of change that must be completed, distance and nearness, cold and warmth, rain and drought. His task, the young Oracle told Tymon, with a shiver of leaves and a soughing of wind through the grass, was to close the circle. He was to gather together everyone he could, all who were lost, and bring them home again. All might see the new world, even the Argosian priests, if they desired it. *All of them*, Samiha repeated ceaselessly. *Tell all of them*. He had one simple task to accomplish for her, one message to deliver. If he had to leave her side for a while, he knew it was ultimately to draw the circle back again.

Another day passed after Jedda's visit, and a night. By the third morning of his vigil, the Tree had grown to the height of a man, its branches spread in a sheltering green canopy over Tymon's head. And he was aware that the time had come for them to part.

'Now?' he sighed, though the question contained no bitterness. 'Must it be?'

If you did not leave, how could you hope to return?

'It's dark and cold out there, without you. What they call life is more like death.'

Without darkness, how would you recognise the light? Without absence there is no reunion.

'That's poetic, but it doesn't help me.'

You will bear it, said the Samiha Tree. *You have work to do. Listen closely, and you will hear my voice anywhere in the world. Look at the hearts of those you love, and find them beating with the Sap-fire. I am with you, always with you.*

Besides, she whispered a moment later, her voice a quiver of sunlight through the branches, *there are those who See clearly, and are ready to help. They are precious: in them I burn bright.*

'Bolas,' exclaimed Tymon in surprise.

For at that moment, he had glimpsed a vision of his old friend in the space between the Tree's branches, limping down the quays in Argos city to fall weeping into Nell's arms. Had Bolas lost a leg? Other brief images followed, though whether of the past or future Tymon could not tell: Masha in her bed, Amu Bibi eternally at work with her broom, and a vision of Jocaste chanting in a prison cell. Where was Anise?

Those are absent friends. Others are already here, of course. The one who arrives now will be the first to champion your cause.

Tymon looked up to find Oren's faraway figure climbing the slope towards him, his face a bright speck in the morning sun.

Oren had delayed as long as possible on that third day, before finally walking up to the grave, reluctant to give Tymon news of their departure. His friend, he knew, would be loath to leave, though Wick was far away or dead by now, and everyone else more than ready to depart. But Gardan had not minced her words that morning: there had been enough mystic communion at Samiha's graveside, Tree or no Tree, she had announced. The scouting expeditions were over, their provisions were running low, and the judges' minds were made up. It was time to go. Other expeditions would set out from the Freeholds in the coming weeks, to further explore the World Below.

But their own task was to return home. As Oren trudged up the slope to Samiha's resting place, the final bundles were being loaded into the air-chariots in preparation for departure. They would leave with or without Tymon. The latter prospect weighed heavily on Oren's mind.

He had expected to find his friend sitting in a half-dream, as had been the case every time he visited him over the past three days. And indeed, when Oren caught sight of the young man at the top of the slope, he was in his usual cross-legged position by the sapling. But as he approached, Tymon rose to meet him, his expression grave and alert. The long blanket wrapped about his shoulders gave him an oddly regal look. Oren came to an uncertain halt before him.

'It is time, *Syon*,' he said apologetically. 'They wait … Gardan and the others. Air-chariots are ready.'

He tried to take hold of Tymon's elbow, to lead him down the slope, but the other lad was immovable, fixing him with his steady gaze.

'Samiha spoke to me,' he told Oren, as if this were a natural response to all questions of staying or leaving. 'She gave me a message for the Freeholders.'

For an instant, Oren felt his heart skip a beat. But he told himself that this was just a grieving man's fantasy. Tymon was in mourning for Samiha, hardly the right frame of mind to experience a proper Grafter vision. Of course he would hear her voice. Oren's duty now was to get him back to the Freehold, and get him well.

'They are waiting for us,' he said gently, and attempted to pull his companion away again.

But Tymon did not budge. 'She told me everyone has to come to the World Below,' he said. 'Everyone, Oren, not just the Freeholders. Do you realise what that means? It means Argosians, too. The old world is dying. In a few years, a century at most, it'll be uninhabitable. We all have to leave.'

Oren gazed wearily at him. He could not move Tymon by main force. If the *Syon* did not follow him of his own accord, he would be left behind. 'Can we talk about this on way home?' he asked. He turned, ready to walk down the slope.

'Home is here!' replied Tymon.

There was a ringing note of assurance in his voice that caused Oren to jerk round and stare at him again. The Argosian had grown up in the last few months, he thought, bemused. Tymon was tall now, his silhouette dark against the white sky. But there was a light in his eyes Oren had not seen before. He searched his friend's expression intently. Could it be …?

'Don't worry, I'm coming back to the Freehold with you,' Tymon continued, with a smile. 'But first I want you to listen to me, because this is important. I need your help, Oren. Samiha told me the World Below doesn't belong to one people or nation. She wants everyone to be able to live here: Nurians, Argosians, Saffid, Jays … all of them. It belongs to all of them.'

A breeze stirred and the leaves on the sapling behind Tymon rippled and danced. Oren shivered, despite the fitful sun shining through the Storm clouds. But it was not because he was feeling cold. He had the sudden and distinct impression that they were not alone by the graveside. There was another presence there, a shimmer over the pool, a glimmer between the rocks. He took a deep breath.

'This will not be easy message to give,' he warned Tymon. 'Even if we come to live here, no Freeholder wishes to share World Below with both Argosians and Saffid.'

'They might, if you help me convince them,' said Tymon eagerly. 'What do you say, Oren? Will you fulfil

Samiha's wishes with me? Will you be a Witness for her too?'

Oren gazed at him a moment longer, in dawning joy and wonder. Then he bowed low. 'To the end,' he murmured.

For he knew, then, that Matrya's patience, and Samiha's faith, had been justified. Tymon had indeed become the *Syon*, a 'Sign of the Sap' or a 'Saint' as the Argosians would call it, in more than just name. And Oren was ready to serve him to the hour of death.

'But this is just the beginning,' laughed Tymon, as they walked together down the mountainside. 'Not the end. A new beginning for us all, if we get it right. You'll see.'

ACKNOWLEDGMENTS

So many people have contributed to the making of this trilogy, it's hard to name only a few. The Chronicles of the Tree went from dream to reality in a little less than four years, from the completion of the first functioning manuscript to proofs of the third book. Throughout the process, I have valued the eagle eye of my editor, Stephanie Smith, as well as that of my agent, Helenka Fuglewicz. I am particularly grateful to my mother, Bahiyyih Nakhjavani, who was my first reader, creative partner, and a staunch support in times of stress. As these acknowledgments cover both *Samiha's Song* and *Oracle's Fire*, I would also like to thank Mitenae for her excellent beta reading on *Samiha's Song*, and all the team at HarperVoyager for their hard work and patience throughout. But most of all, I would like to thank my husband, Frank Victoria, who believed in the dream. I wouldn't be here without you.

Discover the other books in
the Chronicles of the Tree trilogy ...

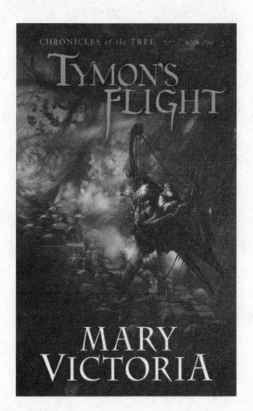

CHRONICLES *of the* TREE ～ BOOK ONE

TYMON'S FLIGHT

MARY VICTORIA

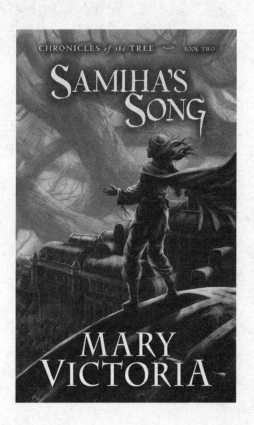

CHRONICLES *of the* TREE ——— BOOK TWO

SAMIHA'S SONG

MARY VICTORIA

MAKE VOYAGER ONLINE YOUR NEXT DESTINATION

VOYAGER ONLINE has the latest
science fiction and fantasy releases,
book extracts, author interviews,
downloadable wallpapers and
monthly competitions. It also features
exclusive contributions from some of the world's
top science fiction and fantasy authors.

DROP BY the message board where you can discuss
books, authors, conventions and more with other fans.

DISCUSS SF/F in depth: take part in the Voyager Book
Club which runs every two months, or look up some of
the available reading guides to your favourite books.

KEEP IN TOUCH with authors via the Voyager blog,
which is updated every week with guest posts from
authors and all the latest news and events on
sf/f in Australia and around the world.

FOLLOW US on Twitter and Facebook.

ENJOY the journey and feel at home with
friends at www.voyageronline.com.au

HARPER
Voyager

www.voyageronline.com.au